The Gods of Nazus Trilogy
Book Two

When The Gods Learn Lies

The Gods of Nazus Trilogy
Book Two

When The Gods Learn Lies

Kefira Zink

When the Gods Learn Lies
Copyright ©2025 by Kefira Zink

Contact Info: kefirazinkauthor@gmail.com

ISBN: 979-8-9928400-6-3

Also by Kefira Zink

<u>Young Adult Fantasy</u>

The Chronicles of AnnaBella Cain Series:

The Trials of AnnaBella Cain
The Warding of AnnaBella Cain
The Name of AnnaBella Cain

<u>Adult Fantasy</u>

The Gods of Nazus Series:

When the Gods Play Games
When the Gods Learn Lies
When the Gods Wage War

Table of Contents

Dedication

When the liars
Say you are unlovable,
When they say you are
too broken to be whole,
Remember...

If you wouldn't take their advice,
Then, don't take their criticism.
Take those pieces of yourself back!

Author Note and Trigger Warning

If you are related to me, either stop here, set the book down, and walk away or get really cool about some stuff really quickly. I'm only going to say this once and it's on you if you don't listen. I will look you straight in the eye, at the next family function, knowing you know exactly what freaky, weird stuff is in my head. Again, I love you, but not every book is for every reader.

Okay, for everyone else and the family brave enough to continue, here's my warnings. This is book two of a trilogy. You should have already read book one and know what's coming. There is still **swearing** in the book. There's **sex** too. They all love each other a bunch and still show it a lot. There are also references to **past child abuse** and **SA**, (all remembrances, discussed in depth on page, but nothing any of the main people did, they were the victims).

Other issues in this book include:
- Forced violence and fighting
- Blood
- Murder and death
- Forced proximity
- Issues with alcohol
- Governmental overreach and abuse with talk of a superior race
- Magical poisoning for forced control

Reader be warned and as before, I care about your mental health more than I do readership. If you have any specific triggers that you would like spoilers on, please feel free to reach out to me on social media/email and I will willingly tell you as much or as little as you want to determine if you will feel comfortable reading this book.

As a final note, my stand on AI hasn't changed. Nothing in this book was done with AI. It was written with my own blood, sweat, tears, sleepless nights and grueling days. Witch hunts should be in the book, not about the book. AI checkers are still feeding the machine. Don't do it.

And family be warned, if you read this, I will ask you about it right in front of my mother with zero shame.

Love, Kefira Zink

Note from the Council of the Gods Games Realms-wide

The following is a recreation of the true events of the Three Hundred and Seventy-Fifth Gods Games, in the city of the gods, Veirveil, on the continent of Nazus. The records have been obtained by audio and video recordings taken from the games themselves, with assistance of Drila, Nazus goddess of games and trials, the current Gods Games officiant. As is required by the official rules of the Gods Games, the record has been written from the perspective of the leading human witch and poetic license has been taken to fill in any details unknown and unknowable for the most accurate creation of the required Manual of the Gods Games record. This is the second half of the manual for the Three Hundred and Seventy-Fifth Gods Games. If you do not have the first half, return to your distributor and obtain a copy before reading this.

In following of the regulations of the creation of Manuals of the Gods Games, this record will be translated into all known languages for available access by all gods and humans after passing their twenty-fourth birthday and, in the case of the humans, a blue blood test. In an effort to allow the greatest understanding by the largest number of readers, all scientific information, including names of animals, foods, plants, medicines, magical workings, etc. will be translated to something of a similar nature known by the realm to which the translation will be sent. Original transcripts in their original language are available by request with proof of the linguistical understanding of requesting persons. Any such requests are to be sent to the officiating council of the gods from which the record originates. The Council of the Gods Games Realms-wide is not responsible for any mistranslations, misrepresentations, or errors within these records.

Gods Games Score Board

This scoreboard can be used to keep track of the witch players and their gods position within the games. The witch is listed first with their god(s) second and the pantheon or suspected mantle of the god listed afterwards in the parentheses.

Suggested use:

Fill in the blank space for each game with the team's total points followed by their current standings. I. E. Under Game 1, Amanda & Tholdir: write 10 points (1st place)

Suggested Pronunciation Guide:

Amanda: ah-MAHN-duh
Aretha: ah-REE-thah
Asteria: ah-STEER-ee-uh
Bokysus: bahk-EE-suhs
Damek: dam-EHKH
Drila: DREE-lah
Esnir: es-NEER
Iella: ai-EHL-ah
Isis: EYE-sis
Jinx: JEENKSS
Kinshra: keen-SHRAH
Leander: lee-AHN-dur
Nazus: NAH-suhs
Raven: RAY-vuhn
Saffron: sahf-ROHN
Tholdir: tohl-DEER
Uesis: OO-ehs-ees
Velmos: VEL-mohs
Wren: REHN
Ydum: EE-duhm
Zodum: zoh-DUM

Cave Trial Arrival & Room Designation	Game 1 (Sept 6)	Game 2 (Sept 13)	Game 3 (Sept 20)	Game 4 (Sept 27)	Game 5 (Oct 4)	Game 6 (Oct 11)	Game 7 (Oct 18)	Game 8 (Oct 25)	Game 9 (Nov 1)	Game 10 (Nov 8)
Designation	Nature	Weather	Protection	Life & Death	Animalism	Strength & Combat	Intellect	Senses	Creation	Wild Card
1st: Amanda & Tholdir (Flames)										
2nd: Isis & Esnir (War)										
3rd: Aretha & Zodum (Charity)										
4th: Damek & Iella (Chance)										
5th: Saffron & Velmos (Sky)										
6th: Asteria & Wilros (Messages)										
7th: Leander & Bokysus (Mockery)										
8th: Jinx & Byder (Hunt), Ydum (Nature), & Anarus (Obscurity)										
9th: Wren & Kutar (Storms)										
10th: Raven & Uesis (Music)										

Chapter One

I AM STANDING IN my bedroom at the Three Hundred and Seventy-Fifth Gods Games. Outside the bedroom door, I can hear the three gods a cave matched me with and I've cemented a fated mate bond with. That have cemented a fated mate bond with each other when the gods usually only bond to the witch. They are quietly moving around the front sitting room of the hotel we've been housed for the Gods Games.

These games are not something I ever thought I would have to do. As a witch, it was mandated I took the blood test on my twenty-fourth birthday. Nothing new. My seven older sisters all took it and got a red test. My parents both took it too and got a red test. Everyone in my village has taken it and gotten red. Not even my parents knew of anyone in the history of our small, poor, and isolated village who had gotten blue and been forced into the games.

When my test came back half blue and half red, ten times, on my birthday, no one knew what to do. Because there was no time to ask. My birthday on September fifth was the same day the games started, so the high priest didn't have time to ask the gods. He also didn't get the time to teach me about these games, from the manuals everyone else got to study from before going. The village tester, high priest, and village healer shrugged their shoulder and sent me to the games anyway. They sent me in blind, no idea what the games really were, and with no time to pack even a change of underwear or put on the shoes I didn't bother with to go to the testing center.

Then Drila, the Gods Games officiant didn't know what to make of the results either. She also shrugged and told me to do the cave trial to find my teammates, what I later learned were more than just teammates but gods I had destined fated mate bonds with. She assumed I would fail to find them and die there, not a strong enough witch to compete.

But I didn't fail, and got matched with three gods. Three gods, three mate bonds. Ydum, my colorblind nature god who is smart and silly, kind and goofy. Byder, my hunt god who can't read the letters right but is strong and commanding but also protective and has a major thing for making sure people eat. And Anarus, an orphaned god with shadows no one understands, classified an obscurity god when there has never been such a thing before because no one knows how he had shadows at birth or who abandoned him only hours later.

A trio god team when even duo god teams is rare. Three? Unheard of. Also unheard of is an end magic witch being strong enough to get a blue test. But I didn't get only blue, and as far as anyone can figure, it's because I'm both an end magic witch and a beginning magic witch, but also neither. And now everyone, even the original gods that made all of the continent of Nazus, humans and the witches, are all shrugging their shoulders and letting it all play out. Never mind the fact that if any of the four of us on my team fail in any of the ten games, we die. Or get made mortal for the gods, an excruciating process for them that is less preferable than death is.

There were originally ten teams, made of twenty-two people, when the games started. But after five of the ten games, we are now down to only eight. Two witches and two gods dead or close enough to it to not matter. Outside this hotel suite's door, down the long hallway, are those teams' rooms. They are probably feeling the same worries and fear my gods and I are.

Once we walk out the suite door, we have to go into the sixth game of this life and death competition, where we will almost assuredly be forced to fight and maybe even kill people, gods and human witches, who have become our friends.

And I will have to do this injured. A recently dislocated shoulder. A just healed broken wrist. A bruise on my hip that even my colorblind god knows is completely black. My birthday means I don't know enough. The poverty of my village means I didn't learn enough. The way my body feels means I'm not strong enough. But it is fight or die in these games, and none so much as this one.

I dress in the best outfit I can from the clothes I had to borrow from people who should be my enemies. Pants from the only goddess in the games, Iella, that fit nicely without being too loose. A shirt from the witch Aretha that's looser than one from another witch, Asteria, but I tuck it in. I prefer the looseness for movement over tightness of no extra fabric for fighting. I try to braid my hair as tightly as I can, but give up when my wrist hurts too much.

In the sitting room, Anarus, Byder, and Ydum are all up before me and waiting. Anarus seems gloomy as he drinks his coffee on the couch, but he is wearing a shirt even though he knows he's not going in the game today. Huh, normally I have to fight him over wearing a shirt to the games. His dark umber skin is covered by the shirt, meaning I can't see the tattoos that cover his arms, chest, and back. I notice his braided coarse hair down his back isn't as neat as it usually is and he hasn't cleaned up his goatee and mustache either.

Byder is eating some fruit on the other couch and just grunts at me. His pelt sleeveless shirt shows off his tan skin and his hunt tattoo lines on his right arm. Thin bands that represent each successful hunt he has completed since he was born lined up neatly from his right wrist to his elbow, a hunt god tradition for all children until they complete these games. His leather pants are tight around his massive, powerful thighs, he hasn't put on the boots sitting next to him yet. Nor has he put up his shoulder-length brown hair, probably waiting for me to help him since he is so bad at it.

He isn't going into the most dangerous game in the already dangerous Gods Games either. We know that only me and one god will be allowed to go this time. The manuals everyone else got made that abundantly clear. Never in over three hundred years has there been more than one god from a multiple god team been allowed in the sixth game of strength and combat. Byder may be powerful, and Anarus may be smart and strong, but Ydum is the best fighter out of everyone here, other teams included. Except maybe Esnir, the god of war we will probably have to fight today.

Ydum is standing over the dining table, a plate of toast in his hands but he hasn't eaten any yet. His knee is bouncing nervously, making his linen long-sleeved shirt and pants rustle as his blond curls bounce. There's no hint of glittery mischievousness in his emerald eyes and his green tinted skin looks paler than normal. Only tight-lipped nerves emanate from his tall, lanky frame as I grab some coffee and go over to Anarus.

"Can you braid my hair for me?" I ask him. "My wrist hurts when I tried to do it myself."

He groans. "Fine. Sit." I sit on the floor in front of him and wonder how much of his coffee he has actually drank because he seems overly crabby. Even for him. As he pulls my hair back to start the braid at the crown of my head, I try to relax and sip at my coffee.

The first sip of my coffee tastes weird. I sniff it. Did they change which coffee they were using? I sip again and taste the sweet peppery edge to it, an edge that makes my throat itch, and my brain explodes.

"Stop!" I shout, standing up.

"What the fuck are you on about?" Anarus grumbles. "Do you want me to do your hair or not?"

"How much of the coffee did you drink?" I ask him, taking the mug from him.

He huffs. "That's my second cup."

"Shit, okay, you're not rational anymore." I turn to Ydum. "Did you eat any of that?"

"Not yet." Ydum furrows his brow. "What's going on, Jinx?"

I reach over and grab the toast out of Ydum's hand. I sniff it and smell the sweet peppery tang. "It's in the food too. Byder, stop eating."

"What the fuck are you talking about, Jinx?" Byder asks.

"They put petunia in the food and coffee." I start pacing. "How many other teams have already eaten? Could we stop them in time? Shit, Aretha. They have probably been doping them for days."

I had wondered why Aretha suddenly seemed to have a vendetta against my team when, only a week ago, everyone was pissing Drila off by working together so as many of us as possible survive. The gods want us fighting to win, but who cares about that when survival is enough to pass and none of us chose to be here anyway? One panic attack where I was screaming and suddenly everyone didn't care about just surviving anymore but blamed my gods, thinking they were hurting me when they weren't. And won't believe me when I tell them that. Aretha had been the first one to band the teams together, but now she was the first one throwing shade at my gods and turning against us. Maybe they've been doping her all week.

"What are you talking about? Why can't I have my coffee?" Anarus stands and gets in my face, angry.

"Byder, take him away." I wave my hands absentmindedly. "He's gonna be pissed for a while. They poisoned the food and drinks to make us angry and resentful. It's in the food. That's why the manuals always made game six seem excessively bloody, Ydum. That's why your parents all said they just knew to fight when they were here. The gods in charge poisoned them to make them angry."

Byder's eyes go wide. "Are you sure?"

I nod at him. "Completely. We learned about the effect of magical workings with petunias in the magical arts classes and how dangerous they are. It creates frustration at the lowest levels and can make someone go into an uncontrollable murderous rage if there's too much. It's banned to even plant petunias in my village because it's too easy to hide the taste. The only time it's allowed is when the High Priest gets it to teach us how to recognize it and what it does. Most people would mistake the taste as someone using too much pepper, but I know exactly what petunias taste and smell like because I'm allergic to them. My eyes itched and my throat was sore for days after we learned about them. And there is petunia in the coffee and on the toast."

"Fuck." Ydum runs his hands through his hair and pulls on his cuffs. "So, we are going out to fight fourteen people under a magical working to be angry and resentful?"

I nod slowly. "They will be but we won't. We'll be rational where they aren't because we didn't eat any of it. At least, not today."

"That is insane. How do they keep people from killing their own teammates?" Byder shakes his head in shock.

I sigh. "They can't. It's possible to create a working where the anger is directed to a specific individual but that's hard and takes a lot of time. Plus, it only works if you are directing one person's anger at only one other person or themselves. This? This would be random and indiscriminate. They can't know exactly who will eat what in each room. Even if they know what we normally eat, like that Anarus only ever has coffee, that's too random. How much coffee will he drink and when? Before me? After? And will he even come into the game with me to have the direction they wanted to give him? Honestly, I'm surprised they haven't had something fuck up and two teammates kill each other before they even get to the game at all."

"They could have." Ydum says quietly, folding his arms over his chest and staring at the floor, his eyebrows pinched. "Who would tell us that happened? The people in that game won't even know what happened afterwards and if the record says they died in the games, who would question it?"

"Your hair." Anarus says, anger lancing his voice.

"You're mad, Anarus." I take a step back from him.

"I know!" Anarus roars. "I'm trying really hard not to be. I'm angry, not stupid. I know what you're saying, Jinx. They fucking poisoned me and it's making me angry for no reason, so I'm going to tamp that shit down and braid your fucking hair so your wrist doesn't hurt because I don't want you to die in a stupid rigged game!" He slams back down on the couch and gestures roughly to the floor at his feet.

I sit and, while Anarus aggressively braids my hair, pulling much more than necessary, Byder gets his daggers from his room and gives them to Ydum. "These are from my father. Don't fucking lose them, okay?"

"Okay, man." Ydum glances at me and I know he's unsure what to do with an angry for no reason Byder who's trying really hard not to be.

I give him a half smile as Anarus pulls my head again, muttering about little humans who can't sit still. As soon as Anarus is done, I stand and come over to Ydum. "We're going to be okay. We won't be as bad as anyone else, at least, if they have been putting it in the food longer than today for us. I'm almost positive they have for some other teams, but I don't think for us. If they knew I'm allergic, they may not have wanted to risk it until the last minute."

Ydum runs his hands up and down my arms. "What do we do with them?" He glances at Anarus and Byder.

"Byder seem almost normal. I don't think he had much. The coffee was strong though. Byder will be able to handle Anarus until he comes down from it."

"And everyone else?" Ydum asks.

I sigh and lean my head against his chest. "Try like fuck not to have to kill them defending ourselves. Hope other people, like Esnir, just happened not to eat today either or figured it out and avoided it long enough."

Ydum doesn't like this answer any more than I do. Instead of responding, he pulls on my pants waistband. "Where can you reach without hurting either your wrist or shoulder?"

I move, trying it out, and point to the small of my back and the front of my right hip, close enough to center line that it won't brush the hip bruise. Ydum tucks one blade into each spot. Then, he hands me a third blade.

"Hide this in your shirt, the way you did in the protection game. If they take the others, they won't find this one. I'm fine with only two." He has me help him tuck the last two blades in the waistband of his pants on his back. He turns back and kisses me. "Don't forget your wolf. Call her if you need to and claw the fuck outta anyone who tries to hurt you."

I close my eyes and use my familiar bond to peek in on Kinshra. She's ready and waiting. I move my shirt around and hide the last blade inside it, in the breast band I made from another shirt since I didn't bring any with me, knowing I might need it today.

I kiss Ydum again. "If it comes down to you or them, you come back, understand?"

"I understand, beautiful." Ydum tell me. "Now, talk to Byder and Anarus. They may be under the petunias, but just in case."

"Just in case nothing. We'll be _fine_." I do as he says anyway and turn to

Byder. I pull him close and hold him, running my fingers over his hunt tattoo lines.

"You are so much stronger than you think you are, Jinx." He kisses the top of my head then my lips. "Fight hard. We will always come for you."

"I love you, Byder." I tell him then move over to where Anarus is still sitting on the couch. "Anarus."

He is gritting his teeth, his jaw twitching. "Come back. Just fucking come back." He looks up at me and, under the anger and swirling shadows, I can see his fear and for the first time I'm actually scared. I can feel through our bond that Anarus is afraid he may be left alone again with no one who loves him.

"I will always love you, Anarus." I tell him, then kiss him. "I will come back."

Anarus turns to Ydum and stands as tall as he can, pointing directly into the taller god's face, growling. "You come back safe or I'll fucking split your lip again."

Ydum nods solemnly at Anarus. "I promise."

The tone calling us to the game sounds and the four of us move to the foyer silently. I try to look at everyone else, see who is affected and who maybe isn't, but everyone looks determined and scared in one way or another, gripping different weapons closely, so I can't tell.

As we line up along the wall, gods behind humans, Drila surveys us all, standing tall in her shimmery pink dress and sandals. Her gaze lands on me and I know she's taking in my bruised face. Esnir, who had been using his minor god skill of healing to help me along after the floor and I had an argument during fight practice, didn't bother wasting energy on the lip and the jaw that ended up turning colors yesterday, so he could save it for the worst injuries. Drila smiles with a sick satisfaction when she sees it. "Well, don't we all look so happy this morning."

"Shit." Ydum whispers behind me. "Pretend to be pissed like everyone else."

I snort softly. "Drila's here. I don't have to pretend."

I can tell Ydum is trying not to smile.

Drila doesn't seem so upset this time when no one responds. "This game is about strength and combat. The goal of this game is to get two pieces of a coin and put them together. The halves of the coins will be located at the top of a tower. One tower will be for the humans and another tower will be for the gods. The two parts of the coin are different, so you cannot take two parts from the human tower and make it work, but all the human halves are the same and all the god halves are the same, so it does not matter which human or god piece you get. You can get the two halves however you want, but only the god can get the god half and only the human can get the human half. Now, so you know, there are only six coins in total."

Oh, fuck. Six coins, eight team. And everyone else is doped up and angry on petunias. And they can get the coin however they want. They don't have to climb the tower to get one but just wait until someone else comes down from the tower and take it from them. And I have to climb a tower with a recently broken wrist, dislocated shoulder, and completely screwed up hip. We are so fucked.

"For the paintings this time, both the gods and humans will be allowed to choose a painting, and a team does not have to choose the same painting." Drila continues, providing instructions that deviate from how the painting choices are different in this game than any of the other games. "Also, multiple people can choose the same painting. The weapon on the painting is the only one you can bring and use in the game. You cannot have multiple types of weapons and you cannot use someone else's weapons if you are able to disarm them. These limits on weapons includes animalistic manifestations, but does not include godly powers. Any available god powers are allowed on top of the weapon chosen. You must provide your own weapons. Since the paintings are not limited, feel free to move to the one you want at any time. If you need to retrieve a weapon from your room, do so quickly, because when I call time, if you are not at a painting, you will not be allowed any weapons."

Ydum and I move quickly to one of the paintings of the daggers. "I can't call on Kinshra." I say.

He slides his hand in mine. "We will be fine. We can do this."

Several people are running to their rooms to retrieve their weapons and arguments ensue as people jostle each other. I watch the hostilities and movement, holding tightly on Ydum's hand, willing my panic to stay away.

After a few minutes, Drila speaks again. "Jinx, who will be coming with you?"

"Ydum." I hear a snort when I say this.

"Of course," Aretha says, "the one who hurt her."

"Fuck off, Aretha." Damek says back.

I ignore all of them and focus on my three gods. "I love all of you."

"Have fun!" Drila says and I find myself magically transported in a blink into a large rectangular room with a sandy floor. The light is only shining in the middle so I can't see the walls and the edges of the huge space are in shadows. Ydum is nowhere to be found. The other humans are all here, but none of the gods. We're all lined up at one of the short ends of the room and far away, on the other end, is a tall wooden tower, lit up with a bright light shining down over it, gold shimmering at the top, draped over the thick tower with red fabric strips. Other than that, the rest of the room in front of me is empty, just a long stretch of sandy floor that seems to go on and on.

I need the coin half that has to be the gold shimmering on top of the tower. I have to run. I take off like Ydum taught me. I don't know where he is but I have to get my half of the coin first then I'll worry about finding him. I make sure my hips are open wide and run. And run. And run.

The tower doesn't feel like it's getting any closer. I keep running. The distance looked like it was so much closer than it actually is. I keep running. I can see motion in my peripheral vision, but I ignore it and run until my lungs feel like they will burst. There are only six coins and eight team. I keep running.

Someone slams into my back and I sprawl to the floor. The sand cushions my fall some but whoever it was steps on my back as they pass me and shove me down again. I push up off the floor and ignore the twinge in my back to keep running. In front of me, I can see that Saffron is at the tower and climbing. Why is that fucking thing not getting any closer for me? I run hard and it moves only slightly closer. I should have been there twice over by now.

I slow my thoughts and try not to panic. What magic would cause this? It's an illusion, I realize. The tower I see is not the real one. I'm not even sure that's Saffron climbing it. I stop running, close my eyes and focus. I need to see the real tower. I open my eyes again and look around. The tower with the gold shimmering at the top is still there, but behind me, back where we started, there's another one. This one is not shimmering with gold but silver.

I turn and run back the other way. It only takes a few minutes for me to make it to the real tower. In the thrall of the illusion, I'd been running in circles around the room and had nearly made it back to the start.

At the tower, almost all the humans are already there and fighting to get on it first. They are clumped together, fighting and arguing. I pull one of my daggers from my waist and hold it tightly in my hand. I don't want to use it. I don't even take off the sheath.

Everyone is screaming at everyone else. I stay silent and focus on how to climb the tower, examine it. It's thick. I don't think Ydum could even wrap his arms all the way around it. The other witches are all bunched up in one spot, right under where the silver half coins are hanging from blue strings at the top. I walk around to a spot where no one is and contemplate what to do. The tower is tall, at least ten feet, maybe more. It's the height of a full-grown tree.

Running a hand down the tower, the wood feels soft. I give a test thrust of my dagger into it and see that the blade can go into the wood, but not very far. I could use the daggers to climb the tower but it won't be great. I try to come up with any other way to climb the tower, but I can't. I keep one eye on everyone fighting, and know I am wasting time. Think. Think. Shit. I can't think.

I shake my head and try to dislodge the lump in my throat that forms as I look up at the half coins so high up the tower. I'm calm. I'm rational. They're not. I can do this.

I look at the knife in my hand, then the tower. It's the best worst idea, but it's all I have. This is going to hurt. I grab the second knife out of my pants waist and take the sheathes off. I tuck the sheaths in my shirt so I won't lose them and stab the dagger in my left hand into the wood of the tower as hard as I can. Then, I brace my feet against the tower and reach higher, stabbing with the dagger in my right hand. I use my feet to brace against the wood as I yank out my left dagger and hold on with my right. My shoulder and wrist scream as I push my knees straight to reach higher and stab into the wood with my left dagger again. Over and over, I stab the wood with one hand, push up with my knees, stab the wood with my other hand, then scrabble my feet up and push again.

By the time I'm at the top of the tower, my entire right side is on fire, my right hand is numb and I'm covered in sweat, my hands slick. Anarus's slightly too big boots are making it hard to brace my feet and my toes are cramping. I have no idea how I'll get back down, but I can reach a half coin. I hold on to my highest dagger with my left hand and brace with my feet so I can reach with my right hand and grab a coin. It tears away from the tower easily and I stuff it down my shirt as well.

Down. I have to get down. I look down and see the problem is not only how to get down but that Wren is climbing up underneath me. To get down, I will have to go around her or push her back down. I don't want to fight anyone while I'm hanging on to daggers only shallowly stabbed through wood. They are barely holding me up as it is. I also don't want hurt her if I don't have to. So, in a crazy thought, I grab a second half coin and lean down to hand it to Wren.

She screams at me unintelligibly and threatens me with her own dagger.

"Stop, Wren!" I yell down. "Here!" I hold down the second half coin to her. When she realizes what I'm holding out to her, she grabs it, wrenching my arm downward and making my sweaty hand almost lose grip on the dagger I'm clinging to. But she moves back downward, meaning I can too.

While I wait for Wren to clear the tower, I think. I know there are only six coins and eight teams so someone needs to fail, but I want as little people as possible to die. And I don't want anyone else trying to climb the tower while I'm trying to get down. The best way to prevent that is stop the fighting over climbing the tower. There are three coins left and, making a rash decision to say fuck these games, I grab all three and toss them to the sandy floor. Now, no one has to climb. Of course, it doesn't stop the fighting, but does break it up for a moment as the witches at the base of the tower scramble to claim a coin from the sandy floor.

Wren takes off the moment she touches the ground, and I know I'm free to climb down. My shoulder hurts so bad and feels like it'll give out from the effort. But, slowly, taking multiple breaks, I make it to the ground. I have to take a moment to catch my breath.

Everything hurts. I gasp in air and am just thankful I haven't had to fight anyone yet. Five people are still crowded around the front of the tower, fighting over the coins I threw down. I can't tell who exactly because they're a tangle of arms and fists, but I know one of them is Damek just because he sticks out as the only male human witch among all the females.

I try to determine where I should go to find Ydum. I can see the other, gold coin tower still, and it dawns on me. That wasn't an illusion. It was the wrong one. I couldn't get there because that was the god tower, not the human one. The game wouldn't let me make it there until I had my half of the coin.

I start trotting towards it, but in an instant, I'm lying flat on my back and my scalp hurts. Someone yanked me backwards by my braid. I try to move but before I can, Damek is on top of me. He's sitting on me and searching my clothes. He's trying to steal my half coin from me. He's my friend, or kind of, so I know it's only the petunias making him act this way. He even continued to train with my gods and me when Aretha split the teams. He was the one pinning me in the air when I accidentally kicked him in the balls and fell to the floor, causing all my injuries. I do not want to have to hurt him.

"Damek! Stop!" I try to buck him off like Ydum and Esnir taught me, but Damek digs into the sand with his feet and I can't get any leverage. He's not wearing a shirt so I can't grab him by it and his pants are slick leather like all of Byder's. I never figured out the maneuver to flip someone with those leather pants.

"Give me the fucking coin!" Damek yells as he grabs both of my wrists with one of his large hands and pins them over my head. His other hand is questing my body, trying to feel where I put the coin. My right shoulder screams in protest at being wrenched that way, my right wrist feels like it's snapping again under his punishing grip, and my right hip hurts even more with his knee digging into it.

"Stop, Damek. Please stop!" I scream. He's sitting on me. My old fears and the panic that always comes with them resurfaces. I can't breathe. I don't know where my daggers went. I can't break free. He's too strong. I fight back the panic. No, Ydum taught me what to do. Don't stop fighting. Ydum said don't stop fighting. I keep trying to dislodge Damek.

"Give me your fucking coin!" Damek is still yelling. I manage to pull one hand free and try to use it to leverage myself, like Ydum told me. Don't panic, remember what you learned, I tell myself over and over. Damek pushes my free hand away and slaps me across my face hard enough for me to see stars.

"Give me your coin!" He shoves his hand through my clothes, his hand pushing in my pants. He moves his fingers, searching and I scream as the thoughts of what he might do race through my mind. Finding nothing, he moves on to my shirt as I continue to fight both him and the panic.

Damek feels the coin through my breast band. I see the recognition as his hand brushes over it. He uses his free hand to yank my shirt up more, tearing the hem from the force of him yanking it as hard as he can. He reaches his hand under my shirt to search the rest of my chest he couldn't uncover. He pulls out the dagger sheathes and tosses them aside, forcing his hand up my shirt again.

"Damek! Stop!" The panic is overwhelming. I fight to think. What do I do? Where are Byder's daggers? "Ydum!" I scream, hoping he has his coin and can hear me. "Ydum, help!"

I keep moving, squirming, fighting. Nothing I do works. All the things they taught me. Damek is too big, too strong. He's sitting on me. He's in my shirt, touching me. He rips at the breast band made from a shirt and the third dagger falls out. He grips it, ready to use it, but then he shrieks and drops it like it burned him. As he shakes out his hand, I try to use his distraction. Keep fighting, Jinx. I can almost hear Byder telling me. I keep fighting, but I can't breathe. He has my hands pinned. I can't reach the dagger that is. Right. There.

Damek screams at me again. "Give me the coin!" His hand goes inside my shirt again and moves under the breast band. I feel him moving his hand over me, searching as he manhandles my breasts.

The panic is so close, I am fighting. Screaming. Twisting. "Ydum! YDUM!! Byder! Anarus! Please help me. Please come!" Anarus's name breaks a tiny bit of mind free. Weapons or god powers. That's what Drila said. She didn't say it had to be the god who wields the god power. I've taken Anarus's shadows before. "Anarus! Give me your shadows! Anarus, I need them, please!"

Suddenly, the whole room goes darker. Without trying to think, without questioning it, I tell the dark to get Damek off me. I need him off of me and far away! The darkness pulses and Damek flies through the air, landing several feet away on his back. As soon as I'm free, I flip over on my stomach and snatch the dagger.

I'm still crying and can hardly breathe. My entire right side feels like someone set me on fire then poured acid on my skin. I can't feel my right hand at all and my left is shaking so hard I'm struggling to hold the dagger. I feel inside my shirt and the half coin is still there, so I tuck the ruined edges of the shirt back in my pants so I won't lose it.

Damek is getting up and charging at me again.

"Stop!" I hold up the dagger. "I don't want to hurt you!"

Damek pauses. His eyes go wide as he looks at me. "Oh, fuck. What did I do?" I can tell the petunia magic wore off. "Jinx, I…"

"Just get a coin, Damek. Not mine, but your own, okay?" I rasp out, still holding the blade between us. I fight to stand, but it takes several tries to just make it to my knees.

Damek runs away from me, back toward the tower. My head is spinning and I feel so weak. I look down the room. It seems so far to the god tower. I struggle again to get to my feet, stand and start walking. I can't run, my hip feels like it was dragged through broken glass. I take a few steps and my right leg gives out.

I struggle to stand again, make it a few steps, then fall again. Ydum, I keep telling myself. I need to get to Ydum.

As I fight to stay on my feet, Aretha barrels past me. She stops, seeing it's me. "Fucking wench." She growls at me. She has a whip in her hand and she brandishes it at me. "That's my fucking shirt."

"Aretha, stop, please." I plead with her.

She ignores my pleading and steps closer. She flicks her whip and it whistles past my face. "Cocky ass witch with her three gods and unfortunate birthday. Boo hoo, poor Jinx." Aretha fakes whining. She flicks her whip again and this time, I feel heat flash on my right hand before it goes numb again. She hit me and it's probably bleeding, but I don't have time to think about that.

I try to move around her, away from her, but I can't move fast enough with my body so sore and hurting. She flicks the whip again and I try to dodge it. I feel fire on my right side. She steps closer again.

"Aretha, don't. I don't want to fight you. Just get a coin and find Zodum." I'm trying to rationalize with her but I know it won't work. I try to move away, move around her, but she's boxing me in, spinning her whip in her hand, letting it just barely lick me again and again.

"You and your violent, broken gods think you are so great." Aretha says. She's almost on top of me and I can't move fast enough. I try to go right, she steps to the right. I try to go left and she moves back in front of me again. I'm too slow, too hurt, and so, so tired.

"Aretha, please don't make me fight you." I try one more time. I'm not sure if Anarus's shadows are actually still with me. I can't feel their coldness against my skin, but that may be just because everything hurts too much and there's too much to feel. I try to pulse them out again, like I did with Damek, but nothing happens.

Aretha reaches for me, grabbing my hurt wrist tightly, making me scream out. She smiles when she sees the pain in my eyes. She brings her whip up, about to flick it at my neck. She'll use the whip to choke me, I know. I have no choice. None. It's me or her. I bring the dagger in my left, trembling hand up and swipe at her chest. A tear forms in her shirt, blood welling from it. It's only a small wound, barely scratching her, but I hope it's enough pain to make her mind clear of the effects of the petunias, like Damek's did when he hit his head.

It doesn't. Instead, it just makes her angrier. Aretha roars at me and yanks on my wrist again, making me stumble towards her. On instinct, I bring my left hand with the dagger up between us as I fall towards her, intending to use my hand to catch myself and not fall against her. As I fall, Aretha catches my left wrist in her hand, not remembering that my dagger is in that hand. She twists my wrist as if she means to break the left one and leave me defenseless with no working wrists. I fight back, twisting my wrist back the other way, the way Byder and Ydum taught me to free it from someone's grip.

We end up pushing and pulling on each other, her fighting to pull me down, make me fall and hurt my wrists so I drop my weapon, while I fight to stay upright and keep hold of my dagger. Neither of us gains leverage over the other for too long. I scream at her the whole time, begging her to just let go and we can both go our own ways. We don't need to fight. But she's too lost, too far gone under the petunias to hear me.

I know I can't stop her with words. Every move makes my body hurt more. My hip grinds and wants to give out. My right wrist and shoulder are so far past painful they are just an agonizing burning numbness. Everywhere on me are licks of fiery stickiness that are the bleeding marks from her whip. She isn't even trying to get the coin, but just hurt me.

I have no choice. I know I have no choice. It's her or me. I give one last try to pull my left arm with the dagger in my hand towards me, out of her grip, but it's futile. Instead, I shift the dagger so that it's pointing towards her and relax my arm completely. The sudden lack of tension in my arm makes Aretha pull that hand straight at herself at full force. I close my eyes and know by sound alone when the dagger plunges into Aretha's chest, buried to the hilt.

I open my eyes again and Aretha looks at me with surprise as she collapses, blood spilling over her shirt in crimson waves. I fall on top of her, and the building panic in me reaches new heights as I feel her blood coat my hands. I want to cry. I'm already crying, but I want to cry again. I didn't want to do it, but me or her. She made it me or her. I shake my head, trying to clear the dizziness and anguish, and yank the dagger out of her. The squelching sound it makes turns my stomach and I vomit. My hands are trembling so badly I can't hold the dagger anymore. I drop it back on the floor and collapse, everything hurting and my heart pounding so hard I can't hear anything but the rush of it in my ears.

I killed her. I killed Aretha. I look over and see her open eyes, staring at me, cold and lifeless. The sand around her is a rusty red. I'm kneeling in that rusty red. I'm kneeling in Aretha's blood because I killed her. My brain riots. I can't breathe. I can't think. She's dead and it's my fault. I can't even blame the petunias because I didn't have any. What will Ydum think when he knows I killed her? Ydum. Fuck. I need to find Ydum. I want to get away from here. I need to find Ydum so we can leave. But that means getting up and I can't. It hurts. I just want to stop here. She's dead and I killed her and I want to just stop here.

No. I can't stop. I can't stop here. I tell myself over and over to get the fuck up and run. It takes two tries, but on the second try I manage to get my trembling legs to hold me and I run. Every step hurts, so I scream Ydum's name as I run. I make it about halfway to the god tower when Ydum come careening at me.

"Jinx! Fuck, Jinx!" Ydum yells as he pulls me towards him. "Are you okay?"

"No." I cry, relief flooding me as he holds me.

"The coin. Do you have the coin?" Ydum is trying to look me over, or at least my face.

"I killed Aretha." I tell him. "The coin is in my breast band."

Ydum actually looks at my shirt, how it's ripped apart from Damek's hands and Aretha's whip. "Oh, fuck. What happened?"

I reach in my shirt and dig out the half coin Damek tried so hard to get. I hand it to Ydum. "I want to go back. Let's go back, please." My hand shakes as I hand Ydum my half of the coin and the panic is the only thing I can feel besides Ydum's arms on me.

Yum pulls a gold half coin from inside his shirt and puts the two halves together. We are back in the foyer immediately and Byder and Anarus, who is not angry anymore, are there, pulling us away to the wall.

"What the fuck happened?" Anarus pants. "I felt Jinx panic and then my shadows were gone. Just gone."

"Damek was hurting me. I didn't stop fighting." I say to no one in particular. "I think I killed Aretha."

"Shit." Byder says. "Whose blood is all that, Ydum?"

"Not mine," is the only response Ydum gives him. "Later, please. We can talk later."

Anarus has his arms around me, holding me tightly. He picks me up and carries me to the wall. "You did good, Jinx. You did really well, but you need to let go. Give the shadows back to me."

I look at him but don't exactly see him. "I have your shadows?"

"Yes, little human. But you need to relax so you give them back."

I sigh deeply and slump against Anarus's chest, tears slowly falling from my face to his shirt. "You came for me. With your shadows, you came for me."

"I did. Now, let go. There you go, little human." Anarus wraps his arms around me tighter and I shudder in his arms. "That's it. You're done fighting."

I can't stop shaking, but Anarus holds me tightly. Drila is talking. I can't listen though.

"I killed Aretha." I whisper to Anarus. "I had to. She wouldn't stop. She was so angry and wouldn't stop."

Anarus smooths a hand over my hair, pushing pieces stuck to my bloody and sweat and tear stained cheeks. "You did what you had to, to come back. We can figure everything else out later. Just rest."

I bury my face in Anarus's shirt and just stay there. After some time, I hear Damek.

"Jinx, fuck. I'm so sorry." He's saying, but Anarus stops him.

"Whatever happened, we will figure out later, Damek. Not now, leave her alone right now."

Drila must have finished speaking because Anarus is lifting me up, carrying me as he walks. I don't take my face out of his shirt as we go back into our room and he settles down on the couch with me.

"Hey, baby girl, can I look at you?" I hear Byder ask, his hand smoothing a trail up and down my good arm. "I want to see your injuries. How hurt are you?"

I sit up and Byder sucks his teeth. "Damn. Okay, the shirt needs to go. I can't tell what blood is hers." Anarus holds me steady by my waist as Byder helps ease my shirt off, wincing when I yelp as we remove my right arm.

"I lost your daggers." I tell him. "I'm sorry. I lost your daggers."

Byder's voice is soft as he looks over me. "Don't worry about it, Jinx. I know how I was this morning about them but that was the petunias. Ydum brought back his two, but I don't care about the other three daggers, baby girl. Fuck, she's a mess." His hands are moving slowly and gently over me. I hiss and squirm every time his fingers brush a cut or bruise and am surprised how many times it happens.

"Ydum?" I reach out for him, realizing Anarus and Byder are only focusing on me.

Ydum comes to sit next to Anarus and me. "I'm right here. I'm fine, beautiful. Nary a scratch. You fought hard, didn't you?"

I try to focus my eyes on him but everything is hazy with pain and exhaustion. "I didn't stop trying. I did everything you taught me and I didn't stop trying."

Byder lets out a small snort. "We can tell. Bruise across her cheekbone, still the split lip but the bruise on the jaw is worse. Shoulder is completely covered in a bruise down her arm and back. The hip is completely black with bruising. That wrist looks like it re-broke and at least two fingers are probably as well. Seven, maybe eight weal marks on her chest, arms, and one on her face. Missed the eye by fractions of an inch. Three of the cuts on her chest are bleeding but not very badly. Where the fuck did all the blood come from, though? Nothing looks bad enough for all that."

Byder's list of my injuries reminds me of them and I feel the pain of each one as he talks. "Blood is Aretha's. My toes."

"Your toes?" Anarus says, confused.

I nod, but it's a mistake as the world dances. "I think I broke some toes. They hurt a lot. The boots kept slipping because they're too big."

Either Byder or Ydum remove my boots. "Yeah, big toe on both feet and the second toe on the right foot are red and swollen, getting worse without the boots now. Probably will be bruised by tomorrow." Ydum says. "You made a right mess of yourself, Jinx."

"Can you tell us what happened?" Byder asks gently. I move slowly to sit up and slide onto the couch next to Anarus. He keeps an arm wrapped around my waist loosely to support me without aggravating any of my injuries.

I tell them everything. I feel their anger flare when I tell them about Damek. "Don't blame him. He was under the petunias. As soon as he broke out of their power, he was immediately apologizing. He must not have eaten much this morning because it didn't last long enough."

Anarus nods. "That's why he was trying to apologize so much the minute he got back."

"Aretha and Zodum never came back." Byder tells me. "Asteria and Wilros either."

"I killed her." I bite my lip and fight back the urge to vomit again. "I killed Aretha."

"There must have been something to this, how everyone targeted everyone else." Ydum says. "Zodum came after me. He tracked me down. He already had a coin and I didn't yet, but still, he tracked me down and came hard. I had to kill him to stop him too. Iella tried as well, but I just disarmed her and was able to

14

get her to back off enough to get away."

"Same teams came after both of you, even though you weren't together." Anarus thinks out loud. "Too much of a coincidence. But Jinx said it was too hard for the gods to direct the flow of the anger through magic."

"Maybe it wasn't purposeful." All three of them look at me. It's the clearest thing I've said since getting back. "Maybe the magic just heightened what was already there. Iella and Damek may have been actually fine with what happened when we were sparring, but any tiny bit of concern over it, or frustration, would be manifested greater and gotten blown out of proportion. That's why they weren't trying to kill us, just angry."

I sigh. "And Aretha? We kept bumping her off winning. And the whole thing with the witch's kit was really her idea, but everyone kept giving me the credit for bringing everyone together. The things she was saying as she attacked me? It was like she was jealous of me. And you three."

"That actually makes a lot of sense." Ydum rubs his chin. "It would explain Esnir and Kutar too. They both attacked me but neither one seemed like their heart was in it. Esnir is a war god but people looked to me to lead the fight training. Kutar and I have always had a friendly rivalry. Storm god and nature god. We are both in the same pantheon but what is his only power is just part of mine."

"How's your head doing, baby girl?" Byder asks me, looking closely at my eyes.

I blink a few times and think about it. "Better. Everything else hurts like a bitch, but my head is better. Damek pulled my braid and slapped me hard." I turn, slowly, to look at Ydum. "How did you climb the tower?"

He smiles tiredly. "I didn't. After Zodum attacked me, and I fought him off, after he." Ydum lets out a shuddering sigh. "After I killed him to stop him, I took his."

"I used Byder's daggers." I turn to him. "Sorry. Even if I hadn't lost them, they would've been ruined."

Byder takes my left hand into his. "You survived and came back. I can get new daggers. I can't replace you."

"I never heard what Drila said. How did we do?" I glance around the guys to see the point board on the back of the suite door. I can see from the couch that four names are now crossed out with a thick red line.

"You came back fifth." Anarus tells me. "We're now in second place."

He gathers me into his arms again. "Now, I say you need a shower and bed. I'd skip the shower but you're covered in blood." Anarus stands with me in his arms, and walks to the washroom. "I'm probably going to need help to do this with all the injuries."

All three of my gods get in the shower with me. I am undressed the rest of the way and Anarus holds me as Byder and Ydum gently clean me. It is completely clinical, with Byder and Anarus still wearing pants as they move back and forth to clean me up. Ydum only gets naked when he starts washing himself after I'm clean. Only then do I notice a few bruises on Ydum's chest and back that he failed to mention. Gods heal quickly, I know, but it makes me wonder what fighting he had to do that he downplayed in the wake of me being such a mess.

After they dry me, and themselves, off, Anarus carries me into the room and gets me into bed. They don't even bother with bed clothes, not wanting to jostle me more than necessary. Anarus stays there in the bed, next to me, and I feel Byder slide in on my other side. I feel movement of the bed that tells me Ydum has found a spot to lie down too, but I don't think too much about it because the exhaustion wins first.

When I wake up in the morning, Ydum is the only one still in the bed with me. He's still asleep and I try to get up without waking him. I roll over and immediately regret it.

"Oh, fuck." I swear under my breath. Everything hurts. My whole body down my right side burns and feels battered. I'm out of breath by the time I sit up. I feel a tug from Kinshra.

Hey, Kinshra, I'm okay, just hurt from the game yesterday.

She growls low in her throat, but I tell her not to worry. I'll heal and the people who did it are either dead or will be taken care of.

Why didn't call on me? Kinshra nearly shouts. *I could have helped!*

Oh shit, I'm sorry. I never told you that it was against the rules. You were waiting for me all day. I'm sorry. I promise to keep you more informed.

She huffs. *Fine. Forgiven. This time.*

Thank you, and I really am sorry.

Kinshra only shakes her fur and mutters under her breath, but I know she doesn't want to actually talk anymore. I let her go.

I go back to trying to get up for the day. Part of me considers not even attempting to put on clothes, knowing none of my gods will mind if I walk into the sitting room naked, but I push that idea away. Instead, I snag Ydum's shirt and slowly get it on, cursing under my breath the whole time.

I gingerly walk out to the sitting room and am very happy I opted to put the shirt on. Damek is sitting on the couch with Byder. I can tell by how Byder is holding himself he's trying not to hate Damek. Anarus is on the other couch, simmering in shadows and not trying to hide his hate. I move very carefully to the table and get coffee. When I sit on the couch with it, Anarus drapes the blanket we keep there over my lap for me. I take a sip of the coffee and grimace as the mug pushes on my very swollen bottom lip.

"Jinx." Damek says. "I need to talk to you. I need to apologize."

I shake my head at him. "You don't have to. I understand."

Damek interrupts me. "No, please. I need to say this." I let him talk. "Anarus told me about the petunia and I actually feel kind of foolish that I didn't recognize it in my breakfast. I remember thinking that the eggs were too peppery but disregarded it. In the game, all I could think is that I'd do anything to get a coin. But by the time I climbed up the tower, they were all gone." I don't tell him that was me. They were gone because I threw them all to the ground. "From then on, it was almost like I was watching myself from the outside. I saw you hobbling so slowly toward the gods. I knew that I could take yours from you. You were too hurt to fight me. Part of me was screaming at myself to stop, not do it, but another part knew I would kill you to take yours from you."

Damek looks at the floor, clenching his fists. "I knew what I was doing. If I made you panic, if I used your trauma against you, maybe you'd just give it to me. My mind rationalized it. Hurt is better than dead. If I hurt you to get you to just give it to me, then I wouldn't have to kill you. I knew it was wrong. I knew what I was doing was wrong, but I couldn't make myself stop. I fought myself as hard as I fought you and only succeeded in convincing myself to not just outright kill you. To not actually assault you. My non-rational brain made me do everything I could to make you think I would rape you, but my rational brain watching from the outside told me to stop, not do that, it wouldn't make you give up the coin but would ruin our friendship.

"When you threw me off you with Anarus's shadows, I hit my head on the ground and it was like it knocked the last bit of the magic out of me. I knew everything I'd done to you. To everyone else. I killed Asteria. She didn't even have a coin yet, but I killed her anyway for nothing. I'm so sorry, Jinx. So very, very sorry. Don't forgive me. You shouldn't ever forgive me for what I tried to do. But I just wanted to tell you how sorry I am. I could say it wasn't me but the magic, but that's no excuse for the thoughts I had. The things I thought about doing."

I close my eyes and roll my lips between my teeth, forgetting that one of them is swollen. I stiffen at the pain and look around. Anarus and Byder are both watching me. I can tell through our bonds they're angry but trying to stifle it, waiting for me to decide how I feel about Damek's admission of what he was really feeling as he groped me to find the coin.

"Did you ever have any thoughts like that before yesterday, Damek?" I don't look at him but down at my mug of coffee. "Did you ever want to hurt me like that before yesterday?"

"Honestly? No, not like that. I thought you were pretty when I first saw you in the cave, with no shoes and so confused. But I knew what the games were and ignored it. Then, I got to know you and thought you were great. By then, Iella and I were very close, so it was just a weak attraction. Nothing more. I thought maybe we could be friends if we all survived. I swear it was never more than that before yesterday." Both Anarus and Byder feel protective and a little jealous at what Damek said, but they simmer down easily.

"And what do you feel now without the magic of the petunias anymore?" I ask.

Damek sniffs. "Horrified at myself. Awful. Like I am a horrible male who would deserve it if you or your gods killed me for this. I know you can never be friends with me now. If someone did to Iella what I did to you, I would take their hands at the very least. I deserve whatever punishment you feel like. I hurt you and I will never forgive myself. Iella won't even look at me, and I deserve that too."

I nod slowly. "You said you can't blame the magic, but I disagree. If you're telling me the truth about how you felt before the petunias, then it really was just the magic taking advantage of our smallest thoughts and blowing them out of proportion. You wanted me as a friend and the gods made that something else, something awful. It's their fault, not yours." I reach out and take Damek's hand, surprising him. "We are friends and I did trust you before all of this. It might take a while, but I think we can get back there." I drop his hand quickly, that small comfort for him making me feel only a tiny bit of panic. I know that Anarus and Byder felt me feel it, but Damek doesn't know it and that's what I wanted.

It's not his fault, I think in my head. It's not. The original gods did this. Damek was just a tool they used in their games to break me. To break all of us. They are the ones who deserve my anger, not Damek. They made us hate each other, hurt and kill each other, for no other reason than their sick, twisted ideas of how to save themselves. They will pay for it, I decide. I'll make them pay for this. For Aretha, Asteria, Amanda, Leander, and everyone in the cave. For what they made Damek do, me do, all of us do. For the three hundred and seventy-five years of torturing gods and witches, and what they made all of us do.

Byder snorts with a smile. "Planning a revolution there, baby girl?"

"Yes." I look at him. "Yes, I fucking am."

"It's about damn time." Anarus says darkly. "I've been planning one since I was old enough to know the word."

Ydum comes out of the bedroom, yawning and scratching his head. "What's everyone doing and why are you all feeling murderous and stabby?"

"We've decided to hate the original gods and that maybe a revolution isn't a bad idea." I tell him. "How are you feeling everyone? Don't you mean just me?"

Ydum stops mid-step. He purses his lips, thinking. "No. Pretty sure I mean everyone. Byder is less mad than he is determined, and Anarus could gut someone with his bare hands. Fuck, okay. New things. Lots of new things. Jinx took over—" He stops, noticing Damek, and picks up a butter knife from the table. "Are we killing him or okay with him right now?"

"Tentatively okay." I tell him. "We'll fill you in later. The stabby stabby is only for the original gods."

"Ydum wielding a butter knife and talking about killing me is my cue to get going." Damek stands and goes to the door, but turns back around before leaving. "Thank you, Jinx, for listening. I didn't deserve even that much from you, so thank you." He goes out the door and Ydum puts down the knife.

"Well, isn't this fun?" Ydum says as he comes to sit. "Forgiving humans we should want to kill, wanting to kill gods that want us to revere them, the four of us having bond connections in weird ways, and Jinx stealing Anarus's power when they are nowhere near each other. Sounds like a perfect start to the morning."

"Not just stealing my power," Anarus corrects Ydum, "but using it in ways even I haven't yet. You threw Damek across the room with my shadows, Jinx."

I shrug. "I needed to do a thing, so I did a thing."

"That end magic of yours doing things it shouldn't again." Byder shakes his head.

Ydum sniffs a piece of toast he brought over from the table. He holds it out to me. "This safe?"

I sniff it and nod. "No petunia."

Ydum takes a bite then and chews thoughtfully. "I don't know that we can call Jinx's magic end magic anymore. It's very evident that it isn't strictly that. You use need, like any end magic witch, but not in the way you should. The way you describe taking Ani's shadows sounds a lot like how a beginning magic witch would call materials to them. And the fact that you used them at all? That's god power through and through. You shouldn't have been able to command them at all, no matter what type of magic you have. You're human."

"Has there ever been someone who could do all three types of magic before?" I ask. "God or human?"

Ydum rubs his knees. "Technically? The original gods would have had to wield all three to make everything, if that story is true. But as Ani said, there's no proof of that."

"What is the story anyway? We talk about the original gods a lot, but I don't really know much about them."

Anarus next to me twist me slightly so that I am laying down. "Rest, Jinx. You're hurt. We can keep talking, but I want you to relax." When I'm situated, lying down on my left side with my feet on Anarus's lap, he continues. It does feel better to not be sitting up anymore. "At the start of time, there were only twenty gods. They all existed in the nether, the nothing, together. Each one had their own desires and loves and focused on their own thing. But one day, one of them, the god of Inspiration, had an idea."

"Of course, it would be the god of inspiration." I joke.

"Shush, I'm telling a story." Anarus grumbles, but he's smiling too. "He decided that all the gods should come together to make something of the nether. He described his idea to everyone else and all of them except one agreed it was a good plan. The goddess of the Sky made the backdrop for everything, adding light with the sun and the stars. Then the god of Nature made the earth. He made plants and trees, rocks and stone, metals. The Water god made rivers, lakes, oceans. The Hunt goddess added animals. She made some live on the land, some live in the water, and some live in the sky."

Anarus moves his hands to my toes, letting his cold shadows hover above my feet, like an ice pack. "The four seasons, the gods of Spring and Fall and the goddesses of Summer and Winter, all added the movement from one type of weather to another. The god and goddess of Fertility gave everything the ability to procreate. The flowers developed pollen, the animals made eggs or wombs. The plants and animals were delightful, the gods thought, but the four Fates, the gods of Happiness and Anger, and the goddesses of Sadness and Peace, could not work with them. So, the god of Knowledge and the goddess of Curiosity made something new. They made humans. The god of Wind added their breath and the goddess of Fire gave them the ability to survive in the cold of winter and stay warm."

Anarus pauses the story while he wanders over to the table to refill both of our coffees. When he settles back down next to me, he continues. "Everything was good and all the gods were happy with what they made. Some of the gods even started sharing their power with humans they especially liked. But there was a problem. Everything they created was taking over. There were too many plants, too many animals, too many humans. The one god who hadn't agreed to the plan, the god of Death, refused to help because he didn't like what his power could do. He knew that what he did would only destroy what the others had made, so he stayed away. But the other gods soon begged him to help. There was too much everything everywhere. Nature's plants were sick because the land was being stripped too fast of all the things the plants needed to survive. The animals were struggling too, many of them couldn't find food and were starving, but without death, they all only suffered in unending agony."

Anarus moves his shadows to my hip and wrist. "Eventually, the gods convinced Death to come see what they had made. He looked at their creation and saw the havoc no death was causing. He laid his hand upon the creation and spoke the word death into the land, giving it a touch of his power. Only a touch. Then he fled, afraid that the other gods would be mad. The other gods saw death work on their creations and did in fact get angry. Death had not stopped the suffering, just changed it. The earth was in balance now, life and death equal, but the gods didn't care. They cursed Death for what he did. The nineteen gods set up the city of Veirveil to live amongst their creations, to watch over them and make sure the Death's gift never went too far. They prohibited him from ever coming to Veirveil and he didn't fight them, ashamed of who he was."

"Time passed and the gods grew comfortable in their new home. They had children and their children had children. Soon, the problem overrunning the world was the gods who could not die. There were too many of them and their powers were mutating badly because they all came from the same nineteen original gods. The nineteen original gods came together again and created the Gods Games. They decreed that the descendants of those humans who had been gifted power in the beginning, called witches, would compete with the gods to find mates. The gods were no longer allowed to mate with each other, but only with the witch they were destined to be with from the magic of the cave trial and only if they survived the games. They put the limits on god powers so that no new children would actually have the power of a god, including full immortality, until they passed the games and were paired with a witch human that had a destined fated mate bond that could temper their powers and help them retain a form of humanity.

With a sigh, Anarus sits back, spreading his arms across the back of the couch. "Now, the original nineteen gods rule Veirveil and the whole continent. Eventually, the non-magical humans grew tired of being left out of everything. They chose a leader who approached the gods and asked them for a chance to live on their own, away from the magical controls on their lives. The gods agreed and made them a new home, far away from this continent and sent them there. Some claim that Death lives among them on the other side of the world, but there is no proof of where Death is now. His power still moves in our world, proving he's still alive somewhere. His banishment meant he didn't have access to the gods or witches he could mate with so probably never had any children to pass his power on to. But he has never been seen again."

"Wow." I whisper when Anarus finishes his story. "Does anyone else feel bad for the god of Death?"

Byder answers. "Not really. Or, well, I never have before but then again, I never heard it told quite that way before. Most of the time, Death is portrayed as bad, like that he added death to the land when the other originals hadn't asked him to and his addition of death to everything but the gods was why the gods had problems. They blame him for everything, but the way Anarus is telling it, Death couldn't help who he was and what his power could do."

"Kind of like Anarus can't either." Ydum says softly, as if his mind is just making the connection now. "Yet the gods all call him bad for his power too."

"Anarus, do you think you could be Death's child?" I ask gently. "You said that everyone assumes you're pure when that isn't allowed, and your power is unlike anyone else's. Could that be because you inherited it from Death?"

Anarus looks down at his lap, his hands fidgeting over my feet. "I've wondered about that sometimes. No one would accept me though, if it were true. I would be shunned."

"As would I if anyone found out I'm colorblind." Ydum tells him. "And Byder would be if his parents hadn't helped him with his reading issue so much. They expected him to die in the games because he couldn't read the manuals and know what to do. But we were all teamed together and help him how he needs it."

I groan. "Yet again, it seems like the original gods are trying to use the games to rid themselves of problems while keeping their hands clean. How many times have they done this before and been successful, I wonder. Did the other gods that failed in cave have issues like you guys do? We'll never know for sure, but fuck."

Ydum shakes his head. "Half-truths and secrets. We can't know anything for sure unless the original gods admit to it. Even then, we have to trust that they're telling the truth, which I don't think we can trust them to do. Jinx's magic, Ani's powers, there's a link there. We know that already. But what and how, we can only guess until we figure out exactly what Jinx's magic is and Anarus has his full mantle to work with. The rest of it? The original gods are using their power in ways that are not right, no matter if the stories they tell are true or not. Starting with the banishment of Death and all the way to these games right now. This is all wrong. But what can we do about it?"

"Nothing." Anarus mutters, his anger at the futility of it all showing. "We can't do anything. At least, not now. After the games, when we have our mantles and maybe understand Jinx's magic, maybe. But now, we can just survive when they don't seem to want us to."

"That in and of itself is a form of fighting back." I say. "Surviving. You said the same thing about my panic attacks after Jacob and his friends hurt me when I was sixteen. I survived how I could when they wanted me not to. We are on the seventh game when I don't think they thought we would survive the cave. We just keep surviving until they have no choice but to accept us, you as fully crowned gods and me as whatever a witch becomes when they complete the games."

"Demi-god." Ydum tells me. "You become a demi-god. You only have the magic you already had, but get immortality like the gods have. Every witch who survives gets that much."

"And if my magic is more than a witch usually has, more like the original gods have, then when they give me the immortality to go with it…"

"You would be no different than they are." Ydum says. "More god than even we are because you aren't limited to one thing. I'm only nature, a descendant of Nature. Byder is only hunt, a descendant of Hunt. Ani is, well, whatever Ani is. But you, Jinx? We haven't found a limit for you yet. You made it rain, that's Nature, Water, and Spring. You made it warm which is Fire. You can create peace, that's the Fates. You can call a wolf, that's Hunt. You moved life from the rabbit to the dead witch, so that covers Wind. You are creative as fuck, which can be Knowledge, Curiosity and Inspiration. And if Ani's shadows are from

Death, well, you did that too."

"Fuck, Ydum." Byder declares. "That's eleven of the original gods. If you think of the Fates as all one type, and the four seasons, that's seventeen of them. She'd only be missing the Sky, which is debatable. She made clouds. Other than that, all that's left is the two Fertility gods and well, I'm not broaching that one right now."

I can't help but giggle at that. "Pretty sure everything's good on that front. Or at least was. We have been here five weeks and nothing."

"Fertility inhibitor in the food takes care of that for the females." Anarus says, getting my meaning before the others do.

"So, then, all the original gods' powers in one pretty little package." Ydum says. "Add in a god guided actual fucking familiar and, if we are right, Jinx, you are one scary witch. Really scary to the original gods if they have to make you immortal on top of everything else."

"If we are right," I sit up, or try to. Anarus has to help me. "If we are right, then the four of us together are a problem for the original gods. Ydum is all of nature. Byder is all of the hunt. Anarus, we don't know about you, but how much you want to bet you are full death or whatever you are? And me, a witch that can do all magic? We'd be scary as a whole, bonded group. A group that is bonded more than just several gods to me, but each of the gods to each other too."

"I am not death." Anarus says.

Ydum tilts his head. "You are not death, or you can't do death?"

"Can't do death." Anarus clarifies.

"Have you ever tried?" Ydum asks.

Anarus opens his mouth to say something, then closes it again.

Ydum holds out his hand. On it is the rosebud we practice my magic with. "Why don't you try it now? Can you make the rose die?"

Anarus looks at the rose, leaning forward to concentrate on it. His shadows swirl out from him and envelope the rose. Ydum squeezes his eye shut, as if something is hurting him. The shadows lift and the rose is wilted, petals dry and stem brown.

"Fuck." Byder stares at the rosebud, pulling Ydum's hand towards him. "Anarus is Death's child."

Anarus sits back, breathing hard but not from the effort of killing the rose. Panic is swirling his shadows around him.

Fuck my pain, I think. I pull him to me and grab his face with both hands to make him look at me. "Anarus. This changes nothing. You know that, right? It changes nothing for me. For Byder or Ydum too. Right guys?" I glance at them only long enough to know they are nodding.

Anarus's eyes are unfocused. He's looking at me but not seeing me. "My father is Death. Death never had any children. He was banished. How is he my father? Who is my mother? How?"

Ydum is still looking at the rosebud. "This cannot leave this room. If the others knew he could do this, they would kill him. Damn the games, the other gods would kill him on the spot. Or worse. Death was banished. Anarus being his son would mean Death broke that banishment. What the other gods would do if they figured out Anarus is Death's child? I can't even fathom..." He closes his hand and crushes the rose. "That never happened."

Anarus's eyes finally see me. "I'm not an orphan. I have a father. No one knows where, but he isn't dead. He's out there somewhere. Does he know about me?"

"We'll find him, Anarus." I tell him. "After the games, we'll find him if we have to go all the way to the non-magical continent. Then, you can ask him. We'll find your father, Anarus."

Anarus looks at Byder and Ydum, questions in his mind. "Sounds like we have a plan for our first vacation together as a family after the games." Ydum says, smiling at Anarus.

Byder nods. "Anyone know what the weather is like there? I hate being cold."

"You're not going to leave? I'm death. My power is death." Anarus asks in an incredulous tone, as if he can't quite believe what he's hearing.

"And I kill animals all the time." Byder tell him.

Ydum smiles at him again. "And the dirt the plants grow in is the decayed material from things that have died. Death is part of life. Just like you are part of us now."

Kinshra pops up in my mind, feeling Anarus's panic through me, and I quickly explain to her what is going on. "Kinshra says wolves cause a bunch of death when they hunt too. And you and I are both already connected to her. Nothing would be in balance without death with life. Her words."

"Well," Byder slaps his hands on his knees and stands. "With that settled, who wants lunch?"

Chapter Two

AS BYDER SERVES US all, we move on to lighter topics. Anarus still seems a little shell shocked, but slowly Ydum brings him back around with bad jokes and stories. I have to rip my sandwich into tiny pieces so eating doesn't hurt my lip and jaw. Ydum teases me about it, but takes pity on me and cuts my carrot sticks into small pieces for me.

After lunch, we move on to discussing the next game. In my pain and despair after the last game, I missed Drila telling us what it is. Ydum reminds me it is intellect.

"This game is usually some sort of puzzle." He explains. "It combines witch's and god's knowledge to find solutions for something. One year, there was a treasure hunt. Another year, there were puzzle boxes. Some years, they let all the gods in a group go and others, they didn't. But every time, the goal is to complete whatever task it is using knowledge and creativity as fast as possible. The intellect game always has the lowest death and failure rate. Basically, no one dies in this game. The biggest problem people have is getting stuck on one part for a long time. Some years it's taken days because one team or another is struggling for so long, but the game waits for them to figure it out and doesn't count them as out just because they take days to solve it."

"Well, that doesn't sound too bad." I say, rather relieved. I'm not going to be physically in a good spot in six days, no matter how many gods and witches help heal me.

Byder agrees. "I think they know that, after the combat game, too many people are battered and bruised and need an easy week."

I chuckle at him. "Well, I definitely have the battered and bruised covered for our team. Although, Ydum, don't think I didn't notice those bruises on you. What happened?"

He shrugs with one shoulder. "Esnir got in a few lucky hits. Nothing too major."

"You will be drinking Damek's grandmother's tea tonight too." I glare at him so he knows I'm serious.

Ydum pretends to hang his head at being admonished, but smiles at me. "Yes, ma'am."

I smile back, letting it go. "How do you guys suggest we prepare for the intellect game?"

"I don't think there really is a way to prepare for this game." Ydum tells me. "The preparation really all happened while we were in school, you included, Jinx. All four of us are smart and capable. It really shouldn't be too hard."

"Three." Byder mutters.

I turn to face him, staring at him hard. "What did you say?"

"Three, all three of you are smart and capable." Byder repeats.

"I thought we covered this with the succubus." I admonish him now. "You are smart, capable, and wonderful. I would gladly go into the intellect game with only you if I had to. You are part of our team, our family, and you have so much to offer, to help."

Before I realize what is happening, Byder is kneeling in front of me, his head in my lap and his arms around my waist. "How do you do that? How can you always make me feel I'm good enough just by looking at me and a few words? It's like magic. Whenever I doubt myself, you are there making me feel like I can take on the world."

I put my hand on his head in my lap and run my fingers through his hair, chuckling. "It's not magic, Byder. It's the truth. You are amazing and I have no doubt you could take on the whole world. All three of you." I look at Anarus, still struggling with his own feelings after killing the rose. I reach out my hurt hand to him and he captures it in his own, gently cradling it, letting his shadows rest on it. "All three of you."

When I turn to face Ydum, he only smiles. "Nope, magic. I'm saying it's magic. Because you're doing it again."

"And you three do the same for me." I tell them. "Never once have you made me feel like I'm not good enough because of my problems or the fact that I know almost nothing about these games. Well, except for Anarus. That was only in the beginning, but he's young so we'll forgive him. Especially if he keeps using his cold shadows to make my wrist not hurt as much."

Byder sits up quickly. "Shit, forgot you were hurt. Sorry."

"We should probably look at the paintings, see what they are." Ydum changes the topic, I think because they are all feeling a little too emotional for their own liking. "Can you walk, Jinx, or do you want us to wait a few days?"

I shake my head. "We need to see what they are. I can manage it." Once I am standing, I remember I'm not wearing any pants. Ydum grabs some from the room and it takes both him and Anarus to help me get them on. My hip and toes hurt far more than I want to let on, but I think they know.

In the hallway, only a few people are moving around. Saffron and Velmos are out, looking at the paintings too. Saffron seems to avoid my gaze. If I'm right that they were getting the petunia long before the rest of us, she may be feeling very foolish and confused about her behavior over the last week. I don't say anything but only smile at her. She'll come around again or not.

The paintings, which it breaks my heart to only see six of them, are all easily understandable even with the messenger god Wilros no longer here to help us. Three of them are paintings of mazes. One maze is made out of bushes, another is made of stone walls, and the third is swirls carved through the dirt. The other three are different types of puzzles. One painting shows many doors and many keys. Another has a wooden puzzle box with pieces that have to be twisted or moved in a certain order to open the box. The third one shows a scroll with letters and numbers on it that make no sense in the order they are in.

I ask Ydum about the last one. He tells me it's a cipher puzzle. "It's a word puzzle where you answer questions and each letter in the answer becomes a number. There is also a phrase or sentence made of numbers and you decode it using the letters from the questions and what number they mean. I can make one for you to try later if you want. They can be a fun brain teaser sometimes, but I don't think we would want them for this game."

"Which one would you want?" Byder asks him.

Ydum wanders the hall looking at all the paintings again. "I think one of the mazes. Puzzle can be fun, but not for something like this. Honestly, I would pick the bushes maze. I can manipulate the plants and mazes can be easy if you know what you are doing."

I look at Anarus. "Do you agree with that?"

"Yeah." He puts his hands in his pocket and isn't quite looking at all of us yet. "Dirt one if not the bushes. Again, Ydum's power can help us find our way."

"Well, we're in second. We should be able to get one of those two." I say. "If Drila doesn't twist the way we choose the painting to screw us over."

"And your order of choice is Ydum, Anarus, me, Jinx. I won't hear any arguments on that." Byder says. "Anarus and Ydum are both really good with book stuff, but Ydum is the better of the two."

"Not arguing that." Anarus says as Ydum just tries to hide a blush that makes the green tinge to his cheeks more pronounced.

"And with the combat game over, there's no reason for you to make me run anymore." I smile at Ydum.

"Oh, ho ho, so you think." He slides his arm around me, and I lean into him willingly. Standing is hard work right now. "There's still the wild card game. Workouts are only paused while you heal, not cancelled altogether."

"Damn, so close." I mutter, making all three of them laugh.

With nothing much needed to prepare for the next game, and my workouts halted until my skin is less of a kaleidoscope of rainbow colors, as Byder put it at one point, our days are pretty much free for relaxing. I spend some time every day still working with Kinshra but other than that, my job is to heal.

I think Byder is right that the games are giving everyone a break. The other humans I see in my occasional ambles through the hallway just for a change of scenery are as sore and stiff as I am. Well, not quite as bad, but still, they are almost all sporting at least a few bruises and when Esnir makes his rounds to our room on the third night to see how I'm doing, he tells us he has helped with healings for all the other humans as well. The gods, fortunately, can mostly heal themselves.

We don't have the same remembrance type meeting for Aretha, Zodum, Asteria, and Wilros as we did for Amanda and Tholdir. For one, with the division that happened before game six, we're still finding our new footing after the haze of petunias has cleared. I'm trying not to hold a grudge against Saffron, Wren, and Raven and their gods for the way they were to Ydum after my panic attack, assuming he had been harming me just because that's what Aretha said must have happened. It's hard though, even knowing they were under a magic working and not thinking clearly.

We also have the issue of feeling our own guilt. I killed Aretha. Ydum killed Zodum. Kutar killed Wilros. Damek killed Asteria. Their deaths are a lot harder to blame solely on the original gods and rally together around when you can still feel their blood on your hands. Add in that Damek attacked me, Raven shot an arrow into Saffron's thigh, and Uesis hit Velmos with half of a fight song, not to mention the myriads of bruises everyone gave pretty much everyone else, we are all struggling with our own emotions too much to come together yet.

Since our discovery about Anarus, Ydum has wanted to work with him and see what he really can do with his power. Anarus knew he could obscure things, make people or things hidden in his shadows, confuse people, and other small things like that. But with him killing the rose with only his shadows, we are curious what his real powers are and what they will be after he's crowned with his mantle.

Anarus seems to only be playing along with Ydum because he's hoping we stumble onto something that gives us an idea who his mother might be. He makes comments often about who the original eight goddesses are and what their powers are. Everyone has just assumed Anarus's powers act like they do, giving him physical manifestations he has a hard time controlling before he has his mantle, because he's too pure, the child of two gods, but somehow he's latched onto the idea that it's not only two gods, but two original gods.

"Who else would have a child with Death but another original?" Anarus says on the fourth night.

Byder disagrees with him. "Which one, though? You can eliminate Sadness. That was Modes's mom and if she had another child when Modes was three, we all would have known."

"My sister said when Modes was born, it was a huge deal." Ydum tells us. "Everyone knew she was having another child because of her position in Veirveil. I don't think any of the original goddesses could have hid being pregnant from the entire city."

My gods are working out in the sitting room while they talk and I'm watching from a spot on the couch since they won't let me participate. Not that I fought them too hard about it. It's kind of fun to watch them try to outdo each other without making it apparent they are showing off for me. And it is definitely fun to watch them do it in their preferred shirtless states. Not gonna lie, all those muscles and tattoos on such blatant display? Kinda hot. Especially since Byder left his hair down.

We are also being very careful. The door to our room is locked, something we haven't done in weeks except when we left for a game or were sleeping. We don't want anyone walking in on this discussion. We also lock the door when Anarus works with Ydum on his powers and I monitor his mood so he doesn't accidentally make another brown out, or worse.

"Why are you so convinced that it's two original gods?" I ask. "What about your powers makes you so convinced that people are right assuming you are pure?"

"The shadows, mostly." Anarus tells me. They are doing pushups much better than I ever have.

"The temper." Ydum adds. "That was a shit pushup Ani, it doesn't count."

Anarus glares at him. "Fuck you, it was fine."

Byder laughs. "Case in point. But beyond that? I don't know, man. Jinx may have a point. Why does everyone assume you're that pure but never thought to ask which gods are your parents? Someone knows who your mom is. She wouldn't have been able to hide a whole pregnancy and birth, then just go back to life like nothing happened."

"If she survived the birth." Ydum points out, and I cringe. I don't think it's a good idea to start worrying about the potentiality that Anarus's mom may have died in childbirth. It happens and it's something to think about, but maybe not right now when all this is so fresh for him.

I try to move the discussion away from the death aspect without being obvious about it. "That's a good point, Byder. Were there any goddesses that disappeared for a long time before Anarus was born, or disappeared altogether?"

"That's tricky." He tells me as they move onto planking. Gods, these gods look good like this. "Actually disappeared for no known reason? No. But Summer and Winter always disappear for most of the year. They and Spring and Fall usually are only around during their season."

"Well, when is your birthday, Anarus? That could narrow it down with those two, or eliminate them completely." I pause in thought. "Actually, when is all of your birthdays? I just realized I don't know anything like that. Birthdays, favorite colors. food, or anything. Heck, it was weeks until I knew Ydum has a sister."

Anarus answers first. "October first, red, cherry ice cream."

"Shit." I say in response. "It was your birthday two weeks ago and you didn't even say anything. You're twenty-two now. I would have done something for you."

"Oh, you did something for me, little human." Anarus gives me a hooded look.

I raise my eyebrows, unsure what he means and then think about what we were doing two weeks ago and blush heavily. Two weeks ago, on October first, was when we were all together in the sitting room, after we helped Asteria with her meditation. "Not what I meant." I mutter and Anarus laughs.

Byder answers my question too, ignoring all of that. "January twelfth, ice blue, fresh venison jerky."

"May twenty-sixth, strawberries, and rude question to the colorblind god. I have the rarest form of colorblindness according to the human doctor my mom took me to, called achromatopsia. So gray, I guess, since they are all gray." Ydum says. "Now, we know your shitty birthday of September fifth, but not the food or color, Jinx."

I smile. "Fresh baked bread right out of the oven with honey butter smeared all over it, and forest green, almost the same shade as a certain god's eyes."

Ydum drops from his plank to lie on his stomach, kicking his legs in the air behind him as he leans on his hands and bats his eyelashes at me, mimicking a swooning young girl. "You don't mean me, do you?" He drops the act and sits up. "No, really. Do you mean me because I know my eyes are green but only because Mom told me once."

I throw a pillow from the couch at him. "Of course, I mean you, silly."

As the three males return to their workout, my thoughts return to the whole reason I asked those questions in the first place. Anarus's birthday is the beginning of October. He's almost convinced that one of the original goddesses has to be his mother, but for that to be true, she had to be able to keep his birth secret from the entire city of the gods, Veirveil. The only goddesses who can regularly disappear for long enough for that are Summer and Winter, who are only seen during their seasons. Summer would have just gone back into her reclusive disappearance a few weeks before Anarus was born, and the people of Veirveil would have noticed if she was pregnant. But Winter would not have made an appearance for several months yet. The math lines up for Winter.

But all this hinges on us being right that Anarus is the child of two original gods and that being the source of his strange shadow power. Beyond his ability to cause a flower to die while held by a nature god, we have no real proof his father is Death, who hasn't been seen since the creation of the world and never had any other children. And we have even less to say his mother is anyone at all. She could be a witch, another god, or any of the children of the original gods. She could be anyone at all.

My mind flits back to Winter, though. Thoughts tease at my brain. Anarus holding my wrist so that he acts as a cold compress on it. Every time, his shadows have made me feel cold before I touch his warm skin. The second game. Byder and Anarus had to defend against Damek and Amanda's weather. Damek got clouds over us. He needed sleet and it had been snowing. I was freezing because it was so cold. Ydum and I had thought that was Damek trying for that perfect temperature for just the right mix between rain and snow, but Byder told us that was actually Anarus using his shadows to make it only snow. It had been so cold, so very cold. But not dark. Anarus made it cold, not dark.

I suddenly feel eyes on me. I look up from the spot on the floor my gaze had landed as I was thinking and see three sets of eyes looking at me curiously.

"You stare at that floor any harder, beautiful, and you'll bore a hole through it." Ydum bends down to squat by me and look in my eyes. "What are you thinking of so intensely you didn't hear us say your name twice?"

I look at Anarus for only a moment, but it was long enough I know Ydum saw me looking at him. "If I said nothing, would you believe me and let it go?" I'm not sure I want to say these thoughts out loud yet.

"Not when you ask us to like _that_." Anarus grumbles.

29

Ydum looks at me for a moment longer, some sort of recognition there on his face. He immediately smothers it and returns to his goofy, light-hearted nature and stands back up, managing to block me to hide my expression from the other two. "Hey now, I think a girl is allowed a few secrets. If she wants to daydream about my pretty green eyes, she should be allowed her fantasies in private."

I roll my eyes. "Ugh, Ydum. You are so modest, aren't you?"

Byder laughs. "Never know, could have been my brown eyes. Oh wait, you wouldn't know that, Ydum."

Ydum places a hand over his heart and pretends to stagger. "You wound me with that very lazy jab, sir."

"Children." I sigh heavily. "You are all no better than children. Now, if you are all done pretending to work out so you can show off, I think Ydum and Anarus have some practicing to do."

Ydum turns academic very quickly. "I've actually had some thoughts, Ani. I thought we could try some things."

"Why is every time you have thoughts, I end up in an experiment?" Anarus complains, but we know it's hollow.

"Actually, I have thoughts too." I change my mind and decide to tell them.

Byder crosses his arms over his chest with a satisfied smile. "See, I knew you were thinking about something."

"Jinx's thoughts." Anarus says, coming to sit next to me. "I choose Jinx's thoughts first. They're usually much more pleasant."

I shift to face Anarus and I'm aware that Ydum and Byder make themselves comfortable to watch. "Try not to think too much about this, okay? Just go with me here for a minute." I hold out my right hand to him. Esnir had checked it over and said I actually hadn't re-fractured it in the last game, but it still hurt a lot. It's been getting better, as have all my injuries, with Esnir's help and healing teas from Damek and Isis. "Take my hand."

Anarus gingerly takes my hand in his. He's watching me while I watch our hands. As he settles my hand in his grip, he rubs a spot on my hand gently with his thumb and it's utterly distracting. "What am I supposed to be doing?"

"Nothing yet. Just wait." I still watch our hands. I can feel the cold just above the warmth of his skin. The duality of the sensations was one of the first things that drew me to him and I still love the way it feels. "Is your hand cold, Anarus?"

He thinks about this for a moment. "No. Well, yes, but not my hands really. The shadows are always cold."

I speak slowly. "Anarus, what shadows are on your hand right now?"

Out of the corner of my eye, I see Ydum walk through the room. Anarus looks down at his hand. "There aren't any."

"Then what's making your hand cold?" I ask him. Ydum comes up behind me and hands me a cup of water from the washroom over my shoulder. I look up at him and can tell from his face he figured out what I was thinking. That male really is a genius. I take the cup in my good hand with a nod, and instead of moving back to where he was sitting, Ydum crouches down and leans on the couch arm to watch.

Anarus looks at us both, startled and confused. "But it's the shadows that make my skin cold."

I take my hand out of his. "Not your skin, Anarus. Your skin is warm, always warm. The cold hovers above your skin." I take one finger and dip it into the water. Then, I hold the finger over his palm so that several drops fall on his palm. "Freeze the water, Anarus. Make the cold actually touch you and freeze the water."

Anarus cups his palm so that the drops of water roll in the middle of the palm. He stares at them and I see shadows start to pull around his hand.

"Stop." I tell him. "Don't use your shadows. You do it."

Anarus looks up at me, confusion marring his face. I look back at him, maintaining even breaths and my face the picture of calm. He turns his eyes back down to the water drops in his hand, then closes his eyes and takes a deep breath. Internally, I feel panic forming in him. He's scared.

I reach out and take his other hand in mine. "I love you, Anarus. I will always love you. You're safe here with us." As I watch, the small drop of water in his palm turns into a small ball of ice.

"Fuck." Ydum says quietly and plucks the ice from Anarus's palm, rolling it between his fingers in the light.

"How did you know?" Anarus looks at me and the panic comes back again.

"You made it snow." I smile at him. "You turned Damek's sleet into snow without your shadows. It never got darker on that island. It was you, not your shadows."

"What is the best way to hide a pure god that's the child of Death and Winter?" Byder's voice call out from his spot on the couch, between gritted teeth. He's not confused like Anarus, or fascinated like Ydum, but angry. "Tell everyone they're a god of obscurity, something no one has seen before, and then tell him that power is rare and strange and he must contain it to be loved and accepted."

"What a horrible psychological trick to play on a child." Ydum mutters. "Tie their ability to be loved to the control over their power they have yet to be granted by the games. He can't win. Because no one understands his power, and no one helps him with it, he can't contain it. He doesn't get that love and acceptance. He'll fight harder to contain it, instead of learning to control it, which makes it break out in even worse ways, making others even more terrified of his rare and strange, and maybe dangerous, power, and shun him even harder."

Byder's cheeks hollow as he grits his teeth, the muscles in his jaw twitching as he tries to contain his frustration. "The child will blame himself for being unlovable, and everyone else blames him for his power being wrong. Never let him actually have that love and acceptance, so he always hides his powers more in hopes of achieving the impossible."

He laughs, a sharp laugh that sounds almost feral. He shoots to his feet and tugs a hand through his hair. "How fucking awful are the original gods? They knew they were making a system where no one would want to be around him enough to figure out why his power is like it is. Everyone would avoid him out of fear and not care what the original gods do to him as long as it doesn't involve them. So, no one would ever guess that he's the child of a forbidden mating. Winter and death go hand in hand often. Without the gift from Fire, humans would die in the winter. Death is so easy in winter. Gods of the hunt know this. The animals are at their weakest, food scarce for everything. Even the plants die in winter, right Ydum? A child from the two of them would have catastrophic powers. They would be the poster child for why two gods should not mate together."

Ydum is still rolling the ball of ice between his fingers, crouching to lean on the couch arm. "That was probably the real problem with the pure gods. Powers that don't work well together. Imagine the child of a fire goddess and a water god. What power would that child inherit? It would be catastrophic, or conversely, nullified to nonexistence. Or what about a god of honor and a trickster goddess? But the other side could be just as dangerous. What about the child of war and hate? They would be unstoppable. So, what would the powers be for the child of Death and Winter? Two powers that are already so strong and only amplify each other?"

"But she was there." Anarus has his eyes trained on me, his whole focus on me, looking for comfort, looking for me to tell him everything will be okay. "Winter was there every time they told me that I failed again. That I had done something wrong and they needed to move me somewhere new again and would convene to argue over where to send me next. She wouldn't have just sat there and said nothing if she was my mother."

"Every time, Anarus?" Ydum asks him, not looking at him to give him space. "Winter was there every time? Even in, say, June?"

I feel the panic and pain bloom as the realization of it all hits Anarus. "We're done. Anarus, we're done thinking about this today. It doesn't matter. We don't need to answer every question now." My words aren't helping. I can feel him spiraling deeper. I grab his face between my hands and close my eyes, thinking peace and love. Only peace and love. I need you to feel my love, Ydum's love, Byder's love. I need you to feel the peace that we accept you just as you are and you can never do something wrong enough to make us not love and accept you anymore. Your powers are beautiful and wonderful, just like you.

"Jinx." Anarus is crying.

I open my eyes and keep his gaze on mine. "It's all true. We love you. All three of us and you are safe with us, accepted by us. No matter who your parents are or what your power is, we will always love and accept you. You are a part of our family forever."

Anarus tries to pull his face away. "It's only the cave magic. After the games…"

I stop him. "After the games, you will have your full mantle, as will Byder and Ydum, and I will get what I get, and we will be a family like the cave magic told us we should be. No one will ever be able to tell you that you are wrong or bad for what your power is because you will have proven yourself worthy of the full crown of your mantle, and will have two other fully crowned gods and one pretty bad ass witch standing by your side, supporting you."

I can still feel his hesitance, so I try one more time. He has been hurt so much, I don't blame him for not believing what's right in front of him. "What do you feel for me, Anarus? Do you love me?" I know he does without him even saying the words. I can feel it through the bond the cave gave us. "Even with my magic being all sorts of wrong? Even with a birthday that means I never learned what I should and I came to the games with no shoes and have to wear your boots that are too big? What about Ydum? A colorblind nature god that can't even tell what color the flowers are on your tattoo? You love him? And Byder who has the letters go funny so he can't read well enough to learn things that way? Do you love him? With all our broken parts and hard things, do you love us? Or is that just the cave magic?"

"I love you more than anything, Jinx. You are perfect. I love all three of you. It's not just the cave, the cave just helped me find you." Anarus says, then the point I'm making gets through. I feel him relent and the pain ebb. It isn't gone. It'll probably never be gone for him, but for now, he can breathe.

As Anarus collapses against me, resting in my arms as he lets the panic go, Byder shakes his head and smiles. "Jinx's magic of words to the rescue again. I think you are forever going to be patching up our broken parts, baby girl."

"As long as you three patch up mine in return, I'm fine with that." I tell him.

Anarus mutters into my shoulder. "Yeah, well can you stop making it actual broken parts instead of just emotional dysfunction, little human? Human bodies are so hard to fix."

That night, as I am getting ready to go to bed, Anarus approaches me quietly. "Can I," he stops and takes a deep breath, blowing it out hard, "I know you are hurt, but can I come with you? I just want to be close to you."

All three of them have been so worried about me that, after that first night, they all have slept elsewhere. I think they got scared when they realized how utterly fragile my body is compared to theirs. But now, Anarus is digging a toe into the floor, ashamed to ask me for comfort when he needs it. "I'm not that hurt, you know? Esnir is really good at healings, and Damek's grandmother's tea is amazing."

I wrap my arms around him and pull him in for a kiss. "Plus, it's been a few days since any of you have checked my wounds. It might be a good idea for you to do that. If you can be really, really gentle."

Anarus's eyes go wide and I feel the need in him. "I can be gentle."

"Then, never be afraid to ask me for what you need." I kiss him again. He kisses me back this time and it's a hungry kiss, tempered but full of longing. He follows me into the bedroom and slowly helps me undress.

He moves slowly and methodically, his hands and lips finding everywhere that is and isn't hurt. He takes off my shirt and skims soft fingertips over my right shoulder, letting the cold seep into my skin. "This is looking better. Not as bruised." He tells me before moving his fingers to my left shoulder, touching just as gently but following the touch with kisses. My spine lights up as desire starts to build in me.

He trails his fingertips lower, tracing my nipples with a cold and hot sensation that makes me gasp. He takes one nipple into his mouth and sucks on it, biting down as he does. "These weren't hurt at all, which thank fuck for that. They are too perfect to be marred." He moves his fingers and mouth to the other nipple and I grip his shoulders as he gives it the same treatment.

His fingers trail down my stomach, tracing a path between the healed weal marks from Aretha's whip. He controls the cold in his hands perfectly so that his touch is cooling on the spots where the cold would help the ache and warm everywhere else. "These look much better. Almost completely healed, I would say."

I lick my lips and drop my head back at the perfection of his touch and the tight coil of need it is forming in me. "You are doing a very good job being gentle, Anarus." I tell him breathlessly.

His hands skim down my sides to my hips, his hand on my right hip cool and his hand on my left hip warm. "We'll still have to be very careful with this. Bruise is better, but still. I see you favoring it. It still hurts, doesn't it?" He lets his hand linger, not actually touching my right hip but close enough I feel the coolness soothing my skin. His other hand has a firm grip on my left hip.

"Not right now, it doesn't." I grip his shoulders tighter. "Nothing hurts right now."

He moves a hand between my thighs, both hot and cold at the same time, making my muscles clench. "This wasn't hurt at all, so no need to be gentle here." He runs a finger along me, pushing on my sensitive skin. "So fucking wet already." He slips his finger between the folds of my skin and pushes it inside me, the coolness in direct contrast with how warm I feel.

He kneels in front of me and runs his warm tongue over my clit. Between the warmth of his mouth and the cold of his finger as he moves it in and out of me, curling it as he strokes me, I have to fight to make my legs keep holding me up. I rest my hands on his shoulders and tremble against him.

He bites down gently on my clit as he add a second finger and a shiver runs through me. I ball up my fists, clutching his shirt in my hands. "Oh, fuck."

"Do you need to sit down, little human?" Anarus's voice is thick and deep and makes my heart pound.

"I need to touch you." I dig my nails into the skin of his shoulders. "Please."

Anarus lifts me and tenderly lays me down on the bed. "Whatever you need, Jinx. Everything you need." He strips and crawls over me, his legs between mine and his hands on either side of my shoulders holding him up so that he hovers above me. He uses his knee to push my left leg wider but lets my right leg stay as it is, in whatever position is comfortable. He shifts and I can feel his hard length teasing and brushing at my entrance.

I bring my hands up to his chest, brushing my fingers against his skin like he brushed his against mine, reveling in the feeling of the cold heat. I love tracing his tattoos, but avoid the wolf on his chest. I don't need Kinshra interested in what is going on right now. So, I limit myself to the flowers and barbed wire on his arms and the moon the bond tattoo of a wolf is howling at.

"You doing okay, little human?" Anarus murmurs softly in my ear. "Is this gentle enough for you?" He moves his hips so that his cock slides against me and I moan every time he brushes my clit, sending scatterings of electric shocks through me.

I move my hands to trace the phases of the moon I know trail down his spine and shift under him. "I need you, Anarus. I need you inside me."

He leans down and kisses my mouth, taking possession of my lip in his teeth. His hips dip and he pushes slowly inside me, giving me time to adjust and shift to keep pressure off my hip. When he's seated fully inside me, he stills. "This what you need?"

"Oh, fuck yes." I gasp and grip his back tighter, my nails scraping against his skin.

He starts to move, rocking his hips in slow, torturous circles. I know he's watching me for any signs this hurts, but it doesn't. All I feel is slowly building pressure in my core at his movements, pleasure feeding fire to my blood.

"More." I moan out as I cling to him.

"You sure, little human?" Anarus groans out. I can feel his need climbing right alongside mine through our bond. Somewhere in the back of the bond, I also feel Byder and Ydum's awareness of what's happening and their satisfaction and pleasure with it. There's also relief from them that my healing is good enough for me to enjoy this. All three of the gods' desire mixes with mine and the headiness of it pushes me higher, the coil in my core tightening at the intensity of feeling four people's pleasure at once.

"More!" I grind out, demanding this time, bringing my hips up to meet his.

Anarus heeds my demand, increasing his pace and pushing deeper. He finds my most sensitive spot and moves one hand under my left hip, angling me better so that he can stroke that spot with every thrust. I moan again and again as he pushes me to monumentous heights, digging my nails in his back as my muscles ripple around him and I fall.

He loses his control and pounds into me, forgetting to be gentle as he reaches for his release. "Oh, fuck, little human. You. Are. Fucking. Perfect." He matches his thrusts to his words and tenses as he spills himself inside me.

Anarus's body slackens as he catches his breath, but he holds his arms rigid, keeping his weight off me. He turns, lying along my left side and helping me roll towards him before pulling the blankets out from underneath us to pull over us. He curls his arm over my waist and pulls me close, nuzzling his face in my neck. "I never want to let you go."

"Then, don't." I pull him closer and think peace over both of us. Just before I feel him drift off, I whisper. "I love you, Anarus."

I have decided that my favorite thing in the whole world is waking up surrounded. I have a vague awareness that, sometime in the night, Byder and Ydum came into the room under the guise of wanting to check on me and Anarus and I just scooted over for them. Byder climbed into the bed and curled himself around the other side of me than Anarus and then Ydum, unsure what to do, just hung back wavering at the door to the room.

Byder eventually rolled his eyes and said, "Get over here," to him, patting the bed behind him. Ydum climbed under the covers and sprawled behind him, his long arm draped over both Byder and me.

There is something there with that, I think when I wake up and find Byder facing Ydum. Byder's arm is around Ydum's waist, his hand absentmindedly tracing up and down Ydum's spine and both of their legs tangled with the other's, sleeping peacefully. I watch them for a moment as they nuzzle closer to each other in sleep, Ydum tangling his long fingers in Byder's hair, before realizing Anarus is also awake, his head propped up on his elbow, looking at them over my shoulder.

"You think that's something?" Anarus whispers in my ear.

I nod. "I don't know if it's something Byder is ready to explore, but I hope they do."

"Me too." He kisses my shoulder gently. "You still good from last night? I didn't make anything hurt worse?"

I shake my head, smiling. "Oh big, gruff Anarus. If only everyone else knew what a softie you really are. No, you didn't hurt anything. You made it better."

He pretends to growl. "Don't tell anyone. I have a reputation to uphold." But he smiles.

"A smile and no coffee yet?" I feign shock. "What a treat for me."

This time Anarus's growl is real and he gets out of the bed. "You said the magic word. I'm up now."

We sneak out to the sitting room, me in only a shirt and Anarus only in pants, letting the other two sleep in for once. After we are situated for caffeine, and snuggled on the couch, I broach the topic we had started the day before. "Last night, you controlled the cold on your hands very well, Anarus, but you didn't use a single shadow. It's made me confused. We thought that you were the child of Death because of the flower. But then because you made the water freeze, we assume because you are the child of Winter. But you have already done things with your power using the shadows and obscurification. I thought every god only had one basic power. Byder's hunt power gives him different skills, but his power is hunting. All his different skills are just manifestations of what it takes to be a hunter. Same for Ydum. I'm having a hard time figuring out how all of your different abilities would piece together."

He takes a sharp breath. "I was thinking about that as well and, if we are right about who my parents are, I think I might have an idea." I raise my eyebrows and give him my full attention. He isn't upset or panicking, a move in the right direction from yesterday. "I think, and it's just a guess, that maybe my real mantle would be the god of the wilde hunt. I want to talk to Ydum before I totally say so, but it's my thoughts right now."

I never heard of that, so I ask. "The wilde hunt? Is that similar to Byder's hunt god?"

"Your village didn't do offerings to the wilde hunt?" Anarus sounds surprised, but then he shrugs. "Well, it has been a long time since the hunt has been said to run. I guess many witches would have abandoned the lore."

Anarus shifts in his seat and, for a moment looks so much like Ydum when he's going into academic mode, I almost laugh. "The wilde hunt is not a hunt like what Byder does. In the story of the original gods making the world, it used to be believed that Death gave his touch to the land in the dead of night between October thirty-first and November first. This act, adding the power of the word death to the world at that exact moment, created a bridge between the living and dead. Every year, this bridge opens for only moments, but it's long enough for the power of the dead to cross into the world of the living. Riding on the bitter freezing winds of winter, causing death to the land wherever they go, and hidden in the long nights and shadowy days, the shadows of the dead travel throughout the world, hunting for lost souls. They are accompanied by wolves, who lead the chase, their howls guiding the dead to their prey much like Byder would use a hunting dog. This amassing of the shadows of the dead is the wilde hunt."

While Anarus talks, I snuggle in closer to him. He wraps an arm around me and I'm pleased to feel how comfortable he is talking about this. "The story goes that if a human is caught outside at night any time between October thirty-first and the winter solstice, especially at a crossroads, they risk encountering the wilde hunt and being forced to join them. They will become confused and forget they are alive not dead. Then, the hunt takes them, and, unless they remember they are alive before the solstice, they will be stuck with the wilde hunt forever."

I feel an edge of discomfort build in Anarus. He's struggling, so I make sure to keep a comforting presence, stroking his arm and leaning my head against him. Reassurance through our emotions that I'm here and love him, no matter what. My reassurance must convince him to keep talking.

"The old stories used to say that the wilde hunt was the god of Death's revenge for his banishment after only doing what the other gods asked him to. But as the story about the gods changed, the idea of the wilde hunt fell away. Humans, both witches and not, used to leave offerings for the wilde hunt to entice them to take the offering instead of hunting in their villages, then it became offerings to the goddess of winter to keep the bitter cold of winter away, and now I'm not sure if the witches do anything anymore. But everything about the story lines up with so much about me, I have to wonder if there's some sort of validity to the old story. Shadows, cold, wolves, making people confused, I have a connection to all of that."

I listen closely. Everything Anarus is saying sounds right. Beyond that, it feels right. It fits everything we have seen Anarus do. "Well, if you're right, wouldn't you notice something with your power on October thirty-first? We'll still be here then."

"Maybe." Anarus wavers. "Maybe not until after I get crowned with my mantle."

I'm about to say something else when I feel something strange. It feels like desire, pleasure, satisfaction, and a little bit of curiosity and nervousness, and just a tinge of fear. But none of those emotions are mine right now. I'm confused and look at Anarus, expecting at least some of it to be coming from him, but he's only hiding a smile.

"That didn't take long." When I cock an eyebrow in confusion, he only jerks his head towards the door of the bedroom where Byder and Ydum are.

"Wait." My mouth opens in surprise. "Is that? Are they? Is this how it feels when it's me and one of them?"

Anarus only nods. "Well, maybe not the nerves anymore or the fear."

For some reason, I feel like laughing. I try hard to fight it back, but a giggle escapes anyway. "Oh, my gods."

"Consider this payback, little human." Anarus jokes, poking my side gently. "And we told you, find a new swear."

After too short a time, the feelings stop, rather suddenly with a burst of panic. Before I can ask Anarus about it, the bedroom door opens and Byder comes out, his face slightly red and he's very tense. He goes straight to the table and spends a very long time with his back to us, examining the breakfast options that have been the same for almost seven weeks.

After a few minutes, Ydum strolls casually out of the bedroom, bare-chested, wearing only pants, his face too neutral for his living vine tattoo that is only on his arm unless he gets emotional to be covering that much of his chest.

He sits down on the couch, says nothing, and is not looking at Byder. He's not looking at anyone.

I look from Byder's back to Ydum's chest and back again. Anarus is looking at absolutely nothing in particular. The silence gets heavy, but not in a bad way, more full of knowledge.

Byder eventually lets out a long sigh. Without turning around, he speaks. "You felt that, didn't you?"

"Yup." I say, biting my lip against the insane desire to laugh that's still plaguing me for some reason.

Byder groans heavily. "I didn't, I mean I've never." His shoulders sag as he gives up trying to find words.

I don't move from where I'm sitting as I say calmly, "Byder, sweetie, did you like it?"

He gives the smallest nod, his attention still completely on the table.

I turn to Ydum. "And I'm going to assume you liked it as well?"

"Yes." Ydum tells me.

"Then, nothing else matters." I tell them both. "You don't have to explain it to me or Anarus, or defend it. Like I told Ydum when he first told us about his sexuality, liking both guys and girls, this is the four of us, not me and each of you. I know we didn't have the connection this strong at the time, but that doesn't change anything. In fact, the way our fated mate bonds are all tangled up, makes that even more clear. This is the four of us in one relationship with each other rather than me in a relationship with each of you individually. Each of us as free to go as far as they are comfortable with each of us, in any combination that's agreed upon by all the participants. If you enjoyed being with Ydum, Byder, explore that. If you don't want to, then don't. That's between you and Ydum."

I pause for a moment, then add. "But I will say, it's interesting to be on the other end of that bond. Why the fuck do I feel like giggling so much?"

"The bonds. Fated mate bonds, or really destined mate bonds, usually aren't this interconnected, from what my past research has indicated. We keep saying fated mate bond but that's inaccurate for what the cave does. Destined mate bonds are not the same as Fate bonds."

I interrupt Ydum, confused. "Wait. Destined mate bonds and fated mate bonds aren't the same thing?"

Ydum relaxes in his seat with the attention off him and Byder and on the academics he feels comfortable with. "Not fated mate bonds, but Fate bonds, Jinx. You called the bond the cave gave us fated mate bonds, as do most witches and honestly a lot of gods too, but that is not strictly accurate. Fate is a very specific term, scientifically. It means something created purposely by the gods of Fate, Sadness, Peace, Anger, and Happiness. That is different than destiny, the way your life is just naturally shaped by some ephemeral force beyond even the original gods, life, free will, all that. It's very confusing to most people so they just say fate and mean both, Fate the gods, fate that is our destiny, whatever. But that gets confusing too."

I snort. "Yeah, sounds confusing."

"To make it simple, academia and science make a clear line of distinction." Ydum holds up one hand as if he's holding something. "Fate is what the gods of

Fate do purposely." He lifts his other hand. "Destiny is the stuff that just happens, that no one controls."

He moves his hands up and down as if they are tilting scales. "Two sides of the same coin with very different purposes. The Fates control certain parts. You will have a destined mate bond, a specific type of magic or power, whatever. Destiny controls the other parts. Who that mate is specifically. How strong your magic or power will be, and what a god's mantle will actually be. Are you a full nature god or just a god of nature that can work with flowers? The Fates determine you are in the nature pantheon, making a Fate bond to your life, and destiny decides how that plays out, how you fit into that pantheon."

"So," Byder is still at the table and only able to glance our way occasionally, "we've been in effect giving the Fate gods credit for something they didn't do when we call it fated mate bonds?"

"Yup." Ydum nods. "But don't feel bad. Everyone does it. The Fates didn't decide that Jinx would have a mate bond with three gods, just that she would be capable of having a mate bond with some god or another in her life. Destiny itself made it three, and the three of us specifically if that's how it works. But that also may have been the cave magic that made it us three specifically."

Ydum stands and I see him starting to lose himself in thought, his brow furrowed. "Mate bonds aren't under the Fates jurisdiction, though, and the cave wasn't made by them either, so maybe they don't make the mate bonds at all. Just leave a spot for the possibility... could be... Landon the knowledge god said in History of the Fates that the Fates are controlled by destiny, but Agor the third contradicted him, saying..."

"Uh oh. I think he lost the thread somehow." I whisper, then louder. "Hey, Ydum? You were telling us why I felt like giggling."

His head snaps up, looking at me like he forgot we were all here. He nods, going back to his seat. "Right, right. So yeah, Jinx, Fate bonds and mate bonds made by destiny itself are different, at least somewhat, and mate bonds aren't usually this entangled. Or no one has ever claimed their multiple god destined mate bonds found in the cave was like we seem to be, but then again there has never been a trio bond either, so..."

Ydum shakes his head, clearing his runaway thoughts yet again. "So, we feel each other's pleasure, probably pain eventually too, who knows. But for now, your body feels someone else's pleasure when you are doing nothing to cause it yourself. I've been thinking of it as bystander pleasure, a pleasure your body didn't know why was happening and didn't know what to do with." Ydum says. "Or, at least, that's my working theory."

"So, it wasn't just me that felt like that?" I look around the room.

Byder finally turns around and looks at us fully. "Do you know how odd it was to hear Anarus giggle the first time it happened to us? He giggled! Moody, shadow boy full on giggled."

"It was once and only because I was caught off guard." Anarus grumbles.

All three of us laugh at him for that.

"Well, either way," I say through my laughter, "our bond, whether it should be called a fated mate bond or a destined mate bond, is ours. We determine how it works and what's okay. And I say if you want to explore your feelings with each other, then do that. We've all told Anarus we love him. What's the difference if you two show it to each other in that way as well as say it?" I pause, then add. "But, for the record, I don't like the idea of giving any of the original gods credit for something they didn't actually do and don't want to call it a fated mate bond anymore."

"Agreed." Anarus grumbles. "Destined mate bond or just mate bond from here on out. I also agree with Jinx on the other stuff too." He glances at Byder and Ydum, then looks away quickly.

Ydum shakes his head, smiling and leaning back comfortably again. "Witch Jinx with her magic words making everything okay once again. I swear you can do more with one sentence than most witches can do with a witch's kit and a larder full of potions, teas, or whatever else they use."

I tilt my head to the side, sitting up straight, thinking. "Say that again."

Ydum repeats himself slowly, confused. "You do more magic with one sentence than most witches can do with a full witch's kit… Shit. Words. Your magic isn't done through need, or end magic or beginning magic but actually is through words. You say peace and create it. You think the words rain and it rains. You tell a life force to move from one body to another and it does. You call for Ani's shadows and tell them to throw someone off you, they come to you and make them fly through the air. You tell us we are loved and important and we know we are loved and important. Your magic is words, Jinx."

"Has magic ever worked that way before?" Byder asks, finally choosing his breakfast and coming to sit down on the couch.

I stop Ydum from answering Byder's question because I have my own. "Wait, but before you said my magic replicates all the magic and the original gods' powers. Now, you are saying it isn't that but the magic of words. Which is it?"

"Both, I think, Jinx." Ydum answers me, then Byder. "No, Byder."

"Actually, yes Byder." Anarus says. When we look at him, he explains. "The god of Death spoke the word death over the land to give it the touch of his power."

"To build the bridge?" I ask him, thinking back to the story of the wilde hunt.

Anarus nods. "And that would explain the connection between us."

"Fuck, do you think your power is god of the wilde hunt?" Ydum shakes his head, grinning ruefully. "Shit. Why didn't I think of that? It's a perfect fit for everything you do, and would explain the connection between your power and Jinx's magic. Death's use of a word of power opened the door for your power, which is the perfect, all-consuming combination of the powers of Winter and Death. And your power would be wildly unstable, especially during the winter months, Ani, until you take your mantle and actually can control the hunt. But it would also be perfectly tempered by, and also useable by, a witch who uses words for her magic that has a wolf for a familiar. Add in a hunt god and a nature god that can undo any damage the wilde hunt does, and you have a perfect team."

Ydum stands up and starts pacing, muttering to himself again. "A nature god who doesn't need colors because the wilde hunt makes the world gray anyway. A hunt god who can't read right because he only needs the spoken word of his witch. Or maybe is actually trying to read the language of the dead instead of what's in front of him? That would mean the language of the dead is a real thing, though. But we thought familiars weren't real, so maybe." Ydum keeps muttering to himself, gesturing as he paces the room.

"Ydum?" I say tentatively, but he doesn't seem to hear me.

"And he's gone in his own world. We aren't getting him back this time." Byder laughs. "If we weren't here, stuck in the games, I would lay money on us finding him in three hours ten books deep in a library somewhere."

I watch him move, tracing patterns in the air only he can see, muttering and pacing, following some path through the room only he knows. "Wow. I've never seen him this deep in academic thought before."

"Doesn't happen often, but I've seen it once or twice." Byder tells me. "Let him go. He's had a lot of academic thoughts he needs to muddle out in his head. He will resurface eventually. In school, the teachers would just let him go off and call his mom to tell her he would be home whenever he comes out of the trance."

There's a knock on the door and when Anarus opens it, Esnir comes in the room. He takes one look at Ydum and snorts. "He on a thought bender again? What tripped it this time?"

Byder covers smoothly. "Old lore stories and the powers of the Fates versus the power of destiny. Nothing important, but you know Ydum. He gets on an idea and he's gone."

Esnir only laughs and moves out of Ydum's pacing path as if this is nothing new to him. "I just came to check on your injuries, Jinx. I'll leave the lost in thought Ydum to you guys."

Ydum has enough sense not to mutter out loud while Esnir is in the room, but as soon as he's gone, Ydum goes back to drawing diagrams in the air and murmuring. I find his thought bender fascinating.

He makes different faces as he thinks. The light in his eyes and the touch of a smile when he has an idea, the furrow of his brow and chewing on his nails when he's stymied, biting his lip and tapping his long fingers on his thigh when he's making connections, the groans and dismay when those ideas fall through. He is so expressive and passionate, it makes me feel like I'm seeing a whole new Ydum.

I sit next to Byder and we watch Ydum while we eat lunch. "In some weird way, this is kinda hot." I think out loud, not realizing I actually said it.

"Yeah." Byder says, then startles as if he didn't mean to say that out loud either.

I glance at Byder from the side of my eyes, not looking directly at him to give him space. "You know you can talk to me about anything, right? Even this? Trust me, if anyone gets being caught off guard by feeling feelings you did not expect, it's me."

"Really?" Byder glances at me the same way.

I don't look at Byder directly. Instead, I let him hide from looking at me by sliding behind him to fix his hair into a smooth bun for the day. "Yes, really. I met all three of you less than two months ago. Sure, we've been forced to basically spend every second together since but I didn't know any of you. In normal situations, people would say that I'm crazy to have moved this quickly with not one but three males I don't know and that there's no way I know I love you and want to plan to be together forever this fast. But the cave, these games, the magic, it isn't the same as forming relationships out there so I can't use out there logic with this. Same goes for you and Ydum." I finish with his hair and move back next to him.

Byder hangs his head down, sighs, then looks back up. "See, that whole part, the magic of the cave and these games, all that, I was raised to be prepared for this. We don't think about making relationships out there, not real ones anyway. We know they're temporary and only for fun. This is the normal for us. We know our whole lives we'll come to the games and find a witch that we'll bond with like this or we die trying. I trusted the system to bring me you. You, I understand. Even there being more than one god matched with you, I understand. I could even maybe understand if the cave had matched me with a male witch when I never thought that way before. It happens, rarely but it happens."

Byder shakes his head and looks at Ydum, who is circling the room, lost in thought. "It's the idea of him, Ydum, another god. I'm bonded to you. Not him. That's how it should be. Him bonded to you. Me bonded to you. Me and him friends, or something closer but because of you, not each other. To be this new type of feelings, here, like this, with another god? I would swear I felt a bond snap into place with Ydum earlier, same as I felt it with you, but that shouldn't be possible. A god with another god. That's why I panicked. Am I confusing our shared feeling about you for feelings for him? I don't want to hurt him if it's just stress or our weird bond or something else. I don't want you stuck in the middle if I'm wrong and I hurt him."

"How many multiple bonded gods have you talked to, Byder?"

He startles. "What do you mean? None. There was a kid in school a few years ahead of me who had two god moms and a witch dad, but I didn't know him really. Not enough to talk to his parents."

I laugh at that. Really laugh and Byder stares at me. "You don't even hear yourself, do you? You're afraid of hurting Ydum. And you just told me the kid had two moms and a dad. He doesn't have two moms, not biologically, does he? You called them his two moms because that's how you heard it talked about, meaning that's probably how they see themselves. One relationship with three people, not two separate relationships sharing one human. How does something like this work? Ydum can puzzle over the scientific academics of it, but my guess? Exactly how the cave wants it to, and we get to figure that out for ourselves. You love me, Ydum, and Anarus. How you love each of us is something we can all figure out together and something that will probably change a lot over time. It's okay to explore, just tell him how you're feeling."

"Witch of words." Byder puts an arm around my shoulder, smiling. "Fixing us with your magic words all the time."

I smile back and shove him playfully. "Most of the time it isn't magic. I'm just smarter than all of you." I look at Ydum. "Well, most of you. He's really fucking smart, isn't he?"

"Too fucking smart." Byder agrees.

Eventually, around dinner, Ydum comes out of his thought bender and slouches onto the couch slightly despondently.

"Did you figure out whatever your brain was working so feverishly on?" I ask him, and hear both Anarus and Byder groan at my question.

"Don't ask him that." Anarus tells me. "Now, we're going to have to hear the whole inner workings of his mind for hours."

"No, you're not." Ydum sighs. "I really got nowhere fast with it. It all goes in circles. If what we think about Anarus's parentage is true, and what we think about Jinx's magic is true, then I think we are on the right path. If we're wrong about any one piece, the whole thing moves like shifting sand, and new questions come up. New problems. And, honestly, at the end of the day, it doesn't matter. We just keep working with Ani's power and Jinx's magic with our hypotheses in place until something doesn't work. Then, we reevaluate and make new hypotheses. But, most of Ani's issue resolve when he gets his mantle, and we can work backwards toward the issue of his parentage, if he wants. And for Jinx, well, none of it matters unless we try to fight the original gods about her having been here in the first place. If we aren't doing that, who cares what your magic is as long as it works?"

"Like I said." Anarus grumbles. "Whole inner workings of his mind."

The rest of the evening and most of the final day before the seventh game is spent between me and Anarus, working on our abilities to find out exactly what we can do. I'm tasked with trying to make things happen just with my words. Anarus keeps working on controlling the cold without using shadows. We also work on his ability to cause death, but with caution. All of us worry about the other teams finding out about it somehow.

Chapter Three

THE MORNING OF THE seventh game, I don't feel worried. My body feels much better. Not perfect, but better. But we don't expect there to be much physically we have to do for the game. I can be slow and cautious. Ydum said the game doesn't care how long you take as long as you're still working on it, and since we don't really care about winning, just finishing, if I need to move around during the game, I can do what I need to do and take breaks when I have to.

My gods don't seem very worried either. Each of us seem to be relying heavily on the fact that Ydum is smart enough to carry us through whatever the games want to throw at us. And if his knowledge fails us, Anarus can fill in the gaps. My only real worry is needing to wear the boots on my still sore feet.

"You can go barefoot if I can go without a shirt." Anarus tries to compromise with me. I just snort and toss a shirt at him, lacing up the boots on my feet.

After all the teams line up in the foyer, Drila stands in the middle in her white shimmery dress and explains what will happen. "For the seventh game, you'll have to use your intellect to solve puzzles. How exactly the game will work will be different for each team dependent on which puzzle you choose. The only thing that will be the same for all of you is that your human will be blinded for the game. Once you enter the game, the human will not be able to see and will have to trust their god to help them complete their parts of the game. Directions for your particular puzzle game will be provided onsite."

Well, that's fun. I'll be blind. This makes me nervous, but only slightly. I look over at Ydum, Byder, and Anarus. They'll protect me. They'll help me. That I can trust implicitly. I smile at them so they know I have no fear over this.

"Let's move on to choosing your puzzles." Drila continues. "First is Saffron. Pick your painting." Saffron moves to the doors and key painting. Drila looks at me. "Jinx." I confidently walk to the bushes maze.

I hear an, "aww," from one of the humans still waiting, but there's not too much complaint from them. Looking back at them after I'm safely in front of the painting, I think the grumble came from Raven.

With all of us so close, and so calm about this, I can watch as Isis picks the stone wall maze. Damek chooses the cypher. Raven, with me at her first choice, chooses the dirt maze. She gives me a small smile as she walks by me, as if to say she isn't mad that I took what she wanted. Wren chooses the puzzle boxes and Drila sends our gods to join us.

"She hasn't said anything about having to choose one of you." I tell my gods with relief. I like it better when it's all of us. We really do work well together in the games as a full team. The cave did good by us, I realize.

Before any of them can respond, Drila sends us away. Instead of feeling like I blinked and am somewhere else, I feel like I closed my eyes and can't make them open. "Guys?"

"Right here, baby girl." Byder takes my hand in his.

"We're in the game." Anarus tells me as he takes my other hand.

"You doing okay, beautiful?" Ydum must be in front of me. He cups my cheek in his hand.

I nod. "It's odd. This feels weird like I can't open my eyes even though I am trying to, but it doesn't hurt or anything. Just, don't stop saying something, or touching me. I feel a little freaked out when it feels like I'm alone."

"We won't leave your side, Jinx." Byder tells me.

I squeeze his hand. "I trust you."

"We're in a large field." Ydum starts explaining what they are seeing. "The bush maze is right in front of us. There's a table to the side. Currently, the only thing on the table is a scroll of paper. I'm betting that's our directions."

I hear rustling and assume Ydum is picking up the directions. He starts reading out loud. "Within the maze are five items. One at each corner, north, south, east, and west, and one more in the middle. The god directs the human to each of these points to collect the items. Each item will require a puzzle to be completed to retrieve the item. The god will direct the human on how to complete the puzzle. The god and human are allowed to discuss any information needed to complete the puzzle, and the god may move the parts of the puzzle as needed to hand things to the human, but it must be the hands of the human that manipulates the puzzle to solve it. You may only carry one item out of the maze at one time, then return to the maze to get the next one. If at any point, you fail to properly solve a puzzle, the maze will reset and any collected items will be returned to where they came from. The maze will change and the solved puzzles will change as well, and you will have to start over. If the god attempts to manipulate the puzzle for the sole purpose of solving the puzzle instead of the human, the game will be failed completely. Once all five items are retrieved, the witch will have to direct the god to craft using all five items. When the prize has been crafted properly, the game will be completed."

"Not too bad." I say.

"Oh wait, there's more." Ydum sounds a little surprised. "It just added itself a new direction. The words just appeared here. Intriguing."

Anarus huffs. "Stop worrying over the magic directions, Ydum, and read them."

"Oh, right. Multiple god adaptation. Ah, this is because there's more than one of us. Only two gods may enter the maze with the human. They must alternate which god enters the maze each time. The third god will remain behind and human will assist them with the completion of crafting with the five items. All four team members may share their knowledge but only one god and the human may enter the maze at a time and only one god and the human may craft."

I nod my head. "Makes sense. Two of you alternate coming in the maze with me and one helps me make whatever we need to make. Anyone got an idea who should do what?"

"Ydum goes in the maze with you." Byder says quickly.

"Ydum and who?" I ask.

"Anarus." Byder answers again.

I hear Ydum hum. "Maybe not. I think it may be better to have Ani helping Jinx craft with the items we collect. The way that sounds, I'm going to bet there's some magic needed to do it, and he would be better for helping with that."

"So, I go into the maze and help Jinx solve puzzles?" Byder hesitates. "If I get something wrong, we have to start over and the puzzles change."

"Come here, Byder." I reach out and Byder steps into my arms. I pull him into a hug. "You are smart too. I trust you. We all trust you."

"Let's do this thing." Anarus says. "Ydum and Byder, you alternate taking Jinx through the maze. I'll help her craft when you get everything."

"Five items." Byder says as he steps out of my arms, but takes hold of my hand. "Ydum first. He'll do three, I'll do two."

"Sounds fair." Ydum takes my arm in his and starts walking forward. "I'm going to leave a trail of flowers behind us as we walk so that we can find our way back out easily."

As we walk, Ydum talks to me. "I'm trailing my hand along the right wall of the maze. If the right wall turns, we'll turn with it. When you come through with Byder next, he can follow my flower path until the first time the path can go left instead of right, deviate from my path there, then keep following the always to the right plan. If he ends up back following my path, he just chooses left at the next option."

"That makes sense." I tell him. "Good idea."

I feel him turn me around a corner, then another. Slowly, we walk through the maze. Ydum keeps one hand always touching me and rambles on about nothing in particular. "My sister is five years older than me. Zimuna and I got along pretty well growing up, as much as siblings can, I think."

I smile. "I understand that. Catarina and I are oil and water. But Ophelia and I get along great. I think Myrna's a little stuck up. Shearah was always like a second mom to me. Ganna and I are okay, but nothing special, and Samantha and Dahlia are so much older, I really just don't know them that well."

"I cannot wait until we are out of these games and I can meet them all." Ydum tells me. "And your parents. You'll love my dad, I think. You two will have a lot to talk about. I told you Mom is a goddess of flowers and Dad has an affinity for metallurgy magic, but he's where I learned to love books and learning. He knows more about Veirveil and how it all works than anyone because he has read all the histories. Zimuna is a goddess of stone. She can work with metals, crystals, minerals, anything mined from the ground. I think she's always felt a little miffed that I can do what she does, Dad's type of magic, and the flowers and plants, Mom's power. They thought that was it for a long time. But then, when I was eight, I got mad and there was a lightning strike right inside my bedroom. That's when they started thinking maybe I'm all nature, not just Mom and Dad's natures."

"You said your mom hid your colorblindness. Does your dad know about it? What about Zimuna?"

Ydum, I think, nods then remembers I can't see him. "Oops, sorry. Yes. They all three know. When I was little, Mom was trying to work with me to figure out where my powers lie, and I kept struggling so much with simple things, identifying a flower or type of metal. For a while, they worried that my powers were the problem. Maybe something had gone wrong and I didn't have any. Or wasn't a nature god like they thought when I was born. It happens, but again, rare. Mom got really nervous over it. It was Zimuna that figured it out. When I was four and she was nine, we were playing a game and she realized that I was guessing about the colors of things. Mom tested it, having me pick out things that were all the same color from a pile, and lost it. She was crying and so upset, I thought I did something wrong. She took me out of Veirveil, claiming to our neighbors we were going on a family vacation, and took me to a human doctor. He confirmed it, that I'm colorblind and gave Mom advice on how to help me hide it. Zimuna and I struggle in our relationship, I think, because of how much time Mom and Dad had to dedicate to helping me. She felt slighted and ignored. We're better now, but I can't blame her for that. Oops, dead end. We need to turn around."

"Definitely understandable for her to struggle with that." I say, thinking about what that would have been like for Ydum's sister. "When Ganna was twenty-four, right at her birthday, she got really sick. Really sick. She was basically living at Granny Helen's, our healer. Dad had to carry her to the testing center on her birthday because she was so weak and frail. She took up so much of our parents' time for weeks. Shearah ended up bearing the brunt of taking care of the rest of us because Dahlia was married and gone by then, and Samantha was working a lot. Sometimes, I think Shearah resents us for that. Resents Ganna for that, even though she knows it isn't any of our faults. Ganna almost died and she still has breathing issues from it."

"We are at one of the five puzzles, Jinx." Ydum tells me. He lifts my left hand and places it on a table. I feel squares of something cool to the touch under my fingers. "It looks like a mystic square. We have to shift the tiles within the frame to make them go in order. But the question is, what's the order?"

"What's on the squares?" I ask him.

"Each square has a picture on it." He explains. "One is four interlocking triangles."

"The Fates." I tell him.

"One has a cloud." He continues. "Oh, these ones I know. The symbols of earth, water, wind, and fire. Also, those two I know well, now. That one's death and the other one's life. There's a spiral going clockwise, a bow and arrow, a question mark, a map of all of Nazus, an oval with a smaller oval inside it, near the bottom right, and two more that are hard to describe."

"Hmm." I think. "A lot of the ones you describe seem to fit some type of god power. Bow and arrow? That's probably a hunt god. The Fates I already told you. The earth symbol could be nature. Water, fire and death are all self-explanatory. The ovals one is the symbol for fertility. The spiral is spirit. The question mark is curiosity. The map is the world maybe? Not all of them fit the whole powers of the gods theory."

"It's creation." Ydum inhales sharply. "It's the story of creation. The spirit is the ether, where it all started and the map is the whole world, where the story ends. We have to put them in order for the story."

"Okay, so what do we do? I have to shift the tiles so that the spiral is the first one and work our way from there?"

Ydum takes my hand and places it on a tile. "We start here. I'll tell you which way to move the tile and when to move your hand to a different one." When I nod at this, Ydum starts. "Go left. Move your hand left through the empty spot to the next tile, now shift it right."

Slowly, one by one, Ydum guides me through moving the tiles around. It feels like we are going so slowly, but the puzzle is hard to figure out. Several times, Ydum tells me to wait while he mutters to himself, figuring out the pattern to move the tiles to get the next one in line. We eventually figure out, by process of elimination, that the two hard to describe symbols were one for all four seasons and the other was knowledge.

Once we have the whole mystic square in order, Ydum tells me that a door on the side of the mystic square popped open, and that he's taking a small vial out of the opening. "It has a label on it that says acemanan. If I remember right, that's aloe."

"It is." I reach out to him. "Let's head back. This felt like it took forever."

Ydum takes my arm and leads me back, following his flower trail. We move a lot faster out of the maze than we did coming in. We don't talk as much and soon he's telling me we are exiting the maze and Byder and Anarus are waiting.

"That took you two a while." Anarus says as Ydum hands me off to Byder.

"Aloe. We had to solve a mystic square." Ydum tells him. "It did take a while."

Byder cups his hand on my face then takes hold of my arm with one hand. "Hello, baby girl. You doing alright?"

"Doing fine. One down. Ready?" I ask him.

He kisses my cheek. "Let's do this."

As we walk into the maze, I tell him Ydum's plan for following the flower path.

"He did a good job marking the path. This'll be easy to follow." Byder says. We walk for a bit, then he stops. "I'm going to let go of you. I have some sticks I collected from the ground outside the maze with me. I'm just breaking them up and making an arrow on the ground with them, so Ydum will know where we moved off his path. I'll do this at every choice we make, making a path for him to follow like he did with the flowers."

"My gods are so smart." I say merrily.

We wander some more and Byder runs into a spot where we cross back over the flower path. "There are two flower lines here. Hm, what does that mean?"

"Could it be we hit a dead end and had to back-track?"

Byder chuckles. "That would make sense. We'll keep straight instead of going right. I'm going to put an X of sticks here too."

We keep going. Byder and I don't chatter like Ydum and I did. We stay quiet, but it's a comfortable quiet. For all the world, it feels like we could just be out on a leisurely stroll rather than in the games.

I hear Byder swear under his breath. "What is it, Byder?"

He groans. "The puzzle is in front of us. There's a piece of paper with what looks like a poem on it and four glass jars. The jars each have a word on the top of the lid. I think it might be a riddle. I'll have to read you the riddle."

Shit. Byder has to read it to me. I can hear and feel his worry. "You can do this, Byder. I have complete faith in you. Just go slow and take your time. We have all the time in the world."

He takes a shaky breath. "Okay. Okay. I can do this." He lets go of me and something rustles. It sounds like he's handling the paper. "Okay. Why. No, My. My life can de, be, wea, measured in hours. My life can be measured in hours. I serve d, by being bev, devou, devour, devoured. Ugh, I'm sorry. I'm taking forever."

"You are doing perfectly, sweetie." I tell him, reaching out until I find his arm and place a reassuring hand on it. "Keep going, you're doing great."

He takes a deep breath and I hear him blow it out. "Fuck, okay. My life can be measured in hours. I serve by being devoured. Thin, I am pick. No. Not pick. Quick. Thin, I am quick. Fa, fat, I an, am, slom, slow. Fat, I am slow. Last line. Min.. Mind is my foe. The whole thing now. My life can be measured in hours. I serve by being devoured. Thin, I am quick. Fat, I am slow. Mind is my foe. That's it, Jinx. What do you think?"

"What do the four jars say?" I ask him. "That will probably give us clues as to the answer."

"Right." Byder takes another deep breath. "One says misteria. One is cinna, cinnamon. One is honey. And the last one is de, bees max, no wax. Beeswax. Misteria, cinnamon, honey and beeswax."

"Could the one that's misteria actually be wisteria?" I ask him gently.

He doesn't say anything for a moment. "Shit, yeah. I think so. Sorry."

I grip his arm tightly for a second. "Don't apologize. You're doing fine. We're doing this together. Okay. My life can be measured in hours. I serve by being devoured. Thin, I am quick. Fat, I am slow. Mind is my foe. Hm, and the options are wisteria, cinnamon, honey, and beeswax. Well, that first line, I think we can eliminate wisteria. A wisteria flower doesn't only live for hours."

"Cinnamon serves by being devoured." Byder offers.

"True. But how is cinnamon only alive for hours? It's tree bark. Trees live longer than wisteria does."

I feel Byder shrug. "How long it takes for us to eat it?"

"How long do you take to eat, Byder?" I smile. "Remember, I've seen you eat. You can eat for hours, but it doesn't take you hours to eat one thing."

"Fair." Byder hums. "What about honey? How long do bees live? How long does it take them to make honey?"

I shake my head. "I don't know, but we devour it too. The fat and thin thing bugs me. How's honey fat or thin?"

"Maybe it's a play on thick or thin?" Byder offers. "Watery honey would be quick, pour out quickly. But thick, sticky honey would pour slowly. That just leaves the mind is my foe."

Twisting my mouth to the side, I keep thinking. "Honey isn't bad for the mind. At least not that I know of. How could honey have the mind as its foe? Okay, skip that for now. What about the beeswax? Could that fit anything?"

"Life measured in hours, serve by being devoured, thin is quick and fat is slow, mind is the foe." Byder mumbles. "If it weren't for the mind thing, I would have a guess."

"Say it anyway, Byder."

"A candle. Candles can be made out of beeswax. They only burn for a little while, hours. And burning uses the candle. Devours it. Fat candles last a lot longer than thin ones. But the mind as a foe doesn't work."

"All of that sounds really right. But the mind part is the problem. Mind. Mind. How is the mind the foe of a candle?" I stop talking to think more. Mind. The mind isn't a foe to a candle. What would be a foe to a candle? Going out would be the foe of a candle. It can't provide light if it's blown out by the wind or something. "Byder, is there a chance that the word isn't mind but wind?"

"Hang on." I hear him shuffling. "Um, maybe. It could be. I'm not sure. I'm sorry, Jinx. I don't know."

"Don't worry about it. It's fine." I shift my feet. "If we assume the word is wind not mind, it all works for beeswax much better than for honey. The answer to the riddle really would be a candle, because a wind blows out a candle's flame. And we make candles from beeswax. I say we try the beeswax."

"But if we're wrong. If it's mind, not wind, we have to start all over." I can feel Byder feeling worried and insecure. "I don't want us to mess up because I can't tell what the word is."

"Trust your intuition, Byder. Do you think it makes sense for the word to be wind or mind? With what we have talked about, what does your intuition tell you?"

Byder sighs again. "I really think it says mind, but my gut says wind just makes sense. The beeswax makes sense. Mind doesn't make sense even if I think that's what it says."

"Where is the beeswax?" I hold out my hand and Byder takes it, placing my fingertips on top of a jar.

"That one, Jinx." I can tell he's holding his breath as I pick up the jar. When it's in my hand, nothing happens.

"See?" I smile at Byder. "Your instinct was right. And you figured it out, the whole riddle. I don't think I would have made that connection, beeswax and a candle."

Suddenly, I feel Byder pull me into a deep embrace. He lowers his head to nuzzle between my shoulder and neck. "Why are you so good to me?"

I can't help but chuckle. "Because you are good, Byder. You are smart, strong, and so very good to me." I wrap my arms around him and we stand there for several minutes before Byder pulls back and takes my hand.

"Okay." He takes a deep breath and lets it out again. "Beeswax. Let's go back to the others."

Once again, the walk back takes less time. Before too long, Byder tells me we are leaving the maze.

"It was a riddle." Byder tells Ydum and Anarus. "I had to read it to Jinx."

"What was the riddle?" Ydum takes my hand from Byder.

"My life can be measured in hours. I serve by being devoured. Thin, I am quick. Fat, I am slow. Wind is my foe." Byder says. He still has the whole thing memorized. "The answer was candle. We had four options. Wisteria, cinnamon, honey, and beeswax. So, we got the beeswax that can make candles."

I hold out the jar and feel Anarus take it from me. "Byder was the one who figured out it was a candle." I want to make sure the others hear how well he did. He needs to hear the praise.

"Huh, smart catch." Anarus grunts. "I don't think I would have made that connection."

Gods, I love that grumbly man. As much as he tries to act so tough and untouchable, and was so sure we were screwed in the beginning, he has become the most supportive of all of us. I can almost feel Byder's heart lifting a little at Anarus's praise. Byder knows Anarus doesn't say kind things often and when he does, he really means them. His words mean more to Byder than even mine do.

"Okay, two down, three to go." Ydum holds my hand between both of his. "Ready, beautiful?"

I nod and we walk into the maze. We follow the paths left by Ydum and Byder, moving to turns we haven't taken yet. Ydum tells me he's marking our trail with a different flower for Byder to follow. At the first stick sign Byder left, Ydum hums appreciatively. "Don't know why he always thinks he's not smart. That's genius, that's a genius solution since he can't make flowers like me."

"I know, right?" I chuckle. "We keep telling him, but he never listens."

Ydum and I talk more as we walk. In my blindness, I'm noticing things about the differences between my relationship with each of them. The way Byder tends to hover around me, close but not always touching, but Ydum seems to always want some form of contact. How Byder and I can feel safe in just quiet togetherness, but Ydum and I talk and talk. Neither are wrong, I know. Just different. Byder is quieter and more stable, while Ydum seems to always need to be doing something and our individual relationships reflect those differences.

We find our way to the third puzzle and I hear Ydum groan. "What's wrong?"

"I think it's going to be a color thing, Jinx." Ydum tells me. "There's a wooden box with a pentagram burned into it. At each point on the star, there's a small hole. In front of the box is five stones. The stones all look the same to me, but if I remember correctly, there's a color associated with the points of the star."

51

"Yeah, there is." I tell him. "But maybe we don't need the colors. Maybe I can tell by feel what the stones are."

Ydum guides my hand to the stones. I slide my fingers along them and know it won't help. They are all smooth, polished stones, almost like marbles. I keep feeling them while I think. How can we solve this if Ydum can't tell me the colors? "Fuck, I feel like the gods controlling this knew exactly what they were doing and are trying to screw us up. Byder has to read and now you have to deal with colors? Too coincidental."

Ydum agrees. "I've been thinking the same thing. I bet the tiles in the mystic square had colors that would have helped us solve it quicker and I just had no idea. How would the original gods be able to do that, though? Change everything like this? I've never heard of them being able to listen into the games or anything. It would have to actually be just dumb bad luck." He is starting to sound as despondent as Byder was about reading.

My first thought is to use my magic and my need to know what color each stone is to have me just know them at a touch. But, as my hand hovers over each stone, I can't get myself to know the colors. I need to know the color each stone is, but I already know the color each stone should be, and the magic can't just give me the sight the game took away. It has to be Ydum who is seeing it for me. I have to give him the understanding of colors so he can see them for me. My thought wanders back to what I said when I made the red bracelets, explaining red to him. I wonder...

"Okay." I purse my lips. "I have a crazy idea here." I reach up my hand and find Ydum's face, placing my fingers on his cheek. With my other hand, I take his hand and let him guide us back to the stones.

I control my breathing and focus. I need Ydum to feel the colors, so he can see them for me. I know the points of the pentagram well and what colors should be there. The first stone is white. White is empty. The absence of color. White needs to feel empty for Ydum since he can't see the colors. "White is empty. We need the stone that feels empty, Ydum." Make white feel empty for Ydum, I tell my magic.

As we move our conjoined hands over the stones, back and forth, Ydum lets his fingertips trail over each one. "This one." He stops his hand over a stone.

I pick it up. "We need to put this at the top of the star."

He guides my hand and I drop the stone in the hole. We bring our hands back to the stones and I think again. Next is blue. Blue is wet, like water. I need blue to feel wet to him. "Find the wet stone. Blue is wet. The wet stone is blue and goes to the right around the star from the first one." Make blue feel wet to him. We need it wet.

Again, Ydum runs our hands over the stones. "This one." We pick it up and he guides my hand to the right hole.

Back over the stones again. Red next. We already told Ydum about red. He knows how red feels and I ask my magic to make him feel it. "Red is hot like fire. We need red to feel hot to you. The next stone is hot." Ydum guides my hand and stops over a stone.

"This stone is hot." He tells me. We put it in its proper space and go over the stones again.

"Green." I tell him. "This color should be very familiar to you. Grass, leaves, the silkiness of new plant growth. Find the stone that is your nature, Ydum. We need green to feel like your nature."

There are only two stones left and Ydum doesn't even hesitate. "This one. This one is grass." We place the stone and Ydum guides me to the last stone. I pick it up and know it's yellow because it's the last one left.

But I tell him anyway. "This one is yellow. Not hot like red, but yellow needs to feel warm like the sun on your face. It is happy. Peaceful."

"I can feel it, Jinx." His voice is soft and I can almost imagine the smile he's giving me. He guides my hand to the last hole and as soon as it's in place, I hear a soft click. "The middle of the star popped up. There's a small envelope inside."

Ydum guides my hand to it and I pull the envelope free. "Any idea what's in it?"

Ydum takes the envelope from me. I hear shuffling. "It's dried petals from a flower. I think they're yellow, maybe. They're warm like the yellow stone was, but some of them aren't quite right. Like they're yellow but not. A little too warm. Not quite red hot, but somewhere in between?"

I figure out what he's describing easily. "Orange. Red and yellow mixed together. I can't believe that magic worked that well."

"I can." Ydum says and I can tell he's looking at me again. His hands drop to my waist and he pulls me against him. "I'm going to kiss you, beautiful."

I turn my face up to him and he kisses me softly. "Such a fucking amazing witch. You can do anything, Jinx."

"We." I correct him. "We can do anything."

We walk back out of the maze together, and give the petals to Anarus.

"Jinx made me feel colors." Ydum tells them immediately. "It was the most amazing thing. Green feels like grass. Orange is warmer than yellow but not as hot as red."

Byder takes my hand from Ydum. "Every day, I swear I understand better how my parents could say that we can just trust the cave. They tried to explain how you just know and can work together with the human you're paired with, but it never made sense until now."

"I had no one to explain that connection to me." Anarus says. "I was told about it in the classes, like all of us were, but never saw that at home in the same way so didn't trust it, especially when it was all three of us in that cave. But now, I get it too, Byder. I get it too."

Anarus must have come to stand near me because I feel him standing close. "How are you doing, little human?"

I try to turn to where it sounds like he is. "I'm doing good. How are you?"

I feel his hand on my right hip. "You're limping a little again. Is your hip hurting?"

"It's been a lot of walking and standing." I admit.

"We're taking a break." Anarus says louder, to the other two. "Sit with me, Jinx."

Anarus guides me to sit on the ground then pulls me into his lap. He places his hand back on my hip and I feel him using his cold on it. I sigh and relax into him as the pain I had been ignoring starts to relent. His other hand lands on my shoulder and I feel the cold there too. "How's the wrist? Be honest."

I flex my right wrist. "Not too bad."

He moves his hand from the shoulder to the wrist anyway.

"You need to tell us what you need, baby girl. Let us take care of you like you take care of us." It sounds like Byder is sitting on the ground next to us.

I feel someone, I assume Ydum by the direction it comes from, taking off my boots. "Don't forget her toes, Ani. They were bruised too and she hasn't worn the boots since the sixth game."

Anarus moves a hand down to rub my feet with his cold. "Better?"

I nod. All four spots do feel a lot better.

"Leave the boots off if you want." Byder tells me. "The ground is soft grass. You'll be fine barefoot."

Anarus helps me stand again, foregoing the boots, and gives my hand to Byder.

"Ready?" Byder asks me. "Two more."

"Let's go." I tell him and Byder leads me back into the maze.

As we walk, Byder stops occasionally, marking the paths we take with his sticks again. "Tell Ydum that the sticks with one of his second flowers on them is the second path we took. We're hitting a bunch of dead ends this time and keep ending up at places we've already been."

It takes us longer to navigate to the fourth puzzle. A few times, Byder swears softly. "Got turned around again. We're back at the start. Let's try this again."

We eventually make it to the fourth puzzle and Byder looks it over for a moment. "Not sure what we are supposed to do here."

"Describe what you see."

"There are a bunch of wood tiles on a table that have letters burned into them. There's a box on the table too with a tray on top. It looks like the box maybe has several drawers in it. There are no directions that I can see. No pictures or anything else to guide us." Byder hums as he looks around. He lets go of my hand and I can hear him shuffling about. "Yep. Nothing to explain this."

I think. "Does it look like the tiles can fit in the tray at the top of the box?"

"Yeah, maybe. If we line them up next to each other. Maybe six of them can fit in the tray side by side." He puts a tile in my hand. "This is what they feel like, if that helps."

I run my fingers over the small square. I can feel the letter burned into it. "This is an A, isn't it?"

"Yeah. Got an idea?"

I nod at him. "Maybe we need to make a word. A six lettered word and set the tiles in the correct order for the word into the tray."

"That might work. There are ten letters altogether." Byder explains. "Two A's, one E, one I, one O, one R, two S's, an L, an F, and one that can be either M or W."

"Hm," I hum, thinking. "Almost all the vowels, that gives us a lot to work with. I wonder if there's one word that's correct or if any word will do?"

"I think if they wanted a specific word, they would have left clues as to what it was." Byder shuffles around again. "I'm looking all over. I've looked at the box on all sides, tried to open the drawers, and looked at all the tiles, both sides.

There's nothing else here."

"The we guess and hope any word works."

"I think I can think of a lot of words we can make with these letters." Byder shifts next to me. "Rose. Safe. Ass."

I chuckle at him. "Of course, you would find the word ass easily. We need six letters though. No ass for you."

"Damn, a guy can hope." He places his hand on my back and gently scratches it, as if he's just letting me know he's right next to me.

When I hold up my hand, he helps me find the tiles on the table, straightening them in a line for me as I rub my fingers over them to think. I feel the F and try to think of words that start with that letter first. "False. That's only five. Float. No T. Few. Fin, nope no N, right?"

"No N." Byder reminds me. "Are you focusing on F for any reason in particular?"

"Long words. I need long words. Just picked a random letter to start with to think of words for."

Byder must decide to pick a different letter, because he starts mumbling to himself too. "Slowly, nope only one L. Simple, no P."

"Flower." I say. "No, there's no, wait, is there an R?"

Byder doesn't answer for a moment. "F, L, O, that can be a W, E, R. Flower works!"

"Hand me the letters in order." Byder hands me the F and helps me find the tray on the top of the box. I orient it carefully and place it in the tray. We continue until the word flower is sitting in the tray. There is a click.

"Did anything open?" I ask him.

"No. I heard the click, but nothing happened." Byder tells me.

I move my hand on the tray again and try to lift it. The top of the box comes up. "Am I lifting the whole box up or just the lid?"

"Not a lid, but just the tray. Those weren't drawers but sections. There's another tray under that one, but smaller. Maybe five letters this time."

"We need to make a five-letter word this time." Excitedly, I set the six-letter tray to the side, and start thinking again. "Flower, we have flower, so let's continue the theme. What can we make from those letters?"

Byder is moving. "I'm taking the letters off the tray and rearranging them. Fires is five letters and we can make that word."

"Let's try it." I say but Byder doesn't hand me the letters. "Byder?"

"I'm thinking. Give me a minute."

"Okay." I wait. It feels weird to stand in the silence with no sight. "Can you at least mutter out loud or touch me or something? Part of me feels very alone when it's so quiet and I can't hear you're still here."

"Sorry." Byder puts his hand on my back again, giving me a touch to know he's still there. "One, two, three, four, five. There are five trays. The top was a six-letter word, the next one's a five-letter word. If we assume that the bottom tray is the item, then we'll also need a four-letter word, and a three-letter word. Flower worked. Would we need to use only those letters now? Or maybe it's a theme? What's a good five-letter word in the same theme as flower?"

"Flora." I say immediately. "Flora is a five-letter word that is in the same category as flower."

"Let's try that." Byder says and hands me the letters as I spell them out. I run my fingers over them to make sure it is the right letter and oriented properly, then load the tray and hear a click. I lift up the tray.

Byder chuckles. "Like we thought. Tray that can fit four letters."

I come up with a four-letter word easily. Byder already said it. "Rose."

He hands me the letters and helps me load the tray. Another click and I lift the tray.

"Three letter tray." Byder tells me.

I scrunch up my mouth, thinking. "Fir? Can we do that? F, I, and R?"

"Yup." Byder says. We load the tray and there's another click. I lift the tray.

"Yes!" Byder's excited. "There's an envelope in the box."

I grab the small envelope and hand it to him. He looks in and says, "Lavender."

"The theme was plants, I'm almost positive you were right, Byder. If we had used fires, we would have had to start over. Good thinking."

He takes my hand and the two of us walk back out of the maze. "Word scramble of plants." Byder tells Anarus. "Lavender."

"Lavender, beeswax, aloe, and some yellow and orange petals." Anarus says. "Any ideas what we could have to do?"

"Sounds like a good start to a balm." I tell them. "Not sure which one without knowing the last ingredient and what the flower petals are, but if the beeswax is soft, it definitely seems like something to soothe the skin."

"Well then, beautiful," Ydum takes my hand in his, "let's get the last ingredient and figure it out. Keep those items in mind, though. Maybe we can bypass solving the puzzle by knowing what we need."

We go through the maze quickly. We get turned around only once or twice, but find the last puzzle. "Alright. This looks interesting. How did the game know we would come here last?" Ydum tells me.

"Why do you think it did?" I ask him.

"There are five jars on a table. Each one has a blank label on it. There's a paper that says 'Take the last ingredient and make the potion.' It has clues on it, it looks like, as well. How does it know this is the last ingredient?"

I disagree with his idea. "Maybe it doesn't. Maybe it means take the last ingredient in the clues."

"Then, why not just only leave that clue?"

I shrug. "Read the clues. Maybe the answer is in them. Maybe we have to follow the order of the clues to figure out which one is the last one."

Ydum clears his throat. "I'm going to read them all off first, then we can go back through them. One, pulverize first but don't add first. Two, start here. Three, too much and the potion is poison. Four, add some but just for fun. And five, just a touch and you are done. Okay, that's confusing. The second clue is start here. Is the second clue actually the first clue and the first clue the last clue?"

"What's in the jars, Ydum?"

He doesn't speak for a moment. "Some of them I can tell. There are whole flower petals, but not the same ones we already have. One of them is a liquid. One of them looks like honey. One is flakes of something. And I'm not sure about the last one. It looks like tiny beads."

"Can we open the jars? Touch or smell the stuff inside?"

"They're already open. There's no lids." Ydum guides my hand to one. "I think this is honey."

I lift the jar and smell it. Then I taste it. "Yup, honey."

I set it down and he helps me to another one, telling me, "This is the flower petals."

I bring them up to my nose but can't smell anything I can specifically place. I rub one between my fingers and try again. I can smell something but still can't place it. I know it, but I can't figure it out. I hold out my fingers to Ydum. "What does this smell like to you?"

"Lavender. That's lavender." Ydum tsks. "I should have recognized that. We already have that, so that's not the last ingredient."

He takes that jar and hands me another jar. "This is the liquid."

I do the same thing, sniff first, but it doesn't smell especially potent. Slightly nutty and acidic. I dip my finger in it. It feels thick and oily. Carefully, I touch my finger to my mouth, and immediately I spit. "Ew, that's castor oil."

Ydum chuckles. "You shouldn't put unknown substances in your mouth, Jinx."

"Do you want to identify this stuff? Because I'm totally willing to let you have to sniff and taste stuff and figure it out." I tease.

I think, based on how well I know his behavior, Ydum is holding his hands up in surrender. "Nope, I will let the witch taste weird things. Next jar. This is the flaky stuff."

I take the jar and touch it, smell it. "That's coconut."

He takes the jar and hands me the last one. "And the little balls."

I pull one of the balls out and instantly know. "Beeswax. Add that to the lavender, honey, coconut, and castor oil and you get a salve for an infected cut."

"Ah. Makes sense. Do you think that's what we're making too? With the items?"

I shake my head. "We have lavender, beeswax, aloe, and petals of some type. Right type of working, wrong ingredients. But we can eliminate the lavender and beeswax as what we need."

There's a loud sound, startling me. Ydum touches my shoulder. "Sorry, clapped my hands together. Forgot you couldn't see it. Let's go through the clues now and see what's last now that we know the ingredients. First clue, pulverize first but don't add first. What do you think?"

"Coconut. You need the moisture from them, but wouldn't start with it as your base. Well, you could but not in that form. You'd want coconut oil, not coconut milk."

I hear the paper shuffle. "Okay, then, start here?"

"Beeswax." I tell him. "After grinding the coconut down to get the milk, you'd warm up those beeswax balls to melt them down. And the next one, too much and the potion is poison? That's castor oil. Too much castor oil can make someone sick."

"You're on a roll here, beautiful." Ydum snickers. "Next is the one for fun. I'm guessing lavender."

"Yup. My thoughts too. Lavender has some good properties in it for healing, but mostly would be used for the soothing smell."

Ydum takes my hand and guides it to a jar. "Then the last ingredient, the just a touch, would be honey."

I pick up the jar he indicated. "Honey, lavender, beeswax, aloe, and some yellow and orange petals. I bet I know what those petals are and what potion we need to make."

"Yeah? We good to go, you think?" Ydum takes my hand again in his.

I nod and he starts leading me out of the maze. "Burn salve. I bet the flower petals are calendula. They're yellow and orange."

"And you thought you were coming to the games completely unprepared." Ydum lets go of my hand to sling his arm around my shoulders as we walk. "Little human knows her potions."

"Hey," I cry, "that's Anarus's name for me. You call me beautiful."

"Eh, you can be both. A beautiful little human."

I laugh at him. "Just don't try to add Byder's nickname for me onto that. Beautiful little human baby girl sounds weird. And why do all of you have nicknames for me anyway? Should I come up with nicknames for you?"

"No clue. Ani's started out as a taunt, but I think you like it now, don't you? And mine isn't so much a nickname, but just a reminder. You are beautiful, beautiful. Plus, nicknames are fun. We are out of the maze." Ydum takes my hand again and walks me over to Anarus. "Your turn, Ani."

I hold out the jar. "Honey."

"Burn salve." Anarus says. "We have to make burn salve."

"Correct." I smile at him. "Is the beeswax in balls, or a cream?"

"Cream." He tells me.

I nod. "Good, that makes this easier. Do we have any tools at all?"

"No. Nothing."

"Okay, then. First step, grind the calendula and lavender petals until they are a fine powder." Anarus is holding my hand, but I let go and come around his back to put my hands on his shoulders. I feel his bare skin. "Hey, where's your shirt?"

He only chuckles. "I told you this morning. No shoes for you means no shirt for me."

I huff but otherwise ignore it. "I'm going to try to think on strength, power, and healing. We want to infuse them with as much of it as possible. Since you have to do the work, I'm going to try to send my magic through you."

"Reverse of what you did with my shadows? Can I grind these together or keep them separate?" I feel Anarus's back muscles moving as he reaches for things and moves his hands.

"Exactly like the shadows, and yes. We'll mix them together anyway." Power, I start thinking, life, vitality, healing. We need these plants to heal.

"That tickles." Anarus flexes and shifts for a bit then says. "Okay, they are powder. Or as good as I could get." He puts something in my hand. It's the ground up petals.

I nod at him. "That's good. Now, make sure you stir them together well. We want both the calendula and the lavender for this in equal measure. Then add two pinches into the beeswax."

Anarus's back muscles bunch. "Done. What next?"

"Now the aloe. Is it liquid or something else?" Anarus holds the bottle up to my hands for me to feel.

"There's a dropper on top of the bottle. I think it's liquid." He takes the bottle back.

"Five drops, then." I tell him. "Add five drops to the beeswax now."

I feel him move and when he stops, I give him the next direction. "Now for the honey. Since we can't measure it precisely, you are going to have to eyeball it. With the size of the jar of beeswax we have, I'm guessing we need about a teaspoon honey. But err on the side of less. Then, stir it all together."

Anarus moves for a bit, then turns under my hands. He puts the jar under my nose. "Does this smell right?"

I take a sniff. "Yes. Now, one more time. Hold the jar in both your hands and place mine over them." Anarus takes one of my hands in his, then brings the jar in the other hand to be cradled between both of his. I place my other hand on top of his. "We are doing the power thing again, okay?"

"Got it. Tell me what to think about."

"Same thing as before with the petals. We want this to be a strong, powerful, healing potion." I think those things for a moment. We need a good healing burn salve, strong and powerful.

When the light of the foyer hits my eyes, it makes them water. I saw nothing but the dark for so long, it takes a minute for my eyes to adjust. Ydum is holding onto my boots and Anarus's shirt. Anarus holds up a jar to me. I look at it and see the jar of burn salve. "This looks perfect."

"Welcome back, Jinx's team." Drila says. "Third place."

I look around and see Damek, Iella, Raven and Uesis are already here. We go to our now normal spot by the walls and take a seat. We know we could be here a while waiting on the other three teams.

"How long has it been?" I ask.

Raven answers. "They fed us dinner already." She points to a table near the back of the foyer with sandwiches and fruit. Byder goes over to it and makes plates for us. We eat and settle in to relax.

"That actually wasn't too bad." Byder says as he eats. "I feel like the game was purposefully playing our weaknesses against us, but I think we figured them out well together."

"Definitely playing on our weaknesses." Ydum agrees.

We lapse into a comfortable silence then and I think of the things Ydum and I talked about while walking through the maze. It occurs to me that the way I was raised, my life, was so different than theirs. They were raised preparing for the games. Everything about their growing up was to get them here and have them succeed. Byder talked to me about how the idea of romantic relationships wasn't something they ever thought about, not for the long-term, because they knew the cave would give them their mate. Ydum talked about his mom working on identifying his magic with him. And they all three have talked about or done things that lets me know most of their schooling was preparation for these games. All of the humans Ydum helped with the meditation for the fifth game, their gods had done the same led visualization technique with them already. It must have been something they were taught, not just Ydum's creation.

Everything I know about their childhoods stands in direct contrast to how I was raised. We were raised with the idea that going to the testing center on our twenty-fourth birthday was an aberration in an otherwise normal life. Going to the games was something you understood might happen, feared almost, but mostly assumed wouldn't happen. We delay doing anything major with our lives just in case, but people would seriously date in high school, make plans for after that birthday as if they already knew their test would turn red.

When people get that blue result, it's a major upheaval of their plans. We know blue tests go to the games and never come back, but I never knew why. If they taught the why, the matching up with a god mate and rebuilding your life in Veirveil as a demi-god after the games, to people in the classes you take when your test turns blue, I don't know. I only know that those whose tests turned blue leave on September fifth and, one way or another, they never come back.

We wait and wait for the others to come back, but we aren't worrying like in the other games. More bored than anything. My hip is bothering me again, so I turn and lie my head down on Ydum's lap and stretch out.

He looks down at me and brings a hand up to smooth my hair. "Hello, beautiful."

Anarus, guessing what I'm doing, picks up my feet and puts them on his lap and rests a cooling hand on my hip.

"Thank you." I tell him.

Other thoughts scatter through my mind as we wait. Some of them I don't want to think about but know eventually I will need to. There's a point to these games. We've been talking about it using words like mate bond and cave magic, but that first day, Byder said it was to find a mating pair, or group in our case. Mating means children. We've already started talking about after the games, as if it's a foregone conclusion that we will stay together after the games. Which, based on how Byder and Ydum talk about their parents and how they were raised and taught, is what the games intends. But it doesn't just intend us to be together, be a family, but have a family.

I've only ever thought about having children abstractly before, a one day, a long time from now, thought. I thought about the fact that someday I might marry and have a family, living in the same village I always have, with my parents and siblings living close by. But now, my gods talk about after the games with the assumption the witches move to Veirveil, and I've never heard of someone coming home again after the games.

Ydum talked about meeting my sisters, though, and about me meeting his parents. How does all this work? Could I visit my parents? Let them know I survived, introduce them to Ydum, Anarus, and Byder? What would they think about that? They never went to the games. They wouldn't understand it the same way. Or would they? Did they ever learn about the games that way even though they didn't have to go?

What about those children the games want us to have? They would be raised as gods, knowing the games are mandatory for them, in a place that's so different than anything I've ever known. I would have to learn the ways the gods' society works, and raising god children works. Plus, we would be living on borrowed time their whole lives. Would we know what's happening in the games or would they just leave and we wait for ten weeks to see if they ever come back?

I hate what these games do and I'm always thinking that someone should change this system. They need to change. I could never send a child to something like this.

"Ydum?" I say quietly. "Can I ask you about something that might be a little uncomfortable?"

"Yeah, beautiful. What's up?" He speaks quietly too.

I fiddle with the hem of my shirt, unsure how to ask about all this. "The games are to make mating pairs. Mating pairs mean having children." I stall, licking my lips and looking down, away from him.

"It does." Ydum waits, then keeps talking for me. "Most don't for several years, though. It's not like they expect us to leave the games and immediately start building a family. You have to remember, Jinx, your timeline after the games changes. You become immortal like us, unable to get sick and able to heal from most injuries. That eighty or so years of life you thought you were going to have becomes significantly longer. There's time. Time to feel each other out in a way we can't here. Learn about each other and make decisions about major life stuff like children. And no one says we have to have children. It's not a rule or anything, expected but not a rule."

"Do you," I swallow, "have you ever thought about having children?"

He looks down at me until I actually look at him. "Do you want me to answer that honestly, Jinx?"

I nod, not sure why he would ask me that.

"Every time I look at you, I think about it. Every time we are together, I think about it and want it. Not now, of course, but someday, Jinx, I would love to see you carry my child." He sighs. "I would never want to send that child here, to the Gods Games, and if that's how the world still is, I don't know that I would want to have a child, but those two ideas war in my mind. Then, I look at Anarus and want to give him a family, the family he never had. I enjoy the idea of you having Anarus's child as much as the idea of you having mine. Byder, too, but it's different with him. Not as potent a thing, still enjoyable and I would love them as my own, but with Anarus, I think it's more because we're it. We are all the family he has and if it comes down to a choice, I would choose you having a child with him over me."

"Same." Byder says, and I realize that he and Anarus had been listening. "Anarus first, but fuck yes. You would be beautiful, pregnant with any of our children."

My mouth is dry. I look at Anarus. He's looking down at my feet in his lap. "Anarus?"

"I always assumed no one would want that with me. I haven't let myself think about it. The more we figure out about me, the more I've pushed any thoughts about it away. Why would we choose me as a father if it comes with all these complications? But now you two are saying me first and I don't know how I feel about it."

Byder reaches a hand out and plays with a loose strand of my hair. "What are your thoughts, baby girl? Why are you asking about it?"

"Ydum and I were talking about our childhoods in the maze and I realized how very different they were." I sit up, so I can look at all three of them. "You were raised with the idea that the games, and finding who you make a family with here, was inevitable. I was raised with it as an aberration. You probably won't go, but just in case, wait to make any huge plans or do anything drastic. Having children was something I only thought about in a maybe someday way. But I always thought I'd have my parents nearby, and sisters, for whatever family I had. Now I just realized, I'll never see them again. No one who has gone to the games has ever returned, that I know of. My whole world will be different, unknown, strange. I can't even fathom having children in a world I don't understand now. Abstractly, maybe, if the games are different. But there's so much I have to learn and know before I can even think about that. The idea of children on top of everything else is scary right now."

"So, bunch of stuff there, beautiful." Ydum pulls me closer to him. "One, yes, we can go visit your family. That's allowed, encouraged even. The ones who didn't come back probably didn't survive. If your society is based on the games being an aberration in life rather than the plan, I'd bet it's easier for the humans to think about it as they are gone not dead, when their children don't return and ignore the possibility. Two, you aren't going to be just thrown into a whole world you don't know and expected to figure it out. You'll have us to help, and our families. My dad, and Byder's mom, have been in your shoes and will help. Veirveil is big, but not that big. Our situation is unique, but most of the time, the bonded pair comes home from the games and lives with the god's parents for a while after. Zimuna and Greg stayed with us for like six months after they came home. Dad and Greg bonded a lot and they still live close by. We'll have to talk about that, because there are two families to choose from here, but we aren't the first in this situation."

"I know my parents expected that I would come stay with them after the games and bring the girl I am mated with. Mom was kind of excited about the idea." Byder chuckles. "I don't have any other siblings so we haven't been through it with an older sibling yet but Mom was already tickled that she would have another priorly human around."

Ydum nods at him. "Exactly. Not only will there be you adjusting to everything in Veirveil, and all that comes with passing the games. But poor Anarus is going to have to adjust to having a crap ton of family he can't get rid of. I mean, you have seven sisters and how many of them are married and have kids? That's a whole lot of family on top of three father-in-laws, three mother-in-laws and my sister and brother-in-law."

"Aw, fuck. I never thought about that." Anarus grumbles. "I only ever thought about you three. That's a fuck ton of family."

I pat his arm. "Don't worry. It's only a temporary foray into the organized chaos that is my family life. Then we can come back and both of us can enjoy the relative calm that is both of theirs and share our discomfort of not knowing what we are doing."

Byder and Ydum both chuckle at this. Ydum looks at me again, bringing a hand up to my cheek. "As for that last part, we will not do anything about anything with children until all of us are ready for it, if we are ever all ready for it and choose it together. No need to be scared, beautiful. We are all in this together."

"Ydum, are you channeling my magic words?" I tease.

He waggles his eyebrows at me and only says, "Maybe."

At that moment, Wren and Kutar return to the foyer, distracting us from the conversation. Once we determine they came back unharmed, in a relatively good mood, and direct them to the provided dinner, I lie back down on Ydum's lap and rest my eyes, trying hard to think of nothing at all.

I must fall asleep because I wake up to Saffron and Velmos returning. Byder is yawning as well like he just woke up. Dinner's still on the table so I'm not sure how long it's been. After they are situated, I snuggle back down on Ydum's lap and sleep again on purpose.

When I'm woken up by Isis and Esnir returning, Anarus is lying down asleep with his head on my stomach. Ydum is sleeping sitting up like only he can. Byder is also sleeping sitting up, but his head is resting on Ydum's shoulder. Damek across the foyer is snoring loudly. Poor Iella. I'm the only one in this group that snores, or so they keep insisting. Damek is really loud, like a growling bear.

As we all slowly wake up, and a very exhausted Isis and Esnir make their way to sit down, Drila lists off the standings. Her heart, though, doesn't seem to be in it. Maybe she's tired as well. "Last place, Wren, three hundred and seventy-five points. Fifth place, Raven, three hundred and thirty points. Fourth place, Isis, three hundred and fifteen points. Third place, Damek, three hundred and five points. Tied for first, Jinx and Saffron, two hundred and sixty points. Next week, senses. See you then."

Drila pops away as we all struggle to our feet and shuffle sleepily to our rooms. Breakfast is on the table, but I ignore it and continue on to the bedroom. I drop into the bed and go right back to sleep.

Chapter Four

WHEN I WAKE BACK up and head to the sitting room, lunch, or I assume it's lunch since there's still light coming in the bedroom window, is on the table.

"No coffee." I grumble.

"No coffee." Anarus repeats from a spot on the couch.

I groan and slump as I walk to the couch to flop onto it next to Anarus. "Seen Byder or Ydum?"

"Nope." Anarus mumbles something else but I don't catch it.

I lay my head on his bare shoulder, still sleepy but knowing if I let myself sleep more, I'll have problems sleeping tonight and will mess up my schedule. "What was that?"

Anarus shifts so his shoulder is lower and I can reach it with my head easier. "They were up a bit ago, though. I know that much."

I glance up at him and he lets out a silent laugh.

"I'm assuming Byder worked out his issues with his feelings for Ydum." Ah. My brain catches up with what Anarus is saying. I'm happy about that. Sure, it makes this whole thing a lot messier and more confusing, but still, I'm happy.

In wonder about how Anarus feels about this, I tentatively probe my bond with him to sense if there's any other feelings in him besides frustration at the lack of caffeine. I don't feel anything except a quiet comfort with having three people caring about him. He could have been frustrated with it and that would be understandable. It does leave him on the outside more, only having me and them two having each other and me. But he's not.

"I'm good with it, little human." Anarus side-eyes me. "I have everything I need and I'm happy they're happy. I never lied about feeling that way."

I wrap my arms through his and snuggle onto his shoulder more. "I know. I just worry about you."

Ydum finally comes out of the other bedroom, far too bright and cheery. "Good morning, all. Or afternoon. Or whatever." He comes over and plants a kiss on my cheek before gracefully dropping himself on the other couch.

"Shh." I tell him. "They didn't give us coffee."

Ydum feigns fear but can't keep the smile off his face. "So, this is the day I die. Well, it's been a good run."

Byder wanders over to sit. "Why do you die today?"

Anarus responds this time. "No coffee, Jinx mad."

"Jinx looks perfectly content in your arms, Ani." Ydum replies with mirth. "You, on the other hand, look positively murderous."

Anarus just shoots him a look, making Ydum laugh more. "That's the look. That one right there, all murdery and stabby."

Before Anarus can get more stabby, I change the conversation. "Next game is senses. What does that entail?"

"Wait." Byder says before anyone can answer me. "Would the maze count as a hunt?"

Anarus answers, no longer grumbly. "I would say so." Ydum and I nod, agreeing.

Byder holds his black bag with the tattoo kit out to Anarus. "Ydum did one. Jinx did one. Would you?"

Anarus's jaw drops. "You want me to do your successful hunt line?" When Byder only nods at him, Anarus reaches slowly out to take the kit. "I would... I'd be honored to."

I move so that Byder can sit next to Anarus. He shrugs. "It'll make me have one from each person in my family. My dad did my first. My mom did my second. Now, I'll have one from each of you too."

While Anarus tattoos Byder, Ydum gets academic. "The purpose of the senses game is both easy and not. The game makes the team use their senses. Normal senses, smell, touch, taste, vision, but also those more elusive senses that gods and witches possess. The ability to feel magic, the senses that come from the witch and god's bond, that deeper intuition that comes from the type of power a god has, or magic a witch has. How the game makes this happen is varied and always creatively different. The fact that we have a hunt god on our team is a clear advantage, no matter how the game works specifically. Without one single thought, Byder is the choice if you have to choose, but I don't think you will have to. The closer we get to the conclusion of the games, the more the games will push the boundaries to test how deeply developed the bond between a god and a witch is. With multiple god teams, the bond between all of them will be tested."

"How dangerous is this game?" I ask.

"Moderately." Anarus tells me, his focus on Byder's arm. "Have teams failed and possibly humans died? Yes. It isn't the intellect game that's basically impossible to fail, but it's not as bad as the combat game where deaths are assured."

"I assume that what we should work on is our senses? That seems kind of obvious but at the same time, it's easier said than done. How do I work on my sense of taste?" I look to Byder, knowing this is his domain. Ydum looks at him too.

Byder flexes the arm Anarus isn't tattooing, as if he's nervous to be the one everyone is looking at for this. Even in the protection game, where we assumed his hunting skills would be beneficial, the focus was more on what I could teach them rather than on Byder. This is the first time he has been the one to lead us.

"I don't think we could practice those types of senses, Jinx. They are what they are. The magical senses and our sensory awareness of each other, that's what our focus should be on."

"To the paintings?" Ydum asks.

"Give me a few more minutes. Almost done." Anarus says.

As soon as Anarus wipes down Byder's arm, and packs everything up, Ydum asks, "Now to the paintings?"

Byder and I both nod in agreement, so Ydum points a finger in the air. "To the paintings!"

We wander out in the hallway and see that everyone else is already out there. Seems like we slept later than all of them. We all stroll away from each other, going up and down the hallway to examine the paintings and chatter with the others. I do one lap of the hallway and see that the paintings are pretty simple. All black and white, five of the paintings are easily identifiable. A hand, an eye, an ear, a nose, and a mouth. Touch, sight, hearing, smell, and taste. The sixth painting gives me pause. It's another eye but looks very different from the other eye, more decorative. It takes me a moment to realize it must represent the eye of magic, that inward focus used when accessing your magic.

I move to the foyer to be out of the way of other people trying to look at the paintings. Ydum, Byder, and Esnir are talking, laughing with each other. I don't want to go back to the room and make them feel like they need to end their conversation with a friend to join me. As I putter around aimlessly, Saffron comes up to me, almost too casually.

"Your team looks rather cozy." She's looking at Ydum and Byder. The two of them are very close to each other, almost touching but not quite. I can't tell by her tone if she is mocking us or just making an observation.

"We are pretty close." I say, noncommittally.

She's still looking at Byder and Ydum. "That looks a little more than close."

I still can't tell her intentions, but part of me feels wary and protective of my gods. "Do you have a point, Saffron?"

"Velmos told me he's seen duo teams, one witch, two gods before, but never a trio." Saffron shrugs. "Just wondering how that works. But based on the way those two are acting, I think I can guess."

I step between her and her line of sight to my gods, my arms crossing over my chest and I know I'm glaring. "How it works is none of your damn business."

"It is if you tricked the cave." Saffron snarls, her actual motivations suddenly very evident. "It is if you're tricking the games. Did they have some arrangement between the three of them? Anarus would find his actual mate and

Ydum and Byder would just tag along with him, pretending they bonded with the same human just so they can be together. Are you really only bonded with Anarus and pretend a bond with them two so they can be together? Are you cheating by having three gods instead of only the one you should have just so those two can have some unnatural relationship?"

An overwhelming anger burns through me and, before I realize what I'm doing, I slap Saffron across the face. Hard enough to leave an imprint of my hand on her cheek. "Fuck you!" I yell, venom seeping from me. "Fuck Velmos. They are mine. All of them are mine. Do not talk about my gods like that. Don't look at them again. Don't even think about them. They are mine!"

Hands are grabbing me, pulling me away. Ydum is practically lifting me off the ground as he wraps his arms around my stomach, pinning my arms to my sides with his, to move me away from Saffron. "Okay, back to the room with you. Sorry, Saffron, she hasn't had her coffee today. Come on, beautiful."

I eventually stop fighting Ydum pulling me away but the anger in me doesn't settle. In the room, Ydum lets go of me and I immediately start pacing and yelling. "How fucking dare she! She does not get to talk about MY GODS that way! I will choke the shit out of her. Velmos too. Fuck them, fuck all of them. We have been nothing but nice, helpful, and this is how they repay us?" I clench and unclench my fists, stomping around the room, gritting my teeth so tight I think they will crack.

"What the fuck did Saffron say?" I hear Byder ask. "I've seen Jinx mad, but this is a whole new level of vicious Jinx."

Ydum shakes his head. "No clue but damn is she angry."

"She asked if we were cheating." I grind out, ripping a hand through my hair, frustrated. "She said three gods doesn't happen and we're faking the bond with you two so you can be together and I should only be with Anarus. That we're lying to protect your unnatural relationship." I go back to pacing.

There's a scuffle behind me and I turn to see what's happening. Ydum and Byder each have Anarus by an arm, gripping him tightly.

"Control your shadows, man!" Ydum is yelling at him.

"Fuck that!" Anarus yells, trying to yank away from them while his shadows stream around him. "I'll fucking end Velmos. That bastard!"

"They're just trying to fuck with us." Byder continues tugging on one of Anarus's arms. "We're tied for first with them. They're trying to make us mess up. Don't let them win like that."

Anarus is unconvinced. "One punch. Just let me get in one punch."

Ydum laughs despite himself. "Anarus, you'd kill him with one punch."

"My point exactly." Anarus says, emphasizing each word.

Anarus isn't convinced but I am. Byder has a point. We've been battling with Saffron and Velmos for first place for weeks now and are tied with them for the second time. As it stands now, we are their only real competition. As much as the four of us don't really care about winning, only surviving, we can't know how much the other teams want to not only survive but win. I would gladly come in last place so that everyone survives and finishes the games, but Saffron may not see it that way.

I take a deep breath and try to collect myself. I cannot let her use words to make me unbalanced. Angry people make mistakes. I take a few minutes to reign myself in, breathing deeply and focusing on peace. Once I have better control, I stand in front of Anarus, with Ydum and Byder still holding him as he struggles, and place my hand on his cheek. Peace, I think.

"We can be upset, Anarus, but not this upset." I say quietly, knowing my rage is only mostly contained, his rage affecting mine.

As I try to keep Anarus's rage out of mine, I feel a sharp pull from Kinshra. *What the fuck happened to my guide? Why is he so angry?*

Human stuff, people being mean to Ydum and Byder, Kinshra. I pause in my thoughts to her. Wait, did you just swear?

I'm learning a lot from you and Anarus. No idea what fuck means but you both have said it when mad, so I figured it meant something like that. Do we need to take some human down to protect my bonded's bonded?

I hide my chuckle at that, and answer her. No, Kinshra. We are overreacting. But good job with the swear. I feel her shake her fur and go back to sleeping. What I told her is right. Saffron is horrible for what she said, but we can't let her do this to us. Make us angry like this.

I tell Anarus. "We need to be in control. We cannot let them win by making us tear ourselves apart. They are words. Only words. She can do nothing with words that we don't let her. Her magic isn't in words, only mine is. Do not give her your power by letting her words work on you."

Anarus relaxes his struggling. A deep growl comes from his throat. His anger is still very much there, but he's taming it. That's fine. Mine is too. Maybe I'm feeling his and Kinshra's too. I look at Ydum, then Byder. They are both angry as well but not as much. I can feel their anger, I realize suddenly. The bond isn't only sharing our pleasure that deeply anymore, like Ydum thought it would eventually become, and I can feel everyone's feelings acutely.

Ydum carries what feels like an old anger newly touched. He has experience with this feeling and knows how he reacts doesn't change anything about how people see him. Byder has a relationship to it, but the focus of it being on him is new. He's used to being able to react, be the anger for the ones who can't like Ydum. He knows he's one of the ones who can't react now and is struggling to make that change in his mind.

But he's struggling with it less than Anarus who has never bothered with this type of anger, ignoring those who try to stoke it as ridiculous and stupid. But now he doesn't know what to do when it's his family, his people. His instinct is to protect, but we're telling him he can't protect this way.

"Are they really thinking that?" Anarus asks. "How can they think that?"

Ydum lets go of him, sighing. "They probably don't even believe their own words. The cave magic is bigger than that. But doubt sown is doubt that grows. They're hoping to make the others doubt us, maybe make us doubt ourselves. We know who and what we are. Esnir, I think, knows too. He and Isis won't fall for it. Damek and Iella, I would wager, won't either. The other two teams? I don't know but I don't really care. We know, everyone else doesn't matter here."

Byder lets go as well. "Plus, our girl got a pretty good swing in there. Saffron will think twice before saying any shit like that again."

"That was a good hit, little human." Anarus tells me, the anger slowly leeching from his voice and body. "Clean, well placed, nice follow through."

"What can I say? I had good teachers." I try for a smile but know it doesn't make it to my eyes. "Let's just focus on the next game and forget them. Byder, how do you suggest we move forward? How do we practice? Which painting should we choose?"

Byder paces away from Anarus, moving to the couches, and waves his arm for us to follow him. Once we are all settled, our anger mostly contained, he answers me. "I don't think we can pick a painting yet. We need to do the work first then decide where we would be strongest, or potentially weakest. It could be that the paintings represent the only sense we can use or the only one we can't use. We should prepare for both ideas. And, like I said before, we can't really do anything with our physical senses, so I say we focus on strengthening our magical one."

"I agree." Ydum says. "How do we work on that?"

"Well, this little issue with Saffron gave me a thought. What did you each feel when we were all angry? Did someone else's feelings overtake your own? Could you tell who was feeling what?" Byder looks first to me.

"I could feel everyone." I tell him. "At first, it was all me. My anger, boiling and overflowing. But then, as I got control of myself, I could feel each of you. How angry you were and how much control you had over it. Anarus's anger tried to feed mine, but I could acknowledge that it wasn't actually mine. Also, Kinshra, who popped in, angry because she felt Anarus's anger and wanted to know if she could help. I'm not sure if I fed her my anger, Anarus did, or we were all feeding each other, but fin side note, Anarus. Kinshra swore, she said fuck saying she learned it from us."

Anarus's anger settles just a bit more as a small laugh escapes him over that. "We taught a wolf to swear." Ydum and Byder laugh for a moment too, but then we all get serious again.

Byder looks at Ydum to answer his question next. "I could feel everyone's anger. I felt Jinx's in the hallway and it was overpowering. I had to work really hard to not just become angry with her when I didn't know why she was feeling that way. I could tell Anarus's anger too, when she told us what happened, and it was rather overwhelming too. Not in the same way, where I wanted to join him in it, but I knew it was wild and uncontained and knew the minute he started to gain control of it. Yours, Byder, was there too, like Anarus's but you had control of it so I could set it aside. Only Jinx's anger tried to become mine."

Anarus answers next. "I felt Jinx's anger in the hallway. I struggled not to let it overtake me too, but was losing the battle. I wanted to go to her and do whatever she needed. It took everything I had to not just flash out at everyone. I was only able to come to the room once I saw Ydum had her. Then, when she told us what happened, and you two got angry too, I knew it was all four of us. It all bled together and I didn't care what anger was mine and what anger wasn't. It was all mine. I would take it all for you and do whatever I needed to make you all safe again."

Byder nods at that. "I was about like Jinx, but more so. I felt Jinx's first but knew Ydum was taking care of it. When it flared again in the room, I knew I needed to come and see what was causing it. When she told us what happened, I could tell I was angry, Ydum was angry, and I could tell that Jinx and Anarus's anger was bleeding into each other."

Ydum strokes his chin thoughtfully. "It sounds like we can all tell whose emotions are whose when we experience them. Jinx has a handle on the depth for each of us, but lacks control when it comes to separating herself from Anarus and maybe Kinshra. I can separate everyone, with less understanding than Jinx has, but know what's mine and what's someone else's. I struggle separating mine from Jinx's, but less than she struggles with Anarus's. Byder, you seem to have complete control. Each of our emotions is our own for you completely. You feel a desire to help Jinx, and maybe all of us, but have the control to know whose is whose and even see when one of us is using an emotion that doesn't originate in us. Anarus, on the other hand, is wildly uncontrolled. His desire to protect and care for not only Jinx but all of us means he doesn't try to separate out anything at all."

"So, the plan needs to be to build up each of our weaknesses." Byder explains. "Anarus, you need to work at separating our emotions and not being affected by any of us. Jinx, you need to work on keeping Anarus's emotions from bleeding into yours. Ydum, you need to work on not letting Jinx's bleed into yours."

"How do we do that?" I ask him.

Byder smiles at me. "We get mad. Or some other strong emotion. We purposely get emotional and Ydum, you try to sense that out in me without feeling Jinx or Anarus. Meanwhile, Anarus tries to block all three of us out and Jinx tries to block out Anarus. Once we can all easily control our emotions, recognize each other's but keep them separate from our own, we move to doing it with our powers rather than emotions."

Ydum tilts his head to the side. "Do you think that's possible? That we could all use each other's powers?"

"Anarus and Jinx have done it twice now, only once on purpose though. If they can, we probably can too." Byder says. "The only thing in a bond like this that I think should be limited to just them two is Kinshra."

As we settle in with dinner, Byder has us try to tease out the emotional bonds. "Ydum and Jinx, attempt to feel something strongly. Think about a memory, make yourself feel that emotion again. I will too. Anarus, try to feel nothing. We will all try to only feel our own emotion and not anyone else's, except Anarus who will try to feel nothing in particular. Try to keep your faces neutral."

The four of us sit quietly on the couches, focusing on our food and whatever we were told to feel. I search for a happy memory, knowing anger is still too close to the surface for all of us to use that one.

I remember a time when my sisters, parents and I were stuck inside for days after a huge snowstorm. We had built a roaring fire in our fireplace and sat around in the sitting room, telling stories and playing games. Mom made hot chocolate. Dad taught us how to make shadow puppets on the wall. We made cookies and Ophelia, Catarina, and I ended up having a food fight with the flour. It looked like it had snowed as much inside as it had outside. Mom had admonished us for wasting the flour but her heart wasn't in it.

Then, Dad threw flour in her hair and the fight started all over again with all ten of us. We went without bread for a week because we ran out of flour and there was too much snow for anyone to make it to the trading market. But none of us minded because, every time one of us would even mention bread, we would all dissolve into giggles over how Dad looked covered head to toe in flour.

"Ydum." Byder says, breaking my reverie. "What's Jinx feeling?"

"Um, don't know. Not angry?" Ydum says.

"Is he right?" Byder asks.

"Yes." I tell them. "Not angry."

Byder talks to Ydum again. "Can you tell what she's feeling?"

"Do you want me to try to feel what she's feeling now or try not to?" Ydum asks.

"Try to now." Byder responds.

Ydum waits a bit, then says, "Happy, she's feeling happy."

I nod and Byder asks Ydum, "Why? What's she thinking about?"

"Her sisters and parents." Ydum says confidently. Then, less confidently, "Snow? No, it's inside."

"Flour." I tell him. "A food fight with flour."

"That makes so much more sense." Ydum chuckles.

"Anarus, what are you feeling?" Byder asks.

"A lot." He grumbles. "I'm trying not to. But, a lot."

Byder doesn't seem disheartened by this. "That's okay. Can you tell what you are feeling versus one of us?"

"I know the happy is Jinx. She just said that but I already knew." Anarus thinks for a moment. "Ydum is sad? Maybe. And you are I don't know. I know I am trying really hard not to feel Jinx's happy and I'm confused because her happy is not as happy as it should be."

"I was feeling peaceful, maybe you couldn't recognize that under Jinx's happy memory." Byder explains. "Look at that, Anarus, Jinx's not happy enough happy. Why isn't it as happy as it should be?"

Anarus doesn't answer Byder right away. "Because Ydum is sad. Jinx's happy is happy. It's Ydum's sad that is making it not feel as happy to me."

"Hold onto the feeling of the difference between Ydum's sad and Jinx's happy." Byder tells him. "Both of you, change what you feel. Choose a different memory."

I search my mind for another memory. I remember a time when Mom and Dad got into an argument. They don't fight often, but when they do, sometimes it's really bad. Stress and worry makes them both boil over sometimes, but they really love each other and the arguments always end with apologies and a long talk.

But when I was five, there was a huge blowout. I remember sitting on my bed with Dahlia and Samantha. I was so scared that Mom and Dad would get so angry one of them would leave and never come back. My friend from school, Natasha, her mom had recently left her dad and that was the first time I realized parents don't always stay together and love each other forever. I was terrified that would happen to my mom and dad. Dahlia soothed me and all the rest of my sisters, telling us that our parents would be fine, adults argue sometimes and it's going to be okay, but I was still scared until Mom and Dad apologized to all of us and told us they still and always would love each other.

Byder speaks up again. "What is Jinx feeling, Anarus?"

"Scared." Anarus says easily.

"Jinx?" Byder asks me.

I nod again. "Yes."

Byder continues. "What is Ydum feeling?"

Anarus blinks a few times. "Scared?" He doesn't sound as confident.

"Yep." Ydum tells him. "Jinx and I accidentally chose the same emotion."

Byder tries again. "Can you tell the difference between Jinx's scared and Ydum's scared?"

Anarus is struggling, his face creased and he's thinking hard. "I don't know. Jinx seems like she is scared of the whole world and Ydum is more this one thing."

Byder turns to me and Ydum. "Does that make any sense to either of you?"

"I was remembering being scared when my parents fought once. Scared they wouldn't love each other anymore." I tell him.

"I was remembering how my bedroom when I was little always had this weird shadowy corner and I would cry until Mom came and showed me it was just shadows." Ydum says.

Byder bobs his head, thinking. "That sounds about right. Jinx was scared her whole world was falling apart, and Ydum was scared of a shadow in the corner. I think that is enough of that tonight, though. Anarus, you look done in."

We stop for the night and over the next two days, we spend time in fits and spurts working on reading each other's feelings without allowing them to take over our own. Byder works us in different combinations. Sometimes, I'm trying to block out them, or only focus on one of them and not feel the others. Sometimes, it's Anarus who is trying to tease apart who is feeling what without allowing any of it to change what he feels. He struggles the most and, when he complains about it, Byder tells him that he shouldn't feel like it's some sort of failure. Instead, having someone so bent on protecting all of us that he will literally take on our emotions for us is a sign of how much he actually cares and how strongly the four of us have been able to bond.

I'm annoyed that, in between emotional bond training with Byder, Ydum decides I'm better enough to start physical training again. My wrist and toes are perfect. My shoulder is close enough to perfect that it would actually help to do more movement with it. The only thing that still regularly hurts is my hip and Ydum isn't fully convinced that will ever be back to normal until I gain the immortality and can just heal it by myself. So, I'm jogging up and down the hallway again. And telling Ydum exactly how much I hate him for it.

On the evening of the fourth day, Byder and Ydum are working on Ydum's ability to block me out. They sit on the floor, playing a game that requires Ydum to focus on only Byder. Byder is holding his hands out, palms up, and Ydum has his hands palm down, barely touching Byder's. Byder is trying to be able to pull his hands out from underneath Ydum's and slap the tops of his hands before Ydum realizes he's moving, and Ydum is trying to know when Byder will move, without focusing on Byder's actual movements. Both of them have their eyes closed so they have to rely completely on thoughts and emotions felt through the bond.

Anarus and I are on the couch, cuddling under a blanket and watching. It's funny to see Ydum twitch his hands when he's mistaken and Byder isn't moving. It's funnier to watch when Ydum fails to move and Byder smacks his hands.

After watching for a bit, Anarus whispers in my ear. "Do you think you could stay silent?"

Confused, I furrow my brow at him. "Stay silent for what?"

Anarus doesn't respond but has a dark grin. I feel his hand under the blanket drift up my thigh, his fingertips moving with the lightest of touches. As his hand cups me between my legs, and I almost gasp out loud, Anarus whispers again. "Silent, little human. Ydum needs to block you out."

I bite my lip. Oh, fuck. Anarus moves his fingers on the outside of my very thin pants and it takes an absolute will in me to control my breathing. He pushes his thumb against my clit, and I swallow a moan. He strokes his fingers up and down while running his thumb in circles and I fight to control my thundering heart, which I swear is loud enough to be heard across the hall. Need fills me, and Anarus leans over to whisper in my ear again. "Are you blocking me out? You need to block me out."

I look at him and, somehow, his face is calm. I know for a fact he is not, the need in him just as high as the need in me. But he doesn't react. His breathing isn't even hitching or stuttered. I fail to completely mask the gasp when he pushes one finger towards my entrance, only the fabric of my pants keeping him out.

Anarus pulls his hand completely away, leaving me hot, bothered and disappointed. "You failed. You made a noise." He whispers. Fuck him. Fuck him. Fuck him. He brings his hand back, slowly following the same pattern again, creeping up my thigh, barely touching, his thumb finding my clit. This time, I grit my teeth and refuse to let one single sound out when he pushes his finger against me, instead only squeezing my eyes shut at the absolute ache that fills me, and he rewards me by moving his hand inside my pants.

His thumb finds my clit again and his fingers are the lightest feather of touches against my skin. A glance at his face says he knows exactly what he's doing. Agonizing, torturous need streaks through me and I fight the urge to squirm against his hand as he runs a finger up and down me, never actually fully touching my skin. He makes only one finger press harder against my core, but then pulls it back again and I know, I know I whimper quietly.

My eyes shoot to his. Did he hear that? The evil grin on Anarus's face says he did. He shakes his head and pulls his hand away completely. I let myself actually voice a whisper of a groan of complaint and he bites his lip to block the sound of his laughter. Fuck you, Anarus.

Anarus starts completely over. His hand trails up my thigh. He teases and taunts me from the outside of my pants. I stay silent, fighting every urge to moan or make a noise. He dips his hand into my pants and starts the light, barely there touches again. When his finger once again hovers right over me, pressing against my opening ever so slightly harder, I bite my lip hard enough to almost draw blood and dig my nails into my own palms. Please, I beg him in my mind as I stay silent, for fuck's sake, please touch me. I close my eyes and scream only in my head. Fucking touch me. I need you to touch me.

"Fuck." Byder swears and is kissing me hard. "Fucking put that finger inside her now, Anarus, or I fucking will." I open my eyes and Byder is standing over me, so much heat in his eyes that I'm melting. Waves of need, not all of it mine, crash over me.

Anarus does what Byder told him to and sinks his finger inside me. I fight to stop the moan as I come undone. Anarus moves the finger inside me while Byder wraps his hand around the back of my neck in a punishing grip and kisses me. My insides twist tighter and tighter and I do everything I can to not cry out. It's not enough. Fuck, it's not enough.

The blanket over me disappears, and Byder is stripping off my pants. "Who do you want, baby girl?"

Anarus's finger is still moving in me and I can't form an answer. I only squirm against his hand, my eyes closed, my head thrown back, need driving me.

Ydum swears. "She looks good dripping all over your hand, Ani."

"Anarus it is, then." Byder growls. Anarus moves his hand and Byder lifts me up, turning me to sit on Anarus's naked lap and guiding me over him. Byder's hands on my hips force me down on Anarus hard cock so roughly that I bite back a cry from how fast and completely he fills me. That momentary pain subsides quickly to be replaced with racing pleasure as Anarus's hands take over control of my hips, moving me in quick strokes over him. I feel Byder still behind me, his hands coming around to rest on my throat and breast, pulling me back onto his bare chest, and another gripping his cock that is pressed tightly to my back.

The pleasure spiraling in me from every thrust of Anarus makes it take a moment for me to realize that Byder couldn't possibly have his hands on my throat, my breast, and his own cock at my back at the same time. Some awareness that the hand on Byder is actually Ydum's flashes through me and I hear Byder groan as his hand at my throat twitches. I feel all three males' pleasure at the same time in my mind and let their feelings flood through me.

"Fuck!" Anarus groans. He moves my hips faster and puts a hand between us to rub circles on my clit. I suck in air, feeling it move down my throat past the slightly tight grip Byder still has on my neck.

Byder leans over my shoulder, nibbles the shell of my ear then whispers, "Let Anarus hear you scream, baby girl."

I shake my head. Anarus said silent. I rock my hips against him as he drives into me, and arch my back, leaning back against Byder as I continue to bite my lip against making a noise. I place one hand on Anarus's chest to brace myself, digging my nails into his skin, and bring the other up to reach behind me and grip the back of Byder's neck, letting my fingers weave through his hair and tug at it.

Byder groans again and his hand on my breast squeezes slightly. He moves his hand under my shirt to roll my nipple between his fingers. I can feel Ydum still stroking Byder's cock that is still pressed to my backside.

"Fuck, baby." I know Byder's groan is for Ydum.

"You like that, handsome?" Ydum tugs on Byder again. "You like the feel of my hand and Jinx's ass working you together?"

Byder's hand tightens around my neck, but the pressure is only slight. He pulls back on me, making me lean against him harder, my head dropping back onto his shoulder. Anarus, seeing this, leans back into the couch and the angle he's pushing into me changes, his thrusts going deeper and his cock filling more than ever before. I focus my eyes on his and see molten desire in them. He bites his lip and it's all I can do not to lean back over and bite that lip myself. I feel Anarus tense and know he is close. I let go and my muscles clench around him, pulling him over the edge with me. He groans and his hands on my hips relax.

As I catch my breath for a moment, I see Anarus give a small nod and wonder what question Byder silently asked him.

Byder speaks softly against my ear again. "Don't move, baby girl. Stay right where you are. Can Ydum fuck you while I fuck Ydum?"

Oh gods, yes. Anarus tightens his grip on my hips again while he moves out of me. I feel Byder step away and Ydum press against my back. His arms circle around my waist and pull up to take off my shirt and claim my breasts in his hands as he enters me from behind so slowly, I grit my teeth to not moan. He pulls me until I'm leaning against his naked back like I had been leaning against Byder. I'm still on Anarus's lap, facing him, and he's holding my hips still, his eyes burning as he watches me.

"Hello, beautiful." Ydum says in my ear once he's fully inside me. He holds still for a moment, but lets out a low moan. "Shit, handsome. Oh, fuck."

Byder moans, his voice so deep its almost gravelly. "Fuck, baby. You feel so good. Choke my cock with your ass."

When Ydum starts to move, I can tell the difference between his own movements, pushing into me gently, and the added rocking forward caused by Byder's thrusts into him. The sensation is new but not unpleasant. I shut my eyes, feeling overwhelmed. "Open your eyes, beautiful. Look at Anarus as I make you come." Ydum croons in my ear, his fingers stroking me everywhere, down my chest, circling my nipples, and along my sides. When they brush against Anarus's at my hips, he lingers only a moment before moving back up my body.

I look at Anarus. His expression is one of awe. He moves one hand from my hip to rub my clit and I lose control. Every fiber of my being fills with my pleasure, Ydum's pleasure, Byder's pleasure, and Anarus's pure love for all three of us. I finally break my silence and cry out as I unravel in their arms.

"That's my fucking perfect little human." Anarus smiles. "Bring them with you as you come."

Ydum doesn't stop thrusting into me with his patient, gentle movements, made fiercer by Byder's thrusts into him. Byder picks up his pace, pushing harder against Ydum, making Ydum drive harder into me.

"Shit." Ydum groans. "Fuck, Byder." Ydum pushes deeply as he spills in me and holds still again as Byder moans out, still grinding into him from behind. I lean back against Ydum again, my eyes unfocused and my body spent.

Ydum's arms hold me tight to him as he struggles to make his breath even again. Byder and I both have our heads resting on Ydum's shoulder. He kisses my temple, then moves his head to whisper in Ydum's ear. "I love you, Ydum. I just. I fucking love you."

Ydum chuckles softly. "I love you too, handsome." His hands loosen around me and go back to stroking my skin softly. "You too, beautiful."

My gods shift around me and, somehow, I find myself cradled on Byder's lap while he sits on the couch between Anarus and Ydum. We all spend a few moments just existing with each other. Anarus has his arm spread out along the back of the couch, behind Byder and Ydum. Ydum tentatively lifts his arm to join Anarus's along the back of the couch. He keeps an eye on Anarus as he moves, making it very clear he'll stop, pull the arm back, if Anarus is at all uncomfortable with the move. I watch Anarus tense for one moment, then rest his hand on Ydum's shoulder. Ydum copies the move and rests his hand on Anarus's shoulder, the two of them effectively holding Byder who is holding me.

"How is it," I ask slowly, looking at the three males who all somehow managed to put back on their pants, but opted to ignore the shirts, "that when all four of us do this, I always end up naked and you three keep most of your clothes on?"

Ydum booms a laugh. "I don't think you can draw a statistical conclusion from twice, Jinx. That's not a large enough sample size."

I scowl at him then nuzzle closer into Byder. "Don't use your fancy smart words when my brain is mushy, Ydum. I'm naked. You're not. Conclusion, why?"

I scowl at all three of them when they all laugh. But, Byder does pull the blanket over me. "Feel better, baby girl?"

"I feel fucking perfect." I tell him, sitting up slightly to look at him. "But I think you lost the game with Ydum. You definitely didn't block me out."

Byder kisses my cheek. "Kind of hard to when Anarus is making you scream in your head that loudly. I swear your feelings were so loud, I almost heard real words."

Ydum cocks his head. "Almost heard words or actually heard words? Because, I know we are taught that the bond should only function on feelings, but if Jinx's magic is powered through words, it's poss—"

"Ydum!" Byder, Anarus, and I all cut him off at the same time.

"New rule. No post-coitus academic discussions or the rule breaker sleeps on the couch." I say, looking pointedly at Ydum.

He holds up his hands in surrender. "That rule feels very singularly focused."

"It is. Now, shush with the smart talk until I have functioning synapses again." I snuggle back against Byder.

"Now who's using smart talk?" Anarus teases.

The fifth day after the seventh game, Byder stops all of us right at breakfast. Well, before we get real food but after Anarus and I get coffee, because Byder likes breathing. "I want to try something for training. We only have two days left before the senses game and we haven't gotten even close to working on magical sense because our bond sense is so messed up."

"Sorry." Anarus instinctively says as we all move to our respective spots on the couches.

But Byder shakes his head. "It's not just you, Anarus. Ydum still gets distracted too easily by Jinx and Jinx still gets too distracted by you. And if I am honest, I think I still get distracted by Jinx, and maybe Ydum too some, but just hide it better from myself. We need to figure it out or we could have a huge problem in the game. So, I propose we don't talk today."

"What, like, at all?" Ydum sits forward, resting his elbows on his knees. "How do we do anything without talking?"

"Yeah," I snort, "you're asking Ydum to not talk? All day? I don't know if he could go five minutes, much less all day."

"Ouch, Jinx." Ydum holds a hand to his heart. "I'm not that bad. But really, what if we need to say something important?"

"You can talk." Byder tells us. "But only through the bonds. To make it work, we will each have to focus on each bond we have with the others, without letting one person's emotions overrun us. And we will have to maintain our focus on all three bonds we carry at the same time as controlling our own emotions. Otherwise, you will miss someone trying to actively tell you something, or overhear things you have no need to."

Anarus sighs. "It sounds right. Impossible, with where we are now, but sounds right."

"Do we agree to try?" Byder looks around the room. To answer, I only think about happiness at Byder's plan. I feel Anarus feel grudging acceptance of Byder. Ydum opens his mouth, realizes what the rest of us have done, then closes it, feeling hopefully optimistic.

As we get breakfast and finish eating, the four of us all seem to be just quietly contemplating what the others are feeling without anyone actually attempting purposely to feel something. Ydum feels frustrated rather quickly.

I'm curious why he's frustrated. I try not to look at him, try not to use my facial expressions to speak instead of our bond.

Kinshra perks up in my mind. She and I talk at least once a day now, in our minds.

You are always trying things. Kinshra huffs.

Two weeks and two days and the games are over. I remind her. Then, we will go to a normal life and won't always be trying to win games.

Ydum's frustration is strong enough to break through the conversation. I realize he'd been trying to get my attention and am not sure how to explain without words that I was talking to Kinshra. So, I just feel sorry and attentive.

Ydum is contemplative then settles on feeling humorous at me particularly. I try to figure out what he's trying to tell me. Oh. It's after breakfast. He wants me to go run. I hate him and his running. His mirth fills my mind and I know I was right. I feel Anarus feel curious about my feeling and, when I look over, he's getting his hands slapped by Byder. They had started playing the game Byder and Ydum had played last night. Anarus was distracted and his frustration flares at Byder for a moment, then settles into disappointment that he got distracted.

Ydum and I head into the hallway. When we get to the end of the hallway between rooms nine and ten, he only feels confident in me and comfortable in how healed my body is. I know he wants me to do the running we had always done before I was hurt.

I start my laps and after I finish the two warm ups, I remember to keep in mind the bonds as I run. I check in on them and feel Byder's triumph and Anarus's defeat. Byder slapped his hands again. Ydum is only feeling satisfied. I'm running well. I start the run from door nine to door seven, touch the floor and turn back and feel a twinge in my hip. I keep going, hoping that it's just the muscles relearning to do this after such a long break. When I get back to Ydum at the end of the hall, I touch the floor, turn again and don't feel the twinge again. But then, when I get to room five and turn, I feel the twinge again, a little sharper this time.

I keep going. Each time I touch and turn leading with my right hip, I feel a sharper twinge. But I don't feel anything when I lead with my left hip. I can feel Ydum's unhappiness with me. By the time I get to touching the floor at the back wall of the foyer, the twinge is strong enough to make me gasp and falter. I stop running, leaning on the wall and take all my weight off that hip.

Ydum is panicked and by me in a moment. His mouth opens, but I shake my head. Byder wouldn't see us, or know, but we won't get better if we cheat. I close my eyes and focus on pain in my hip. Ydum uses one finger to tilt up my chin to make me look in his eyes. He feels intense concern and a need for Anarus's cold.

Anarus comes barreling out of the room, sees me standing with my right foot held off the ground and is very worried. Byder is behind him, arms crossed over his chest, concern his biggest feeling as well. Ydum gives both of them my hip pain and Anarus immediately moves to place a cold hand on my hip. I sink into his touch, feeling relief.

Ydum starts pacing. He's intent on something but I can't figure out what. At the same time, Anarus's concern is still strong. I stress the feeling of the smallness of the pain and the bigger feeling of relief from his hand and he relents some. As I curiously watch Ydum pace, obviously thinking, Esnir and Isis come out of their room, chatting. They look like they are about to start using the hallway for running practice as well, but both stop when they notice us.

I suddenly realize how we must look to them. Ydum pacing, Byder standing farther off, arms over his chest and scowling slightly, me standing against a wall with my right foot hanging off the ground awkwardly, and Anarus standing towering over me, his hand on my leg that's off the ground, scowling deeply. None of us speaking at all. The desire to laugh is overwhelming.

Anarus looks at me, confused, then turns to see Isis and Esnir looking at us, and feels a little silly. Byder's gaze follows Anarus's and he feels a moment of panic, then curious, but I'm not sure of what. Ydum is oblivious, still thinking.

"Hey, guys." Isis says tentatively. "What's going on?"

Anarus and I both look at Byder for instructions, and Byder internally sighs.

"We're doing a training for our bond sense, not speaking. But, Ydum was having Jinx run and her hip started hurting." Byder explains.

Esnir chuckles. "I never thought about how confusing that must be with four of you. Isis and I can communicate pretty well with it, in emotions and desires, but crap, that must be insanely frustrating with three extra people in your head rather than just one. What's hurting your hip about running in particular, Jinx?"

"Only when I turn on that hip."

Esnir purses his lip. "Can you show me?"

Anarus is very worried about me doing it again and maybe actually hurting myself. I give him a small smile, feeling hopeful at Esnir helping.

"That's really odd to watch." Isis says. "Is that what it looks like when we do that?"

All of us, minus Ydum who's still lost in his own thought, only shrug. "Never seen you do it that I noticed, so don't know." I answer. Then, I shoot a quick, loud, I need you thought to Ydum.

Ydum's head snaps up quickly, worried, then startled that there are other people out here. I leave it to the others to explain through only emotions and move to do another run and show Esnir. I move back to the hallway, and he follows.

I start at the first door and only run to the third door before touching the floor and turning. Then, at the first door again, I touch the floor, go to turn and immediately feel the twinge. "Shit." The word slips out and I don't set my right foot down again, leaning against the wall again.

"I see." Esnir nods and comes over close. "Can I touch you?"

"Yeah." I gasp. It really hurt that time. I move my pants waistband down to expose the side of my hip for him.

"Where exactly do you feel the pain?" Esnir asks.

I point to the spot right at the swell of my hip. Esnir runs his hand over that spot gently. Then, he tells me to move the leg as he feels it. I fix my pants and Esnir calls everyone else over.

"I think," he tells us, "that when she fell originally, she strained that muscle with how quickly she tightened everything, bracing for impact with the floor. Then, when she had to climb the tower in the sixth game, she overstressed it again, maybe even to the point it tore a little. If I had my full mantle, I could maybe tell, but without it and with her human, I can only guess at an injury like that. Broken bones, major muscle or tendon tears, internal bleeding or organ damage? That I can tell. Smaller details like this? Not so much. I'm a war god not a healing god. We only look for the big stuff that kills or completely stop a warrior."

"What do you think I should do?" I ask him.

"Well, for one, no more shuttle sprints. At all." Esnir looks at Ydum, pointedly. "None. I would not run either, or no more than gentle jogs. Save the hard stuff for if you have to in the games. Avoid overstraining or over flexing that hip. No acrobatic," he clears his throat, "extracurriculars for a while."

"How do you know all of this if you're a war god?" I ask, curiosity getting the better of me. "Not that I'm not completely appreciative but are you sure you're just a war god, or is there a potentiality that you could get your full mantle and find out you actually are more healing than war?"

Esnir chuckles again. "It's possible, Jinx, that my full mantle might push me one way or another closer to something with healing, like a combat medic god. A lot of war gods have some level of healing ability that goes beyond a normal god's ability to heal themselves. Soldiers obviously put themselves in danger often, and war gods need to be able to fix their soldiers, especially their human soldiers, quickly. But I know most of what I know about healing and injuries because I've always been interested in it. The idea that I'm a war god is very well known. What pantheon a god should belong to is usually discovered at birth." I knew that from my gods.

"Also, parents are always keenly watching their young children for the clues as to where exactly their powers lie, and if they try to ignore some manifestation, or force something else, the power in that child can break out in all sorts of dangerous ways." Esnir explains. "The bigger designations, especially when it's a pantheon power directly related to an original god rather than some sort of offshoot tertiary power, like chance or music, are easy to recognize in even a god younger than five. War is its own pantheon because the original gods created it as such, rather than because it derives directly from one of them. So, war is as much a full spectrum as hunt or nature, rather than smaller spectrum like chance, which comes from a mix of the knowledge and inspiration pantheons. My interests, and ability to sense and fix major injuries, might equate to some finer specialty that emerges with the full mantle, or might just be an interesting hobby. Asking if I'm sure I'm war would be like asking is Ydum maybe actually a war god because he is as good at fighting as I am."

I shake my head. "No way. I've seen him enough. He's definitely a nature god."

"Exactly." Esnir tells me. "And I'm definitely a war god that just likes healing stuff. Now, no more running today. Rest and I assume Anarus can help you with cooling. Or warmth, whatever feels better for you. And absolutely no more shuttle sprints permanently."

I send Ydum a sense of satisfaction that he can't torture me with running anymore. I try not to show it on my face, but I know I am smirking at him anyway. "Thank you, Esnir. I really appreciate it."

"No problem." He turns back to Isis and we four take off back to our room.

Back in our room, we return to our silence. When Byder sits on the floor and sends a thought of expectance to Anarus, Anarus just sits on the couch and pulls me toward him. I lie down and he places his hand back on my hip. Anarus send the feeling of being needed to Byder.

Byder feels undeterred. He moves so that he's sitting at Anarus's feet and hold up only one hand, again expectantly. Even I can tell what he's saying. Anarus only needs one hand on my hip. They can continue the game one-handed.

Ydum comes and sits next to Byder on the floor in front of me. He holds out his hands and feels the same expectancy. He wants to play the slapping game with me while Byder and Anarus play. I only hold out the one hand, my other too trapped under me as I lie on my side to play two handed. Ydum adjusts for this, and we start playing too.

It's actually really hard to play this game. It's even harder to play it next to two other people playing. I keep confusing Byder or Anarus's intention to move with Ydum's. It takes work to eventually drown out their feelings enough to focus only on Ydum without forgetting to leave a small opening just in case they need me.

After several games, when Ydum and I are about even with times I avoided his hits and times he managed to smack my hands, Anarus's hand started to feel uncomfortable on my hip, the cold not helping as much as it had been. I make myself feel that my hip is too cold and instantly he pulls his hand away, concerned. I course correct my feelings, realizing that he thought maybe he lost control of his cold and hurt me. Instead, I send appreciation and a lack of pain. This is actually much harder than we thought, mostly because it's hard to know how to send a clear message with only feelings.

But I notice lunch has arrived so I send a general hungry to everyone. For my three gods, who all are big eaters, especially Byder, that message is completely clear. When we're settled with our food, Byder getting my plate for me after being annoyed with me when I try to get up to do it myself, we sit silently, all looking at each other. All of us have thoughts, I can tell, things we want to say, but no idea how to do it with the Byder-imposed silence.

Ydum squares his shoulders at one point and seems academic. I tilt my head as I watch him, curious. It definitely looks like he would be saying, "I want to try something." He looks at me when I think this, startled, and I realize that's exactly what he was thinking. I knew it just by his mannerisms.

When he has all of our attentions, he closes his eyes and sends a feeling of needing us to come to him. I close my eyes, assuming that's what he means. Ydum sends a feeling of being very young and remembrance. Then, I feel fatherly love. Being outside and enjoying the sunshine on my face, warm sand between my toes. Wet, everything is suddenly wet and scary. Too scary. Panic, and needing to breathe. A desperate need to breathe. Strong arms and safety in the fatherly love again. Warm sand, lungs in pain, but still strong arms. Wet again, but this time still with the fatherly love. Panic, but the fatherly love overtaking it. Determination to make that father happy. Hard work, sore muscles, lots of wet. Fatherly love moving back but still close enough not to be scared. Success! Pride and confidence growing.

I open my eyes and stare at Ydum. He just told us a story about his father teaching him to swim only through the bond and emotions. I send him a feeling of awe, while Anarus and Byder both send pride in him.

We continue the rest of the day, trying to talk to each other through only the bond. At point, Anarus becomes overwhelmed when we are all talking through the bond and, out loud, he asks us to stop. It takes him a moment to separate us all out again and get control. It was the first and only time he failed to keep us all separated and out of his emotions, which was a huge triumph for him.

After dinner, Byder tells us we are done.

"Oh, thank fuck." Ydum says immediately. "I hated that."

Surprisingly, even though Byder said we are done, none of us talk much. We'd gotten almost used to the external silence. The next morning, at breakfast, Byder decides we need a new training.

"Tracking." He tells us. "Can you guys do anything with it?"

I immediately shake my head. I know nothing of tracking.

Ydum twists his mouth. "I know the concepts, but never actively used them."

Anarus says he's the same as Ydum.

"Can you give me some plants, Ydum?" Byder asks. "Some big, some little, maybe grass or detritus?"

Ydum takes a bit but ends up creating a small forest in the corner of the sitting room. Flowers, a small tree that he takes through a season cycle so it drops brown, dry leaves, and grass.

"That's actually pretty." I say, moving through it to admire the tiny pocket forest. "Maybe we should keep it."

Ydum's kneeling, concentrating on one of the flowers, running his fingers over the petals. "Jinx? What color is this?"

"Purple, why?" I ask, kneeling next to him.

"Purple," he repeats. "That makes sense. Blue is wet and red is very hot. Purple is blue and red together. That explains why it feels that way."

I stand up quickly. "You can still do that?"

Ydum nods and looks amazed. "I can still do that. It's," he sighs, "so weird. I can feel all the colors." He reaches out and touches a leaf on the tree. "I know this one, green." He picks up dry leaf from the ground. "This one is confusing. It's wet like blue, warm sun like yellow, and the hot of red, but all in small bits."

"Brown." I give him the color in a hushed voice. "It's brown. Brown can be lots of different shades, depending on how much of each of the three primary colors are mixed in. White is the absence of all of them, and black is all of them, the primary colors and the secondary colors all mixed together. Anarus's hair is black. Byder's is brown."

He reaches out and takes a strand of my hair, rubbing between his fingers. "What color is your hair?"

"Light brown." I tell him. "It's not a true brown like Byder's but has more blonde to it. It's somewhere in between blonde and brown. Blonde is your hair. Like yellow with some white and gold. Gold would be yellow that is shiny. And so you know, silver is like a shiny white."

"Shit." Ydum breathes out as he moves his hand over my face. "You're fucking beautiful."

I smile at him but blush at the same time.

He smiles back, his hand grazing my cheek. "You're blushing. I've seen you, and other people, do it so often, but it's so red. I never knew it's so red."

I take his hand in mine and move it to his own skin. "You're pale like me, but with just the lightest touch of green tint to your skin rather than red, or really pink, red with a little white, like me. I've never seen that before, the color of someone's skin having a green tinge. Humans at least usually range from a very, very light tint of brown, with just a bit of pink or yellow, all the way to a very, very dark brown closer to black. The shade of brown and the tint of pink, red, or yellow can come in all the ranges, but I've never seen green. I wonder if your mom has a green tinge too, or your sister."

I push up his long shirtsleeve to reveal his tattoo, and move his hand to it. "The vines are a greener green than your skin. So many shades of green, made darker with a little black or lighter with a little white. You're beautiful, Ydum."

Byder wanders over. "What's going on here?"

Ydum immediately touches the bare skin of Byder's arms that he can see with his shirt sleeveless then Byder's hair. "His skin is different than yours, Jinx. Or mine. It warmer. A nice warmer, that feels so pretty. Sorry, best word for it. Is it right that it feels a little brown?"

I nod. "Byder is tanner than you and me. My skin but like he spends a lot of time in the sun, getting tan, a sunburn but not painful. Although, it's natural for him, not caused by the sun."

"Someone want to explain?" Byder raises an eyebrow.

"Ydum can still feel the colors. It didn't go away after the game."

"Of course, it didn't." Anarus joins us in the tiny forest. "You did a magical working, Jinx, but did you ever end it? Did you ever say just for now, just the stones, or tell it to stop?"

"No. I didn't even think of that." I say. "I just did it. We needed it so I did it."

Anarus shrugs. "Then, Ydum will be able to feel colors until you tell the magic to stop. And since you gave him all the primary colors in that working, he'll be able to see every color without you adding to it. Although, I wouldn't be surprised if he struggles to connect the shades of gray he's learned the names of with the feelings of colors he hasn't been given a name for yet."

Ydum reaches out and touches Anarus's face, one finger tracing the skin of his cheek then moving to his goatee. Then he touches Anarus's bare chest. "Brown. Dark brown. A lot darker than Byder. I mean, I knew that. Even in shades of gray, I could tell you were darker than Byder and Byder's darker than Jinx and me somehow. But wow. You're beautiful, Ani."

"Um, thanks." Anarus says uncomfortably.

"Sorry." Ydum drops his hand and shakes his head. "It's just new and kind of disconcerting. I have to think about it, have to want to feel the colors, but when I do, it's like they're alive to me in a way they never have been before. It's almost like I can see them through my fingertips."

"Look at that." Byder chuckles. "Jinx's magic words doing things again."

Anarus nods. "Something we definitely need to experiment with eventually. But not now. Now, tracking?"

"Tracking, right." Byder shakes his head, dispelling thoughts. "Okay. You guys go sit on the couches. I'm going to do some stuff with the plants to see how natural tracking comes to each of you."

Anarus, Ydum and I all move to the couches. After a little wait, Byder calls for me. "Jinx, walk through our little pocket forest and see if you can find any signs that an animal has been through there and, if this was a real forest, which way you think it went and how long ago. I'm not going to give you any hints. I want to see what you can do on your own. Try to tap into my power as you do it."

I nod and focus on Byder's hunt god powers, his knowledge about animals and how they move. Then, I look around. I start low, on the ground, and see a small footprint that looks like two thick lines close together. Then, I notice some scat, but it's dry. I look higher. On the small tree, a tiny branch is broken facing towards the wall and a tiny tuft of brown fur is hanging on it. I keep looking but see no other clues.

I come back out and talk to Byder again. "There was a footprint like two thick lines, really dry poop, and a broken branch with fur on it. Not sure what it was, but it was going that way," I point to the wall, "a long time ago."

"Think. Use my power. What has that footprint?" Byder takes my hand.

I try to relax and use Byder's powers like I have Anarus's, but nothing happens. "I don't know."

Byder shakes his head. "Maybe Ydum is wrong, and that's only you and Anarus. But good job. Especially with that tiny broken branch giving you the direction. Other things to look for are blood that lets you know how fast and in what direction it may be moving. An injured animal might have been through an area a long time ago, but would be moving a lot slower so may not have made it as far. Trampled plants and space between plants where you see those broken parts can tell you size which will also tell you speed. Is it tiny and young, so probably slow, or is it huge? Don't forget scents and sounds too. Are they sweating hard? Or filthy? If the smell of their musk is overwhelming, it may be more than one."

I nod, committing these ideas to memory. Byder calls over Ydum and goes through the same thing with him as Anarus and I wait. Then, Anarus takes his turn. When they are done, they both come back to sit down.

"You all seem to have a good sense of tracking easily." Byder tells us. "I wonder if you're tapping into my power and not knowing it. Jinx said she couldn't but she got things someone who has never done this before shouldn't get."

Ydum cleans up the pocket forest, regretfully, and Byder says we are doing another training. "This time, one by one, we're going to go in the foyer and wait. The other three will find someplace to hide, focusing on our own specific magic or power. I asked Esnir, Isis, Damek, and Iella about it. The three of us teams are going to all do this together. We're all going to open up our full suites to each other. So, you can hide here, in our rooms, or anywhere in room two or room four. They'll be moving in and out of our room too, doing the same thing. The goal will be for you to use only your sense of our powers to find each of us, rather than sensing our bonds."

"Are we supposed to be finding the four of them too, or just us?" Ydum asks.

"Oh, no. Sorry." Byder corrects. "They'll each be looking for their own teammates and we'll only be looking for us. We're just all doing the game at the same time to give ourselves more places to disappear to."

"Ah. Makes sense." Ydum says. When Byder gets up, letting us know he'll be right back, Ydum turns to me. "Wait. Jinx, you didn't have the classes before coming here. Have you ever done this before, tried to sense other people's magic or a god's power?"

"No."

Ydum nods. "Thought so. You should be able to, though, even for gods or witches you don't have a bond with. Our powers will feel more familiar, since we are bonded, almost like a scent you can match to us, but the others will feel vaguer, like you could tell a witch from a god, but not which witch it is, unless it's Damek since he's the only male witch here. But the gods will be more specific. Or maybe not for you. I'm not sure how that works for a witch. For us, we can at least sense pantheons."

Byder comes back quickly. "Okay, they're ready too. Who wants to start?"

"You." I tell him. "You'll have the easiest time of it, then you can describe to me how you did it. I've never done this before."

"Sounds fair." He says. "I'm going to sit in the foyer and count to a hundred."

As he leaves, Isis skirts quickly into our room, not even knocking first. "Sorry," she says quickly. "Anywhere you want me to stay out of?"

We all shake our heads. "Have at it." I tell her, smiling.

With Byder gone, I figure if Isis is in our room, I'll go to hers. I sneak into room two, feeling odd to not knock and that neither of them are in here. I slip in their washroom and hide in the shower, focusing on my power of words. Magic, I need my magic to just be. See me, Byder. Where am I?

After a long while, Byder opens the bathroom door. "Got'cha."

I smile at him and follow him back to our room. Anarus is already there and, when Byder comes back with Ydum, he explains.

"I used your scents to start with, but that doesn't help much in our room because our scents are everywhere. Anarus's power feels dark. Ydum's feels alive. Jinx's magic feels white. I can't describe it better than that. Anarus was found first, so you go next."

This feels just like hide and seek from childhood. I hide again, this time going to room four and hiding behind the bed in one of the rooms. Anarus finds me quickly and first. So, after he finds Ydum and Byder, it's my turn.

I go to the foyer and count to one hundred in my head. Then I stand and start slowly moving down the hallway. Dark, alive, and something for Byder. I pass room two and know from the bond that Anarus is in there somewhere. I skip him though. Ydum needs to be found first since he's the only one who hasn't been. Our room is a mess of sensations. I stand in the sitting room for a minute, trying to determine what everyone's powers feel like.

I get the dark of Anarus and the alive of Ydum easily. Beyond that is a determined, focused feeling. That must be Byder. I can also tell there is a faint sense of a female witch that isn't me and assume that's Isis. Ydum was right. This feels almost like a smell rather than a magical sense.

I go back to room four and see if I can find Ydum. He was in here at some point, but I don't think he is now. Maybe he hid here for Anarus or Byder.

I can also smell what seems to be something strongly feminine, but different from Isis. It has a hint of risk taking in it. Iella is a chance goddess, she would be all about the game and taking risks, and this is her room. It would be strong here, as is Damek's magic that smells like mine and Isis's but distinct in its maleness. It all feels very nebulous, and takes work to sus out, but I can tell the differences when I focus.

In room two, I feel the alive that is Ydum too, but stronger. He and Anarus are both in room two. I just need Ydum, I think to myself. I focus on Ydum's alive and try to block out Anarus's dark, moving slowly through the room. At one of the bedroom doors, I know Anarus is in there. I move away and feel Ydum in the washroom. I open the door and see him sitting on the sink counter.

"Hello, beautiful." Ydum smiles at me. "Find me first?"

"Yup." I smile back at him.

He comes over and kisses me gently. "Good job." Then, he heads back to our room to wait.

I move to go in the room I know Anarus is in. He's sitting on the edge of the bed. "You've been in this room a long time to just have found me."

"Ydum was in the washroom." I tell him. He heads off to our room and I move on to finding Byder.

Byder is significantly better at this. I struggle to find a sense of him. I walk up and down the hallway, finding no clear scent of him. Stopping to think, I try to imagine what Byder would do to hide. He would hide his scent under someone else's. I go back to room four. I stand in the room for a moment and think. I get Iella and Damek easily. There's also a small scent of warrior god power. Esnir, I would assume, but only slightly, like he hid here earlier. On top of all that, I smell the very feminine witch power. Strong enough I know that it's in the room currently. I move toward it. Maybe Byder is hiding himself under Isis's magic.

In one of the bedrooms, I see Isis sitting on the bed. She gives me a small wave, but I ignore her. Could Byder also be in here somewhere? Yes. He's hiding behind the bed. I walk around it and see him crouched low in the corner.

"Found you." I tell him, grinning.

"You did." Byder stands and comes over. "Good job. Am I last?"

I nod and, after Byder thanks Isis for hiding him, we go back to our room for Ydum's turn. This time, I try to do what Byder did. In room two, where I already hid before, I crouch in the corner between the two couches, where Esnir and Damek are sitting. Ydum will have to find me under the scent of a war god and a male witch. When Iella finds Damek, he tells her to come take a seat and wait. We are making it hard on Ydum now. Two gods and a male witch. I smile as I realize that I'm very mean for this.

After a long time, Byder comes in the room and starts laughing. "Shit, Jinx. You made that a challenge. Ydum found both me and Anarus a long time ago and had given up on you."

I stand up and follow him back to the room. When Byder tells them what I did, Ydum cries foul.

"Not fair. How was I supposed to find you under two gods and a male witch?"

I pat his cheek. "I guess I win."

"Sock ball." Ydum cries out. "We are playing sock ball. I will not let this defeat stand!"

We spend the rest of the night playing sock ball, with me winning often and Ydum very frustrated he cannot undo his defeat.

Chapter Five

THE NEXT MORNING, I feel ready for whatever the senses game can throw at us. I make sure Byder's hair won't bother him and wait until Anarus finishes his first cup of coffee to argue with him about wearing a shirt. When the tone sounds, we head out and line up with the other teams. Drila is waiting in a silver dress and launches into her normal speech the moment we're all ready.

"This game will test your team's senses. The goal of the game is to find your teammate, or teammates in Jinx's case. You will be separated and can use any method but the sense you choose from the paintings to eliminate. The choices are vision, hearing, smell, anything through the mouth including taste and talking, touch, or magical sense. Since Saffron and Jinx are tied for first, we'll use a tiebreaker to determine which of them chooses first. Saffron has been in first four times, including this time, but Jinx has only been in first twice. Saffron will go first, then Jinx."

Saffron moves to the painting of a hand, choosing touch to eliminate. I look back at my gods.

"Mouth." Byder whispers. "We did it for a whole day already. We should be able to get away with no taste, and if we're far apart, talking won't matter anyway." Ydum and Anarus nod in agreement, so I move to the painting of the mouth.

Damek moves quickly to the ears, choosing to be deaf. Isis chooses the nose, eliminating smell and Raven chooses the magical eye, eliminating their magic, which honestly is smart for them. Music wouldn't help them as much as the actual senses. That leaves Wren the eyes, but it seems like she knew that would be the case being in sixth. She and Kutar will be blind.

Immediately after Wren is in place and our gods join us, I blink and find myself in a forest alone, similar to all the other forests the game has put us in. It's late October and the weather feels right for it, although the amount of sunshine through the canopy makes me think it's late afternoon instead of morning. The state of the leaves on the trees, all shades of red, yellow, and gold, with many of them in piles on the ground tells me it's definitely autumn.

Just for fun, I try to say something. Nothing comes out, no matter how hard I try. I shrug and let it go. Time to focus on finding my gods. I close my eyes and focus on my magic. I need to feel Anarus, Ydum, and Byder. An awareness that they are somewhere near by floods me, but they are all in different directions.

Kinshra? I reach out for my wolf.

She perks up her head. *In the game?*

Yes. I need to find the other three, but cannot speak or taste, or really use my mouth at all, I guess. Can you help?

Can you hear anything?

I think for a moment. I can hear sounds. Not sure what, though. It's very soft.

Focus on my ears. Kinshra tells me. *Use my better hearing.*

Wait. I shake my head. I can't talk, and neither can they. Even if I hear talking, it won't be them.

Then try smell. I can smell better than you too. I know what Anarus smells like very well. I can help guide you to him at least.

That's a good idea. Thanks, Kinshra. I focus on my wolf's nose. I need to smell like Kinshra can. Suddenly, a lot of smells assault me. It's overwhelming. Earthiness, flowers, and many different musks.

Humans. Kinshra tells me. *To the south.*

Do humans and gods smell different to you?

Yes, but this many humans means a village. My guess would be that your gods will try to make it out of the woods to someplace open to be able to see each other. That's what we would do with the pack. A village would work for that for people.

Good idea, Kinshra. I start walking south, constantly checking my sense of smell and sense of their powers for any of my gods. I use my eyes and Byder's tracking tips as well. As I walk, the smell of humans becomes stronger, but I don't find anything of my gods.

The village is a lot further than I thought it would be. I start doubting that Anarus, Ydum, and Byder would go this way, but with nothing else to go on, it's a direction to move. So, I keep walking. After what feels like several hours, and when the sun is moving slowly to the horizon, I start to see the clearing through the trees. I find a road and follow it the rest of the way into the village.

The smells assaulting my nose become completely overwhelming. I can smell what every home is cooking and each of the people inside them. Without even trying, I can tell where the market was three days ago, how many people have horses, where the healer's hut is, and so many other details. I could not find anything about my gods in this if I wanted to.

Kinshra, I think I need to stop the added smell ability. It's too overwhelming.

Okay. I feel her settle back down, curling up with her tail wrapped around her. *I'll take a nap then. Let me know if you need me again.*

Thanks, Kinshra.

With the extra smell gone, the village smells like a regular village. It looks similar to mine, and the one from game five. Mud and daub huts circle around a central point, with dirt roads running in every direction. Far to the north side of the village is a larger stone building I recognize as a testing center, and another that looks like a High Priest or Priestess's house. Since they're the biggest and most recognizable buildings in the village, I head to them and send out feeling of finding the biggest building in the village. I hope my gods are close enough to sense it.

As I walk through the village, many people are outside moving around. Children are running everywhere. Adults are standing outside their huts, chatting and watching over the children in the gorgeous fall weather. The children ignore me, but the adults seem to watch me for a bit in a rather interested but unconcerned way. The gods must have let them know that their village would be used for a Gods Game and some strange new people would be wandering around. If this was my village and someone new was wandering around, looking everywhere but not speaking, the High Priest would be approaching them quickly, wondering at their motive, inviting but protective of our homes.

There are decorations hanging from all the homes. Drying corn husks on either side of the front doors. Pumpkins carved with funny or scary faces sit on door stoops. People are stringing berries together to make garlands, and there are men in the middle of the village stacking wood high for a bonfire. The village is preparing for a harvest festival.

A pang of sadness hits me. My family will be doing the same thing. Mom will spend days canning fruits and vegetables for the winter while Dad will hunt for deer and rabbits, smoking the meat into jerky. Dahlia's husband Finnegan will chop a lot of wood from the forest nearby, bringing a large load to my parents' and sisters' homes as well as his own. Granny Helen will be making huge batches of cough medicine and making sure Ganna has several bottles of it on hand.

I miss them. I will miss this holiday with them. I missed Shearah's birthday already. Do my gods do anything for the harvest? What about the winter solstice coming up or fall equinox we already missed? Would Ydum's dad or Byder's mom want to keep up those traditions I've known my whole life? Do they miss it if they don't do it anymore or does it become something the witches from the games turned demi-god don't care about anymore? I don't think I would ever want to forget them. I would want to teach Ydum, Byder, and Anarus about them and learn about their celebrations in turn. Maybe we can blend them together and make something new, something our own.

Ydum is next me. I was so lost in thought, I missed sensing him until he took my hand. I feel a little concern from him. He felt my sadness. I smile sadly and place a hand on his cheek, thinking about old memories.

We walk together the rest of the way to the High Priest's house and sit outside to wait, both of us sending out the equivalent of pings to say we are here, together, waiting. I lean against him and wish I could tell him what I'd been thinking. He wraps an arm around me and brushes his fingers against my right hip, questioningly.

I shake my head. My hip isn't hurting right now.

A huge burst of fright and pain comes into my awareness. I shoot to my feet and look west. Byder is hurt. Ydum next to me is also on his feet. We look at each other and both take off at a run, following the sense of pain and a desperate need for help. Fuck, fuck! The fear builds so strongly, my own heart is racing.

We run west, going back into the woods. I keep throwing out feelings of immediate need to Anarus, hoping he can feel me if he can't feel Byder. I block out Ydum's worry so that I am only moving Byder's panic to Anarus, so he knows who it is and where to go.

In the woods, I see broken foliage everywhere. There's no pattern to it I can follow and Byder's panic and pain is too tremendous to pinpoint which way he is. Then, I see something that makes my heart jump into my throat. Blood. There's blood on a leaf, about waist high. I point it out to Ydum and feel his own panic jump.

We slow down and look for more evidence of blood. Ydum points to another leaf. There's a swipe of blood on it. Ydum follows it with his finger. It was a purposeful swipe, and it's headed to the northwest. We move that way and I start seeing the broken foliage have a definite pattern. We're going the right way.

Byder! I yell down my bond. Where are you? Only pain returns to me, but it's still too much to figure out a direction. Ydum and I move slowly, no matter how badly I want to run. We have to watch the trail Byder left us. There are more swipes of blood, and some large drops, and we follow them. A tree has claw marks on it that are straight up and down. I look up. Foliage higher in the tree is broken, and one branch is cracked in half, hanging down. Did Byder try to get away by climbing a tree and fell out?

Before we can move away from the tree with the claw marks, Anarus slams into me. He's panicked and wild. He grabs both my face and Ydum's with his hands, looking at me, then Ydum, fear his biggest emotion. I shake my head and think of Byder. He lets out a sigh of relief, but then immediately isn't relieved anymore. Byder, we need to get to Byder.

Anarus perks up his face, looking, feeling for Byder. When he takes off, northwest still, Ydum and I follow him. Anarus has the deepest connection to all of us, so we trust his intuition. We quickly find him, sitting on the ground, leaning against a tree, his left arm cradled in his right. He is pale and shaking.

I drop on the ground next to him and pull his arm into my lap. Four large gouges cover his forearm that are bleeding badly and two of his fingers are bruised, scraped, and bleeding sluggishly. There're streaks of blood on his rabbit hide shirt and tears in his tan leather pants. The arm is the worst, though. I look up at Ydum and Anarus. Anarus's shirt is dirty. Ydum. I think about Ydum bare chested. Confused, Ydum strips off his shirt and I grab it from him, tearing it into strips.

I start wrapping the strips tightly around Byder's arm, hoping to staunch the flow of blood. Once the wound is covered as well as I can make it, with the blood slowing, I grab his face and kiss him, pouring all my worry and love into the kiss. Ydum sets his hand on Byder's shoulder and does the same. Anarus touches his other shoulder and we are back in the foyer.

"Bear." Byder croaks out. "I stumbled into a bear cub, and the mom was not happy. I fell running and scraped my fingers. I used the blood from them to leave clues which way I was going. I tried to climb a tree to get away but the branch broke under me and the mom bear swiped my arm as I tried to get away."

"You scared the shit outta me." I pull him into a hug.

"I scared the shit outta me too." Byder chortles. "I thought I was a goner."

"Jinx's team, second place. Five extra points for the injury." I hear Drila say but I don't care. We help Byder move over to the wall and once he's settled, I see who came before us. Raven and Uesis. That makes sense. They had all their senses but magic, and with Uesis a music god, that really wouldn't have hindered them much. I focus on Byder instead.

"I'm fine, baby girl." He tells me. "It'll heal quickly. I'll have Esnir look at it too."

"You are not allowed to do that." I tell him, as I kiss him then snuggle against his side. "You are not allowed to scare me like that."

"Or me." Ydum kisses Byder quickly as well, then blushes. His eyes glance up to look at Raven and Uesis. That's the first time either of them has done anything in front of anyone else. Raven saw, I can see it in her expression she saw, but she seems unconcerned.

"Me either, but I'm not kissing you." Anarus grumbles, making us all laugh.

Damek and Iella return next. "Easy." Damek says confidently. "Wow, I'm loud." He'd been deaf in the game. I understand. My voice felt scratchy after not using it.

They barely step away, when Saffron and Velmos appear. Velmos is screaming and has Saffron in his arms. Blood is pooling around them. "Help me! Fucking help me!"

I look at Drila but she does nothing. So, I run over. Sure, Saffron pissed me off with that comment she made, but I don't want her to die and that is far too much blood spilling over the floor.

"Where's she hurt?" I ask Velmos. Anarus and Ydum stand behind me, waiting for me to give them directions.

Velmos lifts his hands. There are gouges in Saffron's abdomen that look similar to Byder's on his arm. "I found her like this. I don't know what happened. Saff, talk to me! Please!"

Saffron groans and the sound is so weak. I look at the gouges. They are deep, far, far too deep. I couldn't even stitch them shut. "We need Esnir. We just need slow the bleeding and wait for Esnir."

Anarus hands me his shirt immediately, but I refuse it. "Too dirty, it will cause infection."

Damek is on my other side. "Mine's clean enough."

I nod and Damek has his shirt in my hand quickly. I push it onto Saffron's wounds hard. She doesn't moan this time. "Velmos, put pressure on it. Hold the shirt to her as tight as you can." I pull Saffron from his arms and lay her on the floor. Velmos does as I say while I check the rest of her. There are more gouges on her scalp and thigh. I sit back and start crying. Even with Esnir, this is too much. Saffron is going to die while we watch.

Anger fills me. I get up and storm at Drila. "Do something! They made it back. Do something. She doesn't have to die right now. Drila, do something!"

Drila looks away and does nothing. Anarus grabs my arms as I start to swing, screaming again. "Do something! You can stop this."

I hear Esnir's voice behind me and know he and Isis are back. "Fuck, this is bad. This is really bad. Isis, sweetie?"

I turn back to Saffron and see Esnir kneeling over her, a hand on her head and another over her abdomen. Isis is leaning against Esnir's back, her eyes closed and her mouth moving silently. She's trying to help Esnir with her magic, I can tell.

I lean down and, through hiccupping tears, I tell Esnir that it's her thigh too. He looks at the thigh and groans. "I can't. I, it's too much."

"Try, please." Velmos begs him, crying as well. "I know we were awful to everyone, but please try."

Esnir takes a deep breath and nods. I put a hand on his shoulder and add my strength as best as I can. Healing, give Esnir my magic to heal Saffron with. I need him to heal her. It feels like my words are hollow, though. No magic in them. I glance over at Drila, but see she is still standing there, a blank look on her face. Are they stopping this? Are the original gods preventing us from healing her? I grit my teeth. Fuck them, I think, and push my magic harder. I push my words, screaming them through my magic. Heal her, damn it!

Damek adds a hand to Esnir's other shoulder and Raven puts her hand next to Damek's. Anarus touches my back, and Ydum and Byder each touch Anarus. Uesis is touching Raven and Iella is touching Damek. We are one huge connection of hope and healing. But it still feels like we are throwing magic into the void, nothing actually reaching Saffron. Her injuries aren't changing.

When Wren and Kutar pop into the foyer, they take one look at what's happening and Wren immediately puts her hand on Raven's back as Kutar puts a hand on Wren's. Drila is talking, but none of us hear her. We are all focusing on healing Saffron.

Velmos groans and let out a soul shattering scream. "No! No, Saff, no." I know without even looking she died.

"I'm so sorry." Esnir's voice is shaking. "I tried. I tried. I just couldn't do it. It was like something was blocking my power. I'm sorry."

Before anyone can respond, Velmos and Saffron are gone, the only sign they had been here the blood on Esnir and me. Even the floor is clean. I collapse in Anarus's arms, tears overwhelming me. My gods pull me back to sit on the floor where we were. Drila is saying the results, but no one listens. She leaves and all the teams stay where we are for the longest time, staring at the spot Saffron died and crying together.

"She was back. She didn't have to die. Our magic should have healed her!" I say eventually, anger replacing my sadness.

"I know, beautiful." Ydum tries to be comforting. "I don't think Drila had the power to do anything in the moment, but the original gods did. They should have stopped her dying."

"It's worse than that." Anarus looks at Ydum, his shadows a mess with his anger front and center. "They didn't just do nothing. They actively stopped us from healing her."

I look at everyone's faces as we absorb that. They stopped us. On purpose. My words did nothing. Their magic and powers did nothing. Not because we weren't strong enough, but because they stopped us. But there's nothing we can do about it. Our anger is futile. Eventually, everyone starts slowly moving back to their rooms. We go back to ours and all sit on the couches, saying nothing for a long time.

"Esnir will be blaming himself." Ydum says, standing. He walks out into the hallway and I follow. Anarus and Byder are behind me. We go straight to room two and Ydum doesn't even knock, just walks in.

Like he thought, Esnir was sitting on the couch, shaking and his face red. Isis is next to him, smoothing his hair.

"I couldn't stop it." He's repeating over and over. "I tried, but I couldn't stop it."

Ydum sits down next to him, putting a comforting hand on his knee. I kneel in front of him, blocking the spot on the floor he was staring at.

"There was nothing we could do." I tell him. "It was too much. We all tried, Esnir. We were all trying with you. This isn't on you." Part of me wants to rail against the original gods. Scream how it's their fault and Esnir shouldn't feel guilt over what's their fault. But that won't help him right now, so I stay silent.

Damek and Iella come into the room too, having the same idea as Ydum. They take up positions to support Esnir like we are.

Behind them, Raven is standing at the door, tears falling freely. "I knew her. I knew Saffron from home. Our villages were close by and my older brother married a girl from there. My parents and I would go to visit together. My sister-in-law's older sister was married to Saffron's older brother. She was basically family. I saw her once in a while. I knew her before."

I stand and go over to Raven, wrapping her in a hug. We don't know each other well, but she's hurting. Comfort is all I can offer right now. Raven accepts my hug, clinging to me as she cries.

"How do I tell them?" Raven's shoulders shake as she cries. "How do I tell them she's gone like that? This game should've been easy. She was always in first, or close enough, and I'm usually almost last. How do I tell them I survived and she didn't?"

I have no answer for her. No one does.

Raven pulls away from me, leaning on Uesis. "I want to go home. I'm so tired. I want to go home. I love you, Uesis, but I want to go home."

Two weeks, I think to myself. Two more weeks and we're done. Two more games. Then, we can leave. I know how Raven feels. I love Anarus, Byder, and Ydum, but I'm tired. I don't want to fight or struggle anymore.

Byder senses my feelings and wraps his arms around me. "Come on. Let's leave Ydum and the others to help Esnir and Raven. You've done enough." He leads me back to our room and urges me to take a shower. I do and realize I'm still covered in Saffron's blood. For the second time, I'm covered in someone else's blood because they died in my hands. I sit on the floor of the shower and cry again, watching the red water run down the drain.

"Come here, baby girl." Byder climbs in the shower, fully dressed and holds me again. The strips of Ydum's shirt on his arm get wet and I worry they won't stay on.

"Your arm." I start to pull at them, but Byder stops me.

He pushes away my hands. "I'm fine. Jinx, you always worry about everyone else. Let me worry about you."

I nod and lean against him again. Eventually, the water gets cold and Byder shuts off the shower. We dry off and he tucks me into bed. I fall asleep, but it's a fretful sleep.

The ninth game is creation. Esnir thinks that the best way to showcase his power is to use the healing part of it to bring back everyone we lost in the games. That'll show the original gods. Then no one will have died. I try to yell at him that he shouldn't do it. It's not a good idea to bring back the dead. That's very unstable magic and goes against nature. But he won't listen.

No. It's not that he won't listen, but he can't hear me. The magic from the eighth game didn't undo. I still can't talk. I'm screaming but he can't hear me. Esnir is putting his hands on Saffron and she twitches and moves and stands.

Saffron walks over to me, yelling. The gouges in her abdomen are still bleeding and part of her scalp hangs loose. I try not to vomit looking at her. "You don't deserve them. Why should you get three gods, Jinx? You're nothing. You're no good. You don't deserve them."

No. I try to yell at her. No, I love them. I love all three of them. I turn, whirling, looking for them. Byder is next to me, clutching his arm. I pull at the bandages and, when they come off, his skin is green and oozing. It's infected. Byder is sweating and feverish.

"Jinx, I don't feel good. Can you fix this?" Byder looks at me hopefully. "Use your words, Jinx. Heal me. Why won't you heal me? Don't you love me too?"

I do, I try to yell at him. I can't talk. I can't speak. I can't do my magic if I can't speak. I keep looking around. Ydum or Anarus can help. A rabbit runs by. No. No. No. Where is Ydum? If the rabbit's alive, Ydum is dead again. I see him over in the corner of the sitting room, bathed in a glowing light, his body crumpled on the floor.

I run to Ydum. Byder still yelling after me, asking why I don't love him too. I do, Byder. I swear I do. But I need to help Ydum. Before I get to him, Anarus grabs me around the waist, stopping me.

"You can't go to him, Jinx. If you step in the light, you'll die too." Anarus tells me. "Stay with me. You can't go to him." I turn in his arms and hold Anarus tightly. Over his shoulder, I see Esnir heal Aretha. She's mad and coming straight for us. I try to yell. I beat on Anarus's chest. Let me go! Aretha's coming. I have to stop her. She's going to try to kill us. Why did you bring her back, Esnir?

But I can't say anything and Anarus doesn't understand. He can't hear her.

"You think you're so great, Jinx." Aretha snarls. "Let's see how great you are without all these gods covering for how stupid you are!" She flicks her whip and it goes around Anarus's neck, yanking him away from me.

No! Anarus! I run after him as Aretha pulls him towards her, winding up her whip until he's in her arms instead of mine. I scrabble in my shirt, but can't find Byder's dagger. It's gone. Damek threw it away from me. Anarus's face is so pale. His eyes are bulging and he's digging his nails into his neck, trying to get the whip off. I know the minute his air gives out. He drops, only held up by Aretha's whip. Limp and pale, I know he's gone and I didn't do anything to stop it. I killed her. I killed Aretha and now she killed Anarus.

I run back to Byder. His arm. I need to heal his arm. But I still can't speak. I can't help him either. Drila stops me before I can get to him. She's looking at her nails as if she's bored, her red dress the color of blood.

"Oh, poor Jinx. You have no more gods left. Oh well, I guess you fail." She snaps her fingers at me and I pop into my village. I race to my home, searching for my parents. Mom is in the sitting room, surprised when I walk in.

"Why are you here, Jinx?" She asks. "You went to the games. You don't get to come back. Either you win or you die. Why are you here? Where are your gods?"

I try to tell her. I try to say that Drila sent me back here. But I still can't talk. My father walks in the door and looks me up and down.

"Are you sure, Avalon? Are you sure she's mine?" He asks my mother. "Her test was wrong. She can't be mine. She's a mess. She failed. Send her away. Send her to Sam, maybe he'll still want her."

Dad! Daddy, please! Don't send me away. Don't send me to him. I plead with him with my eyes. Why can't I talk? Why won't the games let me go? But my father is shoving me out the door into Sam's arms. No, please. No.

Sam only laughs. "You're back. Nice. Maybe we can have more fun." Behind him, I see Jacob. He and his friends, Randy and Devon, are stalking towards me, menacing looks in their eyes. No, oh gods, no. Byder! Ydum! Anarus! Please come for me. You said you would always come for me! But they're dead. They can't come for me because they're dead and I'm all alone.

"Jinx! Fuck, Jinx! Wake the fuck up, little human!"

Anarus? I blink and Anarus's face swims into focus. He's holding me, shaking me. "You're dead. You died." My voice finally works.

"You were dreaming, baby girl." Byder is next to Anarus. We're in my room at the games still. "You were screaming in your sleep."

"Byder!" I scrabble out of Anarus's arms and throw myself at him. "I love you too! I swear I love you too."

Byder wraps his arms around me tightly, running his hand over my hair. "I know you do, baby girl. I know you do. You're okay. It's all okay."

"Where's Ydum? Where is he?" I start to twist in Byder's arms, but I feel Ydum stroke my back.

"I'm right here, beautiful." He tells me. "We're all here, and we're all okay. It was just a dream. A bad dream."

"You were all dead." I tell them, shaking. "Esnir brought Saffron and Aretha back from the dead and they were alive. Byder's arm got infected and I couldn't talk to use my magic to heal it so you thought I didn't love you and you died from it. The rabbit was alive and Ydum was dead and Aretha killed Anarus. Drila sent me home and my dad said he wasn't my dad anymore and gave me to Sam, and—" I choke on my words.

"Well, now." Ydum gives a small laugh. "When you have a nightmare, beautiful, you don't do it halfway, do you?"

Byder strokes my hair again, pushing pieces of it off my sweaty face. "None of that it true. Anarus is fine. Ydum is fine. And my arm is fine and I know you love me."

"Let me see it." I tell Byder. "Let me see your arm."

He holds it up and takes off the bandages. The claw marks are half healed already. The new pink skin around it looks healthy and clean. I sink back against him, relieved. He picks me up and tucks me back under the blankets, not letting me go but lying on the bed with me, still holding me.

"We're all right here, and we're all just fine, baby girl." Byder says as we lie down. "None of us are leaving you. We're all staying right here."

Anarus is on the other side of me in the bed, his chest pressed to my back. "We've got you, little human. You're safe."

Ydum, I know, is lying on the other side of Byder. His hand reaches over Byder to brush my arm with his fingers. "Go back to sleep, beautiful. We'll all stay right here with you."

I close my eyes and bury my face in Byder's shoulder and try. I can feel all three of them thinking about peace as they hold me.

The next morning, the real morning, I wake up and all three of my gods are still around me. They are all awake, but not one of them have moved from the bed. I hadn't dreamed anymore as I slept. Part of me wants to feel embarrassed but I push that away. I won't feel embarrassed about fearing losing them that much. That fear is real in me and Saffron's death proves how easily it could happen when we think we're safe.

"Hello, beautiful." Ydum speaks first.

"Hi." I say quietly. My head is lying on Byder's good arm and Anarus has his arm wrapped around my waist. Ydum's fingers are playing in my hair, his arm stretched out under Byder's head. He has such long arms and long fingers. I turn my face up and kiss his fingers.

Ydum pulls his arm out from underneath Byder's head and slides over top of him. "Mm, excuse me, sir." He pauses, half over Byder, and straddles him as he kisses him.

"You are excused." Byder tells him.

Then, Ydum leans over and kisses me, not moving from his spot perched on top of Byder. I smile and shake my head at him.

"Don't shake your head at me, beautiful. Kiss Byder instead." Ydum tells me and I happily oblige.

The hand at my waist tightens its grip. "Feeling a little left out." Anarus grumbles softly.

"Well, we can't have that." Ydum's voice is very cheery and full of mirth. "Kiss Anarus now, beautiful."

"You are all full of orders today, Ydum." I tell him, but I roll over anyway to face Anarus.

"Hi." I tell him once I am looking at him.

"Good morning, little human." Anarus's kiss is deeper than the other two's. "You were very scared last night."

"I was." I sigh deeply and snuggle into him. Byder pulls his arm from under my head and I hear Ydum giggle about something. I ignore him and his far too cheerful for the morning attitude. "But you came for me."

"I will always come for you." Anarus sounds adamant.

"So, you've said and done." I tuck my head under his chin as he holds me closer. Ydum giggles again and I feel the bed dip and move from him and Byder. I glance back over my shoulder and see Byder and Ydum kissing. They've moved so that Ydum is under Byder and I can tell, both through the bond and from what my own eyes tell me, exactly what Byder's hands are doing to Ydum under the blanket. I smile and look back at Anarus. "Alright, I'm done. Those two are far too active for the morning. Coffee?"

"Oh my gods, yes." Anarus says, then stops, staring at me. He groans loudly. "You're rubbing off on me. You were supposed to stop saying that, not get me started."

I can't help but laugh as we move out of the bed and to the sitting room. The giggly sensation of bystander pleasure, as Ydum called it, fills me, but I ignore it for coffee. When we are settled, I ask a question that formed after my dream last night. "Why doesn't anyone kill other teams here? I mean, I would hope that the gods who all grew up together and already lost so many friends wouldn't, but what stops the humans from killing each other to be able to win?"

"Nothing." Anarus tells me. "In the first few years of the games, they did. A lot of them did. But back then, there wasn't only ten teams. The first five years, they let all the gods that got matched in the cave participate in the games. It was only the humans that didn't get matched that died. And it was only the human that won that got anything. The rest, if they survived, went home."

I furrow my brow. "So, you mean that humans would be torn from their homes, forced into these games, matched with a god so that they mate bonded with them. Then, if they didn't win the games just went home like nothing even happened? Did they get to stay with their god?"

Anarus shakes his head. "No. They didn't. The original gods didn't want many new gods being born. So, one mated pair a year was all that was allowed. In the beginning, the humans would slaughter each other to win, especially later in the games, after their bonds were so tightly formed. Could you imagine how it would feel to be Wren right now and know that the chances of you winning are none and that you would have to go home, never seeing any of us again? As it stands, Wren mathematically can't win. We have two hundred and eighty-five points. If we come in last in the next two games, that only puts us at three hundred and eighty-five points, which is still lower than their four hundred and thirty-five they currently have. She can't win."

I wander over to the point board. None of us paid attention when Drila told us the points yesterday. But I look now. Isis is in fourth with three sixty-five. Damek has three thirty-five, and Raven has three forty. If we come in fifth in the last two games, we'll only have three eighty-five, like Anarus said. Damek can't do worse than at least a second and third place in the next two games. Isis would have to win both the games just to tie us for first. Raven can't do worse than second in both games or they lose to us too. If we take fourth in only one of those games, the only one who can even try to beat us is Damek, and he can only do that if he gets at least second in both. We take both fourths, or a third and fourth, he has to take at least first and second. We get two thirds, he has to win both. We get a second or better at all, we can't lose.

When did we become the almost unbeatable team? No wonder Saffron worried about us cheating. She did the same math I just did. The team with three gods went from the team that shouldn't have made it out of the cave to the one most likely to win. If her relationship with Velmos had been on the line, I could see how it would turn bloody and violent quickly. They paired us up, they matched us with perfect mates for us. They did that in the first games too, then they threatened to rip those mates away if you managed to survive but just didn't win. What we have been through is bad, but that? That would be so much worse.

I turn back to Anarus. "So, they changed the games?"

He nods slowly. "The children and grandchildren of the original gods revolted. The first year it was only the gods who went to the games that complained. Everyone believed that the originals gods were right and that, if they had been strong enough gods, worthy of creating more gods, they would have won and were just complaining. Then, year after year, more gods came back, speaking of their deeply held love for the human they had bonded with and the pain of being ripped away from them. Soon, the older gods started listening and they were furious.

"The original gods had to change the system or risk an all-out war. They changed the rules. If a team survived the games, then they could stay together as a mated pair. The human would be given immortality. The prizes would be more complicated and bigger, but the only thing you needed to do was survive to live with your mate. They changed it to only ten teams, though, as a compromise. Gods could fail to find their mate in the caves and would die too. The other gods agreed to the compromise, and that's how it's been ever since. They never changed any rules to say you couldn't kill other teams outside of game six, and it's happened sometimes, but for the most part, teams worry more about survival than winning now."

"The games have been changed before, then." I say, coming back to sit with him again. "What's to stop them from being changed now? We could make the original gods make it not death. No one dies. You fail, you can fail, but no one dies."

Anarus shakes his head, wrapping an arm around me as he drinks his coffee. "Some have tried. The original gods always say if there is no death, then no one has any motivation to actually try. A game where winning isn't important to the ones playing isn't much of a game. If losing just means mortality, but with their human mate, the gods wouldn't try anymore. They've tried, people have tried to get the original gods to change it. It hasn't worked."

"Yet." I say adamantly. "It hasn't worked yet."

Anarus chuckles. "If anyone could do it, I think it would be you, Jinx."

"What could Jinx do? Because whatever you say, I'm going to probably agree." Ydum leans over the back of the couch, a hand placed gently on my shoulder, and glances down at my coffee mug to see how much I drank before kissing my cheek.

I look up at him with a smile and caress his hand as he moves away from me. "Make the original gods change the games again so no one dies anymore."

"Oh." Ydum laughs, and goes to the table, picks up some toast and starts eating without even getting a plate. "I thought we already decided to do that."

"We did." Byder comes over and kisses my cheek too, then shoves a plate of fruit at me. "Eat real food, not just coffee, baby girl. That was one of the vicious Jinx looks stabby stabby things I thought she decided a few weeks ago."

"Well, I've decided it again. Especially since Anarus says they already changed the games once before." I curl up my legs under me, eating the fruit to make Byder happy. "Have you guys realized that basically there's almost no way for us to lose at this point? What really is the prize for winning? You've all alluded to it, immortality that every surviving human gets, the crown of your mantle that every surviving god gets, and what? Riches? Glory? I know you said to the gods it's mostly bragging rights, but what does mostly mean?"

Ydum turns to the leader board and scratches his chin. "Huh, you're right. The only ones who really have a hope of beating us is Damek and Iella, and only if we really screw up and they really don't."

"Should that be something we want to happen? Not win, especially if we want to fight the original gods?" I ask. "Or is it better to win?"

"Better to win." Anarus says quickly. "Sure, it's mostly bragging rights for the gods, but bragging rights that make people listen to you. If the winners of this year's Gods Games say the games are awful and need to be changed, people will listen more than they will listen to the team that almost won."

None of them actually answered the question about what the prize is. I wait to see if they will remember, but they don't. Instead, I turn to Byder and ask another question. "Wouldn't yesterday count as a hunt? Do you need another line tattooed?"

Byder shakes his head at me, frowning. "I would say it was a hunt, but not a successful one. For one, I didn't find anyone, you all found me. For two, I got injured." He holds up his arm, which looks much better. "So, an unsuccessful hunt means no tattoo."

Ydum turns away from the point board. "I doubt the creation or wild card will have a hunt aspect to them. That means you're done getting hunt lines, right?"

Byder nods. "Yup. The tradition is only birth to mantle."

"How many does that give you?" Anarus asks.

"Thirty-seven." Byder says without even counting them.

I look at the lines that go from his wrist to almost his elbow. "Is that a lot?"

"More than my dad." Byder shrugs. "He only has fifteen. But then again, he's not full hunt and we're pretty sure I am. Full hunts would have more."

"Is there any tradition now that you've gotten all the lines you'll get?" Ydum asks in his eagerness to learn anything and everything.

"Nope. Traditions only exist for the tattoos themselves and the first one given to a hunt child." Byder looks at me. "Something I'm excited to do for my child someday. If we have one." I smile at him, thinking back to my thoughts during the game before Ydum found me. That would be exciting to learn.

Ydum goes back to staring at the point board, devising all the ways the points could go depending on which team ends up in which position after the next game. Anarus is brooding into his coffee and Byder is watching me eat. I shove a piece of pineapple in my mouth just to appease him. The juice drips on my fingers so I lick them clean.

Byder makes a noise and I look at him. His eyes are dark and he's watching me closer. He groans low. "The things that mouth could do."

"No." The word is out of my mouth so fast, my heart stumbling.

Byder's face twitches, and he looks surprised. "What?"

I take a deep breath. I trust him, I remind myself. "No." I do not need to panic. I can breathe. I can.

Ydum steps between me and Byder. He's almost rippling with protectiveness. "She told us, man. Nothing with her mouth but kissing. Remember?"

"Shit. Sorry. It just came out. I didn't think." Byder pales. "Jinx."

"It's fine." I reach out and place a hand on Ydum's back. "It's fine. Just. Creation game. What is the creation game, Ydum?"

Ydum turns and watches me for a moment. He must be satisfied with what he sees because he sits down. "Creation game is interesting. It's exactly what it says it is. We will have to create using our powers and your magic."

"How exactly should a god of obscurity create? Especially when that god of obscurity might actually be the god of the wilde hunt, child of Death and Winter?" Anarus points out.

Ydum opens his mouth but I speak first. "Cold, wind, snow, confusion. You can create all of those things, Anarus. You are also currently creating a bond between me and Kinshra. And in a way, death is a creation as well. It needed to be part of the creation story. Without death, everything would have just suffered endlessly, that's what you said. Creating death is creating. You've created healing by using yourself as a living ice pack. You've created a whole bunch of feelings in me, in you, in Byder and Ydum. You can create as much as anyone can."

I turn to Ydum. "You're obviously easy to create with. You already made our cool pocket forest, and everything you did way back at the first game. Byder, might be a little more interesting. What can a hunt god create? Traps, you've said. Anything else?"

"Pelts." Byder says, shaking his hands as if to shake off the remnants of his earlier mistake. "I can create animal pelts that people can make things with. Leather, or well kind of, hides for others to make clothing out of it or blankets, furs. Food is an obvious one as well. What's the point of hunting if not getting food?"

That makes the most sense. Somehow, I never thought about a hunt god's connection to food. I wonder if that's why he's always trying to feed me. "Is the pelts thing why your clothes are always leather or fur?"

Byder nods, leaning forward to brace his elbows on his knees. "Exactly why. Hunt gods wear what we hunt. Same as why Ydum's clothes are always cotton or flax, or something made from plants. Nature gods wear what they grow."

I turn to Anarus, looking pointedly at his bare chest, and teasingly say. "So that's why you always fight wearing shirts. You only want to wear your shadows."

"No." Anarus grumbles. "Shirts are just dumb. Plus, with as often as you walk around here in only Ydum's shirt, I think it's fair I can walk around in only pants. Together, we make one outfit."

"Touché." I nod at him "As far as me creating, it kind of depends on what's needed, what counts. Does creating peace count? Because I can do that one really well."

"You doubting yourself, little human?" Anarus asks.

I tip up my chin, defiantly. "No. Just knowing where my strengths lie."

"You are really good at creating emotions, that's for sure." Ydum chuckles.

I eye him suspiciously. "Why do I feel that has two meaning?"

"Because it had two meaning." Ydum chuckles again as he stands to get more food. I roll my eyes at him.

Anarus touches my wrist lightly and I turn to him. He speaks quietly. "You didn't panic. You said no and didn't panic."

"I almost panicked." I twist my mouth. "It was just Byder but I almost panicked."

"But you didn't."

"He listened." I shrug like that makes the difference.

"Of course, he listened. But you had to trust that he would before he did and tell him no for him to listen to it. Eight weeks ago, you were crying, panicking and screaming at a thought no one was even trying to act on. Now, you just said no." Anarus keeps looking at me.

"Eight weeks ago, you would have punched first, made him listen second. You didn't even flinch, Anarus." I tell him. "You trusted me to be able to say no and him to listen to no without a bloody lip. You're doing better too."

Anarus sniffs. "Look at both of us getting healthier when it comes to relationships."

Like we always do, once everyone is done eating, we head out to see what the paintings are. As soon as we open the door, loud talking fills the air.

"Maybe they forgot?" I hear Damek saying. "Or they won't do it until later?"

We step into the hallway and everyone is clustered around one painting.

"Ydum." Esnir calls out. "Oh, good. Maybe you have an idea what's going on. Or Anarus? Byder?" Esnir gestures at the painting in front of him.

Ydum walks over, pushing through people to stand right in front of the painting between rooms seven and five where everyone is gathered. It's blank, completely blank, a stark white canvas. Ydum stares at it for a moment, then brushes his fingers over it. I know that he's checking for colors he might be missing.

"There's nothing. Not even any paint on it." Ydum mutters. "It's white but not painted white." He wanders up the hallway, checking the other four paintings, shaking his head.

It's me who ends up speaking. "Creation. They are blank because the next game is creation. We have to make the paintings with our magic and powers." All eleven people stare at me and I feel the weight of their gazes. "At least, that's what makes sense to me."

"Do we have to literally create paintings, do you think, or is it merely symbolic? Because I don't know about you, but I'm not sure how music can make a painting." Uesis's worries out loud.

Ydum comes back over, his hands in his pockets, the careful stroll he does when he's thinking. "Chromesthesia. A condition where people see sounds as colors. You could try for that if it's literal. Sounds as colors."

"And chance?" Iella is looking at Ydum now.

She's looking at Ydum but Damek answers her. "Weaving fates, or really destinies. Chance weaves in between the strands of destiny. Just because it's usually a painting on the canvas, doesn't mean it has to be. You could weave strings like the weaves of destiny, Iella."

Iella leans back against him and gives Damek a small smile. He leans down and whispers in her ear and she smiles again.

Kutar tries next. "Storms would be easy. Water from rain can mar a canvas. Lighting burns edges. Thunder not so much help, but it's something."

Esnir nods. "Same with war. Paint the ground with blood. That's a line my mother has said often. Instead of paint the ground, it'd be paint the canvas."

"What about Anarus?" Isis asks. "Ydum is easy. We create so many dyes from natural elements. Byder too. Same as you, Esnir, only the blood or fur of animals. But what can obscurity create that could be a painting?"

I tense at this. I know we're all helping each other right now, and it's an innocent question asked for the purpose of helping, but with us so hesitant about what Anarus's actual powers are, it feels almost combative or prying. I feel Anarus behind me shift uncomfortably. Ydum is still standing with his hands in his pockets, face schooled to be blank. Byder looks anywhere but at the group.

The problem is, if the goal is to make the painting, I'm not sure what he could do either. Even with the extra powers we know about that the other teams don't. How does death or the wilde hunt paint?

Esnir, with a face that says he knows far more than we want him to, casually distracts everyone. "Well, we don't even know that it's creating the painting literally. Or creating the painting at all. There's time for them to figure that out, and with four smart people, they will, I'm sure."

"We know what this game is supposed to be." Kutar adds. "The lead in to game ten. Anarus will figure himself out or not. His odd powers are not new to him."

I think about those words Kutar just said. The lead in to game ten? Game ten is the wild card game. That's what my gods told me. How is nine, creation, a lead in to ten, the wild card that could be anything? The groups break up around me and I know there are more things Anarus, Byder, and Ydum are keeping from me.

Chapter Six

WE GO BACK TO the room and I decide it's time we had a real talk. "Sit." I tell the three of them, channeling my mom's voice. That one that she used when all of my sisters and I were in deep shit trouble and even Dad wasn't going to protect us from the tongue lashing that was coming. All three of them raise their eyebrows but do what I say.

"There are questions you three have been avoiding answering." I say once they are settled. I try not to pace as I talk but keep my eyes trained on them, attempting to appear imposing even though I'm tiny compared to all of them. Just like Mom again. "What is the prize for winning the Gods Games? Don't say mostly bragging rights and other stuff. What is it exactly? And what is game ten that Kutar says nine is a lead up to ten? You said it's a wild card. What is it really?" I channel Mom one more time, using her line that meant she already knew but was almost hoping we'd try to lie. "Tell me everything, in excruciatingly precise detail."

"It's hard to explain." Byder finally says. He's finding it hard to look at me. I wonder for a moment if his mom has the same you're in trouble tone mine does. "Without understanding how Veirveil works, it's hard to explain what the prize really is."

I cross my arms over my chest and tap my foot. "Try."

"Okay. Okay." The way Ydum hangs his head and sighs before he talks tells me his mom definitely has a you're in trouble voice and I hit it spot on. "We've told you that the original gods, the twenty original gods, control Veirveil. Anarus even mentioned it when we talked about who his mother is. The council of original gods. They control pretty much everything. The laws and rules, yes, but more than that. They controlled where Ani lived as an orphan because their rule is ultimate in Veirveil. They say not just what we can do but actually control most of the intimate parts of our lives, dictating who has the ability to use what powers, social controls, that type of thing."

"What do you mean who has the ability to use what powers? I thought that once you had your mantles you will have access to all of your god power." I push for more details.

"We do." Anarus answers, not nearly as cowed as the other two. But then again, he never had a consistent guardian to have that you're in trouble voice the same way. "But access and right to use them are two different things. Take Ydum for example. He's a nature god, and as far as we can tell, he can work with all of nature. Do you know how many other gods in Veirveil can do that same thing? Lots. Nature is an original god. He had lots of children. His children had lots of children. Now, with the children born of a witch and god, there are so many full nature gods and partial nature gods, like Ydum's mom and sister. How many gods should be allowed to have control over nature? If we say all of them, the chaos would tear the world apart. Could you imagine both Ydum and his mom trying to control the flowers in the world? Or his sister and him both trying to control the stones? The original gods decide what god gets control over those things to keep down the chaos."

"Okay, so that makes sense." I nod, but also furrow my brow. "But Esnir said it was possible for him to have a very specific specialty in war, like combat medic. Where do those fall in this?"

"Gods who aren't in charge mostly help out." Byder explains. He's shaken off a lot of the I'm in trouble vibe. "So, someone like Ydum would only help the original nature god. If someone has a very specific power, the god who has that specific thing in their wider pantheon usually has them work with that, the specific power god guiding most of the day-to-day stuff while the wider pantheon god deals with the big stuff. When a power is from more than one pantheon, like Iella's chance power, they wait until the mantle is fully revealed and that god works in the pantheon they are closest to, same as a specific power in a wider pantheon."

"So Ydum, as a full nature god, probably won't do much of anything because the original nature god will be in control?" I shake my head at this idea. "If that's true, then what's the point of him fighting for his mantle?"

"Because my mantle is part of who I am and without the full mantle, I can't fully be me." Ydum makes a good point. "Our access to our power is bound away from us when we are born. We have some, obviously, but could you imagine a three-year-old with the power to control all of the storms in the world? They'd be one tantrum away from drowning the world. So, our powers are bound until we are old enough to handle them."

That also makes sense. With gods born instead of just existing, there needs to be external controls until they are old enough and smart enough to control them themselves.

"The games is when they undo that binding. We get access to all the power we were born with. Our power and our position within our pantheon. The power that comes from being in a pantheon. We become gods and work with the council. The one who wins the Gods Games get to not just work with the council of gods, but on it." Ydum says. "The god who wins gets a seat on the council for their power for the next year, a seat based on where in the pantheon their true, full, unleashed power gives them the ability to sit. If they are very specificized, that doesn't mean much, just having the chance to work on some small subcommittee, as an advising panel for the original god. If it's a full spectrum god, a true full spectrum with all the power one of the original gods has, they unseat the original god for a year, which can be an issue."

"How is it an issue?" I look at Ydum. We know he's a full spectrum god, almost positive about it, so this will affect him the most. Probably Byder too.

"What could I do in a year if I was on the real council instead of the original god of nature?" Ydum says. "How much havoc could I create in that time that the original god couldn't stop?"

Anarus adds to that. "Being in such a position makes you use your power often. The more you use it, the stronger it is. The new god also has a newly immortalized witch that they are bonded to strongly and whose magic feeds their power. What happens if a full spectrum god gets to unseat the original god for a year, and their power only grows while the original god's wanes, and that new god decides at the end of the year he doesn't want to give the seat back? Gods have been killed over that. Only minor gods with a very limited scope, but still. What would happen if Ydum tried it? Ydum, with a bond to a word witch, Byder who may also be a full spectrum god, and the child of Death? Remember Death has never had any children and is banished. Who's sitting on his seat on the council?"

"Oh shit. We would be quite the threat. As bonded mates, we would take over at least two seats on the original council." I say, putting it together. I sink down onto the couch, the weight of that hitting me.

"Four." Anarus corrects me. "Four seats. The new witch demi-god that wins also gets a seat. There are twenty-one seats on the original council. The nineteen you know, the always empty seat of Death, and the one seat representing the humans. The human seat changes every year after the games. That's what you would win, Jinx. A seat on the council for a year. Technically the tie-breaker vote, but with Death banished, that power is almost meaningless because how can there be a tie between nineteen gods?"

"So, me, Byder, and Ydum would be on the council, but how would you be, Anarus?" I ask. "You aren't a full spectrum god as far as we know."

Anarus only grits his teeth and looks away. I feel a war of emotions in him as Ydum answers. "If the original god is not available to sit on the council, and there's no current Gods Games champion to do so in their stead, the oldest child of the original god that has a similar power takes the seat for them, no matter if they are full spectrum or only partial. Anarus, as the god of the wilde hunt, would be the oldest child of the god of Death with an affinity to the power of death."

"That's what happens every year when the season changes." Byder explains. "The gods of the seasons are only out during their season, usually. The rest of the time, their oldest affiliated child sits in their seat for them. That's why we were confused when Anarus said Winter was always in her seat when decisions were being made about him. It should have been her daughter, Phylidria, the goddess of season's change, in any time not winter."

My mind whirls with this information. All four of us would win the right to take a seat on the original council for a year. But not just for a year. Anarus would have that seat permanently. The child tossed around and hated, mistreated and feared by all the gods in Veirveil would take a permanent seat on the council that rules them. No wonder they threw him into the games early. If they knew, or guessed who his father is, they hoped he would be too young and would fail, leaving that seat empty like they want it to be.

That'd be bad enough for them to fear us winning, but it doesn't stop there. Not only would Anarus have that seat, but for a year, so would I, a witch with magic that doesn't work the way it should, making me potentially more powerful than any human has a right to be, and with a familiar. Byder would unseat Hunt, if he's actually full hunt, and Ydum would unseat Nature if he's full as well. And the four of us would be bonded, making a seriously powerful connection between the four of us. Enough power to make them afraid we might try to keep the other three seat permanently.

Four seats out of twenty-one doesn't sound like much, but it really is powerful when I think about it. The seat for the human would actually matter with all twenty seats filled. We'd only need to convince seven gods for anything we wanted to change. Only seven to create a tie that I'd be the tie-breaker for. How hard would that really be?

Modes's mom, Sadness, might be easily swayed to our side. Her son was in the cave with us and died when everyone thought he was a sure thing to win. Would she be as angry and desperate to change things as we are? How quickly would the other Fates follow her? That's four gods. Would Winter actually want to protect her child now? Would she follow Anarus out of some sort of guilt over what she did to him? And if she does, would the other seasons follow her as quickly? That's eight gods when we only need seven. And who knows how many of them also lost children or grandchildren in the games and feel too alone to speak up right now.

We really could be the seeds of a rebellion against the way things in Veirveil, and the whole continent, are right now. The promised prize is a double-edged sword. In our hands, it could be a weapon instead of bragging rights. Now I understand why my gods were hesitant to say anything about the real prize. That's a lot of weight to carry when, right now, we are just fighting to survive.

But that does not explain Kutar's comment about the tenth game. "What about the tenth game? What is it really that the ninth game of creation leads into it?"

Ydum sighs, his head hanging down for a moment. "It's called a wild card, and not described well in the manuals, but basically, it's the crowning of our mantles as far as I can tell. The game will be completely different for every person. Not team, but person. What Anarus has to do will be different than what I need to do, and what Byder needs to do. As a team, we would be able to help share strength and power, but our tasks would be very individual. It'd be based on pulling out and testing the very roots of our powers as gods, proving exactly what we are the god of specifically. If one of us fails, we all fail. For the other teams, it'll be rather simple. Not easy, but simple. They only have one god's full mantle to figure out. We have three, and one specifically who seems to not be what we've been led to believe at all."

"What about me?" I ask. "Where do I factor into that?"

Byder looks at me in a way that tells me he's worried how I will react. "You'll be responsible to use your magic to control us. Remember, the humans that come here to the games are supposed to be beginning magic witches. A god and their witch should work together seamlessly in this game. The god unveils all the parts of their powers and the beginning witch melds it together cohesively into something specific, the mantle the god wears. The problem comes in with multiple god teams. What's the human supposed to do when they have to support two gods at once, controlling and melding both of their powers at the same time? Carrying that balance between the two of them, using their beginning magic to call the gods' powers to them, can be overpowering if the witch doesn't have perfect control and command of the bond with both gods. They can be crushed under the weight of it all. Or mix the powers up, killing the gods by melding the powers together wrong. Most duo god teams fail here, at the tenth game, because the full weight of keeping both gods' powers separate but cohesive is too much for a human who's not immortal yet."

I hear everything Byder is not saying. If most two god teams fail because the human is crushed under the weight of that much power, then how am I to stand under the weight of three gods when my magic isn't the normal beginning magic? Especially if two of those gods are full gods, with the power of all of nature and the hunt, and the third with a power no one has ever experienced before, that we don't even know what really is. We have thoughts on Anarus's real power but no proof. We could be completely wrong and set ourselves up for failure because I'm not able to handle his power as what it really is rather than what we thought it is.

All this time, and I really am the weak link. Not because I'm not strong or don't know enough, but because I'm the only link in a bond that shouldn't exist. My birthday was never the problem. Even if I'd been born one day later and had the whole year to prepare for the games, I would still be unprepared for what I'll need to do, because I don't have the right magic and no magic should be able to do this much.

Mathematically, we cannot lose the Gods Games. But the math of the points is worthless. We probably won't win because we'll fail the tenth game. We may not die, but we won't be successful and they'll be made mortal, to suffer an agonizing life their bodies weren't designed to handle. And I'll have to watch them suffer, knowing it was my failure that made it happen. If I don't die.

The weight of this all falls over me like a wet blanket. We are a threat no matter what we do. Failure is the only option we have that doesn't leave us a threat to the original gods. A revolution under us happens no matter what. Anarus takes that seat in the council no matter what, no matter if we win or just pass, once he has his mantle. He's a threat to their rule, a threat that makes whatever human comes into the council seat now also a threat, even if it isn't me.

"I don't want it." Anarus whispers. "I don't want that seat. I want nothing to do with them, the council."

"If you don't take the seat, Anarus, then your child will have to." Byder tells him.

"I won't have one." Anarus snaps. "You both said me first to Jinx, but I won't have one. We can find my father and make him take it. Un-banish him. Let him know what they're doing and make him come back. He owes me that at least."

"That's not a choice you get to make, Anarus." Ydum says. "If you never have a child, you are the one in that seat. Where is your father? Death hasn't been seen in so long. Where is he? We'd have to find him first, then convince him to come back and challenge the banishment. If we did, maybe he could take the seat that should be his, but meanwhile, you are the one in that seat. We could go into a self-imposed banishment. Say fuck off to all of it and run. But then all the lives lost in any further games is on us. All the abuse of the humans, other gods, it's our fault as much as it's theirs. We know it's wrong. What's happening is wrong and we have the power to do something about it. If we don't, their blood is on our hands as much as it's on the original gods. Could you live with that guilt? I know I couldn't. Vicious Jinx couldn't. Byder, I doubt could either. Could you, Anarus? Allow others to be tortured like you've been? Don't sit on the seat, refuse it, and they win. You'll become the monster they want you to become."

I move off the couch and kneel before Anarus, forcing him to look at me. When he does, I curl into his lap, making him hold me, and take his face into my hands. "You will never be alone again, Anarus. You were alone and scared, a child, when you had to go before the council all those times before. They used that to berate you and make you feel small, powerless, wrong. But you won't be alone and you won't be powerless this time. You'll have us to tell you that you are perfect just as you are, loved just as you are. You'll have a voice. Even if we don't win and aren't actually there with you on the council, you'll have our support, our strength with you. You will never be alone again. You'll be powerful and loved. You already are powerful and loved."

Anarus pulls me closer in his arms, his head falling into the crook of my shoulder as he nuzzles my neck. I can tell he's struggling. There's so much here. We could be wrong and all of this worry is for nothing because his father isn't Death. Even if he is, Anarus's mantle could be something else, something not related enough to death let him take the seat. There are a thousand ways this worry about Death's council seat is nothing that concerns him. But a thousand ways it is and the other original gods would want to stop him from being able to claim it. And we can do nothing until we know the truth, nothing until two weeks from now when he tries to claim that mantle and the seat that may or may not come with it.

The only thing I know for certain is that the original gods tried to break him. They tried to make Anarus feel unlovable. They sent him to the games early, hoping he would fail. But they were the ones who failed. He did find his bond in the cave, and every day he learns more about how to love and be loved. I loved him first. And the bond is so deep in him because he loves us all more than even himself.

All they accomplished by sending Anarus to the Gods Games now instead of in three years is to allow him to find me, a broken magic witch with words that can give him peace, a god of nature that knows what it's like to feel like you are wrong because of your weaknesses, and a god of the hunt who knows what it's like to be different. They gave him his perfect mates.

Maybe the Fates knew what they were doing sending him early. Because instead of hating the original gods for what they did to him, right now I want to thank them for their mistake. Their mistake gave Anarus to me and made him mine.

"If you love me any harder, little human, I think you might explode." Anarus murmurs into my neck.

"Gladly." I tell him. "I will gladly explode. I feel like my heart does every time I look at you anyway."

"I know we are all supporting Anarus right now, but, um," Byder says tentatively, "just checking after my little faux paus earlier, you still feel that way about me too, right baby girl?"

"Of course, I do." I look over at Byder and give him a soft smile. "Always."

"And me?" Ydum is already smiling, his hand brushing my hair off my shoulder, out of Anarus's face as he snuggles me. "I'm pretty sure I know but just asking so I'm not left out."

I capture Ydum's hand and kiss his fingers. "Oh no. Not you." Ydum's eyes go wide with surprise, but before he can speak, I continue. "A completely different part of me wants to explode when I look at you and your long fingers. And tongue."

Ydum raises his eyebrows. "Somehow, I think I'm completely okay with that."

Anarus groans into my neck. "Jinx has the power with words to make us always feel better, but Ydum has the power with words to make everything horny."

"Actually, it was Jinx this time." Byder corrects him.

"Ugh." Anarus sits up. "Okay. Enough emotional stuff. Game nine. We need to prepare. How do we prepare, especially knowing that game nine is really just a set up for attempting to take the crowns of our mantles?"

Ydum becomes the academic. "Jinx. We have to work with you. You'll have to be able to handle all of our power, all three of us at full strength at the same time. Gods do fail to take on their full mantle, fail to be able to handle it, but the majority of failures happen at the human. In only about one in ten duo god teams does the human manage to bear the weight of that much power. And as we know, there has never been a trio team to try it before. We don't have the full weight now, but we can work on it. Try and see how much you can take."

"How do we do that?" I ask. "I've used Anarus's shadows before, held them when we tried it, and used them in the combat game. But I never did anything with either of you two before. Not even tapping into them, like controlling your vines or feeling Byder's tracking senses."

"We weren't trying to work our power through you but let you use them." Ydum tells me. "Think of it like running water. You took Ani's shadows and used them. You diverted part of the stream of his power to you and through you. A good start, but you have three of us and our full powers. Will you be a bowl that fills with us and overflows? Or are you a sieve that our power runs right through? Both are bad. One will make you explode under the weight of our power, the other will leave our power unchanged, uncontrolled, to destroy not only you but the three of us. We need you to be a filter, purifying the water, and a tea bag, adding flavor to the clean water."

"Nice metaphor, Ydum. Directly quoted from Shejun, the professor of our games classes. But that doesn't help with the how." Byder complains.

Ydum gives a sad smile. "Because all I have is that nice metaphor. You were in the same classes with me, Byder. Did Shejun explain to you how the human becomes that filter? I don't remember missing a day of class that might have been when they explained the how. It's not in the manuals either. Unless Anarus read something in them I missed."

Anarus shakes his head. "I read all of them, not just the last fifty years. All of them get pretty hazy when they get to the last two games. Game nine is creation, making something together using your powers and the human's magic. Game ten is the crown of the mantle, determined by what you accomplished in game nine, the first time you access the full weight of your power and must use the human's magic to filter it, contain it, shape it. No matter what the choice method is, our paintings, other games with their flags or flowers or whatever, the manuals mention exactly what choices the teams had, and who chose what, for the first eight games. For game nine, it always just makes some vague mention of the humans making their choices. Ten fails to mention the choice at all."

"So, we have no clue not only what we are supposed to do but how to do it?" I shake my head. "Helpful."

Ydum stands and starts to pace. "We know you can work with Ani's power, at least the shadows. I say we start there. You and Ani. You practice working with his power, doing whatever you can with it. Try to do it purposefully, under controlled conditions, rather than the height of emotions. Then, you can both explain what it feels like, what you feel like you are doing and Byder and I can try to recreate it."

I look at Anarus, who only shrugs. "Worth a shot. What should we do, Ydum?"

"You seem to benefit from touch, Jinx." Ydum goes over to the table, waving over Byder to help him. They move the table out of the way like they did for fight practice. "You and Anarus take up positions here, touching. Whatever feels right and comfortable. You threw Damek with his shadows, so let's start there."

"What should I throw?" I watch them rearrange the room. Ydum takes the couch cushions off and starts lining the walls with them, as if he's making padded landing zones.

"For now, sock ball." Ydum says as he works. "I'm making a kind of soft zone in case something goes wrong and you throw Ani, or Ani throws you."

Anarus and I take a seat on the floor, in the center of Ydum's soft zone. Without discussing it, Anarus sits behind me, my back to his chest and his legs wrapping around mine. I feel his breath on my neck and it does feel right, comfortable. Ydum puts a balled-up sock from our sock ball game on the floor in front of me.

"Now, don't touch the sock, Jinx." Ydum tells me. "Try to reach for Ani's shadows and use them to move the sock. Just like you did with Damek. Anarus, try to let her have them, give them to her."

I close my eyes and take a deep, cleansing breath. I blow it out slowly, opening my eyes to focus on the sock. I need Anarus's shadows to throw the sock. Can you come to me, please? I only want to borrow you for a moment. Just to throw the sock. I need to throw the sock with the shadows.

Shadows wrap around the sock and pitch it across the room. I smile, but when I look at Ydum, he's frowning. "What's wrong?"

"I don't think that was you, Jinx." He says as he retrieves the sock and puts it back. "The shadows seemed to go through you, but not like you were in control of them. What did you do?"

I rub my forehead. "I said that I needed the shadows to throw the sock. I needed to borrow his shadows to throw the sock."

Byder is leaning against the arm of the couch, frowning from concentration. "I think I know where it went wrong. You told the shadows what you wanted them to do. They didn't flow through you to do that, but just stayed with Anarus and worked without him telling them to, something they do often. That's not the goal. The goal is for you to control the shadows then use them. If your magic lies in the words you say, you have to be very careful what words you use. I need you to throw the sock for me is just that. Not the same as I need to use you, then using the shadows to throw the sock."

"Makes sense." I say, a little disappointed.

"But you did command my shadows, so that's a good first step." Anarus says, I think feeling my disappointment. "Let's try again."

I nod then close my eyes. The focus is on me using the shadows, not what I need the shadows to do. I leave my eyes closed this time and take a deep breath again. Blowing it out, I call for Anarus's shadows. I need you to come to me. I need to borrow you, can you please come to me? I will give you back, but I need you.

The back of my neck tickles and feels cold. Come to me, please. Come on. All of you. I need to use you. The cold tickle spreads down my spine and over my skin. I know from when I did this before that the shadows are on me now. Throw the sock, I need you to throw the sock. I feel nothing but the cold tickle swirling.

"Don't tell them what to do." Anarus whispers on the back of my neck. "You want to use them. Just use them. Like you would move your arm to throw the sock, use the shadows to throw the sock. They are an extension of me, part of me. And now part of you."

I open my eyes and focus on the sock ball. I push on a piece of the cold tickle I feel along my skin, the part on my hand, and move it without moving the hand. The shadows swirl around the sock, which lifts up off the ground. The throw is weak, barely moving the sock a foot, but it is a throw.

"Good." Ydum says quietly. "Now, can you do anything with Ani's cold? You have his shadows, but do you have all of his power, Jinx?"

Ydum crouches in front of me, his elbows resting on his knees. I reach out and take one of his hands in mine. Anarus's power. I need Anarus's power. As I reach for Anarus's power, the tickle on my neck gets stronger, almost scratching at me. It feels uncomfortable and burns. But the power is there, almost like a rope I can grab and tug at.

I grab at it, and try to harness the part of the amorphous rope that feels like his power over the cold. I try to direct the cold to Ydum's hand so he feels it, but the scratching burn on my neck is distracting. I grit my teeth and push forward anyway. I need to control Anarus's power.

"Jinx." Anarus sounds concerned.

No, I think. I can do this. It only hurts a little. I can feel it, the rope of his power binding his cold, his shadows and something else. Something churning and dangerous. Something that feels powerful and demanding. It keeps trying to push itself first. Push itself in front of the cold I want. It's so hard to hold it back, keep it in the rope. I fight with the churning power. I don't want you right now. I want the cold, only the cold. You go sit down and wait your turn. The back of my neck starts to really hurt as the power roars in anger over me setting it aside.

"Jinx!" Anarus screams at me, yanking himself away from me, breaking my concentration.

I open my eyes. "I almost had it."

"No, you didn't, Jinx." Anarus is pale and shaking. His shadows are back on him, but they won't settle. They are arcing over him. "Byder, get Esnir."

"Why do we need Esnir?" I ask him.

Anarus's jaw ticks and he's having a hard time looking at me. "To look at your neck. And Ydum's hand."

Byder is standing next to the door, but he seems to be wavering. "Can we trust him?"

"I don't know that we have a choice right now." Anarus answers. Byder only nods and leaves the room.

Confused at how they are talking, I look at Ydum. He's leaning back against the wall, paler than Anarus is, sweating and clutching his hands to his middle. I kneel next to him. "Ydum, what's wrong with your hand?"

Ydum holds his trembling hand out and I see that the tip of his pinky is gray. Completely gray, no green tint, not even a normal pink tint, but the ashen gray of death. Death. Oh shit. Oh shit. That's the power I fought in my head. Death. And it forced itself through me to Ydum's hand and I hurt him.

I scramble away from him, appalled at myself. "Ydum, I'm sorry. I'm so sorry. I knew there was something, but I pushed it away. I thought I pushed it away. I'm so sorry."

Esnir and Byder come in the room and Esnir immediately goes to Ydum, looking at his hand. "What did this?"

For one second, no one says anything. Esnir only looks at us.

Anarus groans. "Jinx was trying to channel my power. She was trying to control my cold but my power slipped through her control and she touched Ydum with my power of death."

If Esnir is shocked to hear Anarus has the power of death, his face doesn't show it. He only turns back to Ydum's hand. "Gods can regenerate skin easily. If it's only skin deep, it should heal fine on its own. Painful like a bitch, but fine. If it's deeper, into the muscle, it'll probably never heal at all. If it's all the way to the bone, it might necrotize. We would need to remove the finger so the death doesn't spread."

"Oh, fuck." I cry and bury my face in my hands.

Esnir continues. "There's not much I can do for him right now. We'll have to wait and see what happens. Maybe I can take the edge off the pain for him. I can try." He places a hand over Ydum's and, at first, Ydum cries out, squirming as if it's making the pain worse. My heart clenches with every cry. I did this to him. But after a moment, he settles and his breathing is easier.

"Thanks, Esnir." Ydum breathes out.

Esnir only pats his knees then stands and turns to me. "Byder said your neck too?"

I shake my head. "My neck is fine."

"Your neck is bleeding, Jinx." Anarus says and I bring my hand up to touch the back of my neck. Pain flares at my touch and my fingers feel sticky. There's blood on them when I look.

Esnir comes behind me and pushes my hair out of the way. "I assume this was the point of contact between your power and her?"

Anarus nods. "I was sitting behind her."

Esnir tries to be gentle but his touch hurts. I refuse to react though. I used death on Ydum's finger. I deserve any pain I feel.

"The skin split." Esnir says. "You said she was trying for cold when she accidentally harnessed death?"

Anarus nods.

"That makes sense. This looks like a cold burn. Frostbite." Esnir explains. He runs his finger down the skin. "I've sealed the split skin but keep it warm and dry until the cold burn heals. Should be fine in a few days."

Esnir moves away from me. "If you don't need anything else?" He starts to go to the door.

Anarus stops him with a quiet word. "Esnir? My power?"

"Is how you were born." Esnir answers simply. "What happened to have you born that way was not in your control and is none of my business. I'm just here to heal them." He won't say anything. He won't tell anyone. He leaves, and I collapse.

"I failed. I failed and hurt Ydum." I look at him. He looks better, not as pale or sweaty.

Anarus actually has the gall to chuckle. "You told death to sit down and wait its turn. Death. You told death to sit down."

"Only Jinx would yell at death." Ydum says weakly.

I huff. "I didn't know it was death. It was just something churning. I thought it was more shadows or something."

Ydum shifts in his seat, grimacing slightly as he does. "So, we learned a few things. Jinx can definitely channel Ani's power. All of it. And use it. Not well, and the point of contact is susceptible to injury when she does. But she can."

Byder leans against the arm of the couch again, crossing his arms over his chest. "That gives us a few things to work on. We need to figure out how to protect your points of contact, Jinx. Could be why duo gods fail so often. Two points of contact stressing the human body. Three would be worse if we can't protect you. Now that you both know the feel, though, you should be able to walk us through doing it too. Would it be necessary for you to know what each part of the power is and control them individually, Jinx? Or just allow them to flow through you without cataloguing them?"

"I think she's just the anchor point for us in the tenth game. Ninth, she may need to do things, but tenth is just temper the flow and bind the pieces." Anarus says.

They seem determined to just talk about the games like I didn't just accidentally kill Ydum's pinky, so I go with it too. A filter, Ydum said I am to be the filter and the flavoring. With what I know about the way human magic works normally, what would that mean? I think about making the salves and creams, Granny Helen's cough medicine. We use the power already inside the plants and other ingredients as the base and use our magic to enhance it. I have to know the pieces, the ingredients, to make the salve. If I don't, I can't just guess. The ingredients make the whole. If I get one wrong, it could hurt or kill instead of help.

A beginning magic witch, I would guess, can add their power at the beginning, to the individual plants. An end magic witch would be able to add their magic to the salve as a whole. I did both with Anarus with the burn salve in the intellect game because I am both. Or neither. Or something else.

This would be the opposite though. Not adding my magic to strengthen to their power, but using my magic to hone theirs. Anarus's power felt like a rope. I would have to unravel that rope and know each thread of it before I can rebraid it back together properly. Their wild power tempered through my magic.

I shake my head. Now, I'm mixing my metaphors. I need to keep it simple. For them and for me. They made the salve with me, so they understand that one. But how would this be similar to making a salve rather than fixing a rope?

Yarrow. It comes to me suddenly. The yarrow plant has so much power for healing and protection, but also can be used badly as well. If I made a salve with yarrow, I would need to strip it down magically to maximize that one specific need I have of it, then spin that specific power through my magic to be crafted into a salve where all the parts work together in perfect balance. Not too much or too little yarrow, and not the wrong power in the yarrow plant used either.

"I need to know all the parts." I contradict Anarus. "You are the salve I build. I need to know all the parts and add just enough of each to make it work right. Not add too little of what you need, but don't give too much of it either. Not try to use what you don't have to give either. Or leave anything behind unused. You choose, or your power chooses really, which salve you are. I just move the pieces around to mix it together."

Anarus figures out exactly what I'm thinking and calls up the same example. "Like the burn salve? How you knew that the flower petals were calendula without even looking because you knew what the other four ingredients could and couldn't be used to make together with only one more ingredient? And how you could tell me from the size of the jar of beeswax how much to put in?"

I nod slowly. "Exactly. Ydum is a nature god. We know that. He's very obvious, with his tattoo and abilities. That's his salve. How much plants should go into that? How much metal or stone? Water and air? Dirt? He needs to know that, and so do I. Byder has more to figure out. You know you are hunt, but what about the hunt can you do? What can't you? Are there any animals you can't work with, hunt for or with? And which ones are which? I bet your dad, with his tattoo what it is, could never hunt a hunting dog, but he could hunt with a hunting dog, and that's very different types of power in his salve. Anarus is trickier because we know nothing about his powers. But I have felt them now. I know what he has but not all of what he can do. Death is strong, very strong, but should it be? Would it overpower the salve if we let it have its way like that? Probably, because it did it to Ydum."

"That makes," Ydum struggles to stand up, "a lot of sense, Jinx. But that doesn't answer the biggest question in my mind. How do we keep you safe while we do this? The skin on your neck got frostbite and split from just Anarus's power. All three of us will kill you."

I shake my head, disagreeing. "No, it won't. That's part of my point. When I make a salve, I'm not doing it myself. The power isn't mine, but stays in the ingredients. I just bring them together and bless the work with my magic. The power never actually comes to me. I just watch it grow under my guiding magic and hands. It would be the same with this. You're not feeding me the power, into me, but past me, showing it to me so I can see what it is and direct it where to go and how. A pinch of this, a whole handful of that, now stir. I'm not throwing the sock with Anarus's shadows, but just directing the shadows that Anarus should have the ability to use the shadows to throw it and telling them how much or little of the powers he can use to throw it."

"I'm not sure I understand the difference." Byder rubs his face. "But if it makes sense to you, that's what matters I guess."

"Would you be willing to trust that, Byder?" I ask him, standing and facing him. I push hard at this. I already hurt one of them. "Could you trust something that doesn't make sense like that? Because I think starting with Anarus was part of our mistake. I've used his power before, actually used it. I know what it feels like to use it, not just direct it. We are too entangled to start with him. I could be convinced to try this again, maybe, but not with him and definitely not with Ydum right now."

Byder fixes a look at me. "I trust you, Jinx. I may not understand, but I trust you."

I nod at that. Not sure it's well placed right now, but I say nothing. "Then, let's sit. Before anything else, I would need to know your ingredients, things you know you can do with your power, what things you know you can't, and what you aren't sure of yet."

The four of us move back to the couches. Anarus offers to help Ydum, but with his legs under him again, and the pain at bay from Esnir, he manages on his own. I hope there isn't a lack of trust making Ydum refuse the help, because, if there is, it should only be directed at me, not Anarus.

Once we're sitting, me closer to Byder than the other two, I lead him to tell me about his powers. "You said you can create with the power of the hunt. Food is a big one, hides and things from the hides, traps to catch the animals, anything else?"

Byder takes a deep breath. "So, the food one is definite for me. I can clean any type of prey, carve the meat for use from them easily, tell good meat from bad without even trying, and am actually a really good cook. I know it sounds weird, but really. Knowing exactly how tough that meat is and what will work to soften it and what spices will balance with its flavor comes naturally to me."

"So, Byder is always on cooking detail when we get out of the games. Got it." Ydum jokes.

"Only with the meat." Byder jokes back. "I couldn't make a cake or bread to save my life. Beyond that, not just traps but weapons too. I know exactly which weapon or trap would be best for what type of prey and can get even more specific once there's a specific prey in front of me. You want to hunt deer in this area? Here is a bow and arrow, that would be best. Oh, you want that deer, that one right there through the trees? This one specific arrow and that specific bow will take him down if you aim it in this position from this spot in exactly five minutes."

He pauses, considering his words. "And it isn't only what people think of as traditional prey. Are you hunting a human who broke the law? Try going to this one village on the third day of next month. You will find them. I can track too, like you know. Every detail about the prey I have chosen comes to me. I can see them like they are almost glowing, screaming look at me, I know where your prey went. And I know when things are going to mess up my tracking, like a storm coming."

"What about the furs?" I urge him to continue.

"I can see their potential uses. How to skin the animal properly to make a hat versus a blanket. Whether the skin will shrink a lot when tanned or whether it will warp or crack. I can't make the blanket from the skin, but I can hunt the animal, kill it, and prepare the skin for someone else to make the blanket, and it'll be just what they need. I also feel connected to the predator animals. I've never been actually able to do anything with this one, but feel it. My dad has that tattoo of the hunting dog that helps him. He also has had a lot of actual hunting dogs while I was growing up. I've always loved playing with them and the falcon he once had for a while. He was only working to rehabilitate the falcon after an injury, but it was like I knew when it was ready to fly again, and it was really anxious to."

"So, you can use your power to hunt anything, track anything, make and wield any type of weapon or trap, know the specific uses of the meat and skins of what you killed, especially the meat, and may have some connection to predator helping animals." I list it off, trying to think of anything we could be missing. "What about the other parts of an animal? The bones, the blood?"

Byder thinks. "Never thought about that. What could the blood be used for?"

"Magic." I tell him. "Not anything I've ever done myself, but blood in magic workings can be potent, and is not always bad like many people think. Bones can be used in art or magic as well. And food too, I guess."

"I think those would have to be on the maybe list." Byder says.

Ydum adds to our list. "Not just killing animals, Byder, but healing too. You said you knew when the falcon was ready to fly again. That's healing, not hunting."

"That's a lot of things in one power." Anarus says. "That's pretty much everything for the hunt. It sounds like you really would be a full hunt god, maybe some special affinity to hunting and food, but not like a specialty, more like a special interest."

"Is there anything you know you can't, or won't do?" I ask.

"Putting down injured helper animals." Byder answers quickly. "My dad has had to put down hunting dogs when they were sick or hurt and he tried to get me to help once. I cried and froze up. I couldn't make myself do it even though I knew the animal was suffering. I can't make animals suffer, any animals, even if they are my prey. I have to do clean, ethical kills or my power literally revolts and makes me sick. But I couldn't end the dog's suffering either."

Softly, I ask him. "How old were you?"

"Twelve."

"Could that have been age, not ability?"

Byder thinks again. "Maybe. I know how much the pup was hurting. I knew it then but I loved that dog. Maybe it would be different now."

I try to line it all up in my mind. Hunting, tracking, trapping, knowing and making weapons, understanding nature and how it can help or hinder, knowing predator animals and how they can help, the uses for every part of an animal killed so that nothing is wasted, the proper care of his tools, whether they are living or not, how to tend the meat to feed everyone, and when that animal has reached its end of usefulness, nothing more to be gained from its sacrifice.

Slightly nervously, I hold my hand out to Byder. He shows no fear in taking it, though. "Don't try to give me your power. Only show it to me. Let me see it and touch it. It stays in you."

Byder closes his eyes and so do I. I take a deep breath and blow it out slowly. I need to see Byder's power. Let me see the ingredients of it. Let me touch them in him. I feel a warmth spread over my hand holding his, but it's contained, as if I'm touching his warmth, not taking it into me.

I open my eyes and Byder does as well. I expect a rope type sensation like I got with Anarus, but that doesn't happen. Instead, I can see the power in Byder's body.

In his brown eyes, there's a silver light. That light speaks to me. I can read its intentions. His eyes hold his desire to hunt, to kill, he can take everything, track it all, nothing lives when he sets his eyes on them, he could take it all. Feed everyone in the whole world to gluttony. I reach up and touch his eyes with my free hand. No, we don't want everything. Just what we need to survive. Just enough to feed us, make our clothes, and things we need to survive.

I look down at his hands. That silver is there too, making his hands weapons. The power to end all living things is in them. Everything he touches can be used for his goal. Everything is a weapon to harm. I run my fingers along his. No. Not everything. Not all weapons. These hands can be soft too, healing and tender. Loving.

In his chest, his heart beats a silver cadence to the song of death. I touch his chest. Not death, but usefulness, I tell it. Need. Actions out of need, not wantonness or just pain caused for pleasure, but sacrifice done as painlessly as possible and only when it serves a noble purpose.

There are shadows I can't understand there too. In his heart, his hands, his eyes. They swim darkly. Not the dark of maliciousness, but the dark of untraveled waters. The powers he doesn't know about yet, or understand.

I pull my hand out of his and let his power go. The feeling of the warmth of his power leaves my hand and I look down at it. A little red and warm but not

117

hurt. But this was only the power he holds now, not his full mantle.

"That was," Byder shudders, "so strange. I could feel every piece of my power, even things that I never felt before. But then you touched them and they wanted to change. It was like they wanted to calm down."

"There were shadows in your eyes, hands, and heart. I think they were the parts of your power you can't access yet." I tell him. "I told your power what we wanted from it. Not all death, everything hunted just because you can, but kindness, ethical killings without pain, for use to fill a need only."

Byder nods. "I could tell. I don't think it stuck quite right. Like my power heard you but doesn't want to listen."

"That would make sense." Ydum answers. "You don't have your mantle yet. It isn't actually your power yet to control. It's in you but isn't yours yet. But Jinx has the feel of it, and so do you. And no one got hurt."

I clench my hand and tuck it under my other one to hide it. It didn't hurt, just looked red and felt warm. That's fine, I tell myself. That's not hurt.

"Do you think you could do that again, Jinx?" Ydum asks me. "Or are you too tired now?"

"I don't know that there's a point to doing it again right away." I tell him. "It's not like something has changed with his power or we are trying something new."

From his face, I think Ydum was suggesting I try it with him. I realize my mistake and correct it. "Oh, well, with you? Not right now. I hurt you and you need time to heal. And, like I said, Anarus and I would be harder. I don't know what we would need to do to figure that out. I want to think about it more, understand everything more, before I try again with him."

Translation? I scared myself shitless with how much of Anarus's power I can actually take from him and use. It's far too much for me to control and I'm terrified if I try again, I'll kill him, me, or someone else. And I feel too guilty about harming Ydum to even look at him much less try to look at his power.

But I say none of this. I don't want Anarus thinking I'm scared of him or his power. I'm not. I'm scared of me with his power. But I don't know if he would understand the difference. And Ydum would try to make me feel better when I don't deserve it. I should have heard Anarus trying to warn me to stop. I should have known when I was in over my head. They're all worried about making sure I don't get hurt by them in this, but are ignoring how much I could hurt them. This is evidence that, if I fail, it's not only me who could burn up or be crushed under the power I don't contain. I will take a red palm to protect them.

"Son of a bitch." Anarus says, then snatches at my hand. I yank it away before he can look at it. He growls. "Show me your hand, Jinx."

"Why?" I ask, trying to sound like I'm confused. Which isn't hard. How does he know? Or think he knows?

"You're clutching it, hiding it, and I felt you just feel like you have to protect us, even if it means you getting hurt. Show me your hand." Anarus demands again.

I groan, slumping, and hold out my hand. Damn this too strong bond. I can't even think in peace. Anarus takes my hand in his, flipping it palm up and sucks his teeth. "Fuck. It did hurt you, looking at Byder's power."

When the Gods Learn Lies

"No." I lie. "It didn't hurt, just feels warm."

Anarus grumbles, but Byder is the one who snaps. "And warm now could be burned and blistered with the full mantle, Jinx. Why the fuck would you hide this?"

I try not to say anything, but can't stop my thoughts and feelings. Why would I hide this? Because Anarus is just now finally starting to believe in himself and isn't feeling like we are doomed at every turn. Because Byder trusts me even when he doesn't understand. Because Ydum has always trusted me, even when I didn't know it. Because the four of us are perfect, matched perfectly by the cave, yet I still manage to be the disappointment that isn't good enough, doesn't know enough, can't do enough, is too damaged and broken to do what they need and they just keep loving me and covering for me. Because for once I could do something big with my magic and I still managed to fuck it up.

"Stop." Byder says harshly. "Stop thinking what you are thinking. You are not a disappointment. You are not too damaged and broken. You are so many things, but none of them that. You are word witch and would use such words on yourself? Jinx," he sighs. "I don't have the words to say like you always do. I don't know how to heal this in you."

"This was not your fault, Jinx." Ydum holds his hand up, making me look at him. "It was everyone's fault. It was mine because I should have said something when you took my hand in the first place. I should have thought about the fact that you threw Damek across the room with Anarus's shadows. Anarus should have stopped us when he felt his powers actually slipping from him like that, when it was more than just shadows and cold. Byder was watching, he could have done something. He saw me start to hurt, that Anarus tried to warn you but couldn't talk well, that you had no idea what was happening at all. He should have pulled Ani away, or broke our hands apart. You should have recognized that you couldn't control that other power and stopped us yourself. We all had a hand in this. It is not your fault. Not only your fault."

Anarus turns my head to face him. "You were doing the impossible, Jinx. You were using a god's power as a human. You contained my power, all of my power I have without my mantle, and used it without dying. The most that happened was a little frostbite on your neck? For carrying the full weight of an un-mantled god's power where one of those powers is death and you just told death to sit down and wait? You should be dead. It's not your fault you hurt Ydum, it's our luck you're still alive."

Byder speaks softly and doesn't make me look at him. "It's more than just this, Ydum's finger, isn't it, Jinx? Please tell us the truth. Tell me why it feels like your heart is being crushed in your chest and you feel like you deserve that pain."

I can't. I can't say it all. I feel like I am back in the last game, unable to speak. I want to scream but my mouth is not working at all. It all just tumbles through my mind. All the times I failed them. I didn't have shoes or even clothes. I didn't have a witch's kit. They had to teach me everything I should have already known. Every game, we've had to waste time teaching me what the fuck is going on. I know nothing about my own magic. Sure, I can do salves and salt circles, but even the lowest witch can do that. I think even humans with no magic could do that.

119

But my own magic? I have no clue. No fucking clue and they keep having to teach me, help me, direct me. And they have to protect me. Over and over again. Panic attacks. Nightmares. They have to be careful how they touch me, how they stand. They don't touch the alcohol the games still fucking give us every week because I might freak out again. They threw Tholdir out of our room when I wasn't even in it because I might come back, and then he died in the next game. They had to deal with teaching me to fight, then deal with me injured over and over again because I did something dumb. Esnir has spent more time in our room healing me than probably anywhere else.

They even have to protect me from each other. Ydum jumping to my defense today with Byder over a harmless comment, what should have been a harmless comment. Something he wants that I can't... They give me everything and I can't even do one little thing that he... The sob escapes me before I can stop it.

"Stop. Jinx, stop." Byder whispers in my ear. He's holding me tightly, his hands smoothing my hair and wiping away my tears. "I'm so stupid. I shouldn't have said that."

"But you want it." I whisper. "You want it and I can't. I'm not enough. I'm not good enough."

Byder leans his head against mine, shaking it. "No. That's not true. You are more than enough. You are everything I want, and all I want. I don't want anything but you. Just as you are. You taught me to braid my hair. You did it for me every day until I learned. You trusted me to read to you in the maze, and never once made me feel bad about how much I messed up. You protected me from the succubus. You trusted me to find the rabbit that literally had Ydum's life inside it. You didn't even think about it but just knew I would find it. You're all I want. Everything you give me is a gift, Jinx. And it is always enough. You are enough."

"Should I say what you've done for me too?" Ydum says, sitting on the other side of me, his hand rubbing my back as he speaks. "You gave me colors. You worked your magic and fucking gave me colors, Jinx. If that's not enough, you listen to my ramblings. You look at me with those eyes and I feel smarter than I ever have. A thousand perfect grades in school couldn't compare to one look from you. You knew me for one day. One day. And you trusted me, believed in me. I said I was a god of nature and you threw everything at me. Who tells a nature god to make ice spears for a weapon? Who believes that they can after knowing them for one day? You trusted me to fight you, to teach you to fight, to run. You were never scared. Not for a moment. I fought you first and you were never scared. You had every reason to be terrified, but you trusted me. You trusted me to come to you in the combat game. You fought hard, but I could hear you screaming for me. When you couldn't move another inch, you knew I would come to you. You trusted me to make you scared on the island with the rain. You think you know nothing about your magic but you fucking gave me colors just because you trusted and loved me."

"They both talk a lot." Anarus says. "You love me. All of me. I have the power of death in me and you still love me. You have never flinched away from me. You trust me. That's all I need. I don't deserve you, not the other way around."

Byder pushes my face up so he's looking at me again. "The cave knew exactly what it was doing. We've said it before and we will all keep saying it until each of us truly believes it. The cave knew exactly what it was doing. It knew who you are, no shoes, shitty birthday, different word magic, old, unhealed scars and all, and it knew you would be perfect for the three of us. That the four of us are perfect for each other. If you can't trust yourself or us, trust the cave. Trust that magic. There are never trio gods. Never. But the cave gave trio gods to you, Jinx. You. It knew what you needed and it knew what you could handle and it gave it to you."

I don't know what to think. Byder says trust the cave if I can't trust myself. I can do that. I can try. I lean against him and let him hold me. Trust the cave. Okay.

After a few minutes, Ydum is rubbing my back again. "So, Anarus had a breakdown. Jinx had a breakdown. I got injured bad enough to reveal Ani's secrets to Esnir. And it's only just now lunchtime. Byder? You need something, man or are we done with emotional upheavals for today?"

"We dug through Byder's powers intimately. He had his turn." Anarus says, making me laugh.

Chapter Seven

FOR THE REST OF the day, we do absolutely nothing. I check Byder's arm from the bear clawing, but it's already healed. Four fresh pink lines across his forearm that he says will fade to almost nothing before we even finish the games. Anarus checks my hand after a while and is pleased that the redness went away quickly. Ydum's finger stays gray from the tip to the second joint, but he can move it without wincing too hard, so that's promising.

When we decide it's time to go to bed, we don't even discuss it. All four of us just climb into the, thankfully large, bed together. Anarus on one side of me, Byder on the other, and Ydum on the other side of him. I recognize, not for the first time, how much something like this would have terrified me eight weeks ago. But now it feels wrong when we aren't like this. When I'm not safely tucked between all three of my gods.

When we wake in the morning, it feels like something has changed. When I wake up, Ydum is already awake and looking at me, but hasn't moved out of the bed. Anarus wakes up soon after, then Byder. We all wait for each other. We do all those incredibly boring morning routine things together. Getting dressed, brushing our teeth and hair.

It's not overly togetherness, we aren't all standing at the sink in the washroom, brushing our teeth in synchronous movements, but instead just moving and flowing around each other. I comb out my hair while Anarus brushes his teeth. When I finish my braid, Byder hands me a hair tie and I help him tame his messy mop which is rather unruly today. Ydum throws me a clean shirt without me asking for it. We just know each other. Anyone looking in would think we have been getting up and ready for the day together for years instead of two months.

Once we are settled in the sitting room, Anarus with his coffee, Byder and Ydum with breakfast, and me with the coffee I chose and the breakfast Byder chose for me, Ydum makes an announcement.

"New rule. We talk to each other. No more hiding, no more feelings we think we can't tell each other. If we feel upset or unsure, we tell each other. If something feels wrong or strange, we tell each other. We are four very powerful people, with powers that are a lot to handle and sometimes fucking scary. With a bond that's deeper and stronger than I've ever heard a bond can be. There are a lot of threats around us and a lot of concerns about the future. We have to rely on each other because we are the only ones we can rely on completely and unequivocally. We trust the cave when we can't trust anything else, and the cave gave us to each other. So, we always trust the cave and talk to each other."

Ydum looks around at the rest of us. Anarus takes a deep breath and nods. Byder nods as well. When he looks at me, I say, "Or the rule breaker has to sleep in the foyer," making Byder and Anarus laugh.

Ydum throws his hands in the air. "I was trying to be serious, here!"

"We're going to have to find a place to live that has a foyer. Too many of our rules have that punishment." Byder says.

I look between Ydum and Byder. "Do either of your parents' homes have a foyer? Because you said we start there, at the god's parents' house."

Byder shakes his head. "Two-bedroom apartment. Well, maybe. The foyer of the building."

Ydum also shakes his head. "Three-bedroom house. No foyer, but a nice front porch."

"Oh, shit." I say, sitting up straighter. "I just realized that in less than two weeks, we have to tell our parents about this, about all four of us. I will meet your parents and we will take over their home. Can either of you imagine us, the four of us, living with your parents? You three walking around shirtless all the time?"

Byder's face blanches. "My mom and dad are great, but we were always such a quiet family. Dad's a hunt god, obviously. But mom's witch magic has bent toward animals over the years of them together. She's such a quiet person, soft and gentle with the smaller animals. Dad's hunting dogs would always sleep on her feet. With Dad they're tools, but with Mom they're beloved pets."

"Mine's different." Ydum says. "Mom's flowers, Dad's metallurgy, Zimuna's stone, and wild me. Our house was always a riot of things happening. The shirt thing from us wouldn't even faze them. The pants thing with you, Jinx, might though." His eyes twinkle as he teases me and I blush. He's right. I go without pants almost as much as they go without shirts. But to be fair, Ydum's shirts are almost as long as a dress on me.

Once I smile, Ydum continues. "I know how I am, all academic then energetic, loud and always talking. My dad's the same way. Zimuna too, to some extent. Mom's the calm in the storm around our crazy antics. When Zimuna came home from her games with Greg, Mom and Dad were worried how her bond might have changed her, who Greg was and how he would fit in. But Greg tells raunchier jokes than Dad, and can sit in the stillness with Mom as she tends a plant. He fit in like a missing piece we didn't know we were missing. We've been through the post-games new person before, so, while it may be a little shocking to them for it to be the three of you instead of just one, I think they'll take it in stride."

"I have so many questions." I try to think of which one to ask first. "Do your parents know each other because you two are the same age? Do any of them know Anarus?"

Byder answers first. "Our parents know each other, at least a little. They would have gone to all the same meetings and stuff for the parents when we were in school and leading up to the games. They would at least recognize each other. Ydum and I weren't friends, but we saw each other a lot, knew each other well. Anarus was three grades lower, so we never had classes with him until the games stuff. We all knew of him, because of the orphan thing, because sometimes he would be staying at one of our friend's houses. But he never stayed with us, so I'm not sure how much my parents know about him."

Ydum agrees with that. "Anarus never stayed with us either. I know I heard my parents talk about him before, but it was always 'that poor orphan boy with the shadows' not anything specific. They mostly felt bad when he was moved around again, then they were angry when he was sent here."

I move to a different question. "You talk about your mom, Byder, and your dad, Ydum, as if their magic is a power like yours. Metallurgy and small pet animals. But when we have talked about my magic, you always say things like beginning magic, end magic, word magic. I don't have any sort of affinity like that. I don't know if anyone I've ever known does, except maybe Granny Helen with healing."

"You wouldn't." Ydum explains. "The potential for an affiliation magic is in each human witch. Some, a very few with a very distinct path, can tap into that on their own. Probably what your Granny Helen did. But, other than that, most witches don't really pay attention to that affiliation and just stay a basic beginning or end magic witch. The gods and games are what hones that affiliation. Everything we do here, all the games, but also the bond with the god, helps craft the magic in the human. That's why it has to be a beginning magic witch. End magic is too narrowed already, too restricted. The mantle of the god will give direction to the magic of the witch. Channeling that much power as we have to do in the tenth game will shape you as much as it shapes us. Then, over the years, our bond, our relationship, will hone it more because you'll be using certain parts often and others not at all. Which, honestly, now that I think about it, will be interesting to see happen for you. Our powers all have some overlap, but not a lot. How will Jinx's odd word magic hone down with the three of us?"

That confuses me more than it helps. "So, I may not be a word witch but something we don't know yet because my magic hasn't been shaped by your powers yet?"

Byder shakes his head, swallowing the last of his doughnut. "No. The being a specific type of magic user is all your own and been that way since birth. End magic, beginning magic, that won't change. What changes isn't how you use your magic but what you can do with it. Some things will just come easier than others. Dad's hunt god power directs Mom's affinity for magic with small animals. During the games, and a little after too probably, she could do anything magically that Ydum's dad could do, but just became better at and feels more comfortable with that. Now, she probably could still do those things Ydum's dad does, but it would be like using a muscle after not using it for a long time. It would feel weak, like the muscle atrophied from disuse."

Anarus finally finishes his first cup of coffee and joins the conversation as he gets a refill. "We've been trying to figure out how your magic is different. How your test came out half red half blue every time. What Drila meant when she said you were both a beginning and end magic witch but also neither. We've started calling you a word witch because it seems like you conduct your magic through words. Asking it to do things, telling it to."

He sits back on the couch and pulls a long sip from his mug before sighing. "But the problem is, we're just guessing at how and why your magic is different as much as we are with what my power is. We've never had magic like you, but power directed by membership in a specific pantheon. Their parents and anyone I stayed with, those witches had been bonded to their gods for too long for us to see how the magic was before. For all we know, the way you use words is exactly what every other witch does, and the difference is somewhere else."

I sit back and think about this abandoning the toast on my plate as Byder only scowls at me slightly for it. "I should talk to the other humans. My village did so little teaching about actual magic, I don't know either. Maybe if we knew what I do different, we could find out better ways to protect me when you get your mantles."

"Sounds right to me." Ydum says. "Who would you trust to talk about this to? I think maybe we only ask one, not all four of them? At least to start."

"Weirdly, Damek." I tell him. "He's a powerful male witch. Male witches are usually the weaker witches, but to be in the games, he must have a lot of power. Myrna had a strong male witch in her year. He had a lot of issues because they were teaching him all the stuff like they expected him to have just that touch most males have. My dad had more magic than most male witches too. They struggled with being different. If it was the same for Damek, he's the most likely to understand what I mean when I say my magic doesn't feel and do things like it should, without me know what should means."

With that decided, we abandon the rest of our breakfast, except Anarus who brings his coffee with him as we head to room four. I feel a little nervous when I knock on Damek and Iella's door. We revealed to Esnir Anarus's secret about his power and now we are going to talk to Damek about mine. He already knew my blood test was not right. Drila told everyone that twice now. But it's one thing to have him know my test is different and quite another to tell him my magic is wrong. And that I know so little about magic to begin with.

When they let us in, I tell Damek I need to talk about witch magic stuff with him and he gestures for me to join him on the couches. Iella wanders away, towards their table and Ydum follows her. Anarus and Byder step out, leaving Ydum to watch over me and give Damek and me room to talk privately.

I twist my mouth back and forth as Damek watches me, thinking of the right words to say. "You know my test for the games was messed up, and that Drila said my magic is both, beginning and end, and neither."

Damek only nods, so I continue. "My village was small and very poor. Our magical classes were pretty basic, focusing on meditating, creating salves, and protection stuff. We learned about the plants, crystals, stones, that stuff, but not much else. And most of the instruction we received assumed we knew how to access and control our magic already. That we knew what our magic felt like. But I didn't. I never learned that and have been kind of just winging it. The guys have helped, but they think somethings I do aren't how it's normally done."

I suck in a deep breath. "What I need is, how do you access your magic, Damek? How do you use it? What does it feel like?"

Damek laughs, his blonde curls bouncing as his shoulders shake. "Oh, that's all you need? Gods, when you came in, you were so serious, I thought it was something catastrophic. I can help you with that, easy."

He sits up straighter, squaring his shoulders. "Your magic is a flow inside you. It's part of your essence, your being. When you strip away everything else, what makes you Jinx instead of someone else? Not your hair color, or eye color. Lots of people have that. Not how you act, whether you are funny or serious or kind. Lots of people are those things too. But that power moving between all those things, binding them together in that perfect mix that is Jinx. Look for that flow of binding power inside the deepest part of you."

I close my eyes, and try. I clear my mind and try to look deep inside myself. I've done this before, digging deep into a meditation to find peace, but never to find myself. All that comes is all those words that describe me.

"All I'm getting is those words, the ones you told me to ignore." I tell Damek without opening my eyes.

"Words? Like actual words?" Damek asks. "Or images you know words for? When I do this, look for my flow, I can see things about myself, how tall I am, how much I like to laugh. But I see them as images in my mind. Then, when I look in between the images I see it, that power binding them together and can follow it to its source."

I try again, rolling my shoulders to relieve the tension. Okay, look for the images. What my hair looks like. My eyes. I get words in my mind. How I told Ydum what color my hair is. Brown but not dark, lighter with blonde in it, whitish gold, shiny yellow mixed in the muddy brown of red, yellow, and blue. My eyes are the same brown without the blonde and gold.

I groan. "There are no images, just words. Real words."

My eyes are still closed, so I can't see Damek's face, but his voice sounds confused. "Everyone has the images. Everyone I have ever talked to gets images. They can see it, then see the magic between the images. We all describe how that magic looks a little different, but it's always how it looks because we can see it. Hmm. Have you ever meditated and gotten an actual image, Jinx?"

I nod. "When Ydum was helping me for the fifth game. I could see the things he said in the guided meditation, then I actually saw Kinshra, my wolf familiar."

Damek whistles. "You have a familiar? So cool. Anyway, later. So, you saw the field, actually saw it and saw your wolf. Do you still see those things? When you talk to her now, do you still see her or is it more words?"

I have to actually consider this. Hey, Kinshra?

Yes? Another learning thing?

Yeah, sorry. We're trying to figure out why my magic is wonky. I was wondering if I saw you when we talk or only get words.

Words. You only get words.

I smile at her. Well, I know that now. Do you know why? I saw you the first few times, but now I don't?

No. I see you. But I know you don't actually see me anymore.

You see me?

Sure. You are wearing a dark gray shirt and a pair of black pants today. Your hair is braided like normal. And you are sitting next to a male I don't know. I can't see him, I never see anyone who is with you except Anarus, but know he's there next to you. I can feel him, like I feel your other bondeds, but he isn't bonded to you. Who is he?

A friend. His name is Damek. He's a human like me.

Is he going to become part of the bond too?

I laugh. No, Kinshra. Just a friend. No one else will ever be part of the bond.

Well, no one else until you have pups, she corrects me.

Not talking about that, Kinshra. Remember?

Yeah, yeah. Silly human.

I turn my attention back to Damek. "I only talk to Kinshra with words. She says she can see me but knows I no longer see her."

"So friggin cool." Damek whistles again. "Okay. So, you are capable of images, but they take a lot of work, or maybe have to be given to you by someone else. When you aren't, your images are only words describing them. That's really different than my magic, or anyone else's I've ever heard of. What's the easiest magic you can do? Something you feel really comfortable with?"

"Making peace." I tell him quickly. "I can help myself feel calm or others."

"Can you do it for me? I want to see what I feel, see, or whatever when you use your magic."

I nod again and reach out my hand. It lands on Damek's knee. I take another deep, cleansing breath. Peace, give him peace. Calm peace. Damek needs calm peace.

"Okay, that's different." Damek is speaking slowly. "What are you doing in your head right now, Jinx?"

"Thinking the words peace, Damek needs peace."

I can tell he's nodding. "Though so. I could almost hear the words. When they came to me, it's like they dissolved in my magic, became the feeling I usually get with emotion magic. Now, let me try something with you."

Damek takes my hand in his. He breathes slowly once, twice, then I see a fuzzy image that looks like a pair of dice. It fades quickly and I hear the word luck. Only for a moment, exceptional luck.

"Tell me what you see, hear, feel, Jinx."

"Luck." I tell him. "Really quickly, there was a hazy pair of dice, then just the words exceptional luck."

"Thought so. Your magic changed my images to words, like mine changed your words to feelings. Open your eyes." I do as he says and see Damek's face is scrunched up, like he's unsure and confused. "I'm a beginning magic witch. I can craft magic with only the pieces, as you know. End magic needs the whole thing."

Damek holds out his hand. He concentrates hard, staring at his hands. A small pile of little card papers appears in his hand and a bottle of black and red ink. As he continues to concentrate, the ink swirls out of the bottles and coats the papers. Then, they shimmer. He holds one piece of the paper up. "A magical deck of cards. The ink and paper are infused with luck. Which card is this, Jinx?"

He's showing me the unmarked back of the card. I look at it and see a shimmering redness and two hearts. "Two of hearts." He flips the card and shows me I'm right.

"An end magic would need a deck of cards already made and wouldn't be able to make you see the card like that." He explains. "You would have to touch it to see what it is or just guess and feel the luck guiding you. Try to make something, Jinx. Call something to you to make something with your words."

"I can't." I tell him. "We've tried. I couldn't make it rain without water already around me to use. When we practiced in the washroom, we had to turn on the sink to give me the water."

"But you just made peace from nothing." Damek frowns. "Have you ever failed to make peace?"

"When I'm panicking."

Damek nods at this. "Your panic attack. You couldn't make peace in yourself because you had none to access. Everyone around you was also upset and scared, so you couldn't use theirs either. That sounds like end magic. You use things either you already have or what's around you. You didn't just make peace from nothing, you used the peace in you, me, maybe even Iella and Ydum and gave me more. But that's not quite right for end magic. End magic should be able to call the fully made things they need that they know where are. You should have been able to pull the water from the pipes in the walls, with that much water needed and you knowing it was that close by, but you couldn't. The water had to be already there and waiting, within your line of sight, real or magical sight. It's almost like you are the furthest end of end magic."

Damek's eyes light up and he stands, tapping a finger on his chin. "Wait. That's wrong. I think I'm wrong. Jinx, when you gave me peace, did you feel like you had less peace in yourself?" I shake my head no. "Iella, did you feel like you weren't as calm and peaceful a minute ago for no reason? Ydum, you too?"

I turn and look at them. They are both shaking their heads no as well.

"Did you feel more peaceful for no reason?" Damek tries again.

Iella furrows her brow. "Now that you mention it, yeah."

Damek hoots and pumps his fist in the air. "Hah! You didn't take peace from them or yourself to give me peace, like an end magic witch would, but you didn't make it from scratch like a beginning magic witch either, Jinx! You built on what already existed in the room. We all felt more peace even though you only purposely gave it to me. You use words, instead of images and feelings, and you can create more of what already exists. You need enough to start with close by you, then can build it up more. I bet your salves are potent, very potent. And I bet, now that you have a better feel for your magic and a deeper bond with your gods, you'd barely need any water to do what you did back then. You are both a beginning and end magic witch, Jinx, but neither too. You need to already have the thing to do the thing, but once you get rolling, it's all you. So cool."

Ydum comes over to sit on the other side of me. "Let's try something." He holds up his hand and the rosebud is on it. "You know this magic, Jinx. We have practiced with the rosebud a lot. But this time, don't try to make it bloom. Make more of them from what I gave you."

I concentrate on Ydum's hand. I need more roses. I need to make more roses. To make more roses there needs to be seeds, right? Or maybe not. I concentrate on a small part of the stem of the rosebud instead of on the flower. Come on, grow another stem, make another rosebud. I need there to be more roses. I need the rosehips for seeds for later. For tea. More stems. More flowers.

As I focus on the plant, a small tendril starts to grow from the stem of the rosebud. I keep encouraging it in my mind. A little more, form a bud. The tip of the tendril starts to swell and open. A new rosebud hangs next to Ydum's. I know that the little plant can't handle much more weight on it. It can't survive with any more rosebuds so I start a new stem. New roots, a new stem that can make a third rosebud. The dirt on Ydum's hand shifts and a small green shoot pushes up through it. A new plant. I made more from the original plant, and now have started a whole new one.

Ydum is smiling. "Beginning and end magic. And, let me guess, all with thoughts of words and need. I'm calling Anarus and Byder through the bond to come see this."

I nod, still staring at the slowly unfurling shoot that's rapidly becoming a new rosebud.

Damek leans over Ydum's hand, his fingers trailing gently on the two plants. "That is so cool."

Byder opens the door and gives it a soft knock before walking in. Anarus comes in behind him. "We were called?"

Ydum answers them. "Yeah, come see this." He holds up his hands. "I made the first rosebud, like always, but Jinx added to it the second bud, then made the new plant all by herself."

"Drila was right. She's both beginning and end magic." Damek adds. "Her magic is in words, she needs to pull from something within arm's reach around her to start her words, but then can take off on her own and make more as she needs it. Her magic doesn't stop when she runs out of supplies, but can build more from what she already has to keep going."

"And that's different from you?" Anarus asks.

"Very." Damek explains. "I can bring all the supplies I need to me. There are rose seeds and dirt somewhere, I can get them and make the plant grow from that. An end magic would need the whole plant already there to make it grow. But for both of us, once the supply is gone, the working is done. Once the plant uses it all, it'll wilt and not grow anymore. Once it's grown as large as it can, it won't grow anymore and I have to get more supplies, or an end magic witch needs a new plant. Jinx just said okay, that plant is as big as it gets, let's make another and make the soil fertile enough to support it. She made more supplies from nothing at all."

"Not from nothing at all." Ydum says thoughtfully. "From what already existed. Like she made what was there divide itself and make more so she would have what she needed. Like making children of themselves in an instant, then she can use that new supply without having to actually call for more."

"How do we know I didn't just call more supplies like a beginning magic witch?" I ask. "I need the thing at the beginning, the actual rosebud, like an end magic witch. But then, once I have the feel for it, I just called more seeds to me like a beginning magic witch."

Ydum smiles, shaking his head. "Jinx, look at the two rosebuds. Ignore the extra part you grew on the original one. The original rosebud and the one you made yourself are identical. Completely identical. Most people wouldn't notice, but, hello, nature god. They are from the same seed and that isn't possible in nature. Not like that. You made an exact copy of the seed from the original rosebud to grow another rosebud."

Ydum finally closes his hand. When he did this before, the rosebud would just crumble and disappear. He opens his hand and his rosebud is gone, but mine is still there. "Oh yeah. Jinx, end the working. Tell the rosebud to go away, you're done with it."

I look at the rosebud I made. Thank you. I'm done now. Go back to what you should be.

The rosebud curls up, dry and dead then sinks away into the small pile of dirt in his hand. Ydum curls his hand closed again and when he opens it, all the plants and dirt is gone.

"That is so cool." Damek breathes out again.

"Thank you, Damek, for helping me. I really appreciate it." I tell him. "I think we have a lot of work to do now."

Damek gives me a wide smile. "No problem. That was awesome. So glad I could help." He pauses for a moment, then continues. "And thank you, Jinx, for trusting me with this. It means a lot to me that, after everything, you trusted me with this."

I smile back at him and then my three gods and I leave him in peace, to return to our own room.

In our room, Ydum wants me to try the power thing with him. I'm worried about his finger, which still looks gray but doesn't seem to be hurting him. I'm not sure if that's good or bad. Shouldn't a dead finger be causing him pain? But the grayness hasn't spread and Ydum is unfazed.

"Now that we know exactly how Jinx's magic is different, we can work on how to use our power and her magic to protect her from the full weight of our mantles." Ydum settles into a spot on the couch comfortably. "We have to learn my ingredients first, though, right?"

"Yes." I reply, setting myself up next to him. "We need to figure out what your power does and doesn't do. We know some of it really well already. You can create and control all types of plants, trees, bushes, make them grow, live through the cycles of life, death, and rebirth from the seasons. You may eventually be able to use the vines of your tattoo to make vines without any power or anything or the tattoo may just be symbolic. You can manipulate water, freeze it or melt it. You can manipulate stones, move them out of the earth. Anything else?"

Ydum thinks out loud. "Mountains, valleys, shaping the earth. That is nature, but I haven't tried to do any of that. Volcanoes, their fire, lava, that would also be part of nature, but again, never tried it. I've made fire before, like with the oleander, but not sure where in my power that came from. If it comes from volcanoes or the lightning I've done before. Lightning probably means storms too. The rain I helped you make. You said stones, and I did that in the first game, but what about minerals, crystals, like my sister? Again, I don't know."

He shakes his head, then looks at Byder. "I know I cannot do anything with the animals themselves. That's not nature the same way. I like them, enjoy animals, but only know what they need in their environment to survive, not manage them themselves."

He turns back to face me. "The rabbit in game four gave up its life force under my power but that was hard and hurt me as much as it hurt the rabbit. I focused more on the force of nature that abides in all parts of nature, the interconnectedness of it all and called on that part of the rabbit to come out. So, nature's connections too, probably."

Doing as I did with Byder, I simplify what he's saying to its base parts. "Shaping the terrain of the land with dirt or lava is a maybe, moving those elements once they are in place is known. Growing plants is definitely, and sensing the connection of all things' life forces to each other is most likely. Working with the seasons, the cycle of death and rebirth, definitely. Working with weather, also definitely. Anything anyone else can think of that nature might be able to do?"

Ydum, Byder and Anarus shake their heads. But then Anarus changes his mind. "The tides, the moon. The cycles of those, the flow of water in rivers and lakes."

I look at Ydum and he's thoughtful. "The water part would probably be linked to the crafting of the land. Rivers shape the landscape as much as shifting dirt and stone or flowing lava does. So, making it's the maybe, moving it once it's in place, more than likely. The tides? Not sure at all. Never tried."

That settled, Ydum and I sit next to each other on the couch and I take his hand in mine. Byder and Anarus stay close, watching for any sign of something going wrong. I close my eyes and try to use my magic the way Damek helped me see it work. Words that need something to start from, then can add to it.

I stop, an idea in mind. "Ydum, as we do this, think about there being a barrier between your power and my magic. Not a full barrier so I can't get through at all, but like a thin cloth, gauzy, that I can see through and feel through, but can't actually touch directly. Then, when I tell you, let it go."

"Like cheesecloth?" Ydum asks.

"Exactly." I settle myself again, his hand in mine. I take a deep cleansing breath and blow it out. No doubts, no fear. I can do this. We can do this. I breathe in and out again. Ydum's power. I need to see his power, touch it, but not have it come into me. There's the feeling of something slick, blocking me. I grab ahold of that feeling and let it melt into words. A thin gauze of separation. Just enough to protect me but not enough to stop me. I think of a thin gauze over my hands. A warmth spreads over my hand, but it's more diffuse than it was with Byder. I hold onto that magic, the gauzy protection and move it to cover my eyes too.

"Okay, you can let go of the gauze, Ydum." I tell him as I open my eyes.

Ydum is nearly glowing, shimmering with a gray light. It's very different than Byder's, that sat in his eyes, hands, and heart. Ydum's is everywhere, filling him completely. As I look, I realize that the light isn't actually gray. It's green, but he sees it as gray so that's how it looked to me at first too. He looks hazy. I think that's the fabric between us, though. The protection.

Ydum is full of connections. His whole body is a spiderweb of interconnectedness. All the ways things in nature work together, all under his skin, pulsing with life. It's almost like his skin has the green tint it does because all that power is so much, it just oozes out of his pores. Some of the life is his to control, some is life that just lives around him. His skin knows how all those pieces, that life, should come together, benefit each other.

His arm and chest glow the strongest with that life. I reach out with my free hand to touch his vine tattoo and the power simmering through it. It feels like it's bursting with life. So much unbridled life. It's beautiful and powerful and completely dominating. It's too much. The rest of his power is drowning in the flowers, vines, trees, bushes, plant life of all kinds. Plants that want to bust out of him, grow, showing all their abilities. They can help, they can feed, they can heal, they can give so much. And they want to. They all want to. But I tell it no, stay in your proper places in your proper ways. You only get to grow so big, and when your turn to die comes, you must be willing to let go.

With that thought, the vines pull back and I see the cycle of that growth properly. Right beneath the vines is the seasons. The warmth of summer, the decay of fall, the cold of winter, and the rebirth of spring. Each season has its weather. Rain in the spring and fall, snow and ice in the winter, the dry summer. Thunder echoes there, and lightning. It holds its balance between the four seasons with the plants calmed down.

Behind the seasons, almost like it's on his spine, there's the pull of the moon. The tides and flow of the water. The stars and the moon and the bond between them and the seasons. Their bond with nature, how the turning of the tides can flood, giving too much water to the life he creates, or pull away completely. How not enough rain makes the power of the moon weak and the tides not able to do their job. It's just a knowledge now. But it can do so much more, it knows.

I look down and see a glimmer coming from inside Ydum's boots. It's trapped and can't get out. It feels stifled and panicky to get out. "Can someone take off his boots?" I say out loud without breaking my concentration.

Hands move to untie his boots and slide them off, but it doesn't help as much as I thought it would. The power still feels trapped. It wants him to walk, his footsteps changing the world under his feet. His footprint can make valleys and riverbeds, shift the dirt and make a mountain between his toes. But it can't. It's not ready yet. It will be someday, but not today.

I look up at Ydum's eyes and see a fire hidden deep in them. It's a patient fire. It wants to move so slowly, but someday it will explode. Molten rock, heated metals, all there just below the surface. When he's strong enough, it'll pour out of him, bringing heat and death to everything. But from that death, from that purging, the world will be built anew, the stone and ash left behind will be better, making the plants stronger, giving the animals a better home. It fears the tides on his back and wants to crush it. The storms too are a threat and must be stopped so it can live.

No, I tell the fire. You're not at odds, but each right in your own way, in your own time. There'll be a time for the slow ember to flash and burn brightly, consuming everything in its path, but then the rains will need to come, the tides pull back in and the fires be put out so the new growth can happen. You are needed, but only in your own time.

I pull my hand from Ydum's and tell the gauzy protection that I'm done. The film over my vision drops away. I see Ydum fully and smile. He has so much power already. His full mantle will be a wonder to behold.

Anarus takes my hand into his and examines it. "Still a little red but not as bad as before."

Ydum is looking at me with a strange expression on his face.

"What are you thinking?" I whisper to him.

"I felt it all. I felt you brush aside my vines. They moved, they actually moved, but I felt your hand move them and I could suddenly feel things behind them. You never once touched my back but I felt your fingers trail down my spine. My feet ached for your touch, but it never came." Ydum still stares at me, his mouth hanging half open in awe.

"Your plant power wanted to take over everything." I tell him. "The seasons behind it were trapped under all that power. The moon and the tides on your spine too. Your feet want to shape the land but isn't able to yet. And your eyes are a smoldering fire that knows what it will one day do, a volcano exploding and wanted to stop the seasons and the tides too, but I told it not to. It's all warring in you, all the power wants to burst out and be in control. It's struggling to stay in balance."

Byder hums, thoughtfully. "That's different than mine. You said mine was like a heartbeat, somethings wanting to take over, but there were things that are shadowy, undiscovered. But Ydum's power is all out there, all fighting to take over. There was nothing shadowy, nothing you couldn't tell what it is?"

I shake my head. "No. All his power knows exactly what it is and what it can do. Some of it knows it can't yet, that it's not ready, but it knows exactly what it will do when the time comes."

"That makes sense." Anarus says, still looking at my hand. "The power of the god of the hunt would be a softer power. Not weaker, but just not as overpowering. Nature is a force, unstoppable. You can't contain it. You can't stop an earthquake or a volcanic eruption or even a storm. You can only ride it out and hope you survive, and tell it to stay in its proper time and place. Hunting is something you choose to do when you want rather than something that happens to you like nature."

Ydum chuckles. "Oh, we so need to do Ani now. If I'm unbridled power, and Byder's a soft heartbeat, what would Anarus be?"

"Anarus would be after lunch." Anarus points to the table, where lunch has appeared. "Jinx needs to rest and let her hand heal first."

We eat lunch, then once Anarus is happy with the state of my hand, we sit on the couches again. Anarus and I face each other the same way as I did with Byder and Ydum.

"Do we need to talk about what my powers can do?" Anarus asks. "Because the answer is I don't know."

I shake my head, smiling at him. "I know what you know already, which isn't nothing. Death, we know. Cold, we also know. The ability to make it snow or at least make it cold enough to make rain into snow. Your shadows are something, but the question is what are they? You can see through them, or hide within them. They are attached to your emotions. You've said you have made people confused or forgetful before. Did you do that with your shadows or something else?"

"I used to think my shadows, but now I'm not so sure." Anarus answers. "I also bind you and your wolf, am the guide for that familiar bond, but I don't know how I do that either."

Byder adds to it. "Your bond is the strongest of all of us for everything. To Jinx and her meditation. You were the first one to notice the bond doing more than it should. It bleeds so strongly through you that you have problems separating it out in yourself, knowing you from us. So, bonds are a thing all the way around. Connecting them, and maybe disconnecting them."

"Bonds, cold, death, emotions, shadows, confusion and hiding, anything else?" I ask.

"Destiny." Ydum adds. "His tattoos. All of his tattoos link us, the people he bonded with, but he got them before the bonds were made. I'm convinced of it even more now. Anarus, you have the phases of the moon down your spine and that's where Jinx said my power for the tides, controlled by the moon, lives in me. Something with his power is about fate."

I nod and take a deep breath. "Bonds, destiny, cold, death, emotions, confusion, and the things he can do through the shadows. Anarus, remember to make the gauzy protection until I can take it over. We will need it more than I need it with the others because your shadows know me already, I think."

When Anarus nods, I take his hand, close my eyes, and take several cleansing breaths. I focus my mind on only looking at Anarus's power. I don't even want to touch it if I don't have to. I only need to see it, not use it. Do not come to me, just show me what and where you are. I feel a thick, heaviness between our hands. I almost can't feel Anarus's touch through it.

"Not so thick, Anarus. The protection is too thick." I tell him.

Anarus grumbles. "I won't hurt you."

"I can't see. I can't feel. It's too thick." I open my eyes and look at him, dropping the magic of wanting to look at his power. "You have to trust me, trust Byder and Ydum to watch us. Trust yourself. If it's too thick, I can't see, Anarus."

Anarus takes a deep breath and groans. He closes his eyes again and so do I. I feel the fabric between our hands again, thicker than Ydum had it, but thin enough I can feel through it this time. Once again, I just want to look at Anarus's power. Not touch unless I need to, not use or have any of it come to me at all. Only look. I think of the thick gauze over my hand and over my eyes. One more steadying breath and I open my eyes.

Chapter Eight

AT FIRST, I THINK we did something wrong. I don't see the power in him like I did in Byder or Ydum. There's nothing there. It feels almost empty. But I realize that the emptiness is not actually empty. It's full, too full, but quiet, waiting, a deep, covered well right over his heart. Is it all waiting for his mantle?

As I look more, I see bits and pieces of power flowing from that spot over his heart. I see his shadows moving around that deep well. They aren't all of them, just some that snuck out. They aren't actually him, not part of him, but they are others that will listen to him, do his bidding.

His shadows are people. They are actually people. They can see and feel and hear and smell because they used to be people. They don't listen to me when I say I don't want them to come to me, but look to Anarus for permission to go to me. They like me. But Anarus tells them no firmly. Don't go anywhere. They listen to him because he controls their destiny. This power used to be someone else's a long time ago but they gave it to him, so that power is his now. Their destiny, a small bit of gold that sits in their chests, where their hearts resided when they were alive, is Anarus's to control now.

An odd thought comes to me. When we thought Anarus was only a god of obscurity, we had him use his power in reverse to translate what the dead witch said. If it's not actually obscurity, then how did he do that? I look at the shadows that are actually people and know it. The dead witch spoke in their language. The language of a long, long time ago. Just like he doesn't actually look at things through the shadows, but the shadows of the people give Anarus a vision of what they see, they knew the language of the witch and gave him the translation. They also do all the work obscuring and confusing people, not Anarus himself.

So much of what we thought was Anarus's powers is actually the shadows just working inside him. Someone else's shadows from a power that was theirs, given to him now. The wilde hunt, they tell me they are the wilde hunt. Someone else made them what they are now when they died, then ignored them for a long, long time. But now, that someone gave the wilde hunt to him and they are his. Or is partially his for now. It could be all his someday. Maybe.

I try to ask them who gave them to Anarus, when they did that, but the shadows don't know. They don't remember who made them so long ago. They don't know time except in relation to the bridge into the land of the dead. When it is time for them to cross it into the land of the living and when it is time for them to go back and rest. But they aren't going back and forth anymore. They don't know why they aren't, just that they can't. They're stuck. Stuck in the well. Stuck with Anarus.

There's still more coming from the dark well. Leaking and oozing out of it is a cold fire. The flames are white and blue, licking at the edges of Anarus's heart. Like the shadows, it shouldn't be out right now, but there's too much in the well to keep it contained. The cold is part of that power of the wilde hunt that was given to Anarus, and now his body is trying to contain it all before it's ready. When it shouldn't be carrying it at all. At least, not yet.

I look at the deep well over his heart again. There's more coming from there. Not there, but from behind there, from his heart behind the well. A rope of gold runs out of him. Like the rope I felt when I tried to use the shadow to throw the sock ball. The rope splits into strands as it wraps around Anarus's heart to flow out of him.

I follow one of the strands that leads away from Anarus and see it ties itself to Byder's heart. There is another one that leads to Ydum and one more for me. Mine coming from his heart splits in two, one piece leading to his wolf tattoo and another leading to me. The rope of gold is our bond. Anarus's heart is directly tied to our hearts through the destiny of our bonds. The strands to each of us, except to the wolf tattoo, pulse with light that runs back and forth between us.

I tell the strings of our bonds to stop. You can exist, but don't share all the time like that. The bond isn't supposed to be like that, that strong. Let Anarus feel only his own emotions as his own, and let the rest of us only give him what we need to. For a moment, the pulsing settles down but then it starts again. It can't listen, not yet.

I look through the deep well, try to see around it, to see if I can find his real power, the one that's his, but I don't see anything past our bonds. The well over his heart is too dark and too deep. It's closed right now, but it'll open soon, it knows. It's almost time. Once it does, maybe then his heart can do what it's supposed to, all of what it's supposed to. But for now, the well of the wilde hunt is too much for his heart to handle and it's suffocating his real power.

Does he have power anywhere else, anywhere that isn't suffocated? I look up to Anarus's eyes. I see glimmers, that golden glimmer that looks like the destiny in the shadows and in our bonds. It's small and so overpowered by the well over his heart. I look at his hands and see the same golden glimmer. Bare traces of it. The wilde hunt, its well, is hiding his real power. I think his real power has something to do with destiny. But it's so weak and so overwhelmed.

I look over Anarus one more time to make sure I haven't missed anything. When I am sure I haven't, I pull my hand out of his and let the gauzy protection go.

Byder takes my hand in his and checks it over the way Anarus did. "Looks mostly fine. A little red again, but that's it."

"The power isn't Anarus's." I say without preamble. "It's the wilde hunt, but it isn't his. Or wasn't originally. It's closed up in a well but the well is too full, straining his heart and leaking out all over him with the shadows and cold because his body can't handle that much power yet. It's not his. He has another power. One that is scared and small because the power that isn't his is so big and overpowering."

"Two different powers?" Ydum asks. "And one isn't his? How do you know?"

I don't look away from Anarus. "His shadows told me. The shadows are the wilde hunt and their destinies were ruled by another before, but that other god gave the power to Anarus, so now he's in charge of it. The shadows that used to be people who have died and the cold fire are leaking out of the well closed up over his heart. The well will open soon, but they aren't sure what soon is. They have no concept of time, the shadows. He has bond lines running from his heart to each of us and mine is doubled, going to his wolf tattoo too. They are gold and shimmer, pulsing too much. He also has that gold in his eyes and his hands but it's so weak and overrun by the power of that dark well. I think his real power might lie in bonds and destiny, but it's hidden under what someone else gave him that he shouldn't have."

"I have someone else's power?" Anarus asks me quietly. "This whole time it was someone else's power?"

Ydum growls. Ydum never growls in anger like that, so I turn to him. His fists are clenched tightly, resting on his thighs. "That shouldn't happen. That should never happen. Trying to force a power in another god, or stop their power from being what it actually is, is so dangerous. We've been taught that parents who've tried have caused their children serious harm, even killed them, or the power has exploded out of the child hurting and killing others. It's dangerous."

Ydum slams upright, standing at his full height and slamming his fist into his own thigh. "It's dangerous and stupid and reckless! Why would someone give Anarus a power that isn't his? How? When? And how the fuck is he not dead from it?"

Byder sounds just as mad, his face tense and frowning. "It explains why it let Jinx use it so easily. It isn't his so isn't part of him. They have a double bond, because of Kinshra. It would be easy for the power that's only stuck in Anarus, but isn't part of him, to move the leaking bits to someone else. I bet with enough time, all of us would have taken on some of that power, on purpose or accidentally, and fuck all knows what havoc and damage that might have caused."

My mind is whirling as I listen to them. I say all my thoughts, let them tumble out and see what sticks. "We thought Anarus might be the god of the wilde hunt, and that's partially right. Someone, probably Death, put that power in him, gave it to him to carry. It isn't open because it's the wrong time of year. October thirty-first is in three days, the day before the ninth game. It's almost time for it to open, but it also may not be able to fully open because he doesn't have his mantle yet. That would explain how he's still alive. The power never came in full force because it needs the bridge made by the god of Death to fully work, and Anarus can't access it all until he has his mantle. But it's suffocating his real power and who knows what will happen when he takes his mantle and that real power is strong enough to fight back."

"You said you could see bond lines and something in my eyes and hands that looks like the destiny inside the shadows." Anarus says. "Would that mean that my mother isn't Winter but one of the Fates? It would have to be Peace, since we know it isn't Sadness."

I rub my forehead, thinking. "I don't think so. Death is the eventual destiny of all living things. Even immortal gods have the eventual destiny of death. Gods can and do die eventually. All the shadows, the people who are part of the wilde hunt in you, all have their destiny linked to them and it glowed like your real power too. Joining the wilde hunt was the destiny of their death. What happens after we die? Are we just gone? Is there an afterlife? Do we become part of the cycle of death and rebirth like Ydum's plants? That would be a part of our destiny, a very different part of destiny than the Fates make while we are alive. A part of destiny that wouldn't necessarily be controlled by the Fates but by Death."

Ydum seems to get excited about this idea, the anger seeping from his stance some. "That would explain your deep connection to the emotions Jinx uses really well through her magic. Your real power could be being the Fate of death. Will it be the peace of a long life well lived? The sadness of a death too soon? The happiness of an end to suffering or the anger of a violent death? All four emotions of the Fates come together in the destiny of death."

"Oh, that makes sense." Byder says. "What about the bonds? How would the bonds be tied to the destiny of death?"

Anarus himself answers this time. "The only thing that ends a true mate bond would be death. If my power is the Fate of death, I could be responsible for ending those bonds, letting the living let go of their dead and the bond mate with them."

"That would make you feel the bonds so much more than the rest of us." I add. "Not just the emotional connection of dealing with destiny, but you also actually hold the bonds in your hands. The living Fates make them, but then would give them to you to hold and protect until the time comes to end them. That's how you knew about our bonds before they happened, but just thought it was you desiring those tattoos. They were important to you because of the bonds you held of your own, but didn't know you held. Because you don't have your mantle, it might be only your own bonds you actually hold right now. After you get your mantle, you might hold all of them, all of them everywhere."

Ydum nods and starts pacing. I can tell he's almost moving towards another thought bender. "Honestly, we may be overcomplicating your power too, saying the Fate of death. It may be as simple as the destiny of the death of a true bond.

You are the keeper and protector of the bonds until the time comes to let death end them. Or only one of the Fates of death where you are only one of the emotions like the living Fates are. The destiny of the hate of a violent death, or something. Exactly how it works is so hard to tell with the wilde hunt in the way."

"We have to be even more careful about Jinx now." Byder cuts him off, stopping Ydum's pacing. "She won't be feeding through three gods' powers in the tenth game, but four. Mine, yours, Ydum, and the two Anarus carries which could be volatile and fight each other."

"Shit." Ydum swears as he plops back down on the couch. "Only one in ten survive duo gods. I thought three was bad enough, but now it's four and one of them isn't supposed to be there? Shit."

"And the wilde hunt will be open." Byder adds, then swears too. "Fuck. This just keeps getting worse and worse."

I see and feel the concern in Anarus. He's starting to feel like he's too much, too wrong, that he's a problem again. "Okay, so we know there are issues to solve. A lot of them for all of us. But we know now. We know that Byder's power wants too much death, and I have to calm that down. We know that Ydum's power wants too much life and to be everything all the time and I have to keep them in their proper order. We know that Anarus has two powers, his own and the wilde hunt that's not his, and those two may fight or struggle. And we know that I can only somewhat protect myself as long as you three make the barrier for me first without making it too thick or too thin. Now, we know all the problems and we can work on how to solve them. But not right now. I'm exhausted and Anarus is struggling with a bunch of new and confusing information that means he doesn't feel so happy about himself."

"Man," Ydum shakes his head, and drapes his arm over the back of the couch behind Anarus, "how can you not feel awesome right now? You have held onto two powers at once for twenty-two years and never killed anyone. That's some fucking amazing strength. You literally hold our bonds in your heart. You are a fierce protector."

"And the center of us." Byder moves to sit on the other side of me to drape his arm over the back of the couch like Ydum, making their arms wrap around both me and Anarus. "We thought the human was supposed to be the center of our bond, but it literally is you, Anarus. All our bonds run through you, not Jinx."

"I didn't think about it like that." Anarus murmurs.

Ydum hangs his hand down to squeeze Anarus's shoulder. "Well, start. Because it's true. You're the strongest of us, and I am literally a force of nature."

"Say literally one more time. I don't think that means what you think it means." Anarus grumbles, making both Byder and Ydum laugh.

"Are we done being all emotional again?" I ask. "Can we do something silly and dumb, like play sock ball?"

"Oh ho ho, no." Ydum stands, a finger in the air. "I know you're tired but the there's one more thing I want to try before we call the magic portion of the day over."

I groan as I look at Ydum. "What?"

Ydum stands and wiggles his fingers at me in a come hither gesture, with a sly smile. "Come on. You two too."

I get up and follow Ydum as he leads us all into the washroom.

"Are we back to hanging out in here again?" Byder asks sarcastically and hops up to sit on the sink counter.

"There's something I've been interested to experiment with since Jinx talked to Damek." Ydum puts his hands in his pockets as he talks. "He said with your magic like it is, stronger now, and with our bonds deeper, you shouldn't need as much water to make it rain. I want you to try."

Ydum goes to the sink and turns it on. He takes the small cup we keep next to the sink and fills it up, then shuts off the water. He holds the cup out to me, saying, "Make it rain, Jinx."

I look at him, then past him to Anarus leaning on the washroom wall, who only shrugs. I look at Byder, who tilts his head to the side, smiling. Then back at Ydum with his shit-eating grin of thinking he knows something we don't.

"Ugh." I snatch the cup from him and sigh, rolling my eyes. "We have to do this now?"

Ydum only nods and joins Anarus leaning against the wall.

Anarus leans over to him and asks, "Which one of us is the asshole? She said she was exhausted."

Ydum laughs slightly. "Which means it's the perfect time to test her control. Where she was eight weeks ago versus now."

I close my eyes and try to take a deep, cleansing breath but all I feel is annoyance at Ydum and his experiments. I grumble and try again. I need to control my emotions. Peace to try Ydum's dumb experiment. I feel the peace move over me, and take another deep breath. More centered, I focus on the water in the cup. I pour some into my cupped hand. I need more water. I need enough water to make it rain. I need it to rain in the washroom. Blindly, I hold the cup of water out and Byder, I think, takes it from me. I cup my hands together and let the water move between them. I feel it in my hands, gathering and stirring.

Rain. Make it rain. Make more water and make it rain. I need to borrow Ydum's power over the seasons and weather and make a whole fucking spring storm right here in the washroom. Something rumbles and I feel rain falling. Not like when I did this for the second game, where it was fat drops that felt more like condensation, or when I actually made it rain for a moment, that first real rain. This is a true spring storm with cool rain coming down in sheets, soaking our clothes, thunder rolling, warm winds blowing through, making the sheets of rain go sideways for a moment before the wind swirls away again.

I open my eyes and hold up my hands. I know I'm grinning like an idiot. "It's fucking raining!"

"You're making it rain, Jinx!" Ydum yells back, excitedly. "Now, make it stop."

I look up at the ceiling. Stop now. You can stop now. The rain continues for a moment, but starts to relent. Slowly, the storm wears itself out and the rain stops. The floor is covered in water everywhere. Most of it is slowly swirling down the drain in the shower and Byder is kicking the water, pushing it through the shower door towards the drain, laughing.

Suddenly, Ydum is standing right in front of me, pushing my hair that is plastered to my face out of my eyes. "Look at our fucking amazing, powerful witch. Just look at how fucking perfectly beautiful she is."

Anarus comes closer, behind Ydum. "She is fucking perfect."

Byder is behind me, his lips right by my ear. "You made it rain, Jinx. You did that, all by yourself."

I can feel it, through the bonds, their pride, their need, their desire. All three of them, standing here, dripping wet, our clothes and hair plastered to us. I can tell Ydum's desire even without the bond. The heat in his eyes sends a shiver down me, lighting me up. The lines of his body, perfectly outlined by the sticking clothes showing me his taut, lean muscles and hardening length. I match their desire and send it back, an answer to their question.

"Shit, beautiful." Ydum's body presses against mine as he captures my mouth, kissing me, sucking my lip into his mouth and biting gently. When I moan, he takes advantage of the opening and traces my mouth with his tongue. Then, he pulls back, lets me go and takes my hand in his.

When Ydum steps to the side, my hand still in his, Anarus moves closer. He reaches behind me, pulling my braid over my shoulder, playing with the end of it. "Her neck good, Byder?"

Byder kisses the back of my neck, sending more shivers down my spine. "Her neck is fucking beautiful." Byder rests his hands on my hips and continues kissing up and down my neck.

Anarus grumbles appreciatively when a small moan passes over my lips. "Little human, you know how we all like those noises you make." He kisses my lips, then up my jaw to my ear and I wrap my one free arm around him.

Ydum is touching my palm, tracing designs on my hand with his fingers. He lifts my hand to his mouth and kisses one of my fingers. When he puts it in his mouth and sucks on it, the feeling shoots straight through me to burn between my thighs, as if his tongue had been there instead. He bites down gently and I arch my back and moan from the intensity of the feeling flying through me.

"You think we could make her come just like this?" Ydum asks, his voice deep and a little breathless. He licks between my first two fingers and I shoot up to my tiptoes, gasping.

Anarus chuckles. "It would be fun to try."

"Mm, challenge accepted." Byder rumbles into my neck, then licks me slowly from the collar of my shirt to my hair line.

"Fuck." I stammer out. "Oh, my gods."

"That's right. We are your gods and we will worship your body as the god you should be." Anarus claims my lips and everything is pleasure. His lips moving back and forth between crushing against mine, sucking and biting, his tongue tracing the inside of my mouth and running up my jaw to my ear. Byder's hands on my hips, flexing and squeezing me, his lips against the back of my neck, trailing kisses and his warm breath teasing my hair. Ydum lavishes my fingers the way I know he can between my legs.

I am boneless and only still standing because the three of them are holding me up. My nerves are sparking and wetness gathers in my center, an overpowering need for touch, friction, anything there, driving me to writhe as I moan.

"Fuck, please." I breathlessly plead with them. "Oh, please." I dig the nails of my one hand into Anarus's back and my other hand tries to curl up to squeeze Ydum's but he doesn't let it, bent on licking every inch of it. My toes curl inside my boots.

Ydum trails his kisses up my arm. When he licks the inside of my elbow, I lose control.

"Fuck! Please. I need something, anything. Please." I pant, unable to catch my breath.

Byder groans. "I want to lose the challenge."

"Fuck it." Anarus drops his hand to the edge of my shirt, hauling it up roughly before lowering his head to take my breast in his hand and cover it with his mouth, sucking my nipple hard, biting and flicking it with his tongue.

At the same moment, Byder pushes his hand down the back of my pants and reaches his hand between my legs to shove his finger inside me. I cry out, rocking my hips back against his hand and break completely. The waves of the orgasm rush over me quickly and leave me only wanting more.

"Fuck, I barely touched her." Byder stammers out, his breath hitching. "She's so fucking tight against me, I can barely move my finger."

My mind's focus narrows down on only Byder's hand and I have desire coursing through me again. Without meaning to I groan. "Byder."

Anarus lifts his head and whispers against my ear. "You want Byder, little human?"

A sudden desire for Byder fills me. I lick my lips, unsure what to do. I love all of them. But, right now...

"Tell us what you need, beautiful." Ydum says softly. "You can tell us what you want. No one will be mad or feel left out. If you want Byder all to yourself right now, and that's what he wants too, then that's okay. You just gotta tell us."

I look at Anarus, worry clouding me. I'm choosing. They're saying I can choose, but I don't want any of them to be hurt or feel rejected.

He only chuckles. "You fucking love me, little human. I know that." He pulls down my shirt and give me a swift, soft kiss. "Go take care of Byder."

When Anarus steps back, Ydum takes his place. His kiss is also quick but hard. "I love you, beautiful and I have no doubts you love me." His eyes flick up over my shoulder. "And I love you, handsome." Their two heads meet over my shoulder for a kiss. Ydum lets go of both of us and for all the world looks like he casually strolls out of the washroom. Anarus follows behind him, and Byder and I are alone.

Even though I made this choice, I suddenly feel more nervous than I ever have with him. As if he senses my nerves, Byder steps away from me.

"You good, baby girl?" He asks, leaning back against the sink counter.

"I, um," I sigh, trying to find the words, "every time we've been together, it's been rushed and sudden and almost always with someone else."

Byder chuckles. "Like a succubus."

I smile. "Yeah. I just am feeling a little," I groan, the words not working for me.

Byder comes back over to me, wrapping his arms around my waist and leaning back to still look at me. "Do you want me, baby girl?"

"Yes."

"Do you want either of them to come back?"

"No."

"Okay, then." Byder kisses me softly. "Do you want to get out of the wet washroom?"

I relax. "Yes, please."

Byder takes my hand in his and leads me out of the washroom and into the bedroom. On the way, I chance a glance in the sitting room and see Anarus and Ydum playing the hand slapping game, like they are completely unfazed and comfortable. They really are okay with this.

In the bedroom, Byder stops to stand in the middle of the room. "You said it was unfair that you always ended up naked and we all always kept on our clothes. So, baby girl, strip me."

My mouth falls open in surprise. "You want me to…"

He takes one step towards me. "Do I need to tell you twice?" His voice is deeper than I've ever heard it. My mouth goes dry and all the feelings that went away from my nerves start churning back. I didn't think I would be someone who likes commands, but damn if it isn't sexy from Byder.

I bring my body right against him, kissing him as my hands pull on the hem of his pelt shirt. I slide my hands inside it, sliding them up over the skin of his chest, making his shirt pull up as I brush my fingertips over every muscle and ridge. He raises his arms as I do until the shirt is bunched at his shoulders, then he reaches behind his back and pulls the shirt over his head and drops it on the floor.

I've seen Byder's chest before. Of course. All three of them walk around shirtless all the time. But I never noticed the small trail of hair that runs from his lower stomach down into his pants. And it dawns on me, for everything we've done, I've never seen Byder completely naked. I run my fingers over that trail of hair until I reach the ties for his pants.

Byder sucks in air and I look up at him. His eyes are dark and fixed on me. I undo the ties and push down on both his pants and underwear, following them down until I am almost crouching in front of him. The leather of them sticks to his legs, making me have to almost peel them off of him. But, when I get down to his feet, I look down in confusion. Why aren't they coming off all the way?

Byder bites back a laugh. "Boots, Jinx."

I sit on my bottom, cover my face with my hand, blushing and embarrassed. For fuck's sake, why am I so skittish and self-conscious? It's Byder. But Byder doesn't say anything, only moves to sit on the edge of the bed and remove his boots and socks. His pants and underwear practically fall off him with the boots out of the way, and I blush again.

"Come here, baby girl."

When I step between his legs and drop my hand on his shoulders, he puts his hands on my hips and looks up at me. Looking in his eyes, I forget to be embarrassed anymore. I look at all of him. His broad shoulders, strong arms, large, powerful thighs. He's beautiful. I lean down and kiss him. Pulling out the hair tie, I run my fingers through his long, damp hair to untangle his bun.

When I pull back, there's a look in Byder's eyes that makes me want to bury myself in his soul. I would do anything for him. Everything. Even the things that scare me. Because he's looking at me like I am the most precious thing he has ever seen, and I know he feels exactly the same as me.

I push on his chest lightly, and he leans back on the bed, sliding up slightly so that his legs are also on the bed and I can join him on it, kneeling between his legs. I lean forward and grab his wrists in my hands.

He doesn't pull away from me, only looks curious. I pull his hands up above his head. "Don't move." Then, I start kissing a line down his chest.

Byder figures out what I'm going to do quickly. He brings his hands down, grabbing me gently by the arms. "Jinx, you don't have to do anything."

"I know I don't. But I want to try. For you." I take his wrists in mine and push them above his head again. "Don't move."

"I'm not moving, baby girl."

Tentatively, I move back down Byder's body, trailing my fingers over his skin until I reach that small line of hair. My eyes follow it to his cock, hard against his stomach. I run one finger down it from the head to the base and he lets out a small stuttering breath. Wrapping my hand around the base, I notice how silky his skin feels and lean over to lick the tip.

"Fuck, Jinx."

I glance up and Byder is watching me, his hands above his head, clenched in fists. He looks like he's fighting with himself to stay perfectly still. I know he will. His eyes say the words. I'm in control. I'm not panicking. Nerves, yes, but panic, no. He wants nothing I don't give him freely.

With a surge of confidence, I wrap my lips around the tip of his cock and slide my mouth down its length. Byder's groan of pleasure urges me on and I move, letting my tongue twirl around him as I take his length deep into my mouth over and over. Byder groans again and I feel him tense his hips as he tries to fight the desire to push deeper into my mouth.

I keep moving, stroking him with my lips and tongue, glancing up occasionally to see his eyes still watching me, riveted as he bites his lip so hard, I bet it's bleeding. I make myself take him in deeper and he brushes the back of my throat. I gag slightly, and, even though Byder groans in pleasure, I move away. The niggle in my gut tells me there's a panic that wants to start forming. I don't want to taint this moment, so I stop, moving away from him, knowing that I have done more than my past fears would ever let me.

As I sit back up, I feel a small sense of pride, like I took a piece of myself back.

Byder sits up, his arms coming around me. "You are a wonder of strength and beauty, baby girl." He kisses me softly, a kiss of tender love. "But you are far too dressed in very wet clothing."

I let out a small laugh and step off the bed to strip myself quickly while Byder watches. Once I am completely naked, he stands and pulls out my hair tie, using his hands to comb through my hair until it's hanging loose around me.

"Now it's my turn to tell you what to do." He says. In a deep, demanding voice that belies kind words he's saying, he asks me, "Do you have issues with choking, breath play?"

My eyes goes wide but I shake my head no. "Never done it before."

"No one hurt you that way?" The gentleness of his question feels at odds with the absolute desire for dominance I hear in him.

"No." When he cocks an eyebrow at me, I amend my answer. "Well, Jacob sat on my chest as other people hurt me, and now when I panic, I feel like I can't breathe. But that's not the same. Not being able to breathe doesn't make me panic, panicking makes me not able to breathe. Does that make sense?"

He nods, but furrows his brow. "It's more of a triggered feeling rather than a memory. But no one actually choked you? Held you down by your throat? Anything like that?"

I shake my head.

He groans, his hands lifting me onto the bed. "You will say the moment any panic starts. You will say if you don't like it. You will say if you get scared or it hurts or is too much. If you can't speak, you will tap twice on any part of me you can reach. No thoughts of I can do this for a little longer, or I want to for him. You even think of wanting to stop, you say stop. Do you understand?"

Something in me turns molten at Byder like this. Demanding, controlling. In charge. Powerful. Somehow, I feel like I can trust him more like this. Like I know he could force his control over everything, but is making sure I know that all the control is really mine. I nod. "Yes."

Byder speaks through gritted teeth. "Say it."

I don't take my eyes off his. "I will tell you if I start panicking, don't like it, get scared, or it hurts. If I can't speak, I tap you twice."

"What's the safe word?"

I glance at Byder, confused, then remember what he's talking about. "Butterfly."

"Good girl." Before I can think, he has me stretched out on the bed, and is hovering over me. One of his hands grazes my breast, softly stroking the skin around my nipple. He takes the nipple into his mouth, tenderly licking it. Then, he bites down, harder than I expected, making me gasp. He repeats the same process with my other breast, and when he bites this time, I moan. Reaching a hand between us and he rubs along my clit, using all of his fingers to rub in quick circles. I'm lost in the rising pleasure so I don't expect it when the soft touch is suddenly a sharp smack. I cry out against the pain, but before I can do much more, his hand is rubbing again, the pleasure mingling with the sting of pain, and every hot desire in me doubles.

"Oh, fuck." I moan out.

He keeps moving his hand in those circles, then again, I feel the sharp, biting pain of a smack on my clit quickly replaced with absolutely torturous pleasure that leaves me writhing. Byder captures one of my nipples in his mouth again, softly sucking and kissing it. Then, without warning, his hand moves from between my legs to flick the nipple as soon as it is out of his mouth. Again, I am surprised by how the line between pain and pleasure blurs as he immediately soothes the nipple with soft kissing.

He gives the same treatment to the other nipple. My body doesn't know how to react as he moves around on it, touching me softly with his mouth or hands or both, only to replace it with the sting of a slap or pinch, then soothe it again with soft touches. The anticipation of trying to predict where he will move next, whether it will be a soft or rough touch, drives my desire higher and fills me with an inexplicable ecstasy.

———

"Do not close your eyes, Jinx." Byder commands. "Look right at me. Two taps."

I nod, and Byder lines himself up to my opening and plunges deep in me. My stinging and sensitive skin explodes in a rush as his body against mine rubs at each spot. I cry out as he begins to move inside me.

His hand slowly crawls up to rest on my throat. His fingers twitch as he finds the perfect spots to rest them as he sets a pace inside me that isn't rushed or hurried but isn't slow and languorous either. I keep my eyes open and on him as I feel the orgasm building.

"Don't come yet, baby girl." He growls. His fingers on my throat tighten almost imperceptibly and he watches my face for my reaction. I move my hips against him, changing his angle so that he reaches deeper, finding the spot that makes me cry out again.

"Fuck." Byder's hand tightens completely and I try to inhale but fail to pull anything past his hand. I don't panic. Instead, I just want more. I reach my hands around his back, grasping at his ass and pulling him tighter to me, my nails digging in.

Byder's eyes go wide for a fraction of a second, then darken again. "You fucking like this, don't you? Don't come. Don't you dare come until I tell you to."

I fight my body that wants to rip open and pour pleasure through me. I moan soundlessly and feel the edges blur. I dig my nails in deeper as he increases his pace. Oh fuck. Oh fuck. I need to come.

He keeps his eyes on me the whole time and. somehow, I feel such a closeness to him. I'm in control. Byder may be being demanding, he may sound like he is the one in control, but I know it is really me. No matter what he does, two taps from me stops it all. He trusts me to know my own limits and I trust him to listen when I say I'm at that limit.

I fight the need to close my eyes. I writhe as every ounce of me is filled with sparking heat. My muscles tense and I fight the need to let that pleasure have control. Stars dance in my eyes as my body writhes beneath his, fighting for air while he mixes pleasure and pain in a dance. Slamming into that spot deep inside me that throws me over the cliff over and over, while denying me the ability to fall. Stroking my cheek gently then pinching my clit.

Right when I feel like I can take no more, my body overwhelmed by too many sensations, Byder lets go of my throat and says, "Now, baby girl. Shatter around me." And my body complies, the orgasm crashing through me.

"Byder!" I shout his name over and over as the pleasure wracking through my entire body makes every muscle spasm and my walls clench around him tighter than I've ever felt before. It goes on and on until I'm almost crying with pleasure.

"Mine." He groans as I feel him push so deep inside me I feel him in my soul, his release overtaking him just as much as he heaves for breath. "You are mine."

As he hovers above me, he opens his mouth to say something but is interrupted by a shout from the sitting room.

"Fuck!" Anarus cries out and it's evident that he's reacting to the feelings through the bond because at the same time, Ydum drawls out a "Shit!"

Byder and I look at each other and immediately both bite back a laugh. He pulls out of me and moves to my side. Once the shakes of laughter, and a powerful orgasm only barely contained, subside, he runs a finger up and down the column of my neck.

"You okay, baby girl?" His voice is the soft tenderness I have always heard again.

I nod at him and capture his hand in mine, kissing his fingers. "I'm fucking fantastic."

Byder smiles, a whole smile that lights up his eyes. "You did that so well."

"Well, I just had to sit back and not breath. Wasn't that hard, honestly." I tease him.

Byder grasps my chin in his hand. "That's not what I meant. I know how scared you were, how nervous to take me in your mouth you were. You didn't have to, Jinx. If you never did that, I would be perfectly happy."

I sigh and snuggle into him. "It felt like taking a piece of me back. They don't get to own me anymore. My body is mine and I get to decide what to do with it. I decide what feels good and what doesn't, what I want to do and what I don't. I won't let fear of people who can't touch me again control me. I have three amazing gods to keep me safe and in a little less than two weeks, all four of us will be more powerful than anyone in my village could dream of being. I will be more powerful than the High Priest and his son could ever dream of being."

Byder shakes his head. "No. You already are more powerful than they could ever dream of being. All on your own."

A voice comes from the sitting room again. Ydum calls out to us through the door. "So, are you two going to want dinner, or did Byder already eat?"

I roll my eyes, not able to stop the laughter this time. "Oh. My. Gods."

For the next three days, we carefully spend time working on having me look at each of their powers, while gauging exactly how thick to make the gauzy protection. We start with still doing it one at a time, but work our way up to me tapping into two of them at once. My hands are red after and, when I do both Byder and Ydum together for the first time, there are actual blisters on my palms.

The rest of the days, we spend thinking on how to protect me better. Or doing nothing in particular, our favorite pastime. Our conversations start to move from being mostly about our lives before these games to our lives after. Ydum and Byder have long discussions about whether we should start our post-games lives with Ydum's family or Byder's and I find myself completely intrigued, listening as the thought of there actually being an after tries to make sense in my mind.

Nine weeks ago, only nine weeks ago, I thought I knew exactly what my life would be like. I would take a little blood test on my twenty-fourth birthday, leave the testing center and start looking for some type of work. I had thought about working at the school in the High Priest's basement. Or maybe going to work with my sister Orphelia at the bakery. Either way, I knew I would probably stay living with my parents for a long time, maybe forever and be the one to take care of them in their old age. It would be a quiet life, I knew, never leaving my village, never actually meeting all those gods we talked about ruling our lives.

But ten finger pricks and those ideas were gone in a flash. I went from my soft boring life to only focusing on survival from one week to the next. How do I survive the only question that really matters. How do we survive. But now, we're leaving even those ideas about life behind and moving on to where do we go from here? What our life will be is such an unknown because there has never been a trio of gods before.

There's so much we want to do, taking on the original gods, fixing the broken systems, but also Ydum wants to take me to the forests outside Veirveil and show me the flowers there. Byder's planning hunting trips with his dad in his mind and can't wait to serve us all his famous venison stew. Anarus is even having thoughts about the future. He's asked questions like when we get our own home, do we each want our own room or just one big one for the four of us?

Those dreams I had before the games are gone completely. And I can't say I regret letting them go. I have three gods now who love me more intensely than I ever thought love could be, and I love them back just as fiercely.

On the day before the ninth game, we all decide to not practice me seeing their powers. We want to stay up late and wait until midnight and have me look at Anarus's power at the moment the bridge between the living and dead is said to appear.

Dinner is an interesting affair. Instead of the normal fare of tacos, or spaghetti, or something else trivial and juvenile, the games serve us roasted venison, cranberries, apples and honey, freshly baked bread, milk and mead. My gods are confused at the sudden change in the quality of the food, but prepare to dig in before I stop them.

"I think there's a point to this feast." I say, looking over the spread. "Anarus, you said that at one time, humans used to leave offerings for the wilde hunt. What were they offerings of?"

Anarus takes a second look at the table heavy with food. "Huh. Would not have noticed that, Jinx. Winter berries, bread with apples and honey, and anything representative of a hunter. Usually milk or mead to drink, as well as incense that represents winter, and any personal offerings that someone might feel connected to. They would leave them in a liminal space, someplace that's a crossing, a place where people meet and pass by each other. A crossroads, the center of a marketplace, a threshold of a public building, or their own home if nowhere else is available."

"Someplace like where the hallway meets the foyer?" I ask him.

Anarus nods, "Exactly like that."

I collect one of the plates from our sock ball game and hold it up. "Something personal from the four of us. Offerings are always taken first from the meal, the first and the best." I start gathering food onto the plate. A slice of bread I break into four pieces, four apple slices dipped in the honey, four small scoops of the cranberry, and two slices of venison roast, each one cut in two.

Byder catches on quickly and pours two cups, one of milk and one of mead. Ydum, only one step behind, steps into the bedroom and comes back out with a hazelwood stick and the matches from my witch's kit.

Anarus frowns, pondering something.

"What are you thinking, Anarus?" I ask gently.

Anarus doesn't answer me, but instead asks Byder. "Can you grab one of your knives?"

Byder only responds by raising an eyebrow but goes to get one anyway. When he hands it to him, Anarus just tucks it into the waist of his pants. We all look at him curiously but say nothing.

The four of us leave the room and go to the intersection where the hallway meets the foyer. I set down the plate. Behind me, I hear doors opening, but I ignore it. Following my intuition, I say, "For the wilde hunt. May your ride be peaceful and lead back to a quiet rest."

Byder sets down the two cups. "For the wilde hunt. May you feel the power of the hunt in your veins and remember the joy of finding a willing prey."

Ydum kneels next to the plate and arranges the hazelwood so that the ash will fall onto the plate. He lights it and, as the fire on the tip flares, he says, "For the wilde hunt. May you feel the crisp wind and the cool swirl of the snow as you ride." He blows on the hazelwood and the fire goes out, only leaving an ember inside it and a slow trail of smoke rising.

Damek comes up behind us, looking over our shoulders at the plate and cups. Quietly he asks, "There's a lot of power moving in the air right now. What are we doing?"

I glance up at him. "Offering to the wilde hunt. It's October thirty-first."

"Is it already?" Damek moves away, but returns in only a second. He and Iella both step around us, each placing a small bronze coin on the plate.

"For the wilde hunt." Damek says.

"May luck be on your side as you ride." Iella completes for them.

They step back and Isis and Esnir come forward, each placing one arrow in front of each of the cups.

"For the wilde hunt." Esnir whispers. "May your weapons always be sharp and your aim true, guided to the enemies of your eternal peace."

When Kutar and Wren replace Isis and Esnir in front of the offering, Kutar balls up his hands, then opens them again, handing something to Wren. When they each add one to each cup, I see they are tiny snow balls.

Wren speaks as they drop them in the milk and mead. "For the wilde hunt. May the storms that swirl around you calm the storms in your heart."

Uesis takes a deep breath and speaks quietly. "I have nothing physical to give, but I can offer a song to the wilde hunt, that you may carry it with you as you ride, remembering with joy the days when you lived and the music remind those who love you of the good memories." As we all listen, Uesis holds Raven's hand and sings a haunting wordless tune that brings the thought of howling winter winds racing through the boughs of ice-laden trees to my mind.

When he finishes singing, Anarus kneels in front of the offering. He takes the knife from his waistband and cuts his fingertip, letting his blood drip onto the plate. "For the wilde hunt. May you travel the bridge well and find your proper course through the lands of the living, harming none but sharing your power with winter and her grip over the land. May you find your way back again when the sun returns and allow winter to release itself into spring at the proper time."

The twelve of us stand there for a few more moments, the power of our combined offerings blending in the air with the smoke from the hazelwood. The air is heavy with magic in a way I've never felt before. Not even in Granny Helen's hut. Slowly, silently, the other teams turn back to their rooms until we are the only ones left in the hallway again.

Finally, Anarus breaks the silence. "We'll come back out here at midnight to look at my power. This offering belongs to the shadows held in the well over my heart. They should be near enough to take it."

"I'll let the other teams know." Ydum says quietly. "Just in case. I'll tell them we will be doing an experiment with your power and to stay in their rooms, even if it gets darker for a bit. Everyone is prepping for games nine and ten, they'll understand."

We eat our dinner quietly after Ydum returns from talking with the other four teams. "They all said they understood."

Somehow, I think there is more Ydum wants to say, but he keeps glancing at Anarus as we eat.

"Just say it." Anarus finally says. "Whatever it is, just say it, Ydum."

"Esnir asked straight out if we think you are the god of the wilde hunt. With what he already knew, I figured I should be honest and said yes." Ydum looks at the floor, glancing up occasionally to gauge Anarus's reaction to what he is saying. "Esnir only nodded at this, saying he had thought already that you might be the child of Death since he felt a connection with you as a god of war, who also has close ties to death. He made the same guess we did, that your mother is Winter just because of the timing and the connection between death and winter. He actually laughed, saying can't wait to see the look on Winter's face when she realizes her son survived the games."

We all sit silently for a moment, letting Anarus take it all in.

"Are you mad I was honest?" Ydum is still hanging his head, ready to feel ashamed if Anarus didn't want this shared.

Anarus just lets out a shuddering sigh. "No. Esnir was halfway there when he came to look at your finger. It would have been worse if you tried to lie. He'll keep our secret."

Just before midnight, all four of us go sit together in the foyer, close to the hallway but not directly next to it. Byder and Ydum will keep a close eye on this since we're not sure what'll happen when the bridge between the living and dead opens.

As Anarus and I sit facing each other, I take his hand in mine. "Anarus, remember, no matter what happens, you are loved. You are precious to me, to Byder, and to Ydum. Whatever your power is, we love you and accept you just as you are. You do not scare us nor will we cringe away from your power unbridled. You are our heart and the keeper of our bonds. We trust you. We love you. Always."

Anarus takes a deep breath and squeezes my hand. We both close our eyes and take slow, cleansing breaths. I can still smell the hazelwood smoke lingering in the air. I know when Anarus has the gauze in place. He has become adept at making it as thick as possible without making it impossible for me to see through. I touch that barrier and ask it to spread, shielding my eyes and my hands as I look at Anarus's power.

When I have it fixed in place, I open my eyes and look at him. I need to see Anarus's power. Stay where you belong, but let me see you. Instantly, I can see the well of darkness over his heart. I reach up my free hand and touch his chest, right over his heart, right over the well. I know the moment it hits midnight because the covering over the well cracks open and shadows fly out of it. The white and blue cold fire shoots around the shadows and a strong gold light emanates from behind the well.

Without letting go of Anarus, I look around the room. His shadows, the shadows of the souls of the wilde hunt, spin and fly around the foyer. Several of them descend on the offering plate and I see a white and blue fire flare across it.

Turning my attention back to Anarus, the well that felt so heavy and overfull feels lighter. Just a tiny bit, the covering barely cracked open, but enough. I push it to the side to see Anarus's heart. It shines pure gold and, when I touch it, an image flares in my mind.

The white of the snow covering everything is blindingly bright, but I can make out a bridge over a frozen river in front of me. Somehow, I had always thought the bridge between life and death would be a sturdy thing, made out of stone, over a raging river. Instead, the river is really no more than a tiny stream and the rickety wood and rope bridge is so narrow that Anarus can stand over it, one foot in the realm of the living and another in the land of the dead. He has one hand on the rope railing in front of him and one hand on the one behind him. He's holding their frayed pieces together in the lightest touch.

Strands of gold, destinies and bonds, run through him, anchored into his heart in his chest. I look past him into the land of the dead and see some of the gold strands separate and run in different directions.

On the side of the land of the living, all the strands braid together as they travel back. I follow their path through the trees with my eyes and see two males and two females weaving the strands together as they make them from their fingers. They look shadowy and I can't make out their details, but I know they are the four Fates. As I watch, the Fates start a new strand of gold that slowly creeps forward to braid into the others and join them anchored at Anarus's heart. The new strand stays there, in his heart, going no further.

A young male I don't know walks through the snow and crosses the bridge. His form passes straight over Anarus's. The male's form just seems to shimmer as he moves over the bridge, his body becoming noncorporeal as it touches Anarus and steps off the bridge into the land of the dead. When the male is solidly on the other side of the bridge, in the land of the dead, a shadowy figure appears.

"Do you wish to sever your bonds?" The shadowy form asks.

The male nods his head, yes, and the shadowy form plucks at one tiny gold strand where it connects to Anarus's heart. With that touch, the gold strand breaks and its light goes out, trailing back from Anarus's heart and to the four living Fates. The shadowy form takes the hand of the male and, as they vanish together, the vision disappears and I see the well has shifted back over Anarus's heart.

I let go of Anarus's hand and drop the gauze protection. I take his face in my hands. "You beautiful, beautiful man."

Shadows are swirling around Anarus, agitated, but it isn't his emotions making them so, but the opening of the bridge. He stares back at me, his face clear of shadows and full of awe. "What was that?"

I smile at him. "You are the bridge between life and death, Anarus. One foot in the land of the living, one in the land of the dead, you anchor all the bonds, mated ones and destiny, that the four living Fates weave. Your heart holds them, as your hands hold the fraying bridge together, so that the dead can cross it safely and your father, Death, can end the bonds if the dying soul desires him to. You are the bridge, Anarus."

"Woah." Byder whispers next to us. "That's... amazing."

"If he's already holding the bridge together," Ydum asks, "what do you think his full mantle will be?"

"Right now, it looks like the dead don't even really notice him there." I say. "It's like the dead just walk right through him. Or really, they become not solid and he's still solid so they move over him as they walk across the bridge. I would think he takes control of it. Can decide to send someone back to the land of the living or let them through to the land of the dead. Maybe he takes over deciding if the bonds of a dead soul are cut or asking them if they want them cut and then cutting them for the dead if they answer yes."

As if he just thought about it, Anarus grabs my hands that were still holding his cheeks and looks at them. The hand that held his is red, as it always has been, and the hand that I touched his chest with is red on the fingertips that moved the well out of the way.

"They don't hurt at all." I tell him.

Ydum brings us back to ourselves. "We need to sleep. We have a game tomorrow and it's already very late." We all agree and stand up to go back to our room. As we move into the hallway, Ydum takes a second to collect the empty plate and cups from our offerings.

I look at the empty dishes then at Anarus.

He only shrugs. "They liked it, even Uesis's song."

Byder chuckles. "In the words of Damek, so fucking cool."

Chapter Nine

IN THE MORNING, AS we move into the foyer, I notice the paintings that everyone basically forgot about are still blank. As we stand against the back wall of the foyer, Esnir comes over and quietly asks, "How was your experiment?"

"The wilde hunt appreciated our offering. It's been a while since they got one." Anarus tells him and Esnir only gives a grin and shakes his head.

Drila starts talking as soon as she pops into the foyer. She seems to have more anxiety, as if the closer we get to the end of the games, the more that she feels the intensity of it all. As a goddess of games and trials, she would. Her gold dress shimmers almost as much as the bonds did in Anarus.

"The ninth game is creation. As you may have noticed, the paintings are empty. This is because you will have to fill them. Each team, as a full unit, will have to create something. This means that the one thing created, and it may only be one thing, must have the essence of the power of the god and the magic of the witch, or all three gods in Jinx's case. When the object is successfully created, it will appear in the painting for your team.

"Your points will be awarded based on two factors. The first factor is the order in which you return to the foyer with a completed painting. The second factor will be an appraisal of that object and how it accurately represents the powers of the god or gods and the magic of the witch. This means it's possible for you to arrive back at the foyer first, gaining only five points, but have your painting judged to be not a good representation of your team and gain twenty-five points, for a total of thirty points all around. Does everyone understand this?"

We all nod and Drila tells us good luck, sending us on our way. In a blink, the four of us are standing in white. I look around and feel almost dizzy. Everything is so white and empty, I can't tell where the floor or walls or ceiling are. We're standing on something solid, but I'm afraid to move around for fear the solidness ends somewhere we can't see. I'm not even sure there are walls or a ceiling. There's no way to tell anything about distance or space here except when I look at one of my gods and see how far from me they are.

Ydum immediately is scratching his chin, thinking. "Okay, a god of the hunt, a god of nature, a god of the bridge between life and death, and a witch who specializes in emotion control through words. What can we all contribute to make?"

"Your pocket forest with my animals added to it might work." Byder offers.

Anarus shakes his head. "I don't think a pocket forest counts as one object."

"That's true," I say, "but one plant might. A plant would always be nature for Ydum."

"What about the hunt?" Byder asks.

I slump slightly. "And that's where my idea falls apart."

Ydum furrows his brow. "Maybe not. What if we made a carnivorous plant?"

Anarus, Byder, and I all look at each other. "How would that work?" I ask.

"Carnivorous plants attract insects to their leaves, or some sort of trap contained on them, and then use something to kill them, break them down, and extract something they can't get enough of from the soil and sunlight." Ydum explains.

"A plant that hunts." Byder says, excitedly.

Anarus smiles. "And kills. Nitrogen. Plants need nitrogen and dead insects could be harvested for nitrogen in the plant instead of the dirt. And that's definitely life and death."

Byder hums. "More likely, the killing of the insect would be just considered death, which could be just part of the hunt power, my power. Do we think that would be enough to show Anarus?"

For some reason, all three gods look at me, making me startle. "Why are you asking me that?"

"You're the one who's looked at our powers." Anarus shrugs. "You know our ingredients better than we do."

Well... true. I think on what I saw last night. Anarus is the bridge between the land of the living and the land of the dead. Or controls the bridge. Something like that. He also holds the wilde hunt, with its shadows of old hunters and the cold fire. None of that feels specifically death-coded to me. Stuff around death, that death has a hand in, sure, but not death in and of itself.

"I don't know." I bite my lip. "I'm not sure his powers actually cause death themselves, just work with the dead."

Ydum holds up his hand, displaying his pinky. "But when you were harnessing his power before, you used something in him to kill my finger. There has to be death in there somewhere. The actual power of death."

"Could we trust that?" Anarus sounds very unsure. "Just say I can do death because somehow Jinx accidentally injured you with some random part of my power and that injury caused part of your body to die?"

None of us speak for a moment, all of us thinking about that. Finally, Byder just shrugs. "I think, if we know so little about how your powers actually work, what are the chances the original gods don't really know either? I mean, they call you an obscurity god when there is no such thing. Maybe they'll be just as confused and accept that, since you did a thing, it must be part of your power to do that thing."

Anarus looks at each of us. "And are you all willing to risk it? Risk this whole game on the original gods accepting they don't understand something and that part of what they don't understand is me somehow being able to control death when Death is banished and shouldn't have a child to have part of his powers?"

I walk over to him, wrapping my arms around him in a hug. "Anarus, is your real worry here about failing the game or the original gods figuring out that what your powers can do means your father is most likely Death?"

He bends down his head to rest it in the crook of my neck. "How do you always get to the heart of my worries that easily?"

"You're not as mysterious as you think you are." I chuckle, but get serious again quickly, pulling back to look at him. "Anarus, they are going to find out in one week either way. What real difference does it make if they find out now? Too many people know for them to act on it, do anything to you before then. Do you think Esnir would keep quiet if we said the original gods did something to you for who your father is, something you had no control over? Isis, who I'm sure he's talked to about it? Damek and Iella would support them and us too."

"Yeah." Ydum puts a reassuring hand on Anarus's shoulder. "The way I see it, either the original gods know all about your true power, which means they know you have one that isn't yours and will need to answer for allowing that, or they don't. If they know, they can't fail us in this game and maintain their innocence. If they don't know, they can't fail us because they don't know if you used your powers well or not. If you can make a way for a plant to kill insects, using a part of your power of death, then that is part of your power and making a plant that kills is a great representation of your power. If you can't do it, we think of something else for you to make the plant do."

Anarus sighs and steps back from the both of us. "If it sounds right to you, Ydum, then fine. We can do that."

I hum a little. "Well, that solves Anarus, but what about me?"

Ydum twists his mouth, thinking. "A carnivorous plant would need to create a calm environment in its trap so that the insects are willing to land there. Do you think you could think of a way to have them create that?"

"Well, what would attract an insect in the usual plants?" I ask him.

"Sweet nectar or pollen." Ydum thinks. "Or an availability to use the plant as a safe point to hide."

"You guys start. I'll think. I'm pretty sure I can come up with something." I tell them and watch as the three gods group close together.

Ydum twirls his hand for a moment, frowns, then immediately starts

155

growing random plants. "We need the base of soil, and, apparently, we can't call things here but have to make it from our powers. Of course." He keeps feeding power to the plants but is scowling. "Why won't they move through the natural seasons?"

"No death here yet." I say, absentmindedly.

Ydum laughs. "Shit, you're right. Anarus?"

"You want me to kill the plants you just made?" Anarus asks.

"Yes." Ydum nods. "Dirt is made from decaying material. We can't make decaying material if we don't have dead material. And we know you can because you killed the rosebud once before, so that at least is definitely in your power."

Anarus inclines his head thoughtfully. "True." He reaches out his hand, touching one of the plants. He has to think about it for a moment, but then, one by one, he touches each plant until they shrivel up and die, turning first brown then then crumbling to land on the white surface that seems like the floor. As Anarus kills each plant, Ydum makes another one. Slowly, a pile of dry dirt forms between them.

Ydum stops making plants and after Anarus kills the last one, he runs his fingers through the dirt. "Now to add moisture and everything else the plant will need besides the nitrogen." He closes his eyes and stirs the dirt with one finger.

"Now, for the plant itself. Jinx, I'll need your help here. I need the colors. It needs to look colorful, attractive to pollinators." Ydum holds out his hand to me and I take it. Holding my hand in one of his, he uses the other hand to keep swirling a finger through the dirt. Slowly a green shoot forms in the dirt, pushing itself upward. A small bulge forms on the top of the growing stem and tiny leaves come off the sides.

When Ydum decides the stem's tall enough and thick enough, he touches the bulge at the top of the plant. "Here's where the color comes in. Bright colors, purple, red, yellow, pink, blue all good attractants for pollinators. Pick one Jinx, and focus on the descriptions you gave me."

"Purple." I say at random while Ydum continues making the thick leaves at the top of the plant bloom open. "A mix of red and blue. The red of the string on your wrist, my protection bracelet, a warm winter's fire, anger, passion. The blue of the cool water, the sky on a cloudless day, peace, tranquility. Purple is soft like velvet, the sweet scent of lavender, richness, a mystery."

Under his touch, the two thick green leaves at the top of the plant turn deep purple in the middle where they connect to the stem. Ydum stands and lets go of my hand. "How's that?"

"Perfect." I tell him as he brushes his hands off on his pants.

"Byder." Ydum says. "You're up. Make the plant a hunter."

"Alright, here goes nothing." Byder kneels down in the dirt and cups the two thick purple and green leaves. Under his touch, tiny spines almost like teeth sprout from the edges of the leaves. "I'm giving it tiny hairs inside it that crave insects. When an insect is sitting on the leaves, the hairs will want to all wrap around the insect and will pull together like a trap. I'm making it have the understanding of what it needs from the insect, the nitrogen, to break it down, carve the meat from the insect to get that. Anarus, you'll have to give it whatever it needs to actually cause the insect to die, the weapon so to speak, because I don't think I can make it have an actual weapon."

Byder stands and moves out of the way as Anarus kneels and cups his hands around the plant. "Somebody got an idea how the plant would kill its prey?"

"Make the hairs sharp, cutting like knives?" I offer.

Anarus shakes his head. "That would kill the insect but it needs to also break down the insect so that it can get the nitrogen. Kind of cause the insect to decay faster than normal."

Ydum answers him. "A digestive enzyme. Like stomach acid."

"That might work." Anarus turns his focus back to the plant.

Nothing happens for a long while. Anarus pulls his hands away, bracing them on his knees. He doesn't say anything but just stares out into nothing. Byder, Ydum, and I stay quiet, letting him think. He replaces his hands, furrowing his brow and a small line of sweat forms on his temples.

Yet again, Anarus sits back, thinking and we wait. His eyes shift right and left, as if he's examining something in the vacuous space. Then he mumbles, "Huh. Could it be that simple?"

He shakes his head and wraps his hands around the plant for a third time. Soon, small tiny drops of a sickly smelling liquid form on the tiny hairs Byder made. The smell of death coming from the flower is less than appealing. He stands up, letting out a tired sigh, and places a hand on the small of my back. "There. You ready, little human?"

I nod and kneel next to the flower the way they did. I know that, with the smell of the death Anarus gave the plant, no insect would ever come close to it. It needs to smell sweet, enticing. I think those words, giving the plant the feelings of being attractive to an insect, being a safe place for them to land, its nectar that isn't actually nectar but Anarus's acid is a great dinner for bees, flies, butterflies, and other insects. I concentrate on these thoughts but the plant doesn't change. I still smell death on it.

"I need help. I need a sweet, alluring scent to give it. I need the start for the smell." I say, not taking my eyes or hands off the plant.

Anarus doesn't speak, but comes behind me. He brushes my braid over my shoulder, then rests his hands on my shoulders. He buries his face in my neck and inhales deeply. "You always smell alluring to me."

A feeling travels down the bond. I close my eyes and think of the bond. I don't need the feeling but the scent. Anarus's idea of the scent of me. All I get is a feeling. The scent is there, but it's not enough. "It's not strong enough for me to tell through the bond, Ani."

Ydum lets out a small chortle. "Not strong enough? I think we can help that." He and Byder both kneel on either side of me and bury their noses in my hair, breathing deeply, sending the scent down the bond.

"Okay, as sexy as this is, it's also really weird I'm trying to make a plant smell like all three of you's horniness." I smile, but the scent does actually come softly through the bonds and I push it to the plant. Make this your scent, your peace that you entice insects with. Cover your scent of death and being a hunter with this.

The scent of the flower slowly changes. Death becomes sweet, like honey and jasmine. Is that what I smell like to them? I shake my head, smiling. The plant under my hands vanishes and we are back, but not in the foyer but the hallway. The painting in the hallway in front of us now contains a picture of the carnivorous plant we created.

"What is that?" Raven asks from behind us.

All four of us stand, and I tell her. "Carnivorous plant. A plant that catches and eats bugs. Ydum's nature, Byder's hunting, my emotional manipulation, and…" I stop talking, unsure what to say.

Anarus finishes for me. "And my death."

"Your power is death?" Uesis asks, incredulously.

Anarus only nods. "The bridge between life and death, we think."

"Oh." Uesis thinks for a moment. "When you have your mantle, I would love to talk to you about some stuff. Some of the death songs I know seem a little weak and diffuse. Maybe you can help me make them better."

Anarus looks surprised at this and just stammers out, "Uh, yeah, okay."

As Uesis and Raven wander away back to their painting, I wrap my arm through Anarus's. "And you were worried they wouldn't accept you. Death is part of life. It's built into not just Ydum and Byder's powers but into all of them. Music, war, chance, storms, all of them have a touch of death or the possibility to cause or be used around death. You are part of all of them."

Isis and Esnir make an appearance by the fourth painting and we all walk over to see what they made. Their painting is of a finely crafted dagger. The metal of the blade seems to ripple in the light. The handle is made of black leather embedded with several stones. Tiny chips of jade, amethyst, pearl, sapphire, and amber color the hilt.

Curious, as the others compliment them on the dagger, especially Byder, I wander over to Raven and Uesis's painting. They were in third place, so their creation is depicted on the third painting. The canvas is covered with sheet music. From the words that are under the lines of notes, I figure out it's a song to work magic over plants, increase their potency within a magical working, salve, or cooking. The song is actually really well-crafted and I can feel the magic in it. I call Ydum over and show him.

He trails his fingers over the notes and hums appreciatively. "This would work really well."

"Wouldn't it?" I agree. "That's some really good magic."

Raven comes over and blushes at our praise. "I wrote the words then Uesis set them to music."

Next back is Wren and Kutar. When we move to look at their painting, we are all confused. The painting seems to be just a swirl of colors.

"What is it?" Isis asks.

"A whirlwind." Wren explains. "Kutar made the storm, with swirling clouds and wind, and I infused attraction into the winds so it brought the things the wind picked up to the eye of the storm. My attraction magic was supposed to only make it pick up conversations, like a way to eavesdrop on people, and it did that, but it also was able to pick up actual things like leaves and trees and stuff, so I only got it half right."

While we wait for Damek and Iella to return, the others who came later circle the hallway looking at the rest of our paintings. We end up explaining our carnivorous plant twice more.

"Nice." Esnir says, raising his eyebrows. "Well, they got first place. Unless

Damek and Iella do something crazy, Jinx's team is the only one that didn't just create something, but actually created something that never existed before."

"Damn," Wren complains jokingly, "and I thought an eavesdropping whirlwind was creative. You had to go and make a whole new plant species."

Ydum hums. "Well, actually, carnivorous plants do exist already. We just stole the concept and made one that doesn't exist here on Nazus yet."

The others all grumble jokingly, making comments about that being a technicality only Ydum would recognize.

When Damek and Iella come back, they seem to be mid-argument.

"All I'm saying is that it's bullshit." Damek's saying, not yelling but definitely loudly. "A cup that makes the dice roll what you want it to. How's that not my magic and your power?"

Iella has her arms crossed over her chest and is glaring at him. "Because you actually made the cup, not crafted it from magic, Dame."

He throws up his arms. "Well, how was I supposed to know they wouldn't count calling the wood to me to whittle?"

"Because I told you they wouldn't! Twice!" Iella huffs and turns her back on him, whipping her hair in his face, which is really hard for her to do accidentally since Damek is so much taller than her.

I lean over so that only Ydum, Anarus, and Byder can hear me whisper. "Hey guys, we aren't the dramatic return this time!"

All three of them cover a laugh under a cough.

Drila pops into the hallway. "Well, with everyone returned, your original creations have been sent to the council of the original gods to be evaluated. They should be shortly ranking them from first, the best, most original creation that represents the powers and magic of the team that made it, to fifth, the most unoriginal creation that least shows off the power and magic of the team. Remember that, if you get fifth place, this doesn't mean your creation wasn't good. It could be fantastic in a crowd of fantastic creations. One of the creations must be the best, but that also means one has to be the worst, even if it's not bad."

Drila waits a bit. After some time, the paintings all glow for a moment. I look at ours and there's now a small number one in the bottom right corner. I point the number out to my gods and we all smile. A carnivorous plant was an amazing idea.

"We won the games." Ydum whispers. "I did the math already. As long as we pass game ten, we can't lose. Even if we come in fifth, we'll have less points than the other teams have now."

As if to prove him right, Drila starts listing off the points. "In fifth place, with their creation of a mirror of decision, that shows the user which choice of two will be the most auspicious, but that was their third attempt to create using both the witch's magic and god's power, Damek's team takes fifty points, giving them a total of three hundred and eighty-five points and third place in the games overall.

"In fourth place, with their creation of an eavesdropping wind, that also unintentionally picks up actual objects, Wren's team takes forty points. This gives them four hundred and seventy-five points and has them in last place overall. In third place, with a beautifully crafted dagger that can store magic through the stones of the pentagram embedded in the handle, Isis's team gets twenty-five points, bringing their total to three hundred and ninety points for an overall fourth place.

"In second place, with a song that enhances the vitality and power of magical plants, Raven's team gets twenty points. They're now in second place overall as well, with three hundred and sixty points. And in first place, with the creation of a new species of plants that hunts insects for nitrogen lacking in their soil, Jinx's team collects fifteen points."

Drila pauses for a moment. "As some of you might be able to deduce, Jinx's team now has exactly three hundred points. Because of this, unless they fail to complete game ten, Jinx's team will have won the Three Hundred and Seventy-Fifth Gods Games. Now, I don't want the rest of you to give up just yet. Completing the games in and of itself has its own rewards. Also, there's no actual assurances that Jinx's team will be able to complete game ten and, if they don't, any one of you could win."

"Except us." Wren interjects.

Drila only inclines her head slightly at Wren.

Ydum also says, "Well, Raven and Isis could also tie for first. That'd be the first time the games end on a tie."

Drila huffs impatiently. "My point is, there's a lot that could still happen, don't count it over yet. Next game is the wild card for the crowns of your mantles, the goal of the whole ten weeks. See you then."

Drila pops away again and I turn to my gods. "Did anyone else feel like that statement about us not having any actual assurances about completing the tenth game was a threat?"

Anarus murmurs. "Only a lot of one."

For one of the few times, we are back from the game before lunch. When we move back to our room, I notice that the painting of our carnivorous plant is now hung over the fireplace. I sit on the couch facing the fireplace to admire it, because damn if we didn't do a good job. Byder loads up plates with lunch and hands them out, while Anarus actually makes a fire in the fireplace that we have completely ignored the rest of the games. Ydum sits on the floor in front of me, his head leaned back on my curled-up legs and looks at the painting with me.

"That's a beautiful, deadly plant." Ydum murmurs as I run my fingers through his hair.

I nod, distractedly. "That it is. You know, your hair might actually be long enough for a teeny tiny braid now?" I look down and Ydum's blonde, curling hair has grown so much that sometimes a curl or two can fall in his eyes when it's wet.

He immediately arches his back to look at me, his eyes lighting up. "Do it! I want a braid too."

I laugh and oblige. "It won't be great, but I think I can do something."

Once the fire is going well, Anarus sits on the couch next to me. "Give him braids of totality. He has enough for that now."

I raise my eyebrows at Anarus. "Braids of totality?"

"Three tiny braids from the temple back to just past the ear on one side of the head." Anarus explains. "One braid for each, mind, body, and spirit. Some people weave magic for peace and health into the braids as they do them."

Ydum gets fidgety and excited. "That. Do that!"

"Well, fine but stop wiggling." I tell Ydum.

He immediately settles and leans his head to rest on my left knee, exposing the right side of his head to me. I flip his head to my other knee. "Left side, closer to your heart." I tell him, then start carefully braiding. Byder gives Ydum his lunch first and he eats while I braid.

"Ew," Ydum says after taking a sip of juice, "that's too sweet. Someone must have used overripe berries." He holds the cup up and asks Byder to give him water instead.

Byder tries a sip and spits it back out. "Definitely overripe berries. I'll get us water instead. Jinx, is the tea okay?" I take a sip to test and nod that it's fine.

As I braid Ydum's hair, three tiny braids, infusing each one with strength, health, and peace in his body, then his mind, then his spirit, we all eat lunch. Byder sits on the other side of me. My mind maintains the magical working, but also drifts over the idea of this being not an afternoon after a game, but just a regular winter day.

There were days like this at home with my sisters and parents, where it was cool enough for that first real fire in the sitting room fireplace and we would all just snuggle in close, quietly enjoying each other's company as my sisters and I braided each other's hair. The idea of that being something we, my three gods and me, do makes me feel a warmth and hope for our future together.

"You're smiling a lot there, little human." Anarus says.

I smile bigger for him. "Just remembering me and my sisters braiding each other's hair in front of the first winter's fire. I can't wait to see our family do it too, in a real home together, rather than here at the games."

"Hm," Byder sighs, as he settles on the couch after retrieving me a handful of tiny hair ties from Anarus's things, "we just need to add some rabbit stew warming over the fire."

"Rabbit you caught, Byder." Ydum adds. "With carrots and potatoes I grew."

"How can you two possibly be making me hungry while I'm eating?" Anarus jokes.

I finish Ydum's three braids and, after he stands and kisses me in thanks, Byder slides down off the couch, looking up at me. "Me too?"

"This again?" But I'm smiling. He leans his head on my right knee and I give him three braids of totality, weaving strength, health, and peace into them.

When I finish his, I pull on Anarus until he sits down in front of me. "Might as well do all of you." I tell him. "But someone is doing mine next."

When I finish Anarus's braids, he pulls me up to stand, spins me around, and sits in my spot on the couch. He gestures at the floor and I sit, leaning on his right leg so he can do my braids. "Won't be as strong of magic as you can do, but it'll be enough."

At dinner, we all avoid the overly sweet juice again, and now the tea too, and gather up the alcohol to give to the other teams. "Water for everyone it is. If they fuck up the coffee tomorrow, Ydum, you and I will have to be very careful." Byder says.

The next morning, the coffee is actually not ruined but better than it has been, which is a relief. The juice and warm tea are still both awful but the milk is fine. We spend the morning working on me handling looking at their powers two at once. My hands feel red and raw by lunch and we know we need a new idea for the protection.

"Do you think any of the other teams would help us with this? Knowing if we survive, we win?" Byder asks.

"Maybe Wren and Kutar." I offer. "Considering they're in the same boat in reverse. No matter what anyone does, they lose."

Ydum shrugs. "Worth a shot. Worst they can say is fuck off."

We all trudge over to the ninth room and, when Wren invites us in and we explain our issue, they're actually both willing to help.

"I've been wondering how you'll figure this out." Kutar tells us. "Two gods is nigh on impossible. Three? Jinx is going to have to be very powerful and very protected."

The four of us glance at each other, and Wren catches it. "What? If you want us to be able to help you, we need to know what we're working with."

I finally speak. "You know that Anarus is not actually a god of obscurity, right? Everyone kinda figured that out yesterday from our carnivorous plant. Well, it's not three gods, three powers. It's three gods, four powers. Anarus is carrying a power that isn't his on top of his own."

"Fuck." Kutar breathes out. "No wonder you were always such an asshole. I mean, not that the council didn't treat you like shit and your attitude wasn't already understandable, but growing up with someone else's power? Shit. What is it? Is it a full mantle power already?"

Anarus doesn't look at them but the floor. "My actual power, as far as Jinx can tell, is the bridge between life and death, which includes the power of holding, and ending, bonds and destinies. The opposite end than the ones the living Fate gods hold onto when they create them. The extra power sitting directly on top of that one over my heart is the god of the wilde hunt."

Kutar laughs. "That explains the offering I didn't think anyone did anymore." He gets serious quickly. "But yeah, that's a full mantle already. The wilde hunt has already been created and was ruled by, I think, the god of Death. Wait, those powers would mean that Death is your dad, wouldn't it? Oh shit. How? Never mind. How the fuck would you know that? Anyway, yeah, it'd be a full mantle. It may seem like it's not, but that'd only be because you'd need the full access to the bridge. Oh shit, the bridge that you literally are."

He chuckles almost ruefully. "Yeah, I'd expect that, once you acquire the crown of the mantle of the god of the bridge, the full weight of the hunt will hit you all at once because it's all already there. And seeing as it's between October thirty-first and December twentieth, oh fuck, it'll be in full swing. Jinx, you are going to have to do a fuck ton and protect the shit outta yourself."

"Hence why we are here." Ydum says. "With her magic the way it is, a little different than most witches, we've been creating a protection before she looks at our powers and she can pick up what we make and expand it, but her hands where she physically touches us are still turning red. When we've tried me and Byder both, they blister. All three of us? She'd burn up, especially if the wilde hunt hits before she can let go."

Kutar looks thoughtful. "Hm. I say we split up. Gods work from our end, and humans on theirs, and see what we can all come up with. Wren? Want to go get everyone else?"

Byder stops her as she's getting up. "I don't know if everyone else will be as eager to help as you two are. They can only win if we fail. They may think it's better to sabotage us than help."

Wren only laughs and continues standing. "Okay, two things. One, I don't know if it's occurred to you, but anytime someone goes against your team, they end up dead soon after. I mean, your name is freaking Jinx. We're human, not stupid. And two, as Jinx has so often said, these games have been truly unfair. Jinx brought here with not a stitch to her name and Anarus is too young. A trio made by the cave when it's never made one before and most of the gods I've talk to thought they weren't allowed. Saffron being allowed to die when she was already back. Now, you're telling us that one of your too large team is already carrying a second full mantle power that isn't theirs? The original gods have a lot to answer for with these games, and I bet a lot of past ones. So, no, no one will sabotage you and they'll definitely be willing to help."

Byder, Ydum, and I look to Anarus. I step closer to him and whisper. "This is your powers, your story to decide if you want to share. You say no, we work with what we've got, no questions asked. No guilt or blame. This is your life. Are you okay with everyone knowing everything?"

Anarus just looks at me for a moment. "You love me, no matter what? I just need to hear it."

"I love you no matter what, Anarus." I tell him firmly, and Byder and Ydum nod their agreement.

"We will always love you no matter what, Anarus." Ydum tells him solemnly, without an ounce of teasing or frivolity.

"Then, okay." Anarus sighs heavily. "The more help the better."

Wren goes and collects the other teams and soon their sitting room is full with all twelve of us. Kutar lays out the basics of the issues of Anarus's powers and our trouble devising a safe enough protection for me. It takes a few minutes for everyone to settle down after they hear that Anarus has two powers, one not his and already a full mantle. But when Kutar gets everyone's attention again, he explains his plan for the gods to work together to find a solution on their end and the humans to work together on our end. Once we have some solid ideas, we'll come back together to test them.

"I think the humans should go back to our room." Ydum suggests. "It's quite crowded in here and we all need space to work and make sure we don't hurt each other."

Agreeing, I take Damek, Isis, Raven, and Wren to our room. Once we are settled, Damek sitting cross-legged on the floor, Raven and Isis on one couch, and Wren and I on the other, I look to Damek. "You guys know the problem with the gods' powers, but there's also an issue with my magic, which you might have already known. Damek, can you explain it? To me, it's just how my magic works. You'll explain how it's different better."

Damek gives the other three a basic rundown on how I work my magic and what it can and can't do.

"Damn, girl." Raven says, "You're name is a little too apt, isn't it?"

I roll my eyes. "Tell me about it."

"Hey, if you gotta be Jinx, whose jinxed, at least you got those three nice eye candies out of the deal." Wren says, a devious smile on her lips. "Now, I know sure as shit you are hooking up with all three, the way they act around you. My question is how do you keep it straight? Do you have a calendar or something? Because unless you are doing all three at once..."

I know my cheeks flame up, but I can do nothing about it.

"You are! Oh shit!" Wren falls sideways on the couch, laughing.

"Wait." Isis says, throwing out her hands. "I was so positive that Byder and Ydum were a thing. Is that not true?"

"Well, they kind of are." I answer honestly.

Isis shakes her head. "Okay, now I'm confused. If they are, and you are, something isn't making sense for me."

Raven leans over and whispers something in Isis's ear. Isis's eyes go wide and her mouth drops open. "No shit?" Isis says, looking between me and Raven as my cheeks burn.

"Ookayy..." Damek says, walking to the door. "I'm gonna go swap with Iella or something. I'm good. I mean, feel to girl gossip but, um, yeah. I'm gonna get Iella."

"Stop, Damek. Wait." I call out to him. "They'll stop and we can get to work, I promise." I fix a hard stare at the other three girls.

"Ugh, fine!" Raven groans. "Work first, then gossip. But, yeah, you are so getting Iella for that, Damek. We need all those juicy details too."

Damek's cheeks turn as red as mine were, and I poke him in the ribs with my elbow. "Not so fun when it's you, is it?"

"It wasn't fun when it was only you, either." Damek grumbles.

The five of us buckle down and try to figure out how I can work a protection magic that still allows me to see and feel the gods' powers like I do, and work with them how I will need to in the tenth game. I explain what we've done and immediately they all know why it wasn't working.

"Have you actually ever worn gauzy fabrics, Jinx?" Raven asks me. "It protects against nothing. Wind, rain, cold, heat, the sun. Nothing. It isn't any good protection, just pretty."

"Have you forgotten everything from the third game, girl?" Damek chides me. "I mean we all know your brain was a little fuzzy after that wonderful performance you gave us when you got back to the foyer, but damn. Protection magic is something even a base witch can do. What are you using to protect yourself?"

I open my mouth, about to say something about Damek being the one who didn't want to talk about the gossip stuff, but then I stop. He's right. I've been overthinking this. Protection is so simple and we already had a game about it. And, I realize, I already have the perfect base. A slow smile forms as I go over everything in my mind.

"Who has yarrow? Someone gave me yarrow for Isis's arm." I ask.

"That'd be me." Damek says. "You need some?"

I nod at him and he leaves. "Raven, you seem really not skittish. Can you help me with something?"

"What do you need?" Raven moves over between me and Wren. Wren scoots away to sit where Raven was.

I take a deep breath. "I am going to channel my wolf familiar. Can you, I dunno, pull some fur off me or something?"

Raven nods and I close my eyes.

"Oh, shit." Isis whispers. "I do not want to see this."

"Would you go get Anarus for me, then?" I ask Isis and she gladly runs out of the room.

Kinshra?

Mm?

I need a super big favor. I need some of your fur.

How can you get it from wherever you are?

I am going to try to channel more of you than I ever have. An actual solid part of you, enough to have fur. Can you help with that?

Where is Anarus?

Coming.

We'll wait for him. I'm going to let alpha know we are doing a big thing while we wait.

Okay.

"Hey." Anarus says softly. "Isis said you are going to channel Kinshra for fur? Did she get that actually anywhere near right? Because you've never done that before, not that much."

I nod at him without losing my focus. "She got that right. Kinshra said I need you for it."

"Why?" Raven asks and Damek, who must be back, shushes her. But she retorts, "Hey, if I'm pulling fur off a wolfy Jinx, I think I deserve to know how it works and how she won't bite me."

Anarus answers. "Kinshra is her wolf familiar. I'm the god guide for the bond, or maybe just the god over the bond. It's confusing now."

I'm back, Jinx. I see Anarus has arrived. Are you ready?

Yes.

Okay, you need to touch his tattoo of me.

"Anarus, I need to touch your tattoo of Kinshra." I say. He takes my hand and guides it to his chest, knowing I want to concentrate. He's actually wearing a shirt today.

Um. Jinx, I know there's a lot of humans around right now and your type is weird about this stuff, but you need to touch the actual tattoo.

Oh. "Kinshra says the actual tattoo. Sorry."

"It's fine." Anarus says quietly. He moves my hand then places it back on his cool warm skin. He covers my hand with his.

Better. Now focus on actually seeing me, Jinx.

I take a deep breath and blow it out slowly, remembering what Kinshra looks like, her black and gray fur, wet nose, perked up ears, the way she shakes out her fur and sleeps with her tail over her nose. Once I have the image in my mind, Kinshra shakes out her fur.

Now, feel me. Feel what it is to be a wolf. Your eyes changed before when you got angry. You've pulled up my claws, too. Feel my fur, know what it's like with the wind blowing through it. How it's coarse in my outer coat, and soft in my undercoat. How the water of the rain is repelled and it flies off when I shake. How my hackles raise when I'm angry.

I think of all these things as Kinshra talks about them. I don't think anything's happening, but then I feel a small tug and both Kinshra and I yip.

I think that human got what you needed. I am going to sleep. That was a lot of work when we didn't get a good hunt last night.

Thanks, Kinshra. Give me a week and maybe Byder can help you guys with that.

You're welcome and tell him he owes me one for you.

I laugh and open my eyes to find myself staring into Anarus's dark eyes. I tell him about our agreement.

Anarus chuckles. "You get to tell him that."

I turn to look at Raven and ask if she got the fur and see three slack jawed humans staring at me. Isis must have stayed gone.

"You were a wolf, like an actual fucking wolf." Wren says.

Raven rolls her eyes at Wren and holds out a small tuft of silver and white fur. "Not an actual wolf. You still had your human shape, but you were definitely very wolfy looking."

"So. Cool." Damek barely breathes out. He shakes his head as if to clear it and hold up a bag. "Yarrow. Oh, and I think I know what you're doing. Flint too." He digs in his pocket and pulls out a piece of flint.

"You good with me, little human?" Anarus says softly.

"Yes, thank you." Anarus stands and kisses my cheek then leaves again, never remembering to put his shirt back on.

"Okay, girl!" Raven says the minute the door is shut. "Damn! We are definitely gossiping later. Those tattoos! And one of them is your wolf familiar? You may be jinxed but it's working for you in all the best ways."

"What would Uesis say if he heard you, Raven?" I tease.

Raven only laughs. "I'm bonded, not dead."

I shake my head and tell them I'll be right back. I go into the bedroom and grab the box that contains my witch's kit and bring it out to the table. I start digging through it and pulling out what I need. The rosemary, basil, and pepper mix. The lodestone. The matches. While I have it out, I remember to pull out the four jade stones. I don't need them for this but want to give them back to Isis, who returned after Anarus went back to the gods, probably telling her it was safe now. Then, I pull out the jar of burn salve we made in the eighth game to be my base.

The others join me at the table and I slide the jade over to Isis. "Thank you for that."

Isis only smiles and puts them in her pocket.

Raven swears under her breath. "Shit. I have to give you back that too. Later, remind me."

"So," I explain as I organize myself. "This is a burn salve we made for game eight. My hands get red and blistered, a lot like a burn. But nothing happens to my eyes. Burn salves, as we know, don't usually protect from getting a burn. But this isn't a normal burn, but a magical one. My thought is, if I mix a burn salve with protection elements, yarrow, the flint and lodestone shavings, the rosemary, basil, and pepper mix, wolf fur, and just a touch of magical strengthening, I could use it as a preventative protection salve."

"Magic sounds right to me." Raven nods and everyone else agrees.

With their help, I enhance the power in each ingredient and mix them together. Then, when I think it's ready, I add more strength and potency and pass it around for everyone to test with their magic to see if they think it needs more of anything. The five of us pronounce it good and we all make our way back to Wren's room.

"Move outta the way, gods." Raven declares as soon as we enter the room. "The humans have this thing cracked."

"Well, maybe." I qualify her comment. "We'll have to try it first."

"Ooh, can we watch? I mean, we helped and I've been doing this, but have never seen it." Wren pouts, her eyes begging us.

I raise an eyebrow at my gods. Ydum sighs, smiling. "I don't see why not. But not in here, too crowded."

The twelve of us move to the foyer, where everyone else takes a seat along the walls and Byder, Anarus, Ydum, and I sit in the middle.

"Who first?" I ask quietly.

"Start with Byder. He's the easiest and burns you the least." Anarus says.

I set the salve down and open it, taking a small scoop out to rub over the entire surface of my hands and dab just a tiny bit on my eyelids.

Byder holds out his hand to me. "Do I need to do anything?"

"Not this time." I say, taking his hand. I close my eyes, trying to forget all the watching eyes. I sense the magical protection salve and push my magic to make it thicker, stronger still, and cover more of me. Then, I focus on Byder's power. I need to see it, not take, but only look and maybe touch.

I open my eyes and can see his power in his eyes, hands, and heart. The overwhelming desire to hunt and kill in his eyes. I brush his eyelids with my fingers again. I know I can't calm it right now, but just want to try touching it. His hands are weapons, I knew that, but they aren't ready to be taught other uses. His heart beats the cadence of death and I touch him there too, knowing the song will change to a better one.

I feel more than see Ydum next to me reaching out to take my hand that I touched Byder with. When I turn to face him, his spiderwebs of power are everywhere. Both my hands are occupied so I can't actually touch him. I ask the vines to move and show me his spine and the tides, then I look in his eyes for the fire and at his feet to see the itch to build lands.

Taking a risk, Anarus sits behind me, placing a hand on the back of my neck. I don't have to turn around to see that well of darkness that's cracked open slightly, and the five bond lines coming from his heart to each of us and his wolf tattoo. I know behind the well is the bridge but I don't try to move the well right now.

I let go of Byder and Ydum and, seeing this, Anarus moves his hand away from my neck. I look down at my hands and see clean, calm skin, no blisters. I hold them up to show the three of them and they each smile.

"It worked." Ydum says to everyone else. "That's the first time she's been able to handle all three of us at once."

Raven snorts and I immediately shoot her a fierce look before she can say anything. She only shrugs and smiles at me. Then, I notice her taking a bite of a sandwich. While we were working, lunch had arrived and apparently the others just gathered it all from every room to bring out here and make one large feast.

I stand up and notice Byder is already headed over to the impromptu buffet to make us plates. Of course, Byder noticed the food first. I go over to sit with Raven, Isis, and Wren, who have taken over one corner of the foyer. On the way, I tap Iella on the shoulder.

"Us girls are over here." I tilt my head to the others. "You coming?"

Iella looks down and away. "I'm not human."

I snort. "But you are female, aren't you? I mean, in less than a week, none of us will be human, so who cares. Plus, you've got to be desperate for conversation that isn't," I look over at the males and make an almost disgusted face, "that." I have no idea what they are talking about, but most of the males are gesturing wildly and flexing.

"You sure?" Iella asks and when I nod at her, she stands. "Thank fuck. I love Damek but I cannot stand talking about swimming leagues or workouts or whatever anymore."

When we sit with the other girls, Raven is excited. "Finally, all the girls together. I've said it before and I'll say it again. I'm only here for the gossip. Iella, I've been dying to ask you, Damek is so tall, and you're, well, not. I mean, that looks awkward."

"Just dive right in with the crazy personal questions, Raven." Isis teases.

They all get silent for a moment when Byder comes over to hand me a plate of food and a cup of water. "Juice and cold tea still taste weird." He kisses my cheek as I thank him then wanders away to join the guys.

"Damn, you got them trained." Raven laughs.

I shake my head at her. "I did not train that into him. He's a hunt god, feeding people is just a thing with him. Sometimes, it's actually annoying, like when he makes me eat breakfast instead of just having coffee."

"Byder mentioned the juice being off." Wren says. "You guys noticed that too?"

I nod and so do the other three. "The coffee is fine and I don't taste anything off with the food. It's just like they used overripe berries to make the juice or someone is a little heavy handed with the sugar. I don't think it's like the petunias again, though, because it's just the juice and tea."

Iella tilts her head to the side. "Petunias?"

"Didn't Damek tell you?" I ask her. "They put petunias in the food for the sixth game. It was a magical working to make everyone angry and vengeful. It's why people were willing to fight friends, and why Damek did what Damek did. Probably you attacking Ydum too, even though we were all working together."

After a moment, I add solemnly. "I think Aretha was getting dosed far longer than the rest of us. I never meant to kill her, but she just wouldn't stop coming at me. It was me or her."

Wren consoles me. "Well, she tried to kill me. I was able to get away. But it was all petunias? In the food? How did you catch that?"

I snort softly. "I'm allergic to them. I noticed my itchy throat with the first sip of coffee and stopped Ydum before he could eat anything. Byder had already had a little breakfast and Anarus had two cups of coffee. He was unhinged rage for a bit. It was too late to stop the rest of you."

"Anarus does seem a little growly and touch her and I'll kill you about you. I was not really surprised way back before the third game when you said you and him were already together." Raven side-eyes me. She's trying to get back to the gossip, I can tell.

I give in to her just a little. "He is a little growly. But, it's not bad."

"Shadow daddy can be sweet while growling?" Wren asks.

I slap my hand over my mouth to stop a laugh. "Do not call him that, oh my gods. But, um, yeah."

"By the third game, you two were already bonded?" Iella purses her lips. "That's quick."

"We were dancing around each other pretty much from the start, but," I clear my throat, "bonded right after the second game. After he hit Ydum in the foyer. You guys know Byder. The third game, you saw it, well heard once Anarus covered us with shadows."

"That was wonderfully embarrassing and so much fun. Drila was mortified!" Raven tells me.

"Anyway," I try not to blush, "Ydum after game four where he temporarily died. Now, you know all three of mine, you four have to say it too. Fair's fair."

Isis offers the information easily. "Fourth game, but I think it would have been sooner if he wasn't so worried about my arm after the third game."

"Sixth game. When we realized we actually survived, but then knew we could never win. Kutar was sweet when I apologized for not being good enough, and he just told me he didn't care about winning because he already won getting me. His words, not mine." Wren tells us.

"Aw, that's sweet." Raven sounds sincere. "I thought Uesis and I were quick at just after the third game, but apparently Jinx is quicker."

Iella picks at something on the floor in front of her, not speaking as we all look at her. Her cheeks are red and she looks uncomfortable.

"You don't have to share if you don't want to, Iella." I tell her gently.

"Yesterday." She whispers so quietly I almost can't hear it.

Raven raises her eyebrows at this. "Yesterday? Really?"

Iella blushes harder. "I had never, well, I was a virgin. Damek is sweet and he was kind about me not being ready for a long time. There aren't that many female gods that find a bond in the games because there are so few male witches powerful enough. Out of the eleven gods that didn't make it out of the cave, seven of them were female."

I do some quick mental math. Anarus had said there were twenty-three gods at the cave. Twelve matched, one female and eleven males. Seven female gods died in the cave, meaning four males did too. That's fifteen males and eight females. That's not too unbalanced between male and female gods. There were thirty-six humans and only a handful of them were males, but I'm not exactly how many.

"Do any of you remember how many human males there were in the cave?" I ask.

"Four." Iella answers. I didn't expect her to know. "Drila told us before we were allowed to go through the caves."

I shake my head, feeling angry at the original gods yet again. "So, unless two of you bonded to each human male, or somehow got the rare female to female bond, you knew before you started that at least four of you would die."

"And this was a big year for human males and a small year for female gods." Iella adds, sniffling softly. "There have been years that there were ten or more female gods and no human males at all."

"Shit." Raven swears. "So, you knew before even coming here that you would probably die in the caves."

Iella wipes tears away as she talks. "My mom cried for weeks before I left. My parents basically started mourning me before I was even gone, and I have a little sister. In three years, they'll go through it all over again with her. The girls in my year were all close friends and now, all my friends are dead."

"Not all of them." I say, with a soft smile. "I know it's no consolation for losing all your lifelong friends, but we're here, and I'd like to be friends."

Iella gives me a watery laugh. "Let's talk after the next game. If we're all still alive, I'd like that."

"So, that's decided." Raven splays her hands on the ground. "If we're all still here after the next game, we find each other in Veirveil and stay friends. And plan a revolution to change these fucking games."

"Sounds good to me." Isis smiles. "When and where do we meet?"

Iella sits up straighter, collecting herself. "Clock tower in the center of town. Say, on December twenty-second? Give everyone time to visit home, or well, I'll visit Damek's home, and get back to Veirveil? And gives Anarus time to corral the wilde hunt back to the land of the dead, if that's his job."

Wren nods enthusiastically. "That works perfectly. It's a plan. We'll do lunch and whichever one of us is sitting on the council, cough, cough, Jinx, can help us start planning."

Iella's eyes go wide. "Holy shit. I just realized. Jinx, if your team wins, which hello? You only need to survive to win, and now that's a for sure thing, you guys will take four seats on the council. The hunt, nature, Anarus will fill Death's empty seat, and you will take the human seat. Fuck."

I nod. "We've discussed that, and how much of a threat it makes us."

Wren moves her hand through the air as if she is counting. "Shit."

"Shit." Raven repeats, nodding.

Isis slouches. "They are not going to let you win."

"We've thought about that possibility too." I say. "Anarus is Death's child. I'm both a beginning and end magic witch. Byder has issues reading and Ydum." I clamp my lips shut. I almost said Ydum's secret.

"Ydum's colorblind." Iella finishes for me. "Isn't he?"

I only nod. "You knew?"

Iella shrugs. "I guessed. Twenty-four years of basically living in each other's shadows, we gods know each other a lot better than anyone wants to admit. I guessed at his colorblindness and the, well, that he and Byder working well together wasn't a new thing, on at least Ydum's side. Byder, on the other hand."

"It was new and scary for him." I tell her.

Raven shakes her head again. "Jinx's jinx getting more and more complicated every time I turn around. But enough of all this serious stuff. I want gossip! Wren, that god of storms you got. Now, tell me honestly, is he just as stormy with other things?" She waggles her eyebrows at Wren, who blushes as we all dissolve into giggles.

We talk all the way through dinner, everyone just bringing their food to the foyer to pass and share again. Eventually, people stop sticking to the girls in one group and the guys in another, and the parties Aretha always tried to make for bonding the teams actually seems to work this time.

Somehow, this becomes the new normal for us all. We all eat breakfast alone in our rooms. Then, at lunch, everyone just gathers everything up and we make a huge buffet in the foyer. One team or another practices their witch managing their god's powers while everyone else eats and offers advice to the practicing team or teams. Then we dissolve into chatter and hanging out with each other comfortably. The games must have given up because by the third day, dinner just appears in the foyer for everyone. We all eat together then separate back to our own rooms to practice what we learned from each other that day or just relax.

On the fourth day, Isis asks me if I can give her the braids of totality too, and I end up doing them for every god and human that has enough hair. Anarus helps when my hands start cramping. I run my fingers through their hair before he braids and then again after, adding in the strength, health, and peace for body, mind, and spirit. All the other witches are shocked as I do their braids with how powerful they say the magic feels.

"You're magic may work very differently, Jinx," Damek tells me, "but, fuck if it isn't strong. I could literally feel the words seeping into my bones and mind."

That night, Anarus and I spend a long time talking after we make love. Byder and Ydum snuck off to the other bedroom for a little alone time as well, so it's just the two of us in my bedroom.

"This is not how I thought the games would go." He tells me. "I really thought I would never make it out of the cave when the council said I would be going to the games early. If I did survive, I was certain I would be the fourth case of a rejected bond."

"People can do that? Reject the bond?" I ask as we snuggle.

Anarus nods. "It's happened three times in three hundred and seventy-five years. Once was a male god and female human matched in the cave seventy-five years ago. They both balked at the match, saying they were both gay, and chose to not continue with the games from the cave, even though it meant death. It's the one time I think the cave magic didn't actually work right. Once was a male god rejecting a female human a hundred and seven years ago. She was, well the manual said, deformed but based on the actual games recorded, it sounds like she had an old injury that made it hard for her to walk right. She kept surviving though, against all odds, but after the tenth game, he chose to abandon his mantle rather than keep the cemented bond with her. They both got made mortal again even though they should have been made immortal. Honestly, from what the manual said, I think she lucked out. That god sounded cruel. The last was two hundred and eighty-four years ago. A male human and female god. They seemed fine all through the games, but just never cemented the bond and, even though they managed to survive the tenth game and she got her mantle and him immortality, they just shook hands and went their separate ways after."

"So, that's what Drila was talking about in the caves. The whole you can forfeit thing." I snuggle in harder against Anarus. "Until Bokysus said what he did, I thought you were going to take her up on it."

Anarus chuckles. "I almost did. After the game seventy-five years ago, they changed the rule about that. Everyone was mad after they found out about that game and that the cave magic tried to force a straight relationship with two people who weren't straight. Now, if all the people teamed up by the cave want to forfeit right then and there, they become mortal, like they failed a game but didn't die. In a duo team, one god can opt out to become mortal alone and leave the other god and the human as a working pair in the games."

He runs a hand through my hair, looking at me with his dark eyes. "I'm glad I didn't. For once in my life, I'm happy Bokysus was a jerk. You are everything I never knew I needed, Jinx. I would give up everything for you. Ask me to become mortal, and I will do it in an instant. Ask me to fight the original gods, I'll get the swords and meet you there. Ask me to die so that you three can survive, I will build my own funeral pyre and light the match. I am darkness and death and you are the peace and life in my every breath."

Anarus kisses me before I can respond and I show him with my body exactly how much he means to me too.

Chapter Ten

IT'S NOVEMBER EIGHTH. I know this date because it's the last day of the Gods Games. I fill my coffee from the breakfast table for the last time in this room. I've already returned my borrowed clothes to the humans and Iella that are still alive to return them to. The rest, I've packed in my gods' bags since we will all go to the same place after today, wherever that might be.

We have pretty much decided that we'll go to Ydum's after the games to start with. We'll settle there for a day or two, recuperating, before heading to Greenbriar to visit my family for a few days, then return to Ydum's parent's home until we either shift to Byder's or find our own place and settle into our own life.

The four of us have discussed this over and over, dissecting everything they read in the manuals and everything Byder and Ydum's parents told them. We still aren't sure how the crowning of the mantles works exactly but we're fairly certain that there is no actual game today, but just that. Ydum steals the painting of our carnivorous plant from where it's hanging above the fireplace and shoves it into one of his bags.

When we all look at him askance as he fidgets with all his thing to make the painting fit, he just shrugs. "It's awesome and I need to show Mom. Plus, it should be ours."

I'm wearing my dress from home that I came in, and it feels almost like a full circle. Here I am again, sitting in the sitting room, on the same spot on the couch, barefoot, in a rough spun cloth dress, my hair braided down my back, looking over the three gods the cave bonded me with.

They have all done the same thing as me. They are all wearing the same clothes they came in, Byder in his dark green sleeveless shirt, black leather pants, and hair down, Ydum wearing the blue long-sleeved tunic and brown cotton pants, and Anarus wearing his black pants and no shirt. I don't fight him to put one on for this game, just like Byder won't put up his hair and I won't do it for him either. We will end as we began, at least physically.

Mentally, emotionally, magically, everything has changed. Instead of strangers, we are a family. Instead of wary, we are in love. Instead of passively accepting what we've been told, we have learned we've been told lies. Lies about me. Lies about Anarus. Lies about magic. Lies about everyone. We hope today confirms those lies, and finally reveals the truths the original gods sought to hide.

When the tone sounds, we head out silently to the foyer and take up our positions along the back wall of the foyer. I have the salve in my pocket, but I also already put some on in case I can't take the jar. The other teams all seem to be as anxious as we are, gods and humans cuddling close like they may never touch each other again.

When Drila pops into the foyer, her dress black, we all hold our collective breath until she starts to speak.

"Welcome to the last day of the Three Hundred and Seventy-Fifth Gods Games. Five teams, twelve people, have made it to this crucial day. This game will work differently than the others since it is the crowning of the gods' mantles. If you will all step away from the wall, please."

Drila waits as we all shift to stand at the spots we've always drifted to after we return to the foyer after a game. Once we're settled, Drila waves a hand. A door appears in the back wall of the foyer, right where I would always touch the floor when I did shuttle sprints. It's a basic wood door, no different than the doors to our rooms.

Drila explains how everything will work. "Instead of all going at once, each team will go through the door one at a time, in reverse order of your standings, meaning Wren and Kutar will be first and Jinx, Byder, Ydum, and Anarus will be last. Once your team goes through that door, you won't return here. Your personal belongings will be transported after it's determined where you'll be going after the game is over. If you succeed in your god taking on their mantle, they'll be transported to the god's parent's home. If you're unsuccessful, they'll either be transported to your assigned mortal home in the outskirts of Veirveil or disposed of should you no longer have need of them." Should you die, I know she means. "Jinx's team, have you decided where you'll go if you're successful?"

Ydum answers. "My parents' home."

Drila nods and records this on her paper. "Jinx's team, I'm sure you know this, but just for the record, if one of the gods fail to take on their mantle, the team as a whole fails. Any god that did manage to take on their mantle will have it stripped and will be made mortal. With all the teams, if the human fails to survive, then that god will also be stripped of any mantle they took on and be made mortal. Points are determined in this game by which teams complete the crowning process the fastest. After all five teams have gone through the process, you'll reconvene in front of the council of original gods to have the crowning of the winner of the Gods Games then be released from the games. Good luck to all of you and it's been a pleasure watching you all compete. This has been a very interesting games cycle this year."

Drila pauses and looks over all of us, her gaze finally settling on Wren and Kutar. "When you are ready, please step through the door."

The rest of us surround Wren and Kutar, hugging them and offering words of encouragement. When the girls all come together for a group hug, Iella says, "Clock Tower, noon, December twenty-second. We will all be there. All of us."

We let go, nodding, and watch as Wren and Kutar walk through the door hand in hand.

We all settle again and wait. About three hours later, Drila, who hasn't left but just waited in a corner by herself, announces, "Isis and Esnir, when you are ready." I'm not sure how she knew it was time for them, but Drila waits while we do the same for them as we did Wren and Kutar.

They go through the door, holding hands as well, and we wait again. This wait is shorter and I don't know what that means. But, after only two hours, Drila calls for Damek and Iella.

"See you on the other side." I say to Iella as I hug her. "You will still have friends in us."

She nods and Damek slings his arm around her shoulders as they walk through the door.

Raven doesn't wait for her name to be called, but she and Uesis come over and sit by us to wait. We still don't really talk, but Raven tentatively holds my hand and we give each other encouraging squeezes often.

When Drila calls for them only forty-five minutes later, Raven and Uesis just nod at us before standing and walking through the door.

With them gone, and me and my gods the only ones left in the foyer, Drila decides to talk to us. "I've been impressed with you, Jinx. For someone so unprepared, you actually figured out a lot of the games others missed. The petunia thing? Especially clever of you. No one has figured that out before. Shame you didn't catch when they did it again." She contemplates that statement, then gives a fake wide smile. "Or maybe not a shame. Only time will tell on that one."

I furrow my brow. What game is she playing with us? Is she trying to psych us out? What does she mean when they did it again? I know they haven't added petunias to the food again. I would know the minute I ate or drank anything.

Ydum swears softly. "Shit. The drinks. The juice and tea were far too sweet. Could they have done something to it?"

All three of my gods look at me. I look at Anarus. "The coffee was better though, right?"

"Yeah," he says, then he sighs, closing his eyes. "Shit, it was sweeter too."

Byder rolls his lips through his teeth. "Jinx, what could they have put in the drinks that Drila would say was a shame, or maybe not, that really only you and Anarus ingested? Something that time would tell us about?"

I let my mind run over ideas. Making a drink sweet for some reason the games would want. The games, that are really a mating game. Oh fuck. "Red clover." My hands start shaking. "Fuck, it's red clover."

"What does red clover do?" Ydum asks.

I don't look at him. Instead, I look at Anarus. I've only been with him since the ninth game. "It nullifies Queen Anne's lace as a fertility inhibitor even in low doses, like only a few sips, and, in higher doses, like a couple of cups of coffee a day, increases fertility."

Anarus immediately pales. "We drank a lot of coffee this week."

"We did." I nod. And we did a lot of other things, a few times. I close my eyes and take a deep, steadying breath. I bring to mind everything Granny Helen taught the girls in my village about this. I try to mimic Ydum's strictly academic tone. "After longer than one cycle using Queen Anne's lace, the majority of couples will need an equal amount of time using red clover or other reversals before their efficacy reaches its full potential. In rare instances, it'll take less time for the clover to nullify the lace and return the female to proper cycles, and occasionally, when the lace has been ingested for longer than a year, it can take longer to be fully nullified."

"So, what you're saying is," Anarus is holding my gaze, "we took the lace for just over two months, the red clover couldn't have worked yet?"

"Shouldn't." I correct him. "Shouldn't have. Very rarely, the clover could have already taken effect, but that's very unlikely."

"She's just trying to rattle us." Byder says firmly.

Ydum nods as well, taking my hand. "Right. Even if it's true, what she's saying they did, she only wants us distracted by a maybe, might be, very rarely possible thing that we have no way of knowing right now and so shouldn't take into consideration. Nothing has changed, has it?" He looks between me and Anarus. "This is a thought for after we all have our mantles and the games are over. Not now. Right now, nothing has changed. As far as we know, nothing's changed."

Anarus shakes his head to clear his thoughts. "Right. Mantles now. Other issues when we know if they're an issue."

We sit quietly again after that, but I spend a lot of time shooting daggers at Drila in my mind. At one point I hear Anarus chuckle. "Vicious little human."

After what feels like far too long, but really is only two hour and a half hours, Drila finally calls on us. "Jinx, Anarus, Byder, and Ydum, when you are ready."

We stand together and, after I rub salve over my hands and eyes one more time, try to be confident as Ydum opens the door. The other side is shrouded in a white light. We step through, and find ourselves in a large, oval room. We're at the most northern point of the oval with a large stone floor stretching before us. I look up and see tiers of seats staggered up around the whole oval, with each row of seats rising higher than the one in front of it, giving the people in the seats all a clear, unobstructed view of the floor. There are twenty people in one section of seats, ten in the lowest row, and ten directly behind them.

Above that, hanging from the ceiling, are several pendant lights that flicker with a magical light. The whole floor is bathed in bright light but the seats are less well lit. On the floor of the oval, below where the twenty people are sitting, are seven chairs that aren't permanent fixtures, but were added.

Ydum leans down and whispers in my ear. "The Veirveil Colosseum. Those are the original gods in the seats and the human who won the games last year."

One of the original gods, Inspiration, Ydum tells me softly, stands to speak. "Ydum, Byder, Anarus, and Jinx. Congratulations on making it this far in the Gods Games. Please step into the center of the floor and stand in a line."

We walk forward until we are directly in front of the original gods, then line up, Anarus, me, Byder, then Ydum.

Once we're in place, Inspiration speaks again. I can see him better. He's darker than Byder but not as dark as Anarus, with pale hair that almost looks silver that hangs down his back in a straight waterfall. His eyes are almost golden in color and he seems slight of build and probably no taller than me. "Please step forward as I call you. Jinx Bloodmorrow, human daughter of Avalon and Maddox Bloodmorrow of Greenbriar."

I step forward and Inspiration continues. "Witch of potential emotional word magic. Byder, son of Xolios, god of the hunt with animal helpers and Daisy, formerly Gnash, witch of small pets. Potential mantle, full hunt god." Byder steps up next to me.

As Inspiration speaks, two people walk in through the door we just came through. They come and stand in front of Byder. I can tell they are his parents. Byder has his mom's eyes and his dad's chin. Byder's mom is wearing a dress like mine, but green, and his dad is wearing a sleeveless shirt and pants made from deer pelts. His dad's hunt lines are clear on his right forearm, if not a little faded from time. They hug him, his dad clapping him on his back.

"You've done really well, son. I'm very proud of you." Byder's dad, Xolios, sounds similar to Byder, same soft voice that hides a deeper power. His parents sit in two of the added seats and Inspiration speaks again.

"Byder, take the hand of your witch." Byder takes my right hand in his. "Ydum, son of Otuna, goddess of flowers and Eiran, formerly Thornheart, witch of metallurgy. Brother of Zimuna, goddess of stone, mated to Greg, formerly Black, witch of crystals. Potential mantle, full nature god." When Inspiration finishes speaking, Ydum steps forward as four more people come in through the doors. Otuna and Ydum are spitting images of each other. Her blonde, curly hair goes past her shoulders, but is exactly the same as his. Her smile is one I've seen Ydum have so many times. Her green eyes twinkle the same as his.

Zimuna looks just like their father. Dark hair and eyes, shorter that Ydum and his mother, and not as lean frames. Greg is entirely different, of course, since he's married in. He's short like Zimuna, with as dark a complexion as Anarus, but instead of long hair and strong like Anarus, Greg wears glasses with short hair and looks like someone who probably has his nose in a book a lot. All of Ydum's family members are wearing clothes just like Ydum always does. Pants and long sleeve shirts made from fabrics that are cultivated from plants. Except Greg, who is wearing the same type of homespun clothes I've seen my dad and other men from my village wear.

Ydum's mom gives him a swift hug and his father only nods at him, his face worried but also proud. Only Zimuna speaks. "Three? Damn. Don't fuck this up, little brother." She follows her parents to the chairs where Byder's parents are, taking her husband's arm in a crushing grip that shows her nerves. The six of them nod at each other as they sit.

"Ydum, take the hand of your witch." Inspiration says.

Ydum comes up to my left side and grabs my hand, winking at me with a smile.

Then, Inspiration speaks again. "Anarus, son of Winter and Death." Inspiration's voice falters slightly as he says this, and looks over the other original gods. It almost seems like he didn't know who Anarus's parents were until he said it out loud. But he straightens quickly, recovering himself. "Anarus, you have no witch's hand to hold, therefore, cannot take your mantle."

"What?" I yell out. "No."

Ydum shakes his head. "If you won't allow Anarus to try for his mantle, you doom us before we even start. Drila said we all have to be successful or none of us are. Why would we bother doing this at all? The cave made this team, you can't defy the cave. Anarus must be allowed, by the rules, to try for his mantle."

Inspiration does not even seem fazed. "A god must take their mantle holding the hand of the human witch the cave paired them with. Unless Jinx has a third arm we are not aware of, how can Anarus do so?"

I yell. "This is bullshit! You purposely called him last because of who his parents are. Why didn't you do it in alphabetical order, making Ydum last? Or some other way to make Byder last? You did this on purpose, just like you made him join the games too early. Winter, this is your son. How can you allow this injustice? After all the injustices of his life, you owe him this. You all owe him!"

Inspiration turns, and looks at the other original gods. I can tell they are having a discussion, but I can't hear anything. I want to cry. "Anarus." I try to let go of Ydum and Byder's hands to turn and look at him, but find I can't. Our hands will not let go of each other.

Anarus walks around to the front of me. He's heartbroken and angry, his shadows swimming. "I'll be okay. I'll be okay, Jinx." He takes my face in his hands and kisses me.

"No." I cry. "No, they can't do this."

Anarus leans his forehead against mine, still holding my face. "I love you. I love you so much." Ydum and Byder step around him, holding Anarus with their free arms.

We stay that way until Inspiration clears his throat. We turn to look at him. "Due to the conflicting rules of the cave magic and the games, the decision has been made that Anarus, son of Winter and Death, will be allowed to try for his mantle, taking his witch's hand once either Ydum or Byder have completed taking their mantle and one of the human's hands are free for him to do so. All other rules still apply. All three gods must survive and take on their full mantles, as well as the human survive, for any of them to pass."

I do not like that wording. Inspiration didn't say Anarus would start the process after he takes my hand, but that he can try and then take my hand when either Byder or Ydum let go. I think they're still trying to make us lose on purpose.

But we have no time to debate with them, because Inspiration snaps his fingers and I know immediately that all three of my gods' powers have opened up completely. All three of them groan loudly and I feel images rushing through me. They're muddled, lying on top of each other. I can't see any of them clearly in my mind, but my real eyes see Anarus screaming and writhing.

I feel Byder and Ydum struggling, but Anarus is struggling more. "Look at me, Anarus!" I scream over and over until Anarus's eyes latch onto mine. "Keep looking at me. Hold on, please."

"Jinx!" Anarus's voice already sounds weak and my heart is breaking. Shadows are flying out of him everywhere and I can see the white and blue fire pouring around him.

I have to get Byder or Ydum done. Byder first, I decide, and turn to face him. I see his power on his heart, eyes and hands. Byder's groaning and in pain under the weight of it all. I start with his eyes. The desire to hunt and kill shines out of them in a silver light. Tracking prey, all prey is his to take now. He can and will hunt the earth of every animal.

I push against that, staring into his eyes. No, you cannot hunt all the time and everything. You must keep the balance. Enough animals to thin their numbers to a healthy herd, flock, or school, enough to provide food and clothes to people in need of them, but not so many as to threaten the survival of the species. Allow the hunt only when the babies are grown enough and the group is ready. His power listens and accepts the limits I gave it.

I look at Byder's hands. Weapons, they know. Weapons, they are. All they are is weapons to kill. No, I remind them, the hunt is about more than the weapons used. Traps can be used in the hunt as well. His hands accept this easily. Don't forget food too, stripping the hunted animal of the parts we can use, making their sacrifice worthwhile instead of gluttonous. Meat to eat, furs and skins for clothes, bones for art and blood for magic, all uses for the animal that use his hands for something other than weapons. Knowing how to kill an animal means he also knows how to heal. These hands can heal too. Kindness, compassion, and help are all in those hands. A swift kill to prevent or end suffering. Death must be balanced with life. His hands agree, happy with their expanded roles.

Finally, I turn to his heart. The cadence of death still beats there. Death is a natural part of life, I tell his heart. But death is not all of life. Life, love, these come from and to animals as well. The love of a pet, the loyalty to a hunting dog, assisting animals with their births, helping an animal to heal when they can be or die peacefully and without pain when they can't, all a part of loving and caring for the land and its animal inhabitants to make a joyful hunt.

His heart accepts this new song, glad it no longer has such a sorrowful tune. It decides to give me a gift in return for the one I gave it. As I watch, a four-part tattoo inscribes itself over Byder's heart, the four disciplines, the symbols for air, water, earth, and fire shimmer on his chest before settling, each taking a color. Air turns yellow, water blue, earth green, and fire red.

Byder lets out a long sigh. I look up at his face and see him, really see him. The silver light fills all of him, glowing out of him for one moment, before turning back in to stay in his heart, eyes, and hands. Byder lets go of my hand and I feel the overburdened mess in my mind relax. Then, immediately, I remember Anarus.

"Byder!" I yell. "Get Anarus. Give me his hand!"

I see Byder kneel, trying to convince a collapsed and screaming Anarus to sit up and take my hand. I want to stay focused on Anarus, but I can't. Without even trying, my mind and my face turns to Ydum. He's panting and sweating.

"Anarus first." He says between gritted teeth. "I can wait. I can do this, Jinx. Ani first!"

But the magic doesn't give me a choice. Anarus is not holding my hand yet, so it immediately focuses on Ydum. I see a green light filling him everywhere. His vine tattoos are a riot, covering his arms, legs, chest, and back. Some are starting to creep up his neck. No. I tell it quickly. You must stay where you belong. Arm only, Ydum will tell you if he needs more. The vines fight me. Grow! They demand. Flowers, trees, grass, spices. Grow! But I shove them back with my magic. Yes, you can grow, but only in the proper amounts and seasons. Let me see the seasons. You need them to be healthy. Let the seasons of birth, death, and rebirth happen. They are nature too.

After a long tug of war, the vines finally relent and pull back to only his arm and shoulder. They're bigger than they were before, but I accept the compromise. When I ask now, they pull away and I see the four seasons, their weather, and additions to the world clearly. Rivers, lakes, snow, rain, and wind. All in their proper places and times. They are happy as they are, no longer choked by the vines. So, I leave them be.

As I attempt to look at Ydum's spine and the tides, I feel Anarus's hand clutch mine. His pain shoots through me, making me scream. His heart is ripping apart. But I know that I cannot stop with Ydum right now to help him. I physically cannot turn away. I have to move quickly, but Anarus's pain keeps distracting me, and every time I get distracted, Ydum yelps in pain as well. I bite my own lip, letting the real pain center me. I start to feel the edges of exhaustion from managing their pain and their powers. But I fight it back.

The tides on Ydum's spine are warring with the fire in his eyes. They both want to exist, to be in control. Ydum arches his back and contorts as they fight. I yell at both of them to stop! You both have a place and a time. I tell the tides to only come as far as they should, follow the rhythms the moon gives them and only defy them when the creating power in his feet ask for it.

To the fire, I take a stern hand. Stay below. Stay in your mountains, where you belong. Ydum's feet will tell you when it's time. When the land needs to be purged and rebuilt anew. But you must follow their guidance, explosions and lava only when asked for, then cool and calm so the earth can rebuild.

I look to Ydum's feet and feel them sighing in relief. They are free. They can create. I nudge them to see if they will overdo it and they smile, happy to create only under Ydum's guiding hands. They'll take the eyes of fire and the spine of the tide under their wing and protect them, from each other and themselves.

With his powers in their proper places, I can see the web of connectivity again. It's spread over his whole body, thick knots tying together the parts of nature Ydum controls to the parts of his power where those live. Other spots know they don't control anything, but seek guidance and knowledge from other gods who do. Byder's name is whispered over a crossing of the web that sees the animals of the world. The seasons have thicker knots that connect to the seasons in Ydum's heart but also know they have two masters, him and another god. That they must listen to both to thrive.

Ydum's power glows green strongly over him, pulsing and vibrating, then settles into his skin. It doesn't hide again like Byder's did but shimmers just under the surface. Ydum stands tall and breathes out, able to finally look at me. "Beautiful." He lets go of my hand and for a moment, he is all I can see and feel.

But a pain surges through me from Anarus and I turn to look at him. He is not there. I follow his hand in mine down and find Byder holding him up. Anarus is on the ground, pale, sweating and barely conscious. The only thing keeping Anarus's hand in mine is Byder's hand gripping us both tightly.

I collapse on the floor at Anarus's head and grasp both of his hands in mine. "Hold on, Anarus. Hold on." I tell him as I force my mind, my tired mind, to turn to his power. Byder lets go of Anarus and I am swept into an image in my mind. Anarus on the bridge between life and death, clutching at the rope railings tightly. There are gold lines running through his chest burning brightly and trying to tie themselves off with his heart as their anchor.

The wilde hunt is buffeting around him, knocking into him and pushing him around. He slips once, twice, his feet on ice that has formed on either side of the bridge. He can't get a strong grip on the fragile bridge.

"Jinx! Help me!" Anarus screams. I rush to his side and try to hold onto him, to stabilize him, but my hands pass right through him when I try. I'm not really here and my magic is not strong enough. I'm too weak after helping Byder and Ydum.

I yell at the wilde hunt instead. "Stop! Stop running over him. Let him settle his mantle first. Please."

"We do not answer to you." The words sound like a howling wind in my mind. "We are not yet his and do not answer to you."

Anarus's foot on the side of the land of the living slips again, and this time Anarus falls. He catches himself as he slams to his knees with his grip tight on the rope railings, but they're fraying and won't hold up much longer if he keeps thrashing as he slips. The gold bonds running through his heart burn as they try to find a permanent spot to anchor within him. The pain from the bonds makes him stiffen, and his foot slips again, the bridge rocking too much. He can't handle both of them. Not at the same time and not with the wilde hunt loose.

I push with my mind. I need all the strength my mind and magic can give me. I reach up and unbraid my braids of totality, asking them to please, please give me the stored magic there.

Before I can reach for him again, Anarus screams as the bonds tug and burn him again, his foot in the land of the living slipping again. The rope railings give way, snapping in his hands. He falls backwards, his head landing in the land of the dead and his feet falling on the collapsing bridge. The bonds that had been attempting to go through his heart spring up and snap out of him, stretching straight out into the land of the dead.

"No!" I scream as I dash over the bridge, which has sunken into the water. My bare feet and the hem of my dress are covered with icy water, but I ignore it. I pull on Anarus, trying to bring him to stand again, but he's no longer awake. I fight with his body to push it into the land of the living, but he's so heavy and I'm so tired and the wilde hunt runs over us, shoving Anarus back down the moment I'm able to get him in my arms. The rest of the bridge falls, planks of wood coming loose and falling off, leaving gaps in the bridge. The remaining bits of tethered rope and wood boards rest on the cracked ice of the river, the icy water swirling through the cracks and over the bridge. I scream.

I'm thrown out of the vision. The single strand red bracelet on my wrist falls off, used up protecting me from what was happening in the vision. Protecting me from Anarus's death throes. "NO! No! Anarus, no! Wake up, wake up!" I cry and beat on his real chest. "Stand up! You have to stand up. Pick up the rope, Anarus, and fix the bridge. You have to stand up." Beside me, Ydum and Byder both are holding one of Anarus's hands, crying and pushing strength to him. Their braids of totality are undone and their hair looks as wild as the pain in their eyes.

Something in my heart snaps and the pain is overwhelming. Our fated mate bond link that's anchored to his heart broke. Anarus is dead. He did not stand back up.

I scream. A long, loud wordless wail. I can't see. I can't hear. All I can feel is the frayed edge of my bond with Anarus that is now dark and cold.

The pressure in the room changes, becomes oppressive, bearing down on us. Then, with a crack that makes my ears want to bleed, a male appears on the floor of the Colosseum. He has no tattoos and is taller than Anarus, taller even than Ydum, but in every other way looks identical to Anarus. The god of death even wears his hair in a long braid down his back like his son does, I think. No, did. Like Anarus did.

Before Death can speak, I'm up and running to him. I beat on him, hitting him with the best punches Ydum ever taught me. "Give! Him! Back!" I scream at Death, punctuating each word with another completely ineffective hit. "Take back the mantle of the wilde hunt and give Anarus back!"

Death captures my hands in one of his, stopping my assault. "What do you mean, little human? The wilde hunt is not mine. Why is my son even here?"

I glare at Death, my eyes full of all the viciousness Anarus ever saw in me. "You don't get to call me that. Only Anarus can call me little human." Then, my heart breaks and all I can do is cry. "They made him come early. The council of the gods made him come early and the cave gave me three. How was I supposed to hold three hands? They did it on purpose. They were constantly trying to make us fail, but we didn't. We didn't and we would have won but Anarus couldn't handle two powers and I couldn't hold his hand. It's not fair. It wasn't his. The wilde hunt wasn't his and they trampled all over him and the bridge collapsed and he died. Take back the wilde hunt. Bring him back, please. Please."

The god of death appears to grow taller as he listens to me. His nostrils flare and anger swirls around him. With a voice so deep that it reverberates in my lungs and I can't breathe, Death roars. "The wilde hunt is. Not. Mine! Winter was to hold it until after my son took his mantle. After!" Death lets go of my hands and Ydum and Byder pull me away. We collapse in a heap around Anarus's body.

Death turns slowly, the air rippling with shadows and the room growing darker and darker. When he's facing the council, Death looks up at them, a cold white and blue fire coming from his eyes. "Winter! What did you do to our son?"

Acknowledgements

Gotta say the most important one first. Brent, I love you. So very much. Sorry that you working nights and me not getting writing inspiration until the afternoon meant you slept while I wrote and I slept while you worked. We'll figure out the schedule soon, I promise. Maybe when you finish your degree and homework isn't taking priority again. I'm so proud of you. So, so proud of you. Thank you for always bragging to new coworkers about me. I promise if I ever have coworkers that aren't fictitious people in my head, I'll brag about you to them too. I'd tell you that I already brag to the ones in my head, but I think it's probably a bad idea to talk about how much I argue with my own characters like they are real people.

Shoshana Kronfeld, Heather Douglas, and the others who do not check their email enough (I sent the one asking for permission to name you here a month ago, check your inboxes!), I appreciate all of the advice and support. Indie authors cannot do it all on our own. We need a crew to help us. You're my crew. You rock.

To my readers, we are 2/3 of the way there. Next up, *When the Gods Wage War*. The manuals for the Gods Games will be complete after that. Expect to find out that everything you think you know is probably wrong. Everything you learned about Nazus and the original gods right alongside Jinx is wrong. Thank you for reading this far. Especially if you had a red blood test and didn't have to.

Thank you for supporting indie authors. Keep it up. And not for just me. We love even the smallest support. Reviews mean the world, no matter where you review it. Send us emails, message us on social media, send a carrier pigeon, whatever. I think I can safely speak for the whole of indie authors everywhere when I say we love that shit. Don't think it's weird or presumptuous. Or just read and enjoy. Whatever. Just... thank you. All of you.

About the Author

Kefira Zink is an author from a little town in Michigan. She has a bachelor's degree in Sociology from Arizona State University and a master's degree in Sociology, with a specialty in Religion and Deviance from American Public University. She loves buying books, especially rescuing old books and giving them a loving home, as well as reading books (which any reader will tell you, buying books and reading them are two very different hobbies). She is married to her wonderful husband/muse and together they have six grown children, two cats, a dog that thinks it is a cat, and a lizard that thinks it is a dinosaur.

Connect With The Author

Website: https://sites.google.com/view/kefira-zink-author
Email: kefirazinkauthor@gmail.com
Facebook: Kefira Zink Author
TikTok: kefira_zink_author